The Walled City

# The Walled City

## RYAN GRAUDIN

Indigo

First published in Great Britain in 2014
by Indigo
This paperback edition first published in Great Britain in 2015
by Indigo
an imprint of Hachette Children's Group
a division of Hodder and Stoughton Ltd
Carmelite House
50 Victoria Embankment
London EC4Y 0DZ
An Hachette UK company

1 3 5 7 9 10 8 6 4 2

The paper and board used in this paperback are natural and
recyclable products made from wood grown in sustainable forests.
The manufacturing processes conform to the environmental
regulations of the country of origin.

A catalogue record for this book is available from the British Library.

ISBN 978 1 78062 200 2

Printed and bound by CPI Group (UK) Ltd,
Croydon CR0 4YY

www.orionchildrensbooks.com

# 18 DAYS

# JIN LING

There are three rules of survival in the Walled City: Run fast. Trust no one. Always carry your knife.

Right now, my life depends completely on the first.

*Run, run, run.*

My lungs burn, bite for air. Water stings my eyes. Crumpled wrappers, half-finished cigarettes. A dead animal—too far gone to tell what it used to be. Carpets of glass, bottles smashed by drunk men. All of these fly by in fragments.

These streets are a maze. They twist into themselves—narrow, filled with glowing signs and graffitied walls. Men leer from doorways; their cigarettes glow like monsters' eyes in the dark.

Kuen and his followers chase me like a pack: frantic, fast, together. If they'd broken apart and tried to close me in, maybe they'd have a chance. But I'm faster than all of them because

I'm smaller. I can slip into cracks most of them don't even see. It's because I'm a girl. But they don't know this. No one here does. To be a girl in this city—without a roof or family—is a sentence. An automatic ticket to one of the many brothels that line the streets.

The boys behind me don't yell. We all know better than that. Yelling attracts attention. Attention means the Brotherhood. The only sounds of our chase are gritted footsteps and hard breaths.

I know every corner I dash past. This is my territory, the west section of the Walled City. I know exactly which alleyway I need to disappear into. It's coming soon, just a few strides away. I tear by Mrs. Pak's restaurant, with its warm, homey scents of chicken, garlic, and noodles. Then there's Mr. Wong's chair, where people go to get their teeth pulled. Next is Mr. Lam's secondhand trader's shop, its entrance guarded with thick metal bars. Mr. Lam himself squats on the steps. Feet flat. His throat grumbles as I run past. He adds another loogie to his tin can collection.

A sharp-eyed boy slouches on the opposite stoop, picking at a Styrofoam bowl of seafood noodles. My stomach growls, and I think about how easy it would be to snatch it. Keep running.

I can't afford to stop. Not even for food.

I'm so distracted by the noodles that I nearly miss the alleyway. The turn is so sharp my ankles almost snap. But I'm still running, body turned sideways in the narrow gap between these two monstrous buildings. Cinder block walls press against my chest and scrape my back. If I breathe too fast, I won't be able to wedge through.

I push farther in, ignoring how the rough, damp wall claws skin off my elbows. Roaches and rats scurry in and out of the empty spaces by my body—long past the fear of getting crushed by my feet. Dark, heavy footsteps echo off the walls, throb through my ears. Kuen and his pack of street boys have passed me by. For now.

I look down at the boots in my hand. Sturdy leather, tough soles. They were a good find. Worth the panicked minutes I just spent running for them. Not even Mr. Chow—the cobbler on the city's west edge, always bent over his bench of nails and leather—makes such sturdy footwear. I wonder where Kuen got them. These boots have to be from City Beyond. Most nice things are.

Angry shouts edge into my hiding place, piling together in a mess of curses. I flinch and the trash beneath my feet shudders. Maybe Kuen's boys have found me after all.

A girl trips and falls, spills into the foot of my alleyway. She's breathing hard. Blood streaks down her arms, her legs, summoned by the glass and gravel in her skin. All her ribs stick out from the slippery silk of her dress. It's blue and shiny and thin. Not the kind of thing you wear in this city.

All breath leaves my body.

Is it her?

She looks up and I see a face covered in makeup. Only her eyes are raw, real. They're full of fire, as if she's ready to fight.

Whoever this girl is, she isn't Mei Yee. She isn't the sister I've been searching for all this time.

I shrink farther into the gloom. But it's too late. The doll-girl sees me. Her lips pull back, as if she wants to talk. Or bite me. I can't tell which.

I never find out.

The men are on her. They swoop down like vultures, clawing at her dress as they try to pull her up. The flames behind the girl's eyes grow wild. She twists around, fingers hooked so her nails catch her nearest attacker's face.

The man flinches back. Four bright streaks rake down his cheek. He howls unspeakable things. Grabs at the nest of falling braids in her hair.

She doesn't scream. Her body keeps twisting, hitting, thrashing—desperate movements. There are four men with their hands on her, but the fight isn't an easy one. They're so busy trying to hold her down that none of them notice me, deep in the alley's dark. Watching.

Each of them grabs a limb, holds her tight. She bucks, her back arching as she spits at their faces. One of the men strikes her over the head and she falls into an eerie, not-right stillness.

When she's not moving, it's easier to look at her captors. The Brotherhood's mark is on all four of them. Black shirts. Guns. Dragon jewelry and tattoos. One even has the red beast inked on the side of his face. It crawls all the way up his jaw, into his hairline.

"Stupid whore!" the man with the nail marks growls at her battered, unconscious form.

4

"Let's get her back," the one with the face tattoo says. "Longwai's waiting."

It's only after they take her away, black hair sweeping the ground under her limp body, that I realize I'd been holding my breath. My hands tremble, still wrapped around the boots.

That girl. The fire in her eyes. She could've been me. My sister. Any one of us.

# DAI

I'm not a good person.

If people need proof, I'll show them my scar, tell them my body count.

Even when I was a young boy, trouble latched onto me like a magnet. I pounded through life at volume eleven, leaving a trail of broken things: vases, noses, cars, hearts, brain cells. Side effects of reckless living.

My mother always tried to reason goodness into me. Her favorite phrases were "Oh, Dai Shing, why can't you be more like your brother?" and "You'll never get a good wife if you keep acting this way!" She always said these on repeat, trying not to let her cheeks turn purple, while my brother stood behind her, his body language the exact dictionary entry for *I told you so*: arms crossed, nose scrunched, thick eyebrows piled together like puppies. I always told him his face would get stuck that way if he kept tattling: an adulthood damned by unibrow. It never really seemed to stop him.

My father's chosen tactic was fear. He always set his briefcase down, yanked his tie loose, and told me about this place: the Hak Nam Walled City. A recipe of humanity's darkest ingredients—thieves, whores, murderers, addicts— all mashed into six and a half acres. Hell on earth, he called it. A place so ruthless even the sunlight won't enter. If I kept messing up, my father said, he'd drive me down there himself. Dump me off in the dens of drug lords and thieves so I could learn my lesson.

My father tried his best to scare me, but even all his stories couldn't cram the goodness into me. I ended up here anyway. The irony of the whole thing would make me laugh. But laughter is something that belongs to my life before this. In the shiny skyscrapers and shopping malls and taxi-tangle of Seng Ngoi.

Seven hundred and thirty. That's how many days I've been trapped in this cesspool of humanity.

Eighteen. That's how many days I have left to find a way out.

I've got a plan—an elaborate, risky-as-hell plan—but in order for it to work, I need a runner. A fast one.

I'm not even halfway done with my bowl of *wonton mein* when the kid zips past my stoop. He's there and gone, running faster than some of the star track athletes at my old school.

"Kid's at it again." Mr. Lam grunts the last of his mucus out of his throat. His turtle gaze ambles back down the street. "Wonder who he snitched from this time. Half the

7

shops round here lost stuff to that one. Never tried these bars, though. Only buys."

I'm just putting my chopsticks down when the others barrel past. Kuen's at the front of the pack, cross-eyed with focus and rage. I struck him off the list of prospective runners a while ago. He's cruel, ruthless, and a bit dumb. I've got no use for someone like that.

But this other kid might just fit the profile. If I can catch him.

I leave the rest of the noodles on the step, yank up my sweatshirt hood, and follow.

Kuen's gang jogs for a few minutes before coming to a stop. Heads swivel around, their eyes wide and lungs panting. Whoever they are looking for, it's clear they lost him.

I slow and duck to the side of the street. None of the breathless boys see me. They're too busy cowering away from a royally pissed-off Kuen.

"Where'd he go? Where the hell did he go?" the vagrant screams, and kicks an empty beer can. It lands against a wall with a tinny crash; an entire family of cockroaches explodes up the cinder block. My skin crawls at the sight. Funny. After all I've been through, all I've seen here, bugs still bother me.

Kuen doesn't notice the insects. He's fuming, lashing out at trash and walls and boys. His followers flinch back, all of them trying their hardest not to be the inevitable scapegoat.

He turns on them. "Who was on watch?"

No one answers. Not that I blame them. The vagrant's knuckles are curled and his arms are shaking. "Who was on the damn watch?"

"Lee," the boy closest to Kuen's fists pipes up. "It was Lee."

The kid in question throws up his hands in instant surrender. "I'm sorry, boss! It won't happen again. I swear."

Their leader steps forward, closing in on a trembling Lee. His fists are tight, thirsty for a fight.

My hands dig deep into the pockets of my hoodie. I feel kind of bad for Lee, but not bad enough to do anything about it. I can't afford to get involved in other people's problems. Not when I'm running out of time to solve my own.

Kuen looks like he's about to punch the poor kid's face in. None of the others try to stop him. They cower, stare, and wait as the oldest vagrant's fist rises level with Lee's nose. Hovers still.

"Who was it? Huh?" Kuen asks. "I'm guessing you got a look at him."

"Yeah, yeah, yeah." Lee nods furiously. It's pitiful how eager he is, how much Kuen's cowed all these boys. If they lived in a civilized world—played football, sang karaoke with their friends—they'd probably have a different leader. One with more brains than brawn.

But this is the Hak Nam Walled City. Muscles and fear rule here. Survival of the fittest at its finest.

"It was Jin. He's stolen a bunch of stuff from us before. A tarp. A shirt," Lee goes on. "You know. The one who showed up from Beyond a few years back? The one with the cat..."

Kuen snarls. "I don't care about his damn cat. I care about my boots!"

His boots? I look down and realize the hulking boy is barefoot. There's blood on his feet from his race through the filthy streets. Nicks from glass shards and gravel. Maybe even discarded needles.

No wonder he's so pissed off.

Lee's back is ramrod straight against a wall. His face is all scrunched, like he's about to cry. "I'll get those boots back. I promise!"

"I can take care of that myself."

The older boy's fist falls. The thud of knuckle on jaw is loud and awful. Kuen keeps punching—again and again—until Lee's face is almost as dark as his greasy hair. It's a hard thing to watch. Way more unsettling than a few bugs.

I could stop it. I could reach for my weapon, watch Kuen's gang scatter like roaches. My fingers twitch and burn with every new punch, but I keep them shoved deep in my pockets.

Kids die every day on these streets—lives sliced short by hunger, disease, and knives. I can't save them all. And if I don't keep my head down, do what needs to be done in eighteen days, I won't even be able to save myself.

This is what I tell myself, over and over, as I watch the kid's face break apart, all blood and bruises.

I'm not a good person.

"Take off your boots," Kuen snarls when his fists finally stop landing.

Lee is on the ground now, whimpering. "Please..."

"Take them off before I beat the shit out of you again!"

Lee's fingers shake as he unlaces his shoes, but he manages to get them off. Kuen snatches them up, puts them on his own bloody feet. The vagrant starts talking to the rest of the boys while he ties his new boots.

"Any of you guys know where this Jin kid camps?"

All he gets in response are shaking heads and blank stares.

"Ka Ming, Ho Wai, I want you two to find out where he sleeps. I'm gonna get my boots back." Kuen's last sentence is more growl than not.

The street bursts alive with yells. At first I think it's Lee, but the battered, barefoot boy is just as surprised as the rest of them. They look down the street all at once, necks whipping around like those meerkat animals that used to pop up on my brother's favorite nature show.

The yells are from elsewhere, back where my noodles are getting cold on the door stoop. So many grown men screaming all at once can only mean the Brotherhood.

Time to get out of here.

Kuen's pack must be thinking the same thing, because they start an instant, scrambling retreat. Away from the screams. Away from Lee. Away from me.

"Please! Don't leave me!" Lee reaches out, his whimper beyond pathetic.

"Don't bother coming back to camp." Kuen spits down at the boy, now outcast, before he disappears for good. I can't help but wonder what will happen to the battered boy. If he's anything like Kuen's other boys, his familial status reads *orphaned* or *parents too broke to fill his rice bowl*. Kids with roofs and hot food have better things to do than play survival of the thuggiest. No parents, shoeless, broken face, winter in full swing... Granted, it's a mild one (it always is), but chilly temperatures still bite when you don't even have socks.

Lee's odds aren't looking too good.

I start walking with my hood up and my hands shoved in my pockets, trying to look as inconspicuous as possible. I blend into the dark of a side alley just as the Brotherhood men pass. The girl they're dragging is more blood than skin. Her hair is loose, weeping all over the ground. Her dress is sheen and silk: one of the brothel girls. She must've been trying to run. What I'm seeing is an escape gone wrong.

The *wonton mein* kicks up hell in my gut. I push away, farther into the dark bowels of the city, leaving the girl to face her fate.

I can't save them all.

*Jin. The one with the cat.* It's not much to go on in a hive of thirty-three thousand people, but Mr. Lam seemed to recognize him. My first lead. I'll have to move fast, find him before Kuen sniffs out where the kid keeps his tarp. He must be a loner, which means, considering what just happened to Lee, that he's smart. Smart and fast. Plus he's lasted a few years on the streets—which is hard to do in Seng Ngoi, let alone this hellhole.

Just the kind of kid I'm looking for. One more step to my ticket out of this place.

Here's hoping he's willing to play the part.

# MEI YEE

*There is no escape.*

Those were the first words the brothel master spoke to me the night the Reapers pulled me out of their van—after endless hours of rutted roads, windowless darkness. I was still wearing the nightgown I'd pulled over my head days and days before—a thin, cotton thing with more than a few holes. A few of the girls beside me were crying. I...I felt nothing. I was someone else. I was not the girl who'd just been snatched from her bed. I was not the one who stood at the front of the line, waiting as the man with the long purple scar on his jaw inspected us. I was not Mei Yee.

That night, when the master got to me, he stared, inspecting me at every angle. I felt the crawl of his eyes on my skin, like insects creeping into hidden places. Places they shouldn't go.

"Her," he told the Reapers' leader.

We watched as the coins changed hands, more money than I'd ever seen in my short life as a rice farmer's daughter. More than ten times what the Reapers' leader paid my father for me.

"There is no escape. Forget your home. Forget your family." The master's voice was flat, passionless. As dead as his heavy, opium eyes. "You're mine now."

These are the words I'm trying my hardest not to remember when Mama-san calls, "Girls?"

I'm sitting on my bed. Dread snakes through my every vein, and I look at the others. Nuo is by the foot of the bed, a cross-stitch dangling from her fingers. Wen Kei sits on the rug, and Yin Yu kneels behind her, weaving braids into the younger girl's dark silken hair. Yin Yu is the only one who doesn't freeze at Mama-san's voice. Her fingers keep moving, tucking strands of Wen Kei's hair in and out and into themselves again.

Wen Kei's mouth is still open, cut off midsentence from one of her endless, amazing descriptions of the sea. I'm trying to imagine what waves look like when Mama-san appears in the doorway.

Mama-san—the keeper of us girls. The one who feeds and dresses us. The one who calls the doctor when we're sick. The one who runs the brothel and matches clients to our beds. Some of the girls think she was brought here like us: in the back of one of the Reapers' vans. It must've been a very long time ago, when her skin was smooth and her back wasn't bent.

14

She certainly doesn't look young now. Her face is pinched in all the wrong places, eyes distant.

"Girls. The master wants to see you. Now. He's closed off the lounge." Mama-san darts out of the doorway as suddenly as she came, off to gather the girls from the other three halls.

"She got caught." Wen Kei, the youngest and smallest of us, sounds like a baby bird, her voice all fluttery and weak.

Yin Yu pulls her hair so tight that Wen Kei squeaks. "None of you breathe a word. If Master and Mama-san find out that we knew Sing's plan...it won't end well." She looks to me as she says this, searching for words of support.

"We say nothing." I try to sound as old as my seventeen years should make me, but the truth is, I feel just like the rest of them: shaking and whiter than rice noodles.

I don't know why I'm so rattled. I knew this would happen. All of us did. That's why we tried to get Sing to stay.

*There is no escape. There is no escape.* We whispered the master's words to her like a chorus, along with dozens of reasons. Here, she had clothing, food, water, friends. And out there? What? Hunger. Disease. Unforgiving streets with teeth like wolves.

But in the end, there was no stopping her. I'd seen it months ago, the wildness that started in her eyes when she talked about life before this. It spread into everything, lit her up inside. Every time she entered my room, she would pull aside my scarlet curtain and stare, stare, stare out the window—the only one in the entire brothel. She was never good at keeping

15

everything balled up inside like the rest of us. Yin Yu thinks this is because Sing's family never sold her. They loved her, fed her, taught her how to read, and then they died. The Reapers came for her at the orphanage.

We find Sing spread out on the floor of the smoking lounge, hair wild and torn, arms bent back at a terrible angle. I don't know for sure if she's awake or even alive until one of the master's men props her up. Blood, bright, shines down her arms and legs. There's blood on her face, too, washing warm over her cheeks and onto the edge of her lips. Her dress—a beautiful piece of sky-blue silk and embroidered cherry blossoms—is ruined.

The rest of us stand in a line as the master paces a slow, endless circle around Sing's fetal frame. When he finally stops, the tips of his lounge slippers are turned toward us.

He doesn't yell, which makes his words even more terrifying. "Do any of you know what it's like out there for a vagrant? For the other working girls?"

Not one of us replies, though we all know the answer. It's one Mama-san drills into us every single time she sees our faces wither with emptiness. The one we tried so hard to make Sing remember.

"Pain. Disease. Death." The words leave him like punches. When he's finished, he brings the pipe to his lips. Smoke pours out of his nostrils—reminding me of the scarlet dragon embroidered on his lounging jacket. "How do you think you'd do out there, on your own? Without my protection?"

He doesn't really want an answer. His question is more of

a quiet shout, the same kind my father used to ask before his first cup of rice wine. Before he exploded.

"I give every single one of you everything you could need. I give you the best. All I ask for in return is that you make our guests feel welcome. It's such a small thing. Such a tiny request."

Just the fact that the master is addressing us should make my blood run cold. Mama-san is always the one who punishes us, with hissing lips and the sharp backside of her callused hand. The few times the master does talk to us, he always makes a point to remind us of how we're treated better than other working girls. We have rooms of our own, silken dresses, trays of tea, and incense. Our choice of meals. Pots of paint to decorate our faces. We have everything because we're the chosen. The best of the best.

"Now, Sing here"—he says her name in a way that crawls under my skin—"has just spit in the face of my generosity. I gave her safety and luxury, and she threw it away like it was nothing. She's insulted my honor. My name."

Sing sits behind him, still bleeding, still shaking. The men in black are breathing hard. I wonder how far she got before they caught her.

The master snaps his fingers. All four of his henchmen pull Sing to her feet. She flops like a doll in their hands. "If you dishonor my hospitality, break the rules, you will be punished. If you insist on being treated like the common prostitutes, then that's what I'll do."

He rolls up his sleeves. Fung, the man with the scarlet tattoo on his face, gives the master something I can't fully see.

But Sing sees it, and when she does, she lets out a shriek that would wake the gods. She comes to life again, with kicks and jerks so awful that the men holding her down can't stand still.

Her screams manage to meld into words. "No! Please! I'm sorry! I won't run!"

Then the master holds up his hand, and I see the reason for Sing's terror. There, wrapped under all those tight, plump fingers, is a needle. The syringe is full of dirty brown liquid.

The other girls see it, too. Even Mama-san grows stiff beside me. There's no way of knowing what lies inside that plastic tube. Pain. Disease. Death.

Sing fights and flails, her screams rising far beyond words. In the end, the men are too strong for her.

I can't watch when the sharp metal plows into her veins. When her screams stop—when I finally look up again—the needle is gone and Sing is on the floor, crumpled and shuddering. The shadows of the lounge crowd around her curled form, make her look broken.

The master's hands brush together. He turns to us. "The first dose of heroin is always the best. The second time, the rush isn't as strong. But you still need it. You need more and more and more until it's everything you want. Everything you are."

Heroin. He means to make an addict of our smart and beautiful Sing. This thought twists inside me: hollow and hopeless.

"You are mine." The master looks down our line of silken

rainbow dresses. He's smiling. "All of you. If you try to run, this is your fate."

I close my eyes, try not to look at the broken-doll girl on the floor. Try not to remember the words the master spoke into the night so long ago. They reach out of time, bind me like ropes: *There is no escape.*

# JIN LING

It's been two years. Two years since the Reapers took my sister from me. Two years since I followed them to the Walled City to look for her. Over these years, I've learned how to move like a ghost, make the most of my senses. That's the only way to survive here: become something more than you are, or be invisible altogether.

I was invisible a lot when I was younger. There were only three years between me and my older sister, but Mei Yee was the one people noticed. Her face was round and soft. Like a moon. Her hair hung straight, sleek as midnight.

But being beautiful did no good on a rice farm. It didn't help you wade for hours in muddy water, back bent under the hot shine of the sun, cutting rows of whipping grass. I was always stronger than Mei Yee. I knew I wasn't beautiful: My feet were tough with calluses, my skin dark, my nose too large. Whenever our mother wound my hair back into a bun and sent me to the pond for wash water, I saw a boy's face staring back at me.

Sometimes I wished it were true. Being a boy would be easier. I'd be stronger, able to overpower my father whenever the alcohol made him rabid. But most of the time I just wished for a brother. A brother to bend over the never-ending rice plants. A brother to stand up to my father's drunken rages.

And, in my deepest heart, I wanted to be pretty. Just like Mei Yee. So I always tugged the bun out. Let my hair fall free.

My hair was the second thing I lost after my father sold Mei Yee to the Reapers. I knew from the stories that I wouldn't survive in this city as a girl. The knife I used was dull. It was a bad haircut, full of awkward angles, one side slightly longer than the other. I looked just the way I wanted to: like a half-starved, dirt-streaked street boy.

And that's what I've been ever since.

My elbows are raw, stinging by the time I reach my camp. I took the long way back, circling the same moldy, pipe-hemmed passages to make sure no one followed me. Long enough for the blood to scab over and split again. If I don't put a bandage on it soon, the wounds will get red and puffy. Take weeks to heal.

I slide through the opening of my ratty tarp shelter, look through my belongings. It's not much. A matchbook with a single flame left. A waterlogged, half-filled character work-book scavenged from a careless student's satchel. Two oranges and a mangosteen snagged from an ancestral shrine. A blanket heavy with mildew and rat urine. One mangy gray cat that purrs and yowls. Does his best to make me feel less alone.

"Got lucky today, Chma." I set the boots down. The cat slinks across the tent. Rubs his whiskers across the worn leather. Plops his downy body on the laces with a *mine* meow.

I reach out for the blanket. It'll have to do. I tug my knife from my tunic, start to cut the blanket into strips. Try to ignore the stench and damp of the fabric.

Mei Yee always tied my bandages. Before. She looked over the cuts my father made, eyes soft. Sad. Her fingers were feather-gentle when they wrapped the fabric. She had to use the strips so many times they were stained the color of rust. But she always made sure they were clean. Always tied them well. Always took care of me.

But I'm alone now. And it's a lot harder to tie your own bandages. I end up using my teeth, gagging on the taste of rat and rank. Mei Yee would be horrified that I'm using this rotten blanket to cover my wounds. Horrified I'm here at all.

Going after Mei Yee was never a choice for me. She was all I had. Without her, I had no reason to stay on the farm, taking my father's blows. Watching my mother wither like our rice crops.

I don't know why I thought finding my sister would be easy. I wasn't really thinking at all when I jumped onto that rusted bike and pedaled after the big white van. I didn't think when I sliced off my hair. Or when I first reached City Beyond and asked questions in my slow, country speech.

Now I know how young and stupid I was, thinking that I could just walk into this place and find her.

The Walled City doesn't cover much land—it's only

as big as three or four rice paddies—but it makes up for all that with its height. Its shanties stack on top of one another like sloppy bricks, crowded so high they blot out the sunlight. Streets that used to be filled with day and fresh air are now just cable-shrouded passages. Sometimes I feel like a worker ant, running these dark, winding tunnels in a never-ending loop. Always looking. Never finding.

But I won't stop looking until I find her. And I *will* find her.

Chma stops nuzzling his new boot-bed. His yellow eyes snap to the entrance of my shelter—wide. Ears pricked high. Fur bristling. I hold my breath, listen through the Walled City's eternal song: the distant rumbling of engines; a mother yelling at her children through thin walls; dogs howling in an alley far away; an airplane roaring over the city every five minutes.

There's another noise. Softer, but closer. Footsteps.

I was followed.

My fingers wrap tight around my knife. I edge over to the tarp flap, fear rattling high in my throat. My thighs cramp tight as I wait. Listen. My knife hand is rice white, shaking.

The steps pause. A voice calls out, husky and doubtful, "Hello?"

Not Kuen, then. But that doesn't mean I'm safe. These streets are crawling with thieves and drunks. People who would knife you in a heartbeat.

"Go away!" I try to make my voice as throaty as possible. All male. All threat.

Through the slit in my tarp, I glimpse my visitor. A boy, older. He's leaning against the alley wall with his hands stuffed in his pockets. One knee up. The sheen of water that always glazes the city's walls soaks the fabric of his sweatshirt. But he doesn't seem to notice or care.

His stare lights straight on the flap of my tent. His eyes— they're different from most people's here in Hak Nam— they're dark brown, yes. But they aren't the same savage cruel as Kuen's. Or the deadpan glaze of the grandmothers who squat on the corners, gutting fish after fish. Day after day.

No. This boy's eyes are more like a fox's. Sharp. Shining. Smart. Wanting something very, very badly.

I'd better be careful.

"It's Jin, isn't it?"

*My name. He knows my name.* It's enough for me to push the flap back, teeth bared. Ready for a fight.

"Get out of here." I raise my knife. Some far-off streetlight glints, echoes the blade back into the boy's stare. He doesn't flinch. "This is my last warning!"

"I'm not going to hurt you." The boy pushes off the wall. Pulls his hands from his pockets. They're empty.

My teeth are still bared when I stop. Look him over again. Black hoodie. Jeans so new they haven't even frayed. Pale, empty, outstretched hands. Then I study his face—his sharp-cut cheekbones. The tight pull of his lips. Arched, cocky eyebrows.

"How'd you find me?" My knuckles are all ache around the hilt of my knife.

"Mr. Lam told me you usually camp in this sector. All I

24

had to do was look. And follow my allergies." As if on cue, the boy's nose scrunches. The ugly agony of a sneeze never freed. "Closest thing I've got to a superpower."

*Mr. Lam.* I think back to the old shopkeeper. Toad-crouched. Collecting spit in a can. Guarding his shop of splintered furniture and antique coins.

And then my thoughts travel to the other stoop. Memories of shrimp and noodles. Eyes just as sharp as the ones watching me now. "You . . . you're noodle boy."

"The name's Dai, actually," he says. "I'm here to offer you a job."

"I work alone," I say quickly. I do everything alone: eat, sleep, run, steal, talk, cry. It's the curse of the second rule: *Trust no one.* The cost of staying alive.

"Me too." Dai doesn't move. His stare is dead on my knife. "But this drug run is different. It takes two people."

I'm no stranger to drug runs. I do them a lot for lesser drug lords, the ones who trade behind the backs of the Brotherhood. Hope not to get noticed. They pay me in bread crusts and spare change. But the real payment is going inside their brothels. I've looked into the faces of many drug-hazed girls, searching for my sister.

"What kind of run takes two people?" I ask.

"It's for the Brotherhood."

*A drug run for the Brotherhood of the Red Dragon.* Just the thought makes my heart squeeze high. Flutter like a dying thing. I've heard too many stories about the gang and its cutthroat leader, Longwai. How he carved out the tongue of a man he caught lying. How he chiseled a bright scarlet character into the cheeks of anyone who tried to cheat him. How he shot one of his own double-crossing gang members in the head, but only after whittling away at the man slowly, watching flesh fall away like wood shavings. How he laughed when he did these things.

"Since when does the Brotherhood use vagrants?"

"Longwai's men keep getting arrested whenever they make runs into Seng Ngoi. He'd rather use street kids. One to do the run and one to sit in the brothel as collateral."

*Collateral.* One of the many tongue-tumbling words I wrestled with when I first got to the city. Tried to get rid of my sun-slowed farmspeak. Didn't take too long to figure out its meaning: "hostage." Waiting, waiting, waiting with a blade to your throat. Your life held tight in the speed of another person's legs.

"You're a good runner," Dai says. "Most kids don't get away from Kuen."

"So I'd run. And you'd sit. Risk Longwai's knife?" My own knife is still high in the air between us.

"Yep. It's good pay." Dai jerks his chin to the shredded edges of my tarp. "You look like you could use it."

He's right. Good pay means I can spend time searching for my sister instead of scrounging for food and clothes. But tangling with the Brotherhood, even for just one drug run, is a bad idea.

There's only one reason I'm considering this. Longwai is the single most important man in the Walled City, the leader of the Brotherhood of the Red Dragon. His brothel is the biggest. It's also impossible to get into. Most of his girls serve important

26

clients, people of power and influence in City Beyond. It's the last large brothel I haven't searched.

This could be my only chance to get in. To look for Mei Yee.

"*You* don't look like you need the job." The tip of my knife waves at his straight white teeth. His clothes without holes. Just the way he stands smells of money. "Not bad enough to risk your life."

Dai shrugs. "Looks can be deceiving. You want to run or not?"

I should say no. Everything about this screams against the second rule. *Trust no one.* But if I say no, he'll move on. Find someone else to do this crazy run. I'll lose my chance to find my sister.

Good pay isn't worth risking my life. Or trusting a stranger.

But Mei Yee is.

The tarp by my foot wrinkles. Chma's silvered head pokes out, his poison-yellow eyes narrow at Dai. I look the boy over, too. There's no trace of the Brotherhood's dragon on him. No jewelry. No tattoos. Just a raised, shiny scar that snakes up his forearm. Knife work. It's too ugly not to be.

Dai catches my eyes, shoves his hoodie sleeve down, hiding the mark.

Chma slinks over, wraps around Dai's legs like a scarf. Lining those nice jeans with silver sheds of fur. His plumed tail climbs high into the air: a happy greeting. After a few circles, Chma settles over the boy's feet. Tucking his paws into themselves with another solid *mine* meow.

If my cat can trust him, then I guess I can, too.

27

For now.

I nod. "Looks like you got a new friend."

Dai's sneeze is a sudden, explosive thing. Mr. Lam's loogie times ten. He throws his arm to his face, but the damage is done. If anything can make a vagrant look less threatening, it's a face full of snot.

I lower my knife. "When's the run?"

The older boy finishes mopping his face, shoves his hands back into his pockets. Chma is still planted on the boy's shoes. Purring.

"The run takes place in two days. Four hours after sunset. We meet in front of Longwai's brothel."

"I'm in." And there it is. The second rule broken. Me trusting a boy with a scar on his arm. A hunt in his eyes. All for my sister's sake. "But I want sixty."

"Done." He says this with a quick, desperate speed. Without even blinking.

I should've asked for seventy.

"I trust you'll show up, Jin. If you don't…"

"I'll be there," I tell him.

Dai nods and turns to go, dislodging his feline squatter with a gentle shake. I watch him leave with a heavy sigh. Part of it's relief. Part of it is weariness. Now that Dai has discovered my camp, I'll have to move. All my secrets, my terror, spill into the cool air. Misty and milk white. Like my sister's skin.

When my breath cloud vanishes, the boy is gone. I stand in the yawn of my alley, fingers ever-tight around my knife. Alone again.

# MEI YEE

It's a wonder Sing fought as hard as she did, with all the blood she's lost. She's not fighting anymore. What Yin Yu and I lift is deadweight. Both of us are panting by the time we lay Sing out on her bed.

There's blood on my hands. I hold them in front of me, stare long and hard at the bright smears. They're bringing back memories. Awful, awful memories of the life before.

Whenever Father wasn't in the fields, he would be all but collapsed in his cheap folding chair, his fist clamped around a bottle. All of us knew to be careful by the time he unscrewed the third metal cap. Most nights he stayed there—arms and legs limp like dead fish. The nights he didn't, our skin flowered purple and pain under his blows.

Jin Ling's eyes hovered constant over that dangerous corner. Her beatings were always the worst because she wouldn't just lie back and take them. She fought, her tiny limbs flailing like twigs caught in a typhoon. Sometimes she even managed to hit him. Our father would bellow and thrash her twice as hard. I think she did this on purpose, to steal all of our father's rage onto herself. He never beat me or my mother after he was done with Jin Ling.

Somewhere in the midst of these thoughts, Yin Yu leaves, returning with a silver bowl of water. I dip my hands in, and the blood that's not mine washes away, swirling like phoenix fire to the bottom of the bowl.

I thought, at least here, I would be done with blood.

I pick up a linen rag and get to work. Try to right all the wrongs gashed deep into Sing's skin.

"She's lucky he didn't use the knife," Yin Yu says.

*Lucky.* I want to balk at the word, but I know the other girl is right. "Longwai wouldn't mark her up. He wants to keep her working."

The drug lord wants to squeeze as much profit as he can from a pretty face. No matter if it's flushed with heroin highs. He'll squeeze, squeeze, squeeze until nothing is left. Until she's a husk.

That's the way it always goes.

"Why did you do it?" Yin Yu whispers as she holds our friend steady. "Why did you have to run?"

No answer. Sing's staring at the ceiling, eyes dull and vacant. I've never seen her so still before. As long as I've known her, she's been a fireball of energy. Always telling stories, stealing cigarettes from clients' coats, teaching us how to curse in clattering sounds she called English. Even in the morning, when most of us would steal some hours of sleep, Sing sat awake with a book in her hands. Reading.

Now the only signs that Sing's still alive are the painfully slow rise and fall of her chest and bursting pink cheeks.

My hands move quickly, like hummingbirds. They fish a large piece of emerald glass out of Sing's bony left knee. The blood there is starting to dry in crusts—making strange, snaking symbols across her very white skin. My rag, now sodden and pink, wipes them clean.

Neither of us expects her to speak when she does. "I had to see it."

"See what?" Yin Yu doesn't miss a beat.

"Outside. N-no more walls." Sing's words stick together, pull long like melted candy. Her voice is fuzzy and sweet and unfocused. Just like her eyes.

Yin Yu and I stare at each other. Then back at her. I don't understand why these things are worth the gashes in her skin, the needle in her veins. Why she just threw her life away.

Yin Yu asks my question for me: "Was it worth this?"

Silence.

Somewhere, in a room far from here, there's a scream. It dies as soon as it rises, stillborn. Somehow I know it belongs to Mama-san, though I don't know how I'm so sure. In the two years I've spent in this place, I've never heard her scream before.

Sing's not the only one who's being punished. We'll all pay for what she did.

Our friend's eyes close—paper-thin lids fluttering like a pulse. I can tell by the way her head rolls back that the heroin is in complete control. A smile curls into the rose flush of her cheeks. It looks strange on her, framed by so much blood.

"The end is here," she slurs on. "It's beautiful."

There's a creep in her voice that makes my shoulders hunch. Yin Yu's hands hold our friend tight. I unravel a long white strand of gauze and begin winding it around Sing's raw pink flesh.

The doorway darkens with shadow. Mama-san's face looks tight, tired. Her makeup is fresh—I've never seen her wear so much of it before. It isn't hard to guess what's hiding under so much powder and paste: the violet beginnings of a bruise, or maybe even the fresh ooze of a wound—remains of the master's anger.

She's still for a moment, filling up the doorway with her weary, false beauty. Those hard, hurt eyes study Sing: her bandaged arms, wild-nest hair, and wasted drug-haze face.

"They'll catch you. He'll always catch you." Mama-san is still looking at Sing, but the words are meant for us. They're broken, ground up finer than cocaine powder.

But when Mama-san's eyes break away from our friend, as if she's pulling out of a dream, she becomes her hard, unforgiving self again. "Leave her."

We leave Sing lying half naked on the bed. Mama-san towers in the doorway, waiting until we slide past to shut the door and lock it into place.

"Both of you are to go to your quarters until further notice. Girls will only be let out to tend to their chores."

Girls with more practical functions. Girls like Nuo, who lulls the master's guests into a deep drug haze with her delicate zither strings, and Yin Yu, who lights pipes and fills glasses of plum wine at every snap of a finger. I have no chores to my name, which leaves me roombound.

"How long?" I ask.

"As long as it takes." Mama-san's voice snaps like a whip, lashing away further questions. "His memory isn't short."

I can't stop seeing the master's face in my thoughts. So stone cold and steady. So lacking fury. The face of a man long dead to any sort of forgiveness or mercy.

Mama-san's right. We'll be here for a long time.

## 9

Sing's words loop through my head for hours. Over and over: *the end, the end, the end.* Their chill stabs my bones, makes my bedroom colder. I want to sleep, but every time my eyes close, there are visions of blood and needles. There's no room for anything else.

I'm still shaking when Ambassador Osamu arrives.

I'm one of the lucky ones. Girls like Yin Yu are forced to take in three, four men a night. The ambassador is my only client. He pays our master dearly for the favor—to have me all to himself. I don't know why he chose me out of all the girls. I just know that one day he stopped seeing the rest of them, and stopped the rest of the men from seeing me.

I'm exclusively his—cornered and prized.

The ambassador isn't as terrible as the men who came to

my bed before. He doesn't hit. Doesn't yell. Doesn't look at me as if I'm gum to be scraped off the sole of his shoe. Instead, he tells me I'm beautiful. Every time he visits, he brings me flowers. Bright, sweet-smelling spots of cheer.

Today they're nestled in his arm like an infant, violet petals standing out against the charcoal sleeve of his pressed suit. Neither of us says a word as he plucks the bouquet of withered roses from the vase. Petals flutter to the tabletop like dried-out pieces of parchment. With one vast sweep of his hand, the ambassador sends them to the floor.

He sloughs off his dinner jacket before he comes over to the bed, where I'm sitting. Shivering.

"I'm sorry I've been away for so long." He sits and the bed shudders. The mattress slopes down under his weight, pulling me closer to him. The heat of his skin bridges the air between us, reminds me how cold I am. "I've been traveling for meetings."

I try to smile, but there's an impossible weight on my lips. I can't stop thinking of the screams, the slurring words. All that noise from Sing's mouth.

"What's wrong, Mei Yee?" My name doesn't sound like my name the way he says it. It took me many weeks to fully understand the strange chop of his foreign accent.

The ambassador's dark eyes push into me. The concern on his face is real, shining through the slight wrinkles of his skin. The round cheeks and jaw that always remind me a bit of a panda bear.

His fingers reach out, resting just barely on my arm. Even that touch is searing. "You can tell me."

What happened in the lounge explodes inside me. The words burst out. "One of the girls…she tried to run. The master had her punished."

"And this made you upset?"

I nod. The question seems silly, but then again, he wasn't there. He didn't hear Sing scream. He didn't soak up tributaries of blood.

"You shouldn't worry. You're a good girl. An exemplary girl. Longwai has no reason to punish you." He pulls me closer, so our thighs are touching.

"I missed you," he says.

"I missed you, too," I tell him, because I know it's what he wants to hear. What I've really missed for the past week are the colors and scent of fresh flowers.

The ambassador leans in to me. So close I can taste his breath. It's heavy with ginger and sesame and honey. My stomach growls, but he doesn't seem to hear it. He's too busy touching, wreathing his fingers through my hair and pressing me closer against his chest and face.

This is what I do not miss.

My eyes are open and I stare past the silvering hair on his temple. There's a shelf on the far wall filled with books I can't read and the tough evergreen leaves of a plastic orchid. At the very end of the shelf is a statue of a golden cat. I stare at its green eyes and the characters on its chest—the ones Sing says are meant for good luck. I count the whiskers, again and again. There are twelve.

*Twelve. Twelve. Twelve.*

The number sticks in my head. Running over and over and over until it becomes only a single humming word, trying its best to distract me.

*Twelvetwelvetwelvetwelvetwelvetwelve.*

When he's finished, the ambassador lies back on the bed, breathing like a horse that's galloped five hundred *li*. His chest—pinched and taut like naked chicken skin—rises and falls in a maddened tempo. His cheeks are the same shade of red my roses were before they died.

I lie still, stare at the ceiling tiles. Whoever lived here before me painted tiny golden stars all over them. After so many months upon months of gazing, my eyes don't need to be open to see them. I know their constellations better than the real stars, the ones Jin Ling and I used to watch through our bedroom window. The ones that crowned the mountains and showered light along the rice paddies. The ones that actually shined.

I watched them for the shimmer. Gems of silver and shiver and beauty. Jin Ling watched them for their names, their stories. When we were very young, our mother told us all she could about the stars. The White Tiger of the West, which rises when the ginkgo trees yellow and shed all their leaves. The Azure Dragon of the East, which crowns spring's first shoots.

But my mother's knowledge wasn't enough for Jin Ling. She kept watching and wondering with a thirst I could never understand. Asking questions none of us could answer.

The times we felt the closest, the times our wonders

collided, were when the stars fell. Jin Ling usually saw them first. Her eyes were quicker, cut light out of the darkness faster. Her breath would draw in, short and excited, and she would point to where sky met earth. Her other hand shook mine.

"Quick, Mei Yee! You have to make a wish!"

I always frowned and stared into the black. There were so many wishes locked up inside my soul. Picking just one seemed impossible. "I don't know."

My little sister sighed, in that sharp, dagger way of hers. "What's the thing you want the most?"

I never knew. Instead, I asked the question back at her.

Her fingers tightened around mine, full of strength that always surprised me. "I wish we could be together forever. Away from here. Away from hurt."

The ambassador drapes his arm around me, frightens off the memory of my sister's voice like a feral cat. His heat is no longer startling. It's everywhere, like a blanket, folding and pressing me together with its warmth.

We stay like this for a long time. Skin to skin under false stars. The ones that never fall.

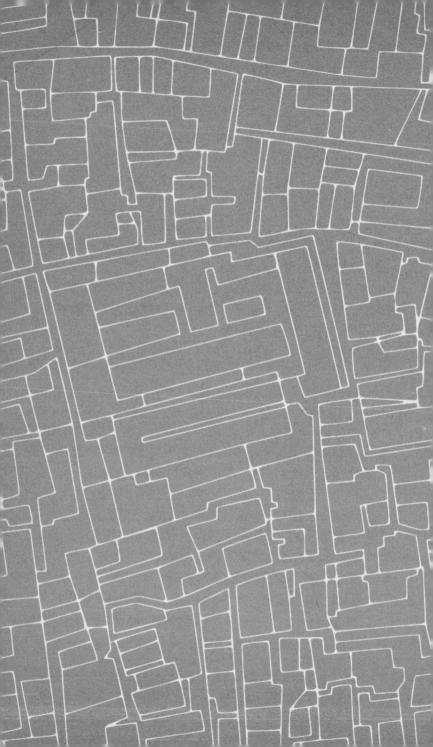

# 16 DAYS

# DAI

I don't believe in ghosts. Not like my grandmother, who knelt at our ancestral shrine every dawn with smoking sticks of incense folded in her palms and offerings of rice liquor and oranges tucked in her pockets. I always thought it was stupid, wasting fruit and good booze on the dead. Those who were long silent and gone.

He haunts me anyway.

My brother comes to me in dreams. It's the same nightmare I have every time I shut my eyes. The "night that changed everything" loops on repeat. My brother's voice rattles and stings, unchanged through all these years of death.

"Don't do this, Dai. This isn't you." He's always reaching out, clawing the edge of my hoodie. Trying to stop me. "You're a good person."

Then comes the blood.

There's always so much of it. On my arm. On him. It pours and gushes in an unreal way. Like the old cartoons we used to watch where the red spurted out like a fountain. I try to stop it, holding his hand as he slips away. His final breath curls out into the winter night like an English question mark. Bad punctuation. It should've been a period. A solid end. Not like this…

I wake up, heart gasping and chest aching. There's no blood on the dingy white tiles of my apartment. Just the marks I drew—charcoal and straight. The marks I've been erasing, day by day, with a smudge of my thumb.

I sit up, blink the terror of sleep from my eyes.

The world is unchanged. My scar is still here. My brother is still dead. I'm still trapped in Hak Nam, and there are sixteen lines on my wall. Telling me that soon—oh-too-soon— my time will be up.

## 9

Half of me doesn't really expect the kid to show up. I lean against a wall across the street from Longwai's brothel, counting the seconds with twitchy fingers. A yeti-size guard hulks by the entrance, watching me with slits of eyes.

I try to ignore him, focus instead on the paper lanterns over the brothel's entrance. Their scarlet light melts into the dragon etched on the door. It's the Brotherhood's symbol: a beast the color of luck and blood inked on the walls of every building in Hak Nam. A reminder that they own everything here. And almost everyone.

The minutes stretch on, and I begin to think the kid I picked is too smart. He must've smelled trouble. My fingers are twitching faster than festival drums by the time Jin dashes out of the shadows.

Maybe it's the bluish quiver of the streetlight hanging from the overhead pipes. Or the pieces of nightmare still crusting my eyes. Whatever it is, the kid's face jars me. It's so full of anxiety and angles. The perfect mix of worry and fierce.

Just like my brother's.

"Something wrong?" Jin steps into the lonely slant of light, and the moment passes. My brother's likeness slips, yanked off like a transparency sheet. It's just this street kid in front of me now. Eyes hard with distrust. Arms crossed tight over his chest.

"Nothing." I swallow back memories (I'm on a steady diet of force-fed amnesia) and push off the wall. "Let's go. We shouldn't be late."

Yeti-guard steps aside, and the door to the dragon's den yawns open. Traces of opium smoke—sweet, earthy, tart, and choking—roll down the hall, past rows and rows of shut doors.

I hold my breath and shuck off my boots, adding them to the neat line of slippers and leather loafers in the marble entranceway. Jin stops behind me, his mouth grim as he looks down at his own boots.

"Nothing will happen to them. If it does, I'll get you new ones with my cut." Promises spill out of my mouth just to get the kid moving. We're already almost late, and I can't afford Longwai getting suspicious. "Ones that actually fit."

In the end, he takes them off. We move down the hall to the lounge.

The smoke is thicker here. Long couches form a ring around a rug. They're full of Seng Ngoi's finest business-men, suits wrinkled and arms dragged to the floor by invis-ible opium weights. The place isn't quite as fancy as I'm sure Longwai wants it to be. There's a poseur quality to it, a faded-ness. One corner of the rug is frayed. There are smoke stains in the couches' fabric. The red-gold wall tapestries all have loose threads. Before the night that changed everything, I would've called this place a dump. After two years of giant rats and streets paved with human shit, it looks like an emperor's palace.

One of the men studies us with quick eyes. He's wear-ing a silk lounging jacket, embroidered with scarlet thread, a dragon snaking up and down his sleeve. A puckered purple scar runs down his jaw. There's a slight bulge of his belly— soft from years of ordering others around.

This is Longwai: leader of the Brotherhood, god of knives and needles, king of this little hell.

"This is the boy you brought to do the job?" The drug lord's voice is like a junkyard dog's. Throaty. Growling. "Doesn't look like much."

I throw another glance at the kid. He's all eyes, shoul-ders hunched and arms still crossed as he takes in the opium smokers. The crimson light of the brothel's lanterns hollows out Jin's face. Shows just how many meals he's missed. One gust of wind could probably knock him flat.

There's a cramp in my stomach, but I push it down, ignore

it. I don't have the luxury of doubt and second guesses. It's this or the chopping block.

"He's the best," I tell the drug lord. "I give you my word."

"No need." Longwai's grin couldn't be more like a dragon's: predatory and sharp. Capped off with false golden teeth. "I'll take your life instead."

The burn in my gut turns into a broil. But then I think of the boots that sit just down the hall. I look back at the dead-coal fierceness of the kid's eyes.

I should be okay.

Longwai nods over to the far corner. A man dressed in a nice black suit appears at Longwai's shoulder. He holds a bag of white powder wrapped in the shape of a brick.

Longwai takes the package and weighs it in his hands. "Do you know where the night market is, boy?"

"In City Beyond?" Jin manages to hide most of the shake in his voice, but it's still in his shoulders.

"Yes. Seng Ngoi." He scowls at the kid's slang. "Take the package to the last stall on the west corner. There's an old man there selling jade carvings. Deliver this to him, take what he gives you, and return here. My man will be watching to make sure that the exchange occurs as planned. Your partner will stay here until your return. And if you don't, then he'll have a nice, long appointment with my knife."

The kid's face goes a shade paler. My fingers start twitching again. They're tapping a frenzied, double-time staccato while I watch Jin tuck the package into his tunic and sprint for the door.

"Have a seat." Longwai's gold teeth flash again as he gestures to an empty couch.

I suck in a deep breath and flop down on the sagging cushion.

Time to get to work.

# JIN LING

Runs into City Beyond are dangerous. The police don't come into the Walled City. But they're always outside. Waiting. More than a few vagrants have ended up in jail for doing outside runs.

There are no police now as I jog through the wide, clean streets. Just flaring neon signs, the slick shine of cars, and an open sky, dark and pouring rain. All of me is soaked when I reach the night market—my clothes, my hair. The only thing that isn't wet is the package. It lies snug between the bindings on my chest and my shirt.

The sooner I get this over with, the sooner I can get back to the brothel. Keep searching all those painted faces for the only one that matters.

The man with the jade carvings makes a point not to stare when I scuttle toward his stall. He busies himself polishing a long line of tiny animal figurines.

"Put it there," the stall-keeper whispers, and nudges the basket by his feet. It lies under his table of merchandise, easily ignored.

I look around. There aren't many shoppers here in the far corner of the market. A young couple stands by the stall next to us, looking at jewelry while the vendor punches numbers into his calculator. The boy has his arm around the girl's shoulder. They're laughing. Together. It's a strange, happy sound. Reminding me of how much I don't have.

My hand slips into my tunic and leaves the brick at the bottom of a shabby, splintering basket. I stay close to the table, close enough to grab the bundle back if I need to.

"Where's my package?" I ask.

For the first time, the jade dealer actually glances at me. I realize how ratty I must look—thin like bamboo, dripping and streaked with mud. I don't belong here. With these happy, laughing people—these crummy, overpriced statues and scarves.

"Tell your … friend … that there's been a slight delay. I'll make up the payment in a few days. Tell him I'll send a boy of my own."

I don't move. This isn't how it's supposed to happen. I'm supposed to get the package … the money … to bring back. If I don't do that, I don't complete my mission. I fail and Dai dies.

This last thought catches me. Sharper than a fisherman's hook. Why am I worried about Dai? He's not the reason I'm running and fighting. If he gets knifed, it's his own fault. He knew exactly what he was getting into when he crossed the threshold of Longwai's brothel.

I tell myself this, but I can't shake this feeling. The crush of this older boy's life on my chest.

"You look like a smart boy." The stall-keeper smiles, flashing a row of crooked yellow teeth. "Your friend will understand, I'm sure. We go a long way back, him and me. My word's good with him."

He's right. I am smart. Smart enough to have rules. Smart enough to survive.

*Trust no one.* The second rule flashes through my head, wailing and police-siren bright. Maybe this man is telling the truth, but there's no way I'm going back to Longwai's brothel empty-handed.

"My friend will understand?" I ask. It's a trick I learned early on in the streets—if you act stupid, people don't pay attention. They don't expect anything.

"Oh, yes." The man's grin splits wider. "He knows where to find me. No?"

"I guess so...."

When the moment is right, I lunge. Throw my body under the table with blind effort. The basket falls over in my rush; the brick spills out. I reach for it, only to have my hand caught by the stall-keeper's fingers. He swears at me, trying to pull me out from under the table. The man's grip is strong. His fingers dig into my wrist so hard that tears blur my eyes.

My knife is under my tunic, easy to reach. I grab it and aim the blade straight into my captor's arm.

His scream is awful. He jerks back. Blood, red and thick, pours everywhere. I grab the brick and do what I do best. Run.

# DAI

Longwai hasn't paid much attention to me since the kid left. He's slouched in his chair, taking long draws from his pipe. Opium smoke spills into the air like ink, making a ghost ring around his head. I watch it, trying to look listless while my mind is racing. From the corner of my eye, I see the guards, black-clad and hulking by the hall.

What I need isn't here in the lounge. Not like I actually expected it to be. Most men don't keep their prized possession lying in the middle of an opium den.

There are four entrances to the lounge. All of them are wide and arched, stretching into dark halls. Four possibilities. My eyes dart among them, trying to get glimpses into the shadows for any hints.

But hints won't help. Not if I can't find a way off this couch.

I look at Longwai. His eyes are closed, face slack like a cat in a patch of warm sun.

"I need to piss." I make my voice hard, matter-of-fact.

He doesn't say anything. He doesn't even open his eyes. But I still know he heard me because of the way his lips thin and twitch.

"You got a bathroom I can use?" I ask, this time louder.

His eyes stay shut. I feel like a kid with a stick, poking not-so-tenderly at a snoozing dragon. It would be stupid to push harder, but today's number burns in the back of my mind. *Sixteen days.*

I think of it, swallow, and make one more prod. "You got anything? A can?"

"Hold it," he growls.

"Can't." I poke back.

One eye opens, dark and webbed with tiny red veins.

"You're awfully demanding for a vagrant." His words all slur together when he says this. "Well-dressed, too."

My chest feels tight, like an empty cola can being crushed under someone's knuckles. I try to breathe long and slow—the way my English tutor used to make me do whenever I panicked over my lessons—but there's too much smoke in the air.

I've never claimed to be a vagrant. It's just an assumption people make. I always let them, because it's better than explaining the truth. Who I am. What I've done. Facts that would change Longwai's attitude toward me very quickly.

"I get by." I shrug.

If he's disappointed with my answer, then he doesn't show

it. He shuts his eye again and waves a hand toward the closest man in black. "Fung will show you where it is."

Fung, a surly man with a nasty red facial tattoo, doesn't look too pleased with this task. He glares and shuffles down the west hall, always keeping me in arm's reach. I walk slow, take in as much detail as I can. Every door we pass is shut, locks on the outside. There are placards in the center, names etched in red paint. These characters blend with the scarlet lanterns that hover over our heads. From some angles they're invisible.

"Here." Fung throws his shoulder against a sliver of door. It's barely wider than my chest, cracking open to reveal a dark, musty space. "Hurry your ass up."

I don't waste time in the filth closet. The only thing I've accomplished on this venture is figuring out that what I'm looking for isn't down this hall. Only girls' rooms and a putrid, open sewer pipe.

My hands shove deep into my hoodie's pockets as I trail Fung back to the lounge. No more using the bathroom as an excuse to look around. I'll have to find some other way. Build up trust and feign interest in the Brotherhood. Create some sort of diversion.

Voices, sharp and sparring, like fencing swords, jerk me out of my plotting. They're so loud they even make Fung stop. He hovers at the end of the hall with me behind him, listening.

"No one else sees her, do they?" a man asks. Something about his voice is familiar, makes me twitchy. It has a foreign sound to it, like a knife chopping liver. The same way my mother speaks. His syllables stab me with homesickness.

Longwai's voice is easy to recognize. "Of course not. You

bought out her time long ago. I'm a man of my word. I thought you knew that, Osamu."

My arm hair prickles. That voice. That name…Osamu. I do know him. I know how he gets drunk on bottles of imported sake and sweet-talks women at his fancy embassy parties. I remember his face perfectly.

He probably won't remember mine—it's been a long time since I've been to any parties or embassies. But I can't take the risk. Not here. I bring my hands out of my pockets and yank my hood up, in case Fung decides we can interrupt.

"If I find out you've been cheating me…" the politician growls. "If I find out she's been with others, I'll—"

"I'd think long and hard before making any threats, Osamu." Longwai's voice is unbending, set in stone. "You might have power in Seng Ngoi, but this is my territory. My rules. Your diplomatic immunity means shit here."

"You aren't as untouchable as you think you are," Osamu rumbles.

No, he's not. Not if I can find what I'm looking for and do what needs to be done.

My heart claws even higher in my chest, up my throat. So many people, so many officials went to great lengths to keep "the day" shielded from Longwai's wide infrastructure of knowledge. They rooted out moles with lie detectors and double agents. Kept all the details on the strictest security level and their one loophole: me.

And now Osamu's here running his mouth, threatening to expose it all.

But Osamu wouldn't know…would he? He's a foreign

diplomat, with no interest in Seng Ngoi's city politics. I'm probably just reading into his words. Sliding my own fears between the syllables.

Longwai laughs. "I'm glad we understand each other. Did you only drop in for a chat or were you planning to cash in on your interests?"

"I was on my way to see her, but I'm afraid I've forgotten my bouquet. The woman who usually sells them on the street wasn't there this evening. I'll have to find another vendor."

The drug lord's laughter continues, gaining speed and volume like an avalanche. "You don't need flowers to get bedded, Osamu. Your coin is good enough there."

"No, I don't suppose a man like you would appreciate subtleties." Osamu says this without fear. "I need the flowers. I'll be back."

I hold my breath and listen, but all I hear are footsteps in the other direction. Osamu is gone. Good.

When Fung leads me back in, the men are laid out on the couches, stoned and still, like nothing ever happened. Only Longwai is visibly awake, his normally lazy eyes bulging and agitated.

"Can you believe it?" He seems to be talking to no one in particular, but his eyes are quick to find me. "Threatening me? Over something as trivial as that girl...Fool's obsessed with her. He brings her flowers and gifts like an actual lover. He even paid for a whole extra month of services so I'd move her into the only room with a window."

*Window.* My mind snags on the word. If there's a window, then there's another way in.

The shine of ranting slips out of Longwai's black eyes. He studies me, intent, and I realize my hood is still up. "How old are you, boy?"

For a brief moment I consider lying, but that would be unnecessary. Not to mention stupid. "Eighteen."

"And you haven't joined any of those ragtag groups that fancy themselves gangs? Most boys your age were snatched up long ago. Unless you've been holding out for an invitation..."

It's not hard to guess what he's hinting at—an invitation to be inducted into the Brotherhood. To officially join the ranks of murderers, thieves, and drug addicts. To organize my crimes. In a completely different life, I might've leaped at the invitation. If I were starving, living day to day like Jin or Kuen or so many of the other vagrants here, I would have screamed yes. Begged it.

But Longwai's not offering. And even if he were, I wouldn't take it. While it would be a surefire way of gaining his trust, joining the Brotherhood as I am now—going through its elaborate, invasive rites of passage—will expose me. Get me knifed into little pieces and killed. My secrets would not keep if Longwai looks close enough.

It's not worth the risk. Not yet.

"I prefer to be on my own. Fewer complications." Because this is true, I have little trouble saying it.

"What about the other boy? Jin?"

*Shit. The old man doesn't miss much.* I manage to keep my face straight. "You said this job took two, so I brought two. He's disposable."

"And yet you're the one facing the knife if he doesn't come back with what I want. . . . The disposable one." His last sentence hangs in the air like bait, begging me to bite, wrestle, fight.

I stare down at my toes. They remind me of the freshwater eels in the tanks of the seafood restaurants, alive but cramped, stacked on top of one another until I don't see how there's any room for them to move at all.

*Don't fight him. It's not why you're here.*

I look at my toes and think of the window. My next move in this intricate game of escape.

"Kid's back," a guard calls from the front hall.

"Is that so?" Longwai settles back in his chair, resumes his sleepy-cat-king position. "Well, boy, we'll see if you made the right choice, trusting that kid."

*Trust.* The word buzzes funny in my head, like a hangover. I guess that is what I had to do. Trust him to come back. Trust him to spare me Longwai's knife. We'll see if I was right.

Even though my hoodie is thick and almost too warm, I can't help but shiver.

about to burst into flame. He laughs and I know the stories are true. All of them.

When the noise dies, I realize the room is completely silent. The girl in the corner has stopped plucking her stringed instrument. Dai's foot is flat on the rug.

"I wish I'd been there to see it." Longwai wipes the corner of his eye. "Bring me the package."

I hold the brick as far away from me as possible. He takes the block and studies it for a minute.

"All there," he says. "I'm not surprised this happened. He was a new client. He's given others trouble before."

Stale breath stutters out of my lungs. I look over at Dai, expecting the older boy to be happy. Or at least not so green.

"It was a setup, then?" Dai's voice is cool, but his foot is tapping again. Faster than ever.

"More or less." Longwai shrugs, unconcerned. "I've been looking for some good street boys. Runners I can trust aren't easy to come by.

"But you've proven yourself today. How would you feel about becoming my personal runner for my more…discreet jobs? I pay well. Both you and your friend here will get a cut. He'll need to stay here during the runs. As continued insurance, you understand."

It's strange, almost eerie, that Longwai thinks human collateral will work. That he thinks we're capable of trusting each other. I wonder if he would've done the same with other vagrants, or if he looked at me with those black scalpel eyes and cut straight to my weakness. My need to protect.

I say nothing. The third rule burns in my calves. All I

59

want to do is run. Far, far away from this place of stinking smoke, filthy money, and fear.

A sharp snap fills the air—Longwai's fingers striking together. "More wine! And a light!" he calls over his shoulder.

I'm about to tell him no when a woman edges into the room. Wait. Not a woman. A girl dressed in women's clothing. Her face is caked in makeup. Just like the girl in the alley. The sight of her—tight red serving dress, tray balanced perfectly in her hands—chokes off my answer. I remember why I'm here.

This girl. I know her. She's from my province. From the farm four *li* west of ours. Her name was—is Yin Yu. I saw her face in the back of the van that took Mei Yee away. She was taken the same night.

"Have a fancy for flesh?" Longwai laughs as more wine is poured into his cup. It smells disgusting. Like alcohol and sappy, sweet plums. "Got plenty of that around here. If you're willing to pay."

I shake my head. The girl—Yin Yu—walks away. Her silk dress flashes red before it disappears back into the shadows.

If Yin Yu is here, Mei Yee could be, too. It's not much to hold on to. It's nothing at all, really. But right now, it's all I have.

I have to accept Longwai's offer. I have to keep looking.

"Yes." I say the word with dry lips, knowing I can never take it back. "I'll be your runner if Dai wants to sit."

If he's willing to risk his life every time I go out into the streets. If he thinks he can actually trust me.

"I'll sit."

Apparently he is. He does.

Longwai doesn't even smile. He takes a long drink of wine. Some of it spills onto his hand. The trailing, deep red streams remind me of the jade dealer's blood. "Come back at sunset tomorrow. I'll have another job for you then. My man will give you your payment at the door," he continues with a wave of his free hand. A sign for us to go.

We follow Longwai's man to the entrance, where he hands us an orange envelope. Stuffed full of cash. All the doors along the hallway are still closed when we pass. I can't help but wonder if my sister is behind one of them. Waiting.

# MEI YEE

There's a single window in my room. It's a strange gap, the only one in the whole building. Six cinder blocks forgotten by the construction workers—filled in with afterthoughts of metal bars and glass. It hides behind a bright scarlet cloth, blocking my view of the outside. There isn't much to see there. It isn't even a proper alleyway—just a gap between buildings used by street children and cats. The ghost lights that shine from the main street don't make much of a difference here... only enough to see forgotten piles of trash.

It's a disgusting sight—all gray and rot. I never understood why Sing loved it so much. During the early-morning hours, when our clients were elsewhere, she sat on my bed, shoved the red curtain aside, and stared through the metal lattice. There was always a glaze in her eyes that made me wonder if she was really seeing the view in front of her.

After two days alone, when the walls start to close and

choke, I pull back the tapestry and look out the window. At mildewed cinder block, snack wrappers, and shattered liquor bottles. I stare at the sight and try to see what Sing saw.

Something moves on the other side of the window. I can't see much, only the reflection of the latticed metal and fragments of my face. Maybe I just imagined the movement.

But then the glass rattles. A spread palm, white and startling, swallows the space where my face just was.

My heart shudders as much as the window. I blink—again and again—but the hand doesn't leave. It's still there—five fingers, palm creased like a cobweb. The lines are deep and tangled, with just a hint of dirt in them.

I'm just wondering what to do—if I should draw the curtain or scream out to Mama-san—when a voice speaks, too strong for the thin glass to hold back. "Hello."

I lick my lips, trying to think of something to say. "Who... who are you?"

The hand pulls away so the window is all darkness again. And then, a face. At first it's just traces, collections of light and shadow curving and colliding to show the person on the other side of the glass. But then my eyes adjust to the streetlamp's damp glow.

He's young. I can see the strength of his arms even through his hooded sweatshirt. There's no bulge where his belly should be. He looks as men should—active and fighting. Not made pasty fat by cakes and lazy with smoke.

And his eyes—they're as clear as a night over the mountains. They stare hard at me, outside looking in.

"You... you're one of Longwai's girls," he says finally.

I nod. I know the boy sees me. It would be impossible not to, with the light of so many paper lanterns rising up behind me.

He stays quiet. Those sharp eyes keep staring. They make the insides of my stomach lurch and flutter in a way I've never known before.

I don't know what to say or what to ask. My mind is blank. All I can hear is the flow of water, the *tik-tik-tik* of drips that means somewhere, far above us, it's raining.

I shouldn't be asking anything at all. If I were a good girl—an exemplary girl—if I knew what was best for me, I would drop the curtain. I would forget about the boy, roll over, and gaze at my painted stars. I would wait for the ambassador to come with a new bouquet of flowers.

But the rain. The dirt. His eyes. The flutter in my stomach. Things both forgotten and new. They keep me at the edge of the window, make me lace my fingers through the lattice.

"What's your name?" the boy finally asks.

My name. Mei Yee. It was my mother's choice. I remember her telling me about the moment. She was standing outside, letting the early-night breezes tangle her hair. Her face was turned to the setting sun, cast entirely in gold. It was strange seeing her so clearly. The house, the kitchen where she spent most of her living hours, was so dark.

We stood together under the fanning yellowed leaves of a ginkgo tree, watching as the mountains grew purple and ragged, like the back of a sleeping dragon.

"It's so beautiful," my mother said, "just like you."

I felt my cheeks grow hot, turn into the color of not-so-ripe plums.

"I knew you would be a beauty as soon as the midwife placed you in my arms." Mother's throat caught, as if she was getting ready to cry. "You made my life bright and new. That's why I gave you your name. Mei Yee."

Mei Yee. Refreshing beauty.

I don't want to tell this boy my name. Too many people have stolen it, used it in ways I never intended. You never know what a fragile thing a name is until it's used as a weapon, screamed like a curse.

"What's yours?" I ask through the glass.

He ignores my question. "What's it like in there?"

I look back at the room. Nothing is new. It's what I've seen every day after day after day. A bed. A washstand and a tin chamber pot. Crimson drapes and paper lanterns. The shelf with the golden cat. My rainbow row of silk gowns. Violet flowers, now wilting. Dying petals, withered leaves: the only things that ever change.

Even when the door is unlocked, I can't go far. Just my hall and the other girls' rooms. Sometimes the lounge, if the ambassador wants to smoke and chat at the same time. He usually doesn't.

It's a small world.

"What's it like out there?" I ask instead.

It seems all we want from each other is answers.

"Cold. Wet," he says.

Beads of rain gather like crystal ladybugs on the end of the boy's nose. I find myself staring at how they glint and shimmer against the street's dim light. I can't remember the last time I felt the hush of rain on my skin.

"Your turn." The boy nods and the drops fall, glimmering bursts of silver light. Like wishing stars.

"Warm. Smoky."

"What else?"

"It's your turn," I point out.

"What do you want to know?"

What *do* I want to know? Why am I even here, face pressed anxious against the grating? Why am I tormenting myself with tastes of a life I'll never have again? I should pull back, let the curtain fall.

But the boy...he's looking at me in a way I've never been looked at before. It's a stare that turns my cheeks the color of plums again. What started as a flutter in my stomach is now a burn.

What do I want to know? What did Sing want to know? *Outside. No more walls.* I think of Jin Ling leaning against our window, hungry, so hungry, for the secrets of stars. Watching to catch them and pull them inside. I lean against my own window, feel the same stir, the same want and sick storm cloud in my chest.

"Anything," I tell him. "Everything."

"That's a lot of things." The boy frowns and his arms cross over his chest. For a moment I fear our game is over. That he'll vanish down the alley to the song of bottle shards and dented cans. "Maybe we can arrange a trade."

"A trade?"

"Yeah, a trade. My information for yours."

"My information?"

"Stuff about the brothel. Do you...see them? Longwai and the other Brotherhood members?"

"Sometimes." My mouth is dry—the same way it was when the Reapers gagged me with a cotton kerchief for the pitch-black van drive from our province to the city. What started off as a game is quickly becoming dangerous. To talk of the Brotherhood, to share the things I've seen, could end very badly for me.

"Don't ever order shrimp from Mr. Lau's booth. He keeps them out far too long. It's a surefire way to get sick. Last time I got a dish there, I couldn't eat again for about three days."

"W-what?" My tongue still stumbles from the dry, feels as if it's tied up in knots.

"We're trading. Remember?" the boy reminds me. "You answer, I answer."

"Oh." *Anything. Everything.* Spoiled shrimp sold by a Mr. Lau. It wasn't what I was expecting, but it's something. I never knew there were shrimp booths so close.

"They hold their meetings in there, yeah?" His question is so quick and intentional that I suddenly don't believe his appearance at my window was an accident. All our words and pauses have been dancing up to this: The boy wants something in here. Something he can't reach.

And I want to know what it is. What can he want so badly in this place of smoke and locks? There's a gleam in his eyes that reminds me of Sing's fire. But while she was looking out, he's staring in.

There's the slick sound of metal sliding against itself. Behind me. I hardly have time to piece the two together. I jerk the tapestry back over the window and dive into bed.

The first thing I see are his flowers. A dozen white chrysanthemums burst through the door, and the ambassador follows. He's a big man, and his steps shake the room. I smell the wet on his coat as he sheds it, but I can't see any drops. He must have used an umbrella.

My pulse is all race and beat when he comes to my bed. There's something in his hands: a gleaming gold box with a ribbon. The ambassador sets it in my lap.

"I brought you chocolates." His voice is calm. Steady. Just the sound of it reminds me of how flustered I am.

I smile and say thank you. I untie the ribbon slowly. All I can think about is the window at my back. Is the boy still behind it, waiting for me? The burn of his eyes stays in my stomach. I pray to the gods that my cheeks aren't flushed.

None of the lace-cupped chocolates are the same—they aren't circles or squares, but strange shapes I've never seen before.

"Seashells," the ambassador offers when he sees the bewilderment on my face. "What clams and oysters come from."

"Seashells." I trace the edge of one. "From the sea?"

"Yes."

Wen Kei always loved to describe the sea. She could talk about it for hours. How it rose and fell with the size of the moon. How it gnashed like an angry cat on windy days. How its waters gleamed like fire against the sunrise. It was always impossible for me to imagine that there was so much water in the world. Sing even said there were mountains underneath—something she'd learned in school long ago. None of us believed her. "Have you ever been to the sea?"

"Many times." He smiles. "I grew up on an island. I couldn't go anywhere without crossing water."

I know I'll never be able to imagine so much water until I actually see it with my own eyes. "Do you think, maybe one day, you could take me to see the sea?"

The smile vanishes. "That's not a good idea."

Normally I wouldn't push—I would stay demure and quiet, the way he likes, follow our unspoken rules—but my heart is full and thrumming from my meeting at the window. "Why?"

"You're my princess. This is your ivory tower. You have to be protected. People outside…they wouldn't understand us. It's best if you stay here."

These walls are made of cinder block. Not ivory.

I'm not sure I understand us, either.

But I'm not brave enough to tell him these things.

We go through our ritual. Our dance. By the end, my cheeks are hot. This time, instead of gazing at the stars, I look at the window and its crimson curtain. I think of the night behind it. The sharp dark of the boy's eyes.

Maybe it wasn't the cinder block and trash Sing loved. Maybe it was the possibility, the knowledge that the universe isn't all opium smoke and cross, sweating men. There *is* a world outside, with shrimp restaurants and star secrets. A place where it rains and handsome boys get dirt wedged into their palms. A place where the sea stretches all the way out to the sky.

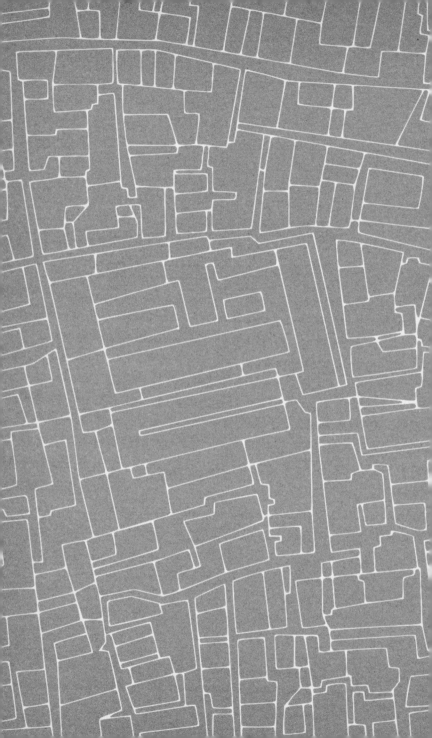

# 15 DAYS

# DAI

The window was hard to find, even after I knew it was there. It took me a good half hour, dodging the storm leaks in the pipes above while I circled the brothel, trying not to be seen, before I spotted the patch of scarlet from the other end of the alleyway. But if finding the window was hard, then facing what was behind it was even harder.

I wasn't ready for the girl.

*City of Darkness.* That's what the people of Seng Ngoi call this place when they glimpse it from their penthouse apartments and high-rise offices. A black spot of slum and crime in their shining city. A better name, I think, would be *City of Pain*.

The suffering is everywhere here. Crouching inside the steel workshops and weaving mills, where workers hunch over their machines for fourteen hours every single day. Threading through the corridors of strung-out prostitutes and knife-scarred youths. Lurking around the tables where drunken men toss money at one another and curse at the speed of their betting pigeons.

Usually I can ignore it, look the other way, keep walking. Not this time.

I don't really know *who* I expected to find. A prostitute, yes. But the girl behind the glass was nothing like Hak Nam's other prostitutes—the ones with bloodshot eyes who hover in doorways, trying to lure men with bare shoulders and heavy lids. Her eyes weren't bloodshot, but they were full. Full and empty at the same time. When she stared at me, I knew she was both young and not.

Haunting. Yearning. Hungry.... Her eyes showed the bars for what they are: a cage. Her want reached through the grating and lodged its claws in my chest, made me babble about food poisoning and second-class seafood. Made my palms sweat like a lovesick middle schooler.

I looked at this girl, saw myself staring back. Ghosts of Dai etched in glass, fragmented, held back by the metal weave of grating. The trapped soul wanting out.

Other than the haunt in her eyes, she was beautiful. I can see why Osamu is obsessed with her—black hair woven into a braid over her shoulder, like night against her star-white skin. The kind of girl my brother and I would've whispered about while the maid brought us puffed rice chips and scolded us to finish our homework. The kind of girl I might've asked to a movie or played the street arcades for just because she wanted the prize.

But Hak Nam doesn't have any feature films or cutesy plastic kittens with bobbly heads. And I'm not going to ask her on a date. I'm going to ask her to spy on the Brotherhood. To find the thing I can't.

Hunger preying on hunger.

*Will she have what it takes?* This is the question I ask as I shove my hands into damp pockets and duck through Hak Nam's cursed streets.

I don't know. It's a huge gamble I'm making. If worse comes to worst, I always have a second door into the brothel. As long as Jin keeps running for me. I can get all the key information from the girl and make a break for it at the last possible moment. A suicide mission at best.

That's my Plan B. There is no Plan C.

Most of the shops are dark as I glide past, but a few are still lit, their keepers hard at work. A clock on the far wall of a dumpling shop tells me it's three fifty. Early morning. If I don't hurry, I'll miss my meeting at the Old South Gate, where I'll give my report and he'll remind me in his stern voice that my time is waning.

I start jogging. The shoestring cinch of my hood taps against my chest as I run through the city, dodging the crumpled, blanket-covered forms of sleeping vagrants.

The Old South Gate is the oldest, largest entrance to the Hak Nam Walled City. In the daylight hours it looks like the entrance of a beehive, hundreds of people moving in and out. Postal workers lug satchels of envelopes. Vendors carry piles of fruit on their backs or wheel them in carts. A few even balance boxes on their heads. But in the hours between midnight and dawn, it's gutted and empty, a yawn into the world outside.

My handler is already here. He leans against the entrance, one foot planted in Seng Ngoi and the other edged into Hak Nam. His cigarette burns bright against the dark, lighting his face like a steel mill. When he sees me, he flicks the butt on the ground, grinds it with his shoe.

There are two cannons on either side of the gate. Relics from the ancient days, when Hak Nam was a fort instead of a dragon's den. Before the government left it to rot. The cannons are so covered in rust that they look like giant, weeping boulders. They're my markers. When I reach them, I stop. Not one step farther.

"You're late," Tsang says when I sidle up to the far cannon. The last dregs of his cigarette slide out of his nose.

"I was working." Rain still falls in sheets over the streets of Seng Ngoi. It runs through the Old South Gate like a river, licking the edges of my boots. I pull my hood over my head.

My handler didn't bring an umbrella. The storm has soaked him through, but he doesn't seem to care. "How was the infiltration? Did you get a look?"

"Not much of one. Longwai's keeping me on a tight leash."

"So you didn't see it?" Tsang asks.

My teeth clench together. I've got enough pressure without his barbed questions. "Oh yeah. He handed it over to me right after he gave me a foot massage. Gift-wrapped and everything."

"This isn't a joke, Dai," he growls. "There are things at stake here. Lives. Careers."

76

Tsang's face is hard to read without the glow of his cigarette. I don't like it.

"I don't see Longwai giving me free rein around the brothel anytime soon. If you want to know the layout, you should ask Ambassador Osamu. Hell, I bet you could walk right in and pay for a girl if you wanted."

"What the ambassador does behind this line is his own business—you're in no position to be slandering his honor." My handler produces a shiny cigarette case from his coat pocket. "You saying you can't do the job?"

"No," I say quickly. "I found another avenue. A girl. On the inside."

"One of the whores?"

*Whore.* The word has never bothered me before. But for some reason, I find my fingers twitching, tapping out Morse code obscenities. "One of Longwai's girls. Yes."

My handler frowns and wedges the cigarette between his teeth. His other hand holds up a lighter. "What have you told her?"

"Nothing. She just knows I want information on the Brotherhood. She doesn't know what or why," I tell him.

"And you really think you can get her to talk? That's damn risky." It takes three tries for the flame to catch the cigarette and hold.

"Yeah. Well, nothing about this is safe," I quip back.

"Fine. It's your ass on the line," he says, like I don't know. Like I'm not spending every waking moment thinking about it. "Test her. Something simple, to make sure she can deliver.

Something you can verify so you know she's not making things up."

"I plan on it." I hate it when he talks to me like I'm stupid or slow. Like I wasn't raised through Seng Ngoi's finest, most expensive schools. "But I'll need to give her an incentive."

A bus chugs down the street just a few yards away. Tsang and I both stiffen, watch as its wide lit windows string past. Its only passengers—a tousled university student and a foreign backpacker—have their faces slumped against the glass. Netting precious more minutes of sleep with open mouths.

Tsang waits until the bus turns the corner to speak again, "Like what?"

"Getting her out. Safely."

"There's no way I can guarantee that. Longwai's whores will be the least of our problems when all this shit goes down. I'm already stretching my bounds with what I promised you...."

"So what should I tell the girl?"

"Tell her whatever you want." My handler laughs. The cigarette shudders, shedding ashes and smoke into the puddle at his feet. "Whatever you think will get her to talk."

"You want me to lie?" My whole hand is shaking now. I have to curl it into a fist to stop the trembling.

"What? Growing a conscience?" Tsang smirks. "You, of all people..."

I glance down at the swelling river by my feet, the currents of trash and filth. A molding orange peel bobs by my boot, alongside something that looks awfully similar to human shit.

Just one more step. My ticket out.

It shouldn't be so hard to lie. Not when that's all I've done for the past two years of my life. It shouldn't be, but I think of the girl's hot bloom cheeks, the stretch in her voice. My insides twist like a rat held by the tail.

"Need anything?" my handler asks. "Before I go?"

*Anything. Everything.* I think back to the voices through the red and glass of the girl's window. Just after the curtain fell. The girl sounded like one of those caged nightingales that tenants keep on the rooftops. Osamu just sounded like a self-ish bastard.

"Get me a seashell," I tell him. "A nice one."

"Stop shitting me."

"No, really. I need a seashell." I need the girl behind those bars to trust me. I need to give her the things Osamu won't. I need to stop this sick swirl in my stomach.

"Anything else?"

I shake my head.

"Fine. Tomorrow. Same time. I'll have your shell."

"Wouldn't miss it." I don't try to keep the snark from my voice.

My handler slides back into the curtain of rain, into Seng Ngoi. I watch him walk until all I can see is the pinprick light of his cigarette. I watch even when that disappears, taking in every sight I can of my old city. The wide, even pave of its streets. The unbroken glass of its doors and windows. Lights in all neon hues advertising everything from dancing and drinks to jewelry and manicures. The trash receptacles on every corner.

I watch until the darkness of the streets starts to grow inside my chest. I push myself off the cannon and duck back into the tunnels of Hak Nam. Away from home.

More shops are open now, getting ready for the dawn rush. Smells and sizzles spill from their doorways, awakening growls in my empty stomach. Fried rice, vegetable rolls, every kind of meat, savory noodles, and garlic. Vendors call morning greetings to one another, borrow ingredients, trade dishes. Most of them nod at me as I pass, calling out the merits of their food.

"You look like you need some eel this morning, Dai-lo!"

I always wince a little at this nickname, so close to my real one. *Big brother.* They mean no harm by it. But it still stings, always stings. Reminds me of what I'm not anymore.

"It's hearty food!" The vendor goes on. "Good for winter!"

"No eel!" The vendor on the other side of the street scowls, pointing to his own steaming pot. "You need snake soup, for strength and cunning!"

A third seller laughs. "For breakfast? No, Dai-lo! You want rice porridge and tea! It will set your digestion right!"

Good digestion or not, it's a bun morning. I decide this as soon as the smoky smells of dough, pork, soy, ginger, and honey swim like hot gold through the air. I watch Mr. Kung slide a fresh tray of *cha siu bao* from his oven's shimmering heat.

He gives a knowing smile. "Three?"

"Six today." Usually I have breakfast alone. I have every meal alone. But I think of how much Jin looked like a skeleton under those brothel lights. He needs better food, and I need him running fast to keep Longwai's blade off my throat. Plus I want to make sure Kuen hasn't torn his camp to shreds.

Mr. Kung scrapes six disks of dough from the tray and drops them into a paper bag. "Have a good day, Dai-lo."

I nod, wishing his words could come true. But I have a feeling that Day Fifteen will be like every other day before it.

# JIN LING

Rain has leaked into my shelter. Everything is wet and shivering: my teeth, fingers, toes. I strip off my clothes and try to ignore how badly I'm shaking. My bindings stay tight against my breasts, protecting my knife. The orange envelope with my share of bills.

Chma yowls as I settle in, clawing his way into my lap. He's warm enough to make me stop shaking. I wrap the blanket around my shoulders and watch my breath shimmer in the air. Here, in the dark quiet of night, I can't help but think of the jade dealer. There was so much blood. I wonder where he is now. If some doctor sewed up the hole my knife made. Or if he bled out, right there in the market.

*It was us or him*, I tell myself. *A cut in the arm for two lives. A fair trade.*

*Us.* How long has it been since I used that word? Not

since the Reapers pulled my sister from our bamboo mat, and I watched, screaming. My twiggy, twelve-year-old frame helpless against so many men. I couldn't fight. Couldn't stop them from taking her.

Since then, it's been only *me*. No one to slow me down. No one for me to protect. No one to betray me.

But now I don't have a choice. If I want to keep looking for my sister, I have to keep working with Dai. The idea makes me uneasy, but it's not all bad. It'll be nice to talk to someone whose vocabulary is wider than a meow....

...

The sound of footsteps jerks me back into full consciousness. It's still dark—but my body has that sluggish ache that means I've been asleep. I don't have time to wonder about it. Someone's coming.

"Jin?"

My heart slows its rapid rabbit race. It's only Dai. Again. "What do you want?"

"You haven't moved," he says.

"I've been too busy," I tell him. This isn't completely true—I realize as soon as I say this. It's actually because I'm not afraid of Dai.

"I was sure you wouldn't still be here."

I remember, in a panic, that I'm not dressed. I've just thrown the still-damp clothes over my head when Dai pokes his head through the tarp's hole.

"Couldn't sleep. Got us some breakfast."

New smells slide through the mildew stench of my tarp.

Wonderful smells. Dough and sweet, tangy meat. My mouth waters. The hunger that's always inside me stretches. Roars.

But why would Dai spend his hard-earned money on breakfast? For me? I never even buy food for myself. Money, when I do have it, goes toward tarps and knives. Things I can't steal quite as easily.

"What's the catch?" I ask.

"No catch." Dai's stare flicks down to my tunic. I realize my hand is tucked there, reaching for my knife. Pure instinct. I pull my hand back out. Leave the blade hidden. "Let's just call it a *thank-you* for keeping me alive back at Longwai's."

"Did you know he was looking for permanent runners?" I watch Chma slink closer to Dai. The smell of meat makes him give a long, low whine.

"No. He made it sound like a onetime deal. I had no idea it would be a test." Dai sticks the bag of food through the hole in the tarp and waves it around. Chma yowls louder, swiping a paw at the brown paper: *Miiiiiiiiine.* "Now, come on. Let's go eat some buns."

"Go where?"

"You and your questions." He rolls his eyes, pulls his head out of my makeshift tent. "Come on. It's stopped raining."

I stare through the hole for a moment. Into the dark chill. My body aches for sleep, the warmth of my blanket. But I want the buns more.

I follow Dai to the end of my alley through the twists and nooks of squalid shanties. We go up and up—up stairs, through hallways of peeling paint and spidery mildew stains, up ladders, across bridges of bamboo and wire. I keep the older boy at a distance, hand always waiting to jump to my knife. He leads me through one more narrow passage to the foot of a rusting ladder. When I look up, my breath catches in my throat. At the top is—nothing. A far, black stretch of sky. If I look close enough, I can actually see some stars. They're faint and chipped. Broken. Every constellation—both the real ones and the ones I invented—has a piece missing. Torn apart by the overwhelming presence of *city*.

I follow Dai up the ladder. By the time I reach the top, the older street boy is already far off, weaving through lines of drying laundry. Forests of antennas. When he reaches the edge, he sits there with his feet dangling, paper bag at his side. One push or hard gust of wind could send him over to certain death. He's either incredibly brave or really reckless.

I'm not sure which.

"Come sit," he calls over his shoulder.

I walk forward. The lights of City Beyond shine bright— like stars that fell to earth and got wedged in its streets and sidewalks. The kind Mei Yee and I used to watch for. Some of the taller skyscrapers are still lit. More stars, trying to climb their way back home. Make the constellations whole again.

"It's been so long since I've seen them," I say, and crouch next to the older boy. He's watching the stars, too.

The air wrinkles with the sound of Dai opening the bag. A nudge against my elbow causes me to jump. It's only Chma, rubbing his nose and whiskers over my sleeve. I don't know how he got up here, but this isn't the first time he's appeared in impossible places.

"I come up here sometimes. When all the stuff down there gets too much." Dai pulls out a bun and pushes the bag closer to me. I don't hesitate. "I like to remember there's a sky."

"Those are my favorite." I point off to a cluster of stars, stronger than most, at the crown of one of Seng Ngoi's tallest buildings. "They always reminded me of a rice scythe."

Dai quirks his head, eyes narrowed, seeing that herd of stars in a whole new light. "That's a unique way of looking at Cassiopeia."

"What's Cassapeah?" The word is eel-slippery on my tongue. I'm sure I've said it wrong.

"Cassiopeia? She was a queen long ago, in a different part of the world. The stories say she was very beautiful, but very proud. Too proud. She smack-talked some goddesses and got herself stuck up there for all eternity."

I look back at the group of stars, try to see this beautiful queen. But only the crescent curve of a blade stares back. Glint and hard hours under the sun. Maybe he's making it up.

Maybe. But something in his words makes me believe. Makes me want to remember. *Cassiopeia.* I tuck the name away. The story that goes with these stars.

"How'd you know that?"

"It's . . . not important." The older boy goes to take a bite of his bun, only to find Chma pinned to his side. All rub and purr and *please feed me* eyes. "Hey, cat."

"His name is Chma." I pull my bun apart. Golden juices leak through cracks in the dough. Run hot down my arm.

The meat is still burning, too hot to put on my tongue. I nibble at the bread instead.

"Chma. How'd you come up with a name like that?"

"You're not the only one with allergies. He sneezes a lot." I toss a pinch of bread in Chma's direction. He pours out of Dai's lap the way only a feline can: full of frantic dignity. "You know. *Chma chma!*"

The street boy's stare is almost as withering as the cat's. "*Chma chma?* Not *hat-chi?* Or *achoo?*"

"Cat sneezes sound different from human sneezes!"

"Okay." He takes another bite of his stuffed bun, but even a full mouth won't hide his smirk. "Whatever you say."

"I swear, it sounds like that," I mumble, and look over at the cat in question. He has no interest in sneezing. Instead, he scours the rooftop for more crumbs.

We eat fast. Three buns each. By the end, my belly is almost full. I pat it with one hand and lick the juice from my fingers. Chma moves on to the empty bag. He inches in: head, shoulders, body. Only his tail curls out.

The sky in front of us grows light. No more stars—just a lesser darkness. We've been so quiet during our meal that I almost forget Dai is here, sitting next to me. That I'm not alone.

"What brought you here?" I jump when my companion finally speaks. "You're a good thief. Not to mention whip-smart. You'd do well in Seng Ngoi. Why stay in Longwai's territory?"

I've never told anyone about my sister. Not even Chma. It's too painful to talk about her.

"I'm not ready to leave yet." Really, there's nothing else to tell him. I don't know the answers. I don't know where my sister is. I don't know what I'll do when I find her. Where we'll go. What we'll eat. How we'll live.

"What about you?" I ask, pushing those worries into a far, dusty corner. "Why are you here?"

Dai stares out at City Beyond. Light is coming. Shining soft, clean colors between the skyscrapers: the purple of lotus petals, the dusty pink of Chma's tongue, and blue. So much blue.

"I've got nowhere else to go," he says. The want I saw that first night swims in his eyes. Shimmering with city lights and sun fire. Reaching for the skyscrapers. The sea beyond.

"You look like you've got money." I glance at the bag Chma is buried in. Those stuffed buns aren't cheap. "Why don't you just move?"

"It's not that easy." A story lurks behind his words. I wonder if it has anything to do with his scar. With the reason he's agreed to risk his life every time I run. But I can't ask him these things without having questions thrown back at me. I don't want this boy of scars and secrets digging into my memories.

I don't trust him that much.

An airplane stretches out just over our heads, eating Dai's words with its ear-throbbing roar. The hot air of its engines bellows down. Tears at our hair. Gnashes at our backs.

Dai is so, so close to the edge. Too close. When the wind hits us, my fingers fly out. Snag the edge of his hoodie. A motion made of speed and instinct. The same way I always reach for my knife.

The plane disappears. My hand is still digging into the

softness of his hoodie. Dai is still on the edge, sitting solid. He looks at my hand. His face drains: pale, paler, palest.

"Sorry." I let go. Cross my arms back over my chest. "I-I thought you were going to fall. I was trying to stop you."

Dai keeps staring at me. The way he did when I met him in front of Longwai's brothel. His eyes are on me, but he's not really looking. He's seeing something—someone—else.

Then he blinks. And the spell is broken.

"It'll take more than an airplane to send me over the edge," the older boy says. "You always so protective?"

I look down at my bare arms—so white after two sunless years. Scars cover them. Shiny lines and circles. My father's fists wrote them all over my skin. Stories he wanted to tell Mei Yee. My mother. I never let him.

I think about when I found Chma—a shuddering whimper of a kitten—being battered like a football among a group of vagrants. I was outnumbered. Four to one. It didn't matter.

I've never been able to sit back and watch things happen. Not without a fight.

"It's a good thing." Dai doesn't wait for my answer. His hands are out of his pockets, gripping the roof's ledge hard. His knuckles look as if they're about to break. "My brother was like that."

"You've got a brother?"

He blinks again. As if he's just now realized what he told me. A secret he let slip. "He's…gone now."

*Gone.* Just like Mei Yee.

Maybe Dai and I have more in common than I realized.

The sun rises fast. Reminds me that the world isn't all

gray cracked concrete. Its orange fire licks the buildings. Sets the world ablaze. Everything around me, everything the light touches, is beautiful.

"I always wanted a brother." I don't know what makes me say it. Maybe it's the buns in my belly. Or the warm sun on my skin. Maybe I feel like I owe Dai a secret in return.

"Why?" he asks.

"Because then life would've been different." My nose wouldn't be crooked and broken. My mother would've smiled. The crops would've grown. My father wouldn't have sold Mei Yee just so he could have money for rice wine. I would still have a family.

"Funny," Dai says. "Sometimes I wish the same thing. Just opposite."

I don't know what he means until he continues, "Sometimes...sometimes I wish I'd never had a brother. Because then life would be different."

We're both silent for a minute. Both staring at the yellow sun. Both wishing for different lives.

"But this is it." Dai wads the empty bag into a ball. Tosses it far into the air. "This is it. And we do what we can. We keep going. We survive."

I watch the bag fall. Down, down, down. Until it's gone. Swallowed by the streets below.

# DAI

Jin's gone now. His cat, too. Swallowed back into the labyrinth of Hak Nam's alleys and stairwells. Off to sleep in that ramshackle shelter of his.

This is the first time I've brought someone up here, to my thinking spot. The place I go when I'm at my lowest. When I sit on the very edge of Hak Nam and trace the scar on my arm. Round and round.

*Don't do this, Dai! This isn't you. You're a good person.* My brother's final words float up on the wind, fill the empty space where Jin just sat. Another 747 rips across the sky. Its wake rakes through my hair and crams my eardrums. It should be all I hear: molecules of air splitting and screaming, torn apart forever.

I've tried my hardest to escape him—to forget all the things that happened between us—but my brother's ghost is hunting me down. Slipping into my waking hours through Jin's face, his motions. The kid even looked at the night sky with the same gleam in his eyes. I wonder what Jin would think of my brother's brass-plated telescope, or the encyclopedia of star maps he read to pieces during his *I'm going to be an astronaut* phase. My brother always stayed up way too late, barefoot and bursting onto his bedroom balcony, babbling if I got too close about whatever new formation he saw. I always pretended not to care, but some things stuck. Like Cassiopeia. Like regret.

And the way the kid grabbed my hoodie and tried to stop me from falling: It was the exact same way my brother seized me that night. Same wide eyes. Same tight fingers.

My brother's voice keeps swirling, reaching, clawing. Trying to stop me again.

*Don't do this, Dai!*

"Get out of my head!" I scream the memories away. It's so much better when the amnesia settles in and I'm numb.

I think about the kid instead. Part of me wishes I hadn't brought Jin here. Hadn't bought him breakfast. Hadn't started to care. My risky-as-hell plan was so much easier to carry out when the people helping me were just chess pieces. Polished pawns without faces. Not a starving street kid and a trapped girl whose beautiful eyes twist and tangle my insides. Show me pieces of myself.

Hunger preying on hunger.

*This isn't you.*

The dead don't sleep easily. Just like me.

I shut my eyes, feel the wind whip up stories and stories of these rotting buildings into my face. I don't see the long fall just inches from my toes. I don't see the skyscrapers stabbing the morning sky.

*You're a good person.*

I wish my brother had been right.

But he wasn't. And now—instead of dreaming about dancing in zero gravity, making footprints in moondust—he's six feet under. Shattered beyond repair, broken just like everything else I leave behind.

# 14 DAYS

# MEI YEE

Since the ambassador's last visit, my life seems all stillness. The door stays locked, and Yin Yu is the only person I see. Every day she comes in to clean my room and collect my dirty clothes, hanging new silks in my wardrobe. She slips in a few extras: a cross-stitch, a sticky bar of rice candy, some gossip from the other girls. Things to free up the endless sludge of hours.

"How much longer?" I ask her. It doesn't matter if they're made of ivory or cinder block—the walls around me already feel tighter than I can bear. "Has Mama-san said anything?"

Yin Yu's eyes slide toward the door. She's not supposed to talk to me. "I don't know. She still has a bruise, from where Master hit her."

Mama-san still has her bruise. How long has it been since Longwai's strike? Weeks? Months? Only days?

"It can't be too much longer." I say this without thinking.

Yin Yu comes a little closer to my bed, pretending to

smooth out the wrinkles in the sheets and fluff the decorative pillows. "I've been in Sing's room a few times. It's bad, Mei Yee. Really bad. They're still injecting her...."

This last sentence makes her voice break. I hear the edges of tears in it.

When Yin Yu leaves, I lift the curtain and stare through the glass. It's still black. It's always black. I sit and stare at my spotty reflection until my vision turns blue.

The boy hasn't been back for me. During the first day of silence, I tried to list all the reasons he wasn't there, behind the glass. He could've gotten stabbed. He might have forgotten about me.

I know I've tried to forget him. But his face is there, just behind my closed eyes, as clear and strong as it was that night through the window. His eyes go deep, stir the heat in my stomach, my chest. So unlike the way the ambassador stares. The difference between them is rice wine to water. I feel drunk just thinking about it.

But I've seen what drunkenness does. I've cleaned Jin Ling's blood after my father's wasted beatings. I've watched Sing's blood dry on her skin after her binge of freedom.

If I know what's best for me, I'll stick with water.

# 9

*Tap, tap.*

Here I am, wrapped up in sheets and night, when the window rattles. Whispering in its fragile glass language:

*Tap, tap. Tap, tap.*

I'd been trying to sleep. My brain is filled with fog and half-woven dreams where I was braiding Jin Ling's long, beautiful hair. I can't decide if the sound is real or if I've wanted it so badly that phantoms are rising from the gray matter of my brain.

But when I peel the fabric back, it's those eyes of flaring dark I meet.

"There you are," the boy says.

I almost start when my nose presses into the metal. I hadn't realized how close I was. "I thought you weren't coming back."

"I've been busy with . . . things." His mouth pinches.

"You look tired." I don't know what makes me say this. It's true. There's a deeper shadow nested between the boy's lashes and his high-edged cheekbones. But I would never say such a thing to the ambassador. Maybe it's the safety of the metal and glass between us. Or the orange flare of the coals in my chest. "You didn't eat more of Mr. Lau's shrimp, did you?"

The boy blinks, as if by fluttering his lids he's actually shuffling my words, rearranging them into something his weary mind can grasp.

"No. No shrimp." There's a taut in his lips—fossils of an almost-smile—before he goes on. "I don't sleep much. The past catches up to me too fast. I haven't had a good night of shut-eye in two years."

"That's all I can do in here." Sometimes I sleep so much that I wake up tired. But dreaming for hours is better than staring at the door. Waiting.

"Too bad we can't trade that, too. Longwai doesn't give you much freedom, huh?"

*Longwai.* The sound of the master's name jars me like the first lurch of an oxcart. Reminding me that the boy isn't here just to chat. He isn't here to stare through the grating with his crystal-dark eyes and make my insides hot. He wants something.

"The last time you were here, you asked about the Brotherhood. Why?" I've thought about this almost as much as I've thought about him. No matter how hard I stretch my mind, I can't seem to imagine what he wants. Or why.

He stays still, weighing my question like precious spices, sifting and sorting the pieces he'll answer. I try my hardest to follow, try not to get distracted by the curl of those lashes. They're perfect for catching raindrops.

"I brought you something," he says finally. "From the outside."

His arm comes up so fast that I flinch away from the window without thinking. But what I thought was a fist is actually a flat palm, knuckles straight and unfurled, offering. In his hand—coiled in perfect shades of cream and rust—is a seashell. The exact same spiraling shape as one of the chocolates. It looks so *other* in his palm—strong and fragile all at once.

"I didn't stay long," the boy says quickly, "but before I left I heard you liked seashells."

The ambassador has given me many gifts: silk scarves, artisan candies, jewels that glow like cats' eyes. All lavish, all extravagant. Many worth more than my father could earn in a year. But none of them has made my throat swell the way this simple seashell does.

"It's—" I stop speaking as soon as I start. There are so many words that could fill the gap: *beautiful, flawless, perfect.* Just as there were so many wishes in my soul. I could never pick only one.

The boy doesn't prod. His palm twists, places the seashell on the window's ledge as carefully as one might handle a fledgling. "It's called a nautilus."

*Nautilus.* The word sounds funny. I want to say it out loud, perfect it, but my throat is still tighter than a straw.

"I asked about the Brotherhood because they have something I need. I think your information can help me get it."

I look up from shell to boy. "What?"

"I think . . . it's best for both of us if I don't tell you."

Again, the voice in my head—the sensible, docile Mei Yee—is telling me to pull away. To let the red fall. To wait, always wait and play it safe. But the window is like a magnet. I can't look away from the seashell, how the boy's fingers still linger against its curves. The rain is gone, but there's still dirt under his nails.

Fear brews strong, but my curiosity is stronger. "What do you want to know?"

"A lot of things. We'll start off simple, though. Names."

What seemed so light and airy before is now a very real weight on my chest. This is information I might actually have to find. . . . "Whose names?"

"Longwai's leaders. The top tier of the Brotherhood. I need to know their names," the boy explains.

Even when I wasn't trapped behind this door, I never saw much of the Brotherhood. I've never been allowed near the meetings the leaders of the Brotherhood hold twice a week, where they talk business and drink vast amounts of plum wine.

But if I tell my visitor how much I don't know, he'll disappear through the valley of trash. I'll never see him again. He might even take the shell with him.

My insides are now equal parts fire and fear. I'm playing with flames—my fingers are tingling with the cold just behind the glass.

Names. That's all the boy wants. Just syllables strung together like herbs drying from rafters. Sounds to mark out faces from a crowd. But somehow it seems like something more. Something dangerous.

"Why should I help you?" I try to sound tough, the way my little sister always did when she came nose-to-nose with the province bullies.

But the boy isn't a bully. He's weighing my question again, his hand curling tighter around the shell's coils.

"I can get you out." His words howl through the glass, prickle my skin like an old sage's prophecy. Tempting and haunting, but somehow impossible. Out. Outside. Under stars and rain. Over dirt. Beyond these walls.

*There is no escape. There is no escape. There is no escape.*

Or is there?

In this moment, staring at this shell, anything seems possible.

"They meet here twice a week. Every three or four days," I tell him. I'm not sure which days. All of them run together here because we're always working. "There's about ten of them."

"And their names?"

"I don't know. *If* I decide to tell you, it's going to take me a while to get into one of their meetings."

His face is all frown. Even still, he looks handsome. "I don't have much time. I'll give you four days."

Four. He says the number with an expression that makes it look as if someone is prying his fingernail off. I feel the same way, but for a different reason. Four days. That's nothing. Mama-san could keep my door locked for months. Any promise I might make comes up dry. It's just as well. They'd be spoken out of thrill, out of nautilus dreams. "I'll . . . try. . . ."

"I hope you do," he says, and lets go of the seashell. It almost doesn't fit on the edge of the concrete, but the boy balanced it well. It's there to stay, less than an inch from the glass. If the window were shattered, I could reach out and touch it.

"If it isn't safe, I'll put a flower in the window."

"I'll be back."

"Wait—" I call out, but the boy hasn't moved. He's still just beyond the glass, a fingertip away. "I told you about when the meetings are. Tell me something. Please."

The boy's eyes drift down to the shell, remind me that he doesn't owe me anything. Not even something. But his words—he can't know how I've held on to them—how I've spent hours imagining Mr. Lau bent over a bucket of spoiled shrimp. Peeling their skins off with hands of practice and calluses.

I need more.

"I watched the sun rise yesterday," he tells me. "I've had insomnia for two years, and it was the first time I'd ever thought about going up and watching the daybreak."

"What was it like?" My voice is eager—hungry for colors and light and everything I don't have. Everything this boy has seen.

But he doesn't tell me about how the pink of the sun spread like afterglow on the cheeks of the sky. Or how the clouds chorused brighter than he could stand.

"Beautiful," he says instead, his voice hesitant and hazy. "Sad. It made me wish I were somewhere else. Someone else."

I wait for him to go on, but he doesn't. He's given me everything he can.

"I think everyone wishes that," I tell him. *I know I do.*

He's still looking at the shell. The edges of his mouth screw tight. And I just want him to smile. To let the years and strain and weary insomniac nights he gathers inside fall away.

"I'm glad you're here," I offer. "I'm glad you're you."

His lips twist more. It's not a smile, but not a grimace, either. "I have to go. I'll be back in four days."

He turns. I let the tapestry down and look at the vase standing guard by the door like a lone soldier. Its flowers are shriveled, fighting off death's brown edges.

I should start watering them.

# DAI

I don't leave right away. I didn't really have to go, just needed to get away from so many dangerous feelings, bull's-eye words. Instead, I stand and stare at the shell. It's a flawless thing. Almost too perfect. When I was younger and the summer days grew too long, my mother and Emiyo used to take us walking along the seashore to look for shells. My plastic pail was always filled to the brim with chipped oysters and hollowed-out crab carcasses. Things Emiyo always chucked in the garbage when we got home.

I never found anything as perfect and whole as this.

It makes me wonder where Tsang got it. He doesn't strike me as the *walk along the seashore with your pants rolled up searching for treasures of the sea* type. Besides, I'm not even sure nautiluses live around here. (My brother would've known. It would be an encyclopedia factoid he gleaned from his *I love dolphins and want to be a marine biologist* phase.) Tsang probably bought it from the gift shop at Seng Ngoi's Grand Aquarium or from a grungy stall at the night market.

Most likely it was made in a factory with chemicals and synthetics. It's probably not even a real shell at all. As glamorous and hollowed-out and fake as me and my promises.

My stomach churns, and for just a minute I want to rap on the window again. I want to look through the lattice and tell the girl it's all a mistake. I can't promise her freedom. I can't even free myself.

But I don't. Maybe it's because I think I really can pull this off. That against all the odds, all of Longwai's men and their guns, I can get the girl out. Fill the emptiness of her eyes. Of my own echoed stare.

*Beautiful. Sad. It made me wish I were somewhere else. Someone else.*

Was I talking about watching sunrises or seeing her? I'm not so sure.

Whatever the subject matter, it was the truth.

So is this: I'm not a good person. I'm a selfish bastard, needing and taking, leaving her behind with nothing but trinkets. Just like Osamu.

*I'm glad you're here. I'm glad you're you.*

Salt words rubbed in a wound. Stinging like a few dozen obscenities strung together. If the girl has any sense at all, she'll forget about the names. Forget about me. And a small part of me—the same hint of Dai that wishes we'd met in a

106

completely different life, the pieces of Dai the window doesn't reflect—hopes she does.

I shove my hands into my pockets, where they twitch and tap and curl into fists.

I walk away.

# 13 DAYS

# JIN LING

My next few runs are smooth work. There aren't so many shadows in City Beyond, but I'm learning that the same tactics work there. Make no noise. Walk with your shoulders hunched. Keep to the sides of buildings. Do all this and no one will notice you. Not even the police who circle the Walled City. Vultures with handcuffs and guns.

I haven't seen Yin Yu again. There are other girls: faces trapped in makeup and forced smiles. Every time one of them walks into the lounge, my heart jolts. Every time, I think it's Mei Yee. Every time, I look and realize it's another nameless girl. Another not her.

Every time, I look. Every time, I hope. I won't stop until I find my sister.

Chma greets me before I reach our alley, my belly still warm and full of the pumpkin porridge Dai bought. I think it's strange that he's so free with his money, but he doesn't seem to mind. We haven't been back to the rooftop. After every run, he takes me somewhere new. Today we sat across from Mrs. Pak's storefront. Watching her beat rice noodles into long, thin strands; teaching her daughter to do the same. We ate in silence and dark, positioned just right so we could see pieces of a cartoon program flickering through a family's window: a cat and a mouse chasing each other. The cat was a terrible hunter. Not like Chma. He let the mouse run between his legs, skip across his back. The kids inside giggled, pointing at the screen and munching on a plate of rice cakes. I couldn't laugh with them. I kept imagining how hungry the cat was. How quickly he would fade in real life.

Something about the way my own cat moves makes me slow. He hops to my side, an angry howl in his throat. His eyes glow through the dark. Electric and wide. All his back hairs stand straight.

I look around, but there's nothing. Just a crumpled plastic bag rolling down the street. It tumbles by rows of hurried, spray-painted characters. None of them dried before the red paint dripped down. The walls look as if they're bleeding.

I walk closer to the mouth of my alley. Chma slides in front of my feet so fast I almost trip. He yowls again. Not a *mine* meow, but something more urgent. With more tooth and *hiiiiiiisssssss*.

Something's wrong. He never acts this way.

My fingers wrap tight around my knife.

*Don't be afraid*, I tell myself. *It's nothing. Probably just a monster-size rat.*

As soon as I round the corner, I know I'm wrong.

My camp lies in ruins. The tarp is destroyed. Its battered blue body scattered in pieces all over the alley. The cuts on the edges are jagged but clean. A knife did this.

My blanket. The melted half of a chocolate candy bar Dai gave me. The workbook of characters I was trying my hardest to learn. The set of hole-riddled slippers I snagged from a door stoop. My matchbook. All of it's gone.

Wind barrels into my corner, whipping pieces of tarp all over. I shake, full of anger and chill. A deep breath reminds me of the envelope at my chest. Nothing I lost was important. I have my money and my knife. I have Chma.

"Nice boots you got there."

I snap back around. My knuckles grow white against my blade.

Kuen stands at the alley's entrance. His burly body blocks the streetlamp's weak rays. He stands by himself, but I know he's not alone. Kuen's never alone.

My feet start a slow, sure retreat.

"They've been useful." I hate how my voice shakes. Kuen leers at my willowy frame, focused on how thin my shoulders are. He doesn't pay attention to where my feet take me. "You want them back?"

The smile on the street boy's lips twists. Turns into something ugly. "You, Jin, have been a pain in my ass. Ever since you showed up from Beyond. I think it's about time we took care of that."

Shadows gather behind Kuen. First heads and then torsos. Other, slightly less hulking boys. Their bodies block the way out. Make sure I don't run. Running is my biggest strength. Everyone knows that. Kuen planned this—used his brain for once.

Kuen's hand slides to his hip, where I'm sure there's a knife as sharp and nasty as mine. He's stronger than me, no question. All the boys are.

I count my steps back. Three. Five. Eight. Each one makes Kuen's lips curl wider. Shows more teeth. They're yellow and sharp. Too many for his mouth.

Ten steps. I pause, my calves grow hard like rocks. I pray to the gods that I counted right. If I look up, Kuen will know.

I crouch close to the ground. Then, with all the energy in my screaming, cramped thighs, I jump.

I've practiced this move before. When sweltering summer nights wouldn't let me sleep. But I always knew where the grip was. The exact spot on the jutting tin roof where my fingers could clasp and pull. Drag me, inch by painful inch, to safety. But that was when I was looking. When there wasn't a seething boy and his army of knives just feet away.

But the gods and their spirits must be watching over me tonight, because somehow my hands find the rusted dip of metal. My fingers latch onto the tin edge. Pull.

It always feels like this when I'm running. As if I'm not in my body anymore. Some savage survivor takes over, does things I can't. She can leap over ten-foot gaps and jump into a half-filled Dumpster from three stories up. She can squeeze through impossible, crushing spaces. And she can pull my full weight onto a slanting roof with only her arms.

I hear Kuen cursing, lunging forward. My body jerks. Strains under the weight that isn't mine. A look over my shoulder shows Kuen, beet-faced and spitting, his hand wrapped around my right foot.

The sight is so terrifying that I might have let go, but the survivor holds tight to the roof. She lifts her free foot. Brings it down onto Kuen's face with a gut-twisting crunch. If I hadn't been wearing his boots, I might not have been able to break his nose.

The vagrant lets go, howling in pain. I don't pause to watch his face run scarlet with blood. The other boys in Kuen's gang are close, frozen by their leader's animal wails. They won't be still for long. *And they*, the survivor reminds me, *can still climb*.

I hoist myself onto the sheet of slanting, rippled metal. Climb as far as I can. For some reason, this section doesn't connect with the other rooftops. It's a forgotten, lonely stretch. A metal island jutting into a sea of cinder block walls. I have the high ground, but I'm still trapped.

"Ged 'im!" Kuen gasps under blood and broken face. "Someone ged 'im, dammit!"

The tin around me shudders as the first boy starts to climb. He's smaller than the rest, even tinier than me. A skeletal wisp. One of the bigger boys has hoisted him up so he can reach the metal.

I stay close to the edge, where I can bottleneck them. Keep them away with quick swipes of my knife. I glare at the boy, flashing my blade. He pauses, his feet still digging into his pack member's shoulders.

115

"Bon! Get your ass up there!" one of the other boys crows.

*Bon.* I know the name. I look closer and realize I know the boy. The last time I saw him he was just a kid. A *kid* kid. Not more than six or seven. Scrawny. Freshly orphaned. Begging for rice on a street corner. He looked so pitiful that I handed him one of the oozing mangosteens I'd filched from an ancestral shrine.

Not much has changed. He's still scrawny. Long meals away from bright button eyes, cageless ribs. His face is the same—smudged in dirt, terrified.

But now he's a part of Kuen's pack. Now he's dangerous.

Instead of sneaking him bruised fruits, I have to stab him if he keeps climbing. I don't want to. I want him to let go of the roof's edge. I want him to drop back to the ground and walk away.

I make my eyes hard and shake my head. *Don't do it. Don't do it.*

For a moment I think my wordless pleas work. Bon hangs on bony arms, exaggerated joints. Looking as if he wants to fall. But the others keep calling under him. Their yells blend into a terrible chorus. It's the threat, the courage of the pack. Bon takes all this in, licks his lips. Starts to pull.

I have to stab him. Kill this boy I once tried to save. I am so sorry, so scared. But the survivor doesn't wait. She holds the weapon and jerks her arm back. Ready to slice.

There's a noise so loud—so *all over*—it almost makes me drop my knife.

The pack shrinks back, one solid motion. Bon grips the

tin's edge, his face colorless with fear. Kuen is the only one who hasn't moved. His hands keep clutching his bloody mess of a nose.

I look over toward the bone-shaking sound. Dai stands in the street, his arm raised so everyone can see the revolver. He points the gun straight into the alley. Kuen's pack backs into the wall. Their feet trample all that's left of my camp.

"I have a bullet for each of you, even with that one gone." He looks straight at Kuen. "I thinks it's best if you leave. Now."

"This nud a yer bidness!" The pack leader snarls fury and tears. "Dat wat stoled from me—"

"It's plenty of my business, Kuen," Dai says, interrupting him. His manner is sharp, cold. Like a razor's edge. "Believe me. I'll shoot you if you don't get out of here."

Kuen slinks away. His elbow stabs the air like a bird's broken wing, trying to stop the blood. His followers give Dai a wide berth as they disappear down the street. Bon is the last to leave the alley. He darts out faster than a dragonfly.

My knife hand is shaking. Haunted by the possibilities of what could've happened if Dai hadn't shown up. I'm glad, so glad, I didn't have to stab Bon. But this feeling is short-lived. Kuen's not finished with me. And the city's boundaries are tight enough to guarantee I'll see him again. Soon.

Dai stands, looking down the street. He clutches tight to his gun, every knuckle painfully white. His hands are shaking, too.

"You okay?" When he looks up, I realize that I'm still crouched at the edge of the sloping tin sheet. I slide off slowly.

Test each limb to see if anything hurts. An angry red line throbs through the crease in my palm. I must have cut it on the edge of the tin.

"I'm fine." I wipe the blood onto my tunic. Another smear. Another scar.

Dai has moved to the middle of the alley. He's poking the tarp's tattered carcass with his foot. My throat squeezes when I see the gun, still there, in his hand. "What are you doing here? Were you following me?"

"Just checking up on you." Dai glances up from the rubble. His eyes are so dark, like tar. The adrenaline of the moment swirls behind them. Something like terror and…sadness?

"Look who's being protective now." I slip my knife back into my bindings. Cross my arms. "I was doing fine on my own!"

"Were you?" He glances at the outcast roof. Something about his face seems raw. Shaken. "It was a good plan. But I'm not sure how long you would've lasted up there."

I swallow when he tucks the revolver into the waist of his jeans. It disappears. A skeleton of danger, power, buried under fabric and denim. I never would've guessed what Dai was hiding there. There are plenty of guns floating around these streets, but they never belong to vagrants. Guns are expensive. Impossible to steal. It's usually members of the Brotherhood whose fingers pull the triggers.

But Dai can't be Brotherhood. Can he?

No….No one in the Brotherhood would feel bad about firing a bullet. Their hands wouldn't shake as Dai's do now.

"Where'd you get that?" Dai seems different now that I know he has a gun. He looks a few inches taller.

"Mr. Lam's shop."

"How'd you get past him and those bars?"

"I bought it. With money."

My lids narrow. Not even all the cash stuffed into my orange envelope could buy me a gun. Where did Dai get the money?

He knows I don't believe him. "I've been making runs for a while now, Jin. I've got stuff saved up from over the years."

Something doesn't sit right. It doesn't fit together. The gun, the nice meals. His clothes without holes. Dai shouldn't have as much money as he does. Not if he's just a drug runner. Not if he's telling the truth.

Questions edge my crooked teeth. Ready to sink into the meat of Dai's lie. Rip it apart. Hound the truth out of those cornered fox eyes. I open my mouth to attack.

But the questions don't come. I think of the gun in his jeans. The one he just fired to save my life. Pumpkin porridge sits heavy in my belly, still warm. A reminder that I haven't been hungry for days.

Dai might not be telling the truth. But he's given me every reason to trust him.

I breathe deep. The bindings squeeze against my budding chest. The girlhood I keep hidden to survive.

Everyone in the Walled City has secrets. I might want the truth, but I need my sister more. I can't risk losing my only way into Longwai's brothel. Not over this.

I exhale. My breath turns to steam, clouds the air between us. "You've had a gun this whole time?"

"I don't want people to know. But I guess all that's gone to shit now." He sighs and grabs a fistful of hair. The clump is so black it's almost blue. His hands still shake. "I've never fired it before."

"Guess I should feel special," I mutter, and kick at a lone tarp piece. It flops on the alley floor like a dying fish.

The older boy gives me an odd look. The blue plastic shred licks the edge of his shoe. He kicks it back to me. "They didn't leave much, huh? You should come stay at my place."

"I can't." My reply is automatic. Ever since the night I rolled off the bamboo mat I shared with Mei Yee, I've slept alone. Too much can happen when you're asleep. Dead to the world.

Dai shakes his head. "Don't be stupid, Jin. You saw the look on Kuen's face—he'll be looking for you."

Dai's right. It's exactly the kind of thing someone like Kuen would do. He didn't strip me of my tarp to use it. He destroyed it. Took away another piece of my armor for survival. And now that I've gone and messed up his pretty face...

Chma settles in the slight break between my legs. His bushy tail twitches back and forth like the hands on those fancy fake watches the street hawkers sell.

"We've got a good thing going over at Longwai's," he goes on. "I don't need you getting cut to pieces in some alley."

"I can take care of myself." I bend down and pick up my cat. My hurt hand throbs against Chma's fur. I don't even have a blanket to wrap it in.

"Stubborn, aren't you?" There's no humor in the way he says this. "What do you suggest I tell Longwai next time I see him? That you got knifed in the back because you were too proud to sleep somewhere safe?"

He's right. I am too proud. Too proud, too tired, too cold. I can't save myself. Not this time. I have to follow Dai back to his shelter. If I want to live the night, I have to trust him. Let him protect me.

I let out another cloudy breath. "Fine. I'll go to your place."

I squeeze my cat tighter. Holding him helps keep me from shaking. Chma seems to know this, because he doesn't try twisting his way out of my grasp. He lies as limp as a dead thing on my shoulder while I follow Dai to some mysterious corner of the city.

# DAI

The gun in my jeans weighs tons. My hands are in my pockets, trembling like a dog spooked by a foghorn. Shivering and burning from the power of the metal.

I've carried the same gun for two years, but this is the first time I've pulled the trigger. The first time I've fired a weapon since the night that changed everything. I had no choice. I had to fire it. Unleash a shot that tore the air apart, unraveled every nerve in my body at once.

My emotions are like pounds of overcooked rice noodles. Spilling everywhere. Impossible to gather back together again. I blame them for my split-second decision to bring Jin back here.

Of course, if I were following my old rules, I would've stayed out of the alley altogether. Kept walking with my head down. Let nature run its course, the way it did when Kuen pounded Lee's face in.

But, like Jin said himself, he's special. I need him.

Questions are all over the kid's face when we stop at the gated door. Of course he always thought I was a vagrant, surviving on drug runs and luck. A persona I'm now shattering by pulling oil-stained keys out of my pocket.

The door to my apartment building is identical to almost every other door in this city. It's barred, crammed between a seafood restaurant packed with smoking diners and a dimly lit noodle-maker's shop. First I unlock the gate, then the door behind it.

"This...this is your home?" The boy blinks.

*Home.* The word fills me with an ache. I shove the door open with a rusty squeal. The stairwell behind it never really grows less ugly. Its walls are soaked with water, crumbling like a sand castle on its last legs. A few years ago someone decided to paint them green, but only patches have lasted. Even those are peeling off in rot and curls, like a snake shedding dead skin.

Not *home.* Never *home.*

"I'm just staying here awhile." My answer climbs the steep, narrow stairs.

Jin follows in silence, but I can still feel his questions. The apartment, the gun, the money for these things...none of them add up in his mind. Not that they should; my story isn't the easiest equation.

Maybe it was a mistake to bring him back here. Tsang would certainly have my head for it. He'd call it something like a "leak" or a "compromise." But Tsang's an asshole, and there's no way I was going to leave the kid stranded in that alley. Not with Kuen's wolf pack circling, waiting for my gun to disappear.

The old rules are changing.

We climb the thirteen stories to the second gate. I unlock the door and let him in.

I try to see the apartment through Jin's eyes. A single room covered in yellowing coin-size tiles and more peeling green paint. No decorations, furniture, or food. The only signs that a person lives here at all are my pile of essentials in the corner and the charcoal marks on the far wall.

Jin steps into the room, cradling that cat like a little girl would hold a doll. He shucks off his boots and stares at the emptiness. His feet make soft sticking noises on the tiles as he walks over to the window where the veranda is and looks out. The window and its veranda are the only things I don't absolutely hate about this apartment. Every once in a while a breeze will dip down from the open sky, and around noon there's a crescent of sunlight that hits the tiles.

But, like every other veranda in every other Hak Nam apartment, mine is covered in bars. They're supposed to keep thieves out, but on my darker days all I see is the cage that's keeping me in.

"You're not a vagrant, then." Jin turns, lets the cat down. I can feel my nose starting to itch. Damn allergies.

"Never said I was."

"But if you don't work for the Brotherhood or a gang… how did you get this apartment? What do you do?"

*What do I do?* What a question. I feel like I'm taking an

exam, holding my pencil over a row of bubble answers. Trying to pick the best one.

A) Stay awake for days at a time to avoid my own nightmares.
B) Sit on the edge of Hak Nam's rooftops, waiting for a wind that's strong enough.
C) Always wear my hoodie so I never have to see the scar on my arm.
D) Lie to a beautiful, desperate girl to save my own skin.

The truth is all over this list, but none of the choices is the best answer. So I write in my own half-truth, cheat a little. "You know. I'm a runner. Freelancer. I find jobs and take them. Or give them to people like you."

He's looking around again, eyes as wide as the cat's. They scour this place like my grandmother's willow broom, picking apart every groove in every tile. It's odd how I feel like so much is hiding here when the only things that are mine are the T-shirts and jeans and jacket stacked in the corner. And, of course, because it's the one place I don't want him to be, the cat plants his pounds of fur and dander straight on the folded fabric. I'll be gracing the world with my nasal linings for months.

"By all means"—I glare at the cat—"make yourself comfortable."

The animal yawns—white fangs, sandpaper tongue—and stretches as long as he can over my jacket. Jin ignores him.

His stare is on the far wall, where the charcoal marks grin at us like rows of rotten teeth.

"What are all those lines?"

I look to where he's pointing and remember that I don't have months. Just days. *Thirteen*. It's not a tight number, but it certainly feels that way when I think about it, squeezing like a rope around my neck. I bring a hand to my throat. "It's a... calendar. Of sorts."

Jin's eyes grow thin with study. His head tilts just a few degrees. "Who are you?"

More bubbles. More terrible, true choices.

A) Not a good person.
B) A selfish bastard.
C) A murderer.
D) A liar.
E) All of the above.

There's no writing in this answer.

I look at the kid again. Ever since I pulled the trigger, my whole body has been on pins and needles, waiting for my brother's ghost to shine through. But Jin's face stays Jin's. Though some of the fierceness is gone. His expression is softer, less like that of a tiger about to maul my face off and more like a pampered shih tzu's.

Something about the way he's standing feels off. I can't seem to place it. Maybe it's the smear of still-bright blood on his shirt. Or maybe it's just that I don't like him asking. I don't want him looking at me like he looked at the room, trying to pick me apart and figure me out. Finding the dirt between the cracks.

"Sun Dai Shing," I tell him. *All of the above.*

"Sun," he repeats my family name. It echoes over the marked tiles, through the window, to the bars. Ties my past and my present prison into a neat little bundle.

I walk over to my pile of stuff, like I could actually run from the fading sounds. The cat doesn't move, just voices his opinion loudly when I root through the things. There's a first aid kit somewhere in here. A scarlet pouch with a white cross crammed full of things I never use. (Tweezers and tongue depressors don't do much when your hurts are inside.)

"What's that?" Jin blinks at the pouch.

"Let me see your hand." I nod at the kid's fist. It's clenched against his chest, tight as a furled poppy. He offers it slowly. Fingers blooming to show the still-oozing gash striped across his lifeline. *An ill omen*, my grandmother would have called it.

"It's not bad."

*Not bad.* The cut is so deep I'm surprised the kid can still bend his fingers. He needs stitches and a tetanus shot. Not some flimsy cloth and a bottle of peroxide.

But they're all I have.

The peroxide fizzes and foams over Jin's cut like a rabid wolf. It has to hurt like a bitch, but the kid's face stays tough. Under this light, I can see all his other scars, spreading up his arm like lace. Some are shiny and white. Others, angry and red. Just like mine.

But Jin probably didn't deserve his marks.

I wrap the gauze tight and knot the fraying ends. Jin eyes the bandage, flexes his hand in and out. In and out.

"Try not to move it," I tell him.

"It's fine." He clenches his hand into a fist again. Tough as nails.

I wish I could be fixed that easily.

"Right. Well, it's late. We should crash. Pick a spot anywhere. If you can move the king from his perch over there, you're welcome to use my jacket as a pillow."

I reach out and flick the light switch. The room pitches into a startling darkness. I can't see Jin's scars anymore. Or the lines on the wall.

"Dai?" Jin's whisper is light and high. Not like him at all.

"What?"

There's a pause as I fumble through the dark to the center of my room.

"Thanks."

*You're welcome.* The answer sticks inside my throat like an octopus tentacle. I can't bring myself to say it. Not when I know the real reason I did all these things.

Tonight I don't bother unzipping my hoodie and using it as a pillow. I lie flat on the floor, curl my knees up to my chest. In my mind I map out where the wall with the marks is. I turn my back to it.

# JIN LING

My hand has stopped hurting. I keep it close to my chest. My finger brushes the bandage—the cleanest one I've ever had.

Sleep comes easy when there's a roof. Four walls. I make my bed in the far corner, back to the tiles. Chma has left Dai's laundry pile in favor of my warmth. He curls against my full belly, rattles me with a lullaby of purrs.

No knives. No rats. No hunger. Just rest.

And Dai.

The older boy lies in the middle of the room. Coiled like a snail. Hidden deep in his shell. His breaths echo all over. Remind me—even when the dreams start edging in—I'm not alone.

I could get used to this.

# 12 DAYS

# JIN LING

The rice cake is sweet. Honey drips over its sides, makes my teeth ache when I sink them in. Mei Yee sits behind me. Her fingers run through my thick, tangled hair. Soft, gentle, never hurting. She pulls it apart into three sections. Starts to weave them into one.

"The braid is always stronger than the strand." Her melodic proverb floats over my shoulder.

I should tell her that my hair is too short. There's nothing left to braid. But honey sticks in my mouth. Catches all my words. I try to turn, try to see her. But the dark is closing in. Dream's end.

The sweet of honey on my teeth, my long hair, my sister's voice. All of it's gone.

The dark in front of me shifts. It's Dai. Getting up. Creeping toward the door. Like a ribbon through the air: silent, graceful. The way some people move when they don't want to be followed.

I don't move until the door clicks shut, the stairwell's light swallowed back into pitch dark. Dai's footsteps sound like raindrops. Fading fast.

He's leaving. *But why?*

I pause at the door. Each step grows fainter. Slipping away. If I wait too long, I won't be able to track him. Part of me wants to go back to sleep. Forget this ever happened. It's the same part that wants to trust Dai. That wants to believe he's worth trusting.

But trust hasn't brought me through two years of knife fights and hunger. Dai's hiding something.... This might be my only chance to find out what.

I don't bother knotting my bootlaces before I rush out. Stairs whip under my feet. Two, three at a time. Threaded through with my silver cat stalker. Soon I'm out in the streets shadow-hopping and alley-weaving. An awkward rush to catch up to Dai.

It's so late even the restaurants are empty. Tanks of fresh fish and eels bubble like electric crickets. No cigarettes burn in doorways. No old men crouch on steps sipping cheap liquor. Even the vagrants are asleep.

Dai moves ahead of me. He walks fast, hands shoved in his pockets.

I follow. Keep my distance. He moves to the end of the street, where the line of hanging pipes stops and the buildings' soggy concrete walls fold open to air. The outside, star-studded night. I look for Cassiopeia, but the angle isn't right. All I see are a truck's taillights—red and shouting—like dragon's eyes. A wind knifes through the gap, cool and careless and dark. This is the end of Longwai's kingdom. The entrance to City Beyond.

But Dai doesn't step over. He leans against the wall. Arms crossed. One knee up. Minutes pass. I crouch in a shallow doorway. Watch the older boy as he watches City Beyond. Waiting.

Then he stands straight again. His shoulders go rigid. A man-shaped shadow appears. Fills the empty space next to Dai. The hood of his jacket drapes far over his face. I can't see anything past the bridge of his nose.

I hear him, though. Every word. His voice is brassy. Not loud, but strong. Like a temple gong. "Are you staying out of trouble?"

Dai nods. The action looks more like a bow.

The man-shadow pulls a tightly bound wad from his pocket. He offers the package to Dai. It hovers between them.

"Take it," the man says. "You know how she worries."

"I'm doing well enough on my own." Dai frowns.

"You mean risking your neck?" The man pushes the parcel into Dai's chest. His voice drops low. "You've been doing work for the Security Branch, haven't you?"

Dai stares at the man, his mouth grim.

His visitor sighs. "Look, I know—I know they've made promises, but you have no obligation there. You need to stay safe. That's your biggest priority until we can get you out of here."

"And when will that be?"

"We're getting closer...."

"It's been two years!" Dai's yell isn't very loud, but it sets me on edge. He's always so calm and even-keeled. Like a paper boat set in a shallow puddle. Something about this man is wrecking him. "Two years! If you could've pulled me out, you would've by now. I'm running out of time. I can't just sit and do nothing!"

"Nothing," the man continues, unshaken, "is exactly what you must do. Stay here. Stay alive. If Longwai finds out who you are..."

Dai looks away from the hooded man and the package pressed against his chest. His eyes bore back into the streets. This dark maze of silent doors. His stare slides past my stoop. My heart turns to lead.

"Where's your jacket? Are you even staying in the apartment?"

Dai shrugs, but he still isn't looking at his visitor. He's staring at the ground. At the shards of liquor bottles, layers of mortar and filth. And my stare is on him. Trying to answer the monsoon questions rumbling in my head.

*Who is this man? Who is the "she" he talks about? Who is Dai?*

"She worries about you. I worry about you. We already lost—"

"Don't!" Dai's head snaps up. Jaw set. Chin sharp. "Don't talk about him."

Some agreement I can't hear or see passes between them.

Dai's arm closes across his chest, tucks the bundle like a sleeping child. The same way I hold Chma.

"We won't lose you, too. This will end," the man says. "I promise."

"Why do you even bother?"

"You know why," the man says.

Dai isn't smiling or frowning. His face is flat when he turns away.

I shrink back, but Dai isn't looking at the hidden corners he passes. His walk is full of energy. Purpose. He stares straight ahead, as if he wants nothing more than to get away. The man-shadow stands on the edge of City Beyond, watching Dai's every step.

Then they're both gone. Wind howls through the gap they left, a lonely, wailing sound. It cuts into my bones. Punches a hole through my chest. My fist clenches tight. Remembers the hurt under the bandage.

The wad the man-shadow pressed into Dai's chest had to be money. How else could he hold keys to an apartment or wedge a gun into his untorn jeans? But why would the man-shadow give him money? And if Dai has money, why work for Longwai? If the man-shadow wants him to stay hidden, why is he sitting right under the Brotherhood's nose? What is the Security Branch? How is Dai working for them?

And the biggest question of all: Why can't he leave?

It seems Dai has more secrets than scars. Secrets that involve Longwai and Dai's risking his neck. Which means, all this time, he's been risking mine.

Kuen and his knives, I can handle. Dodge, duck, hide. That's all it takes. But Dai...he's a different kind of danger. Made of sweet and sleep and safe. The kind that creeps up while you're dreaming. Stabs you in the back.

I never should've broken the second rule. Never should've let myself get closed in by his four walls. A place with no room to run. What good is a locked door when the threat might be inside?

I've survived two whole years on these streets. I don't need anyone to save me.

# MEI YEE

Every day the walls shrink smaller, smaller, smaller. Even staring out into the alley doesn't hold them back. The nautilus shell sits, a marker of the boy and his promise. A reminder that it's out there and I'm in here.

The painted stars above me are stale, old. I soak them in anyway. I've picked out all the blemishes, every point where the painter's hand trembled. I shut my eyes, try to imagine how she stood with the brush tucked between her fingers like a chopstick. I decided long ago that the creator of this mural was a girl. The master and his men would never create something so desperate and beautiful.

As I stare, I wonder about the girl. What was her name? Where did she come from? What was she thinking about when she sketched the stars onto the tiles? Was she still brave, still hopeful enough to place a wish on each one?

There are dozens of them, flecked over my bed. But there are still more wishes in my soul than there are stars.

I wish I could hold Jin Ling's hand in mine.

I wish Sing never tried to run.

I wish the boy didn't make my chest burn, make my thoughts soar like a phoenix.

I wish every girl in this brothel could be one of the lucky ones.

I wish, like the boy, I was somewhere else. Someone else.

And on and on and on.

# 9

The time the window-boy gave me is half vanished when the ambassador comes for a visit. Two days lost to staring, wondering, and worrying at my bedroom door. When it finally opens, my heart paces inside my chest like a tiger trapped in a bamboo cage. It drips with the ache of so many wishes—heavy and bloated. The ache the boy started. The ache so deep not even the ambassador's flowers can distract me. Their petals are a yellow and orange so bright that I can't look at them for long. Colors so exaggerated they seem fake.

His coat is heavier today, and his skin feels like marble against mine, an unyielding cold. He notices, too, but in a different way. "You're warm."

The ambassador draws into the heat my body offers. His hands tug on my dress, my hair, but all I can feel is the window at my back. The thin veil of the curtain and the nautilus behind it. Taunting and tempting with promises of something more.

And then it comes to me. I know how to make Mama-san unlock my door, if I'm willing to take the risk.

The ambassador is my key. His money is more powerful than Mama-san's anger or the master's apathy.

"You're very cold," I say once he's finished and rolled over onto the silky, rippled sheets. Once his arm drapes across me like a sash.

"I'm sorry." His honey-drip murmur fills my ear. Slows with encroaching sleep.

I shift and turn so that his hand slides off me and we're face-to-face.

I don't know if the scarlet slant of my lanterns' light is just right or if it's just the haunting youth of the window-boy's face. But today I notice how the ambassador wears his years in so many places: the fine fan of lines spreading from the corners of his lids, age spots the color of fire-singed bread, veins on the backs of his thighs that writhe and bulge like eels. I've always known he was old, but something about it today makes me uneasy.

*Pace, pace*, goes my heart. Back and forth. Back and forth. A restless beast.

I can't stay here anymore.

"Mama-san has been locking our doors."

"What?" His jowls tighten, snarl like a moon-crested black bear. Everything about him is sharp now, shot through with anger and business. This is the side of him that makes my fingertips tremble. "Why would she do that?"

"She told me not to tell. I'll get in trouble." I swallow. My mouth is edged with salt and bile. "Please don't tell her I told you."

He does not answer my plea. "She's kept you locked in this room? For how long?"

"I don't know. All I want is to talk to the other girls. I get so lonely in here and there's nothing to do!" Except stare at stars and a shell, talk to a mysterious boy.

The ambassador sits up. He looks around the room, his eyes mirroring every inch, every corner of my cage. I think this is the first time he's really looked at it. Noticed the chip in my flower vase, the small snag in the edge of the wall tapestry. Every muscle in my body cinches when his gaze slides past the window.

"Mei Yee—I've been thinking. About the day I gave you the chocolates."

The day I first saw the boy. *Don't*—I catch myself—*don't think about him. Not now.*

The ambassador looks at me down the slant of his nose, from a great height. "What if I took you away from here?"

For some reason his accent sounds extra foreign at this question. I can't quite believe what I'm hearing. "Away?"

"You've been exclusive to me for over a year now. I don't think it would be unreasonable for me to make a deal with Longwai."

"W-where?" I stammer.

"An apartment. In Seng Ngoi. Close to where I work. There's a pool. And a garden on the rooftop. There's a gourmet food service. Guards at the door. Everything you could possibly want."

From where I'm lying, the ambassador could be a god. He looms, stretched out like a temple idol. Golden skin, stomach round against the sheets, pushing into mine.

*A pool. A garden. Gourmet food.* The words feel like blessings misting my head, promises of heaven. A utopia far from this place of syringes and slaps. The thing Sing bled for—a way out—is being offered to me on a silver platter. I should snatch it, seize it before it disappears.

A week ago I would have said yes. But a week ago there wasn't a nautilus balanced on my window ledge. There wasn't a boy staring in, making me feel naked when I was fully clothed, promising his own way out.

Is escape enough? Is it even the thing I want most?

I don't know.

*Yes.* It's such a small, fleeting word. So easy to say. Even a nod would do.

I open my mouth. Crimson-bright drapes flare in the corner of my vision. No words come out.

"Mei Yee?" A fledgling frown hatches on the ambassador's lips. He reaches out, strokes my arm. The touch, this barest graze of fingers, startles me out of my whirlwind head. His hand trails down, comes to rest on the curve of my hip.

I should say it. I should, but I can't.

"I . . . I have to think about it," I tell him.

The frown deepens, storm clouds roll up behind his face. Gray. "I thought you would say yes."

I thought I would, too. But it seems that *out* and *away* are two different words.

There's a darkness behind his eyes, his face. A flash of something that makes me shiver. His hand is heavy on my hip; fingers pressing, pressing, pressing.

"There's someone else, isn't there?" His accusation is a lightning bolt—sudden and splitting. "Is Longwai forcing you to take other clients?"

Those fingertips, the ones on my hip, suddenly become crush and bruise. A whimper leaves me—half surprise, half pain. He's never touched me like this before, never hurt me.

The ambassador jerks his hand away at the sound. He stares first at his palm, then at me. "Sorry. I'm sorry. It's just that you've seemed different lately. And I thought…"

"There's no one else." This feels like a lie when I say it. Because of the boy. Because of Sing and Wen Kei and Nuo and Yin Yu. So many faces I'll never see again if I agree. If I take the safe route. "I just need time to think. It would be hard to leave my friends.…"

The storm cloud has vanished, yet his eyes are all haze and confusion. He pulls away, and cold air ribbons over my skin, calling out gooseflesh. The ambassador dresses slowly, carefully. He buttons up his dress shirt and twists in the cuff links. His fingers are so steady as he works these small items into place. There's not a trace of emotion on his face as he shoulders his dinner jacket and retrieves his topcoat.

"I'll get Longwai to unlock your door."

He's gone, through the door without even a good-bye.

The doors open, just as the ambassador promised. Mama-san doesn't linger. She continues down the darkened hall, undoing locks with iron twists of her key ring. I hover at the threshold and watch her. I look for her bruise, but it's gone. Healed or hidden. I'm not sure which.

The skin on my hip is splotchy—blood that can't be freed—pooling in shapes and shades that remind me of an exotic flower. The same flowers that freckle the other girls' bodies. The same flowers that used to circle my mother's wrists whenever my father gripped her too tightly.

I had them, too, my first few months in the brothel, when there was no limit on who came to my bed. Before the ambassador arrived and rescued me from all that. Or so I thought.

*It was a mistake*, I tell myself. *He didn't mean to.*

My hip throbs with every heartbeat, reminding me that those are the same words my mother said every morning after. She wouldn't even look at Jin Ling's bandages or her own battered limbs. She slouched over the cooking fire, waiting for the water to hiss like a dragon caught in a pot.

"He didn't mean to do it. He already told me he was sorry."

But the bruises kept blooming—yellow, green, bright pink, purple, blue—a whole garden of marks to undo my father's words.

"Why doesn't Mother leave?" Jin Ling asked me one night when I was cleaning out a terrible split over her left eye. "We could go and start another farm. Or move to the city."

My sister made it sound so easy: leaving. As if we could just load up the oxcart and go. And I could never find a way to explain it to her, why our mother stayed. It was just something I knew in my heart. Father was the familiar, the known. It didn't matter that his breath stung like pine needles every night, or that his knuckles battered our flesh. We expected that.

She would never leave him. Not for the world. Not even for us.

My mother was not a person made of risk and run. Not like Jin Ling. Not like Sing.

And me... I don't know what kind of person I am.

The girls come, one by one. Crowding my doorway like sparrows jostling for spare crumbs. I know it hasn't been *so* long since we last glimpsed one another, but their faces could almost belong to strangers. Even tiny Wen Kei, the youngest, has a weight in her eyes that wasn't there before.

"I didn't think they'd let us out so soon," Nuo says once we're all in the room. "I wonder why."

I wonder, too, what the ambassador said to sway the master's decision to unlock not just one but an entire score of doors. Whatever it was, it worked. I have no doubt he could talk me out of this brothel altogether.

My thoughts are still a raging typhoon—speeding around and around—so loud I can barely hear the other girls as they talk about their time behind the doors.

"And then he tried to make me..."

*A pool. A garden. Gourmet food.* Heaven on a platter.

"...I had to yell for Mama-san."

*Yes.* Why didn't I say yes? Any one of them would. In a heartbeat. *Yes. Yes. Yes.* A heartbeat.

"...haven't slept for days...I keep hearing her scream...."

Sing. Would she have said yes? I'm not so sure. She was all fire, all risk. Her heart might as well be my seashell. Sitting on the other side of my window. Unhindered by bars. Just out of reach.

"Wen Kei?" I speak out.

The other girls stare at me.

"Have you ever seen a nautilus?" I still stumble over the word, uncertain.

The girl's eyes brighten. A twinkle that waltzes with the weight. "Oh yes. My father used to catch them sometimes. He sold the shells to tourists in the market. If you split the shell open, you can see how it's grown. Whenever it gets too big to fit in its old space, it seals it off. Over and over again. Until it's all curled up."

The last image makes Nuo sigh. "Like a fern? My grandmother used to grow ferns in her garden. And radishes, and carrots, and—"

"We shouldn't talk about home," Yin Yu interrupts. Her voice is itchy and distracted. Hotter than usual. It makes me notice the stain of wine on her serving dress. Still wet and dark, like a wound. "All we're doing is hurting ourselves. Nothing good can come of it. This is what got Sing into trouble in the first place...talking about home. It got in her head."

No. It didn't get into Sing's head. It sabotaged her heart,

fed it so it grew and grew and grew. Until she was forced to seal everything off—try for a wider, better life.

I wonder if the boy knows about what's inside the nautilus. If those moon-clear eyes can see how my own shell is squeezing tight. How soon it will be more than I can bear.

It's not so simple as a *yes* or a *no*. It's not even a matter of escape. It's a question of what I want more. The ambassador's penthouse or whatever lies past the bars of that window. The familiar or the risk.

I'm not like my sister. I never was. Jin Ling always ran faster, fought harder. Whenever she was around, I didn't even bother.

But I don't want to be like my mother, either. Waking up every morning and watching the sun rise on fresh wounds, wondering in the secret chambers of her heart if there was something more. Through the rice fields and over the mountains.

And this is my race. My risk. Jin Ling's not here to take it for me.

Maybe I'm a faster runner than I realize.

## 9

I don't know why I thought getting the names would be easy once I found a way out of the room. As if I could just walk up to the master's henchmen and shake their hands. The only way for me to get the names, to wander freely around the brothel without suspicion, is to ask the master for a job. A job that will get me the closest to the Brotherhood's secret meetings. A job serving plum wine and lighting pipes.

Yin Yu's job.

There are leaping frogs in my stomach as I get closer to the unsettled smoke of the master's den. I've thought of how to ask him, so the request will sound innocent. But the master is smarter than his drooping lids suggest. How else would someone become law in a lawless place?

The lounge is almost empty. There are no clients stretched out on the couches, no long pipes spewing smoke into glazed faces. Nuo is not in the corner; the silence of her zither is deafening. I hear every one of my footsteps, creaking and sliding against weathered wood.

Master sits alone. His legs are crossed, tucked with a flexibility I'm surprised he still possesses. There's a pipe in his hands, but it stays down.

"Mama-san says you requested to see me. Normally, I wouldn't bother, but after my most recent discussion with your client, my curiosity is piqued."

He tilts his head at the last word. All I can look at, all I can see, is that awful purple hook of a scar. I turn my stare down to the floor. All ten toes are curling beneath the silk of my slippers, like worms stabbed, sacrificed to find fish.

*He knows. He's smart.* My fears whir; cautious, docile Mei Yee is scrambling, trying her hardest to stop me. *Don't ask. Just go back. Sit. Wait. Say* yes.

I wet my lips, gather up all my scattered fragments of courage. They're sharp, spinning, and newborn, enough to push out the words. "I was wondering if, maybe, you might let me take up some duties. I'd like to learn how to serve wine."

"You want me to give you chores?" His eyes slit, like a cat half asleep but still watching. My neck feels akin to a chicken's, stretched tight, waiting for a blade. I wonder, not for the first time, why I'm standing here. Why I didn't just say *yes*.

I stare into the lusty gold links of his necklace. "The other girls have tasks. I don't like feeling as if I'm not earning my keep."

From the way his mouth is set, all crumpled and caved into the side of his face, I wait for his *no*. Instead, he nods slowly.

"Very well. You have fortunate timing—Yin Yu was foolish enough to spill wine on a client just this morning. Have her show you the trays and the lighting procedures. You can take her place this evening."

He says this, and I remember the heat in Yin Yu's voice. The stain on her dress. I wonder at how I could be so fortunate, to ask on the same day Yin Yu's perfect service failed.

Then again, I am the lucky one.

I leave with a long, low bow, with a hope beyond hope that my luck will hold.

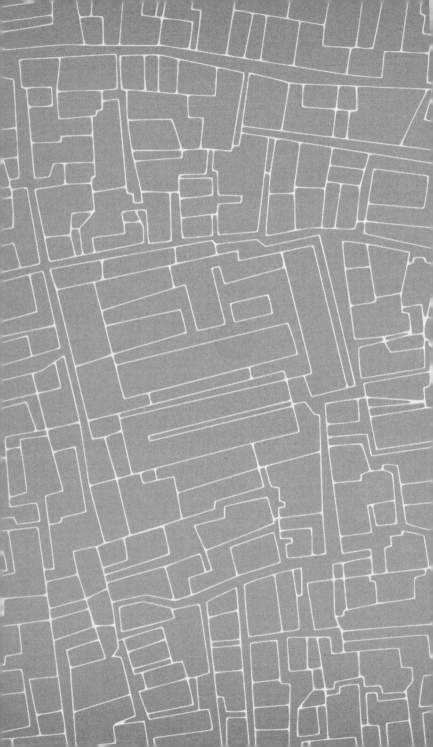

# 11 DAYS

# DAI

My whole body bounces as I stand by the rusted-out cannon, full of wild, untamped nerves. Up and down. Up and down. I wish Tsang would hurry his ass up. We never seem to get here at the same time. One of us is always late.

I see his cigarette first. Bobbing through Seng Ngoi's almost-dawn dark like a firefly from hell. The very first time I saw Tsang—the night I drew the marks on my apartment wall—he was smacking the pack of cancer sticks against his palm. Pulling out the perfect one and setting it ablaze. That was many weeks, many charcoal lines, many clandestine meetings ago. I'd bet the number of cigarette butts he's left at the Old South Gate would add up to cartons.

I stop bouncing, hold my breath when Tsang gets closer. Smoking is one of the few vices I never really took to. Probably because my father forced me to smoke an entire pack when he caught me lighting up in the rock garden. By the time it was over, I was the greenest, sorriest eight-year-old in Seng Ngoi.

It makes me wonder what my life would be like if he'd taken that approach for everything else.

"What've you got for me?" My handler hasn't even stopped walking.

"Longwai isn't budging. He's keeping me in the lounge. I've still got the boy doing runs...." I trail off, wonder if I told the truth. Jin's gone now—leaving just enough cat fur in my apartment to give my allergies hell. Not that I'm surprised. He's one of the smartest kids I've come across. He probably figured out what I was up to and ran.

I wish he'd thought to snitch my first aid kit. That wound of his is going to need another cleaning.

"What about the whore?"

*Whore*... Tsang's talking about the window-girl. It takes me a moment to realize this. To reconcile this brutal, bat-bashing word with the girl who's been on my mind the past few days. I keep remembering the look that washed over her face when I set out the shell. The joy and longing. One hundred percent concentrate.

She looked at the nautilus like it was sunlight on a string. The most beautiful, pure thing in the universe.

She looked at me the same way. Like I was someone worth seeing. A goddamn hero. It was a stare that made me want to stand straight, look the part.

Too bad she's wrong. For both of us.

"I'm testing her." I spit the truth out like a bad pill: *no hero here.* "She's trying to find out their names."

"Still?" Tsang growls.

"I gave her four days."

"Four days!" He sucks a sharp breath. His cigarette flares, lights his face like anger. "That's awfully generous."

"It's what she needed." Four lines. It's a lot for me to give, but what I'm asking for is worth so much more.

"You've got to move faster. Get rid of the boy. You don't need him anymore, and the last thing I need is you getting gutted for a failed drug run. Focus on the whore."

*Get rid of the boy. Focus on the whore.* Up and down. Up and down. Maybe if I jump hard enough I can shake off his words. I go faster. Up, down. Up, down.

"Are you even listening?" Tsang's cigarette is down to the nub, which means he's getting crabbier than usual. His eyes gleam with its last ashes as they watch me jumping. Up, down.

"I need both of them." Plan A *and* Plan B. "The boy is my only way into the brothel. I'll need that when the girl comes through."

"Why not let the whore do it all?"

My feet land flat on the ground. Stay there. I stare straight at Tsang. At the orange fire choking in a wreath of smoke. Almost dead.

"Stop using that word," I tell him.

Tsang's features twist into a smirk. He starts to laugh. "Sounds like someone's got a crush. Now there's a match made in heaven: a prostitute and a—"

"We done?" I cut off my handler. His cigarette winks out on cue.

"Next time we meet, I want results." Tsang plucks the dead, smoking thing from his lips. Tosses it into a grimy puddle, where it hisses its own pitiful eulogy. "Stay focused, Sun Dai Shing. Your time is running out."

# MEI YEE

Yin Yu's fingers were too tight on everything when she showed me the lacquered cabinet of servingware. Her knuckles were so white and strained I feared the decanter would shatter under her touch.

Serving wine and lighting pipes are simple tasks, but Yin Yu treated them as if they were the most sacred things in the world. She handed me a shimmering, holly-red serving dress, and endless instructions spilled from her mouth:

*Come when they call.*

*Watch their glasses; keep them full.*

*Bow before and after every pour.*

*Don't look them in the eye.*

Her list went on and on, in a voice neither soft nor sharp, but strained like a rope twisted tightly. I couldn't blame her for being upset. This was her job since the first day, when we were dragged fresh from the back of the Reapers' van, bleary-eyed and shaking. It was her first step to becoming a Mama-san of her own. And there I was, taking it without word or explanation.

"I didn't want this." It was the closest I could come to an apology, to the truth.

Yin Yu's smile was as woven as her words. She looked down at her too-tight fingers. "You weren't the one who spilled a whole decanter on Mr. Smith. Honestly, I was afraid something worse would happen. It seems I was lucky."

I wanted to tell her. I wanted to tell all of them about the window-boy and his seashell and the promise of a world outside.

But then I thought of Sing, and that was enough to silence any words I might be tempted to say.

So I picked up the tray and started serving. The first night it was only clients who filled the couches of the lounge. No Brotherhood in sight. And now, the second night, I'm chewing the insides of my lip, trying to keep the fear from showing. Tomorrow is the fourth day, which means the boy is coming back to my window soon. If the Brotherhood doesn't meet tonight...if I don't have the names...

I don't know why the possibility makes me as sick as it does. There's still a Seng Ngoi apartment waiting for me. A pool I can't even swim in without drowning.

But I walk into the lounge, and the first face I see is the master's. I look from couch to couch and see that every man is wearing black and scarlet. Only three of them have pipes.

Their eyes are fastened to the room's most commanding presence, the one all of us fear.

I keep to the corner, my shoulder pressed against the serving cabinet. Across the room sits Nuo, dressed in the same low-cut scarlet dress, her fingers skipping over steel strings. The notes she plays are so soft I'm not even certain I hear them. But my ears are trained in other places, listening as the men offer their reports.

There are ten men in the circle; several of them are older, with silvering hair and creased brows. The only one I recognize is Fung. He sits in the far corner, face almost as fierce as the dragon inked onto it.

I listen for names, but these men are not friendly with one another. They toss around titles instead. Fung is called "Red Pole." The man with golden incisors and the four deep nail marks down his cheek is the "Incense Master." Another, a snow-haired member, is known as "White Paper Fan." I lock the titles deep into my chest and try not to panic.

Why panic when there's a rooftop garden? Will the ambassador still bring me flowers if I have an entire garden to smell?

The meeting stretches long. Each man gives a report filled with numbers and profits and loss and death. The master listens, his mouth set like stone as he scratches down notes in a book of parchment and red leather.

I keep listening, my ears straining for names until they ache. In the end, I walk away with four: Fung. Leung. Nam. Chun Kit. Five if you include Longwai. But I don't. His name is everywhere.

161

Fung. Leung. Nam. Chun Kit. I keep the names on the tip of my tongue. Mouthing them silently to keep them fresh in my head. Again and again and again. Until they become one long name, without break: *Fungleungnamchunkit*. I recite it over and over—a silent prayer—as I wash out the glasses and put away the slender pipes.

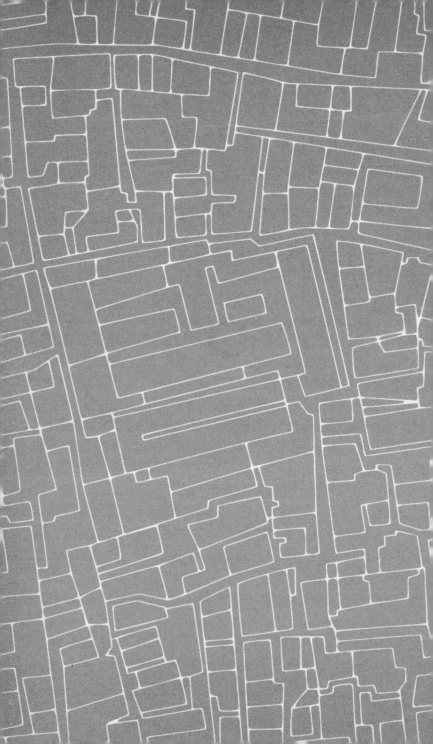

# 10 DAYS

# JIN LING

It took two days to find a replacement tarp. Two days of picking through disgusting piles of rubbish. In the end, I had to go
to Mr. Lam's shop. Use the money in the orange envelope.

And now that I have a tarp, there's no perfect place to pitch
it. My favorite spots are claimed. Some by the older vagrants.
Men and women who cram into the warmer corners with
wadded newspapers and moth-eaten, mildewed coats. Others
by groups of twig-limbed orphans. Who watch me pass with
hungry, wide eyes. Bare-toothed snarls. I walk quickly. Head
down, hoping none of them remember my face. Hoping word
doesn't get back to Kuen. Other spots, by the water spigots and
sewer grates, are too exposed. I need a place that's out of the
way. Hidden from Kuen's pack.

For two days I've avoided the thug. Not an easy task. Even
in this maze of corners and ever-night. He's on the hunt: Three

times I've slipped into a shopfront or alley crack, watched his pack pass. They've spread out, roaming the streets in pairs. Raking every walkway and back again. Knives glinting.

Kuen's out for blood.

I just have to stay one step ahead of him.

So I keep walking. Searching for a place out of sight. Safe. I stay off the main streets. Away from the grandmothers gossiping around soap tables, dealing black cards and coaxing fortunes from one another's palms. Away from mothers kneeling by water stations, scrubbing sauce stains out of their families' shirts. Away from the factory men standing long hours, pouring liquid plastic into molds.

But eyes are everywhere. Even in the loneliest corners. An old man shuffles by, picking out scrap rods for recycling the way a sparrow selects straw for a nest. He tosses them into his wheelbarrow with a crash that makes me shiver. Walk faster. Around another corner. Too fast. No pausing to listen for other steps.

I see the boys first. Two of them, walking slow. Combing the stoops and barred windows with eyes and knife-points. My feet are still in a hurry, still rushing forward when they see me.

The closest boy stops. His nose scrunches, then flares. "It's him!"

The survivor kicks in. She twists my hips midstep. Lights blur. Gravel hisses under my feet. Lunge, lunge, stretch. I'm running before I can even see where this street will take me.

There are no gaps or alley cracks for me to vanish in. The

corner I turned is long behind. This stretch belongs to store-fronts and gated stairwells. One of these apartment doors swings open. Nearly catches me in the face with white grating.

*Get off the street!* The survivor doesn't hesitate. She jumps. Into the doorway. Past the startled old tenant with the key in his hand. Up, up, up the steps.

This complex is like Dai's. With stairs that wind up like a never-ending paper clip. Noise carries far in the hollow space. I hear Kuen's two boys panting and plodding up the steps. I take my precious, flapping tarp, spread it wide, and let it fall. Curses and the sound of wrestled plastic push me higher— past door after gated door. Ten floors of this.

And then, the end. The final door. This one isn't gated. It isn't even really closed. There's no fight when I slam into it, burst into the open free.

Water. Everywhere. Falling from the dark, dark sky. Bursting like freckles across my face. Drumming the puddles at my feet. Wet sinks into my boots. My steps *slosh, slide* through rising pools, past someone's abandoned sunbathing umbrella, between two trashed mattresses. All the way to the ledge.

This building's rooftop is shorter than the others around it, stunted by at least four stories. There's only a single edge, a gap where the fourth wall doesn't fuse to the building I'm standing on. It's too far to leap across. And I'm not even really sure what I'd jump to. All the windows in front of me are flat, barless.

The only way off is down. Where raindrops shimmer,

dim, and die. Swallowed by the canyon. It's not all black. Verandas jut out the side, their slanting tin roofs clinging like fungus to the far wall. But getting to them...

It's a drop that makes my hairs bristle and rise.

Behind me the stairwell door smacks open. Both boys spill out into the rain.

"Gotcha!" The first boy sees me on the ledge, slows down. His steps don't splash anymore. His blade stays straight. "Kuen's been looking forward to seeing you, Jin!"

Fight or flee. I look away from their knives. To the slippery, wet metal roofs. To the fall.

"He's got plans for you," the boy goes on. Steps closer. "I wouldn't want to be in your shoes for all the porridge at Mrs. Pak's."

"Or boots!" His partner snickers.

I can't make the jump. It's too far. Too wet.

And I can't fight the boys. Not without getting cut or killed.

The survivor turns back to the edge.

She jumps.

My stomach is high, high, high in my throat. My hands are clawing, scrabbling at air as empty as my gut. The rain around me catches the window lights, twinkles like stars. They look almost still. But we're falling together.

My boots meet the tin first. Their City Beyond soles grip through the wet. Stick. My knees crumple and my hands splay, steady me.

I made it. For a few seconds I'm frozen in my frog-squat.

Stunned. My chasers' curses fall with the rain. I look up and see the first boy has sheathed his knife. But he's not walking away. He stands on the ledge with nervous lips, wide legs.

He's going to follow me.

I scramble to the edge of the roof. All around are laundry lines and pipes. None of them appear strong enough to hold me. Every veranda is barred. There's a crossway between the two buildings, woven together with bamboo and wire. Reaching it would take another jump.

This time I don't hesitate. Kuen's boy is crouched, ready to spring. We take to the air at the same time. Desperate birds, clipped wings, deadweight.

I land. The bridge sways. Bows low. I grip the wire edges, pull myself up, run into the new hall. Its lamps are old, shuddering just like the bridge. On and off again. I'm not sure if Kuen's boy made the jumps. If he's still behind me. I run as if he is. Flying past doors like cages. Loafing bags of trash. Walls cramped with mildew and weeping paint. Under the ill light, everything looks black and white. Like a nightmare.

It ends in another stairwell. Another choice. Up or down?

A shout from the other end of the hall cuts my debate short. Kuen's kid made it. His silhouette grows. Moves too fast in the flickering light. Like some kind of shadow monster.

I choose up. My thighs are screaming now. Knit too tight. Cramped with fire and flash. My lungs feel so full and empty at the same time. Starving for air, unable to hold it. I fight all these things up the steps. All the way to the second rooftop.

This is the highest level. Where everything is open and

wide and wet. I don't know where I'm going, but my feet fly. Through dripping clotheslines of faded shirts and pants. Past rows of potted plants, their stems bent by rain. Through towering antenna forests. Past a pair of pitiful nightingales, left in their domed cage by some forgetful owner. So drenched even their song sounds heavy, soaked.

One foot in front of the other. On, on, on. That's what the survivor demands. That's what I give her.

But then I see something that makes me slow. Stop.

Dai. He's hunched on the ledge. Where we sat so many mornings ago. With stuffed buns and sunlight. He's staring out, out. The way he was that morning. At the skyscrapers, thick and tall as a bamboo forest. Their windows twinkling madly through the falling rain.

He must have come to watch the sunrise. He's out of luck. There won't be one today. Not with this storm.

Dai might be out of luck, but mine has turned. There's no way Kuen's lackey will come after me once he sees the older boy. The one who pointed a gun at him just days before.

I'm right. My pursuer swipes through a string of sopping jackets and jeans. Halts. His eyes narrow, aim straight at Dai's still-turned back. We stand across from each other—tense, panting, staring—waiting.

Kuen's boy steps back. Slowly, slowly. Behind the laundry. Gone.

Dai has saved me again. Without even knowing it.

I let out a deep breath. My knees are shaking.

"Jin?" I turn back to see Dai staring at me. His hood is

pulled up. All I can see is his face, all the dozens of drops sliding over his skin. There's something behind his expression. Some feeling that hasn't completely washed away. Sadness, anger, *need*. I can't pinpoint it, and the fact makes me uneasy.

I don't go near his ledge. There's too much slick and wet up here. One slip could sling me off. Dai's legs dangle the same as last time, waving over the streetlights of City Beyond. Reckless and wild. As if they want the fall.

"Where've you been?" His eyebrows fold into his face. "I was getting worried."

*Was he?* I look at his face again. There's too much emotion there. Too much raw. I can't tell if he's lying or not. My instincts are going soft.

Dai's many secrets still cram my head. As thick and blurring as the rain around us. While I'm here, I can at least try to ask for the truth. Dai's truth.

He turns his face away. Back into the flush of falling rain. I take a deep breath. Too deep. My lungs shudder. As if they're drowning. "I saw you."

His shoulders grow still, and I realize there's another reason I'm standing so far away from him. I want room to run if things go sour. If I uncover some secret Dai can't let me live with. If he's really as unstable as I think.

"I saw you," I say again, "with that man. The one who gave you money a few nights ago."

For a long time Dai doesn't move. Drops smack into the soak of his sweatshirt: pellet drumbeats. He's a temple idol, crouched and constant. I start wondering if the wind stole my words away.

But then he turns. The look on his rain-stung face tells me he heard every word.

"Who is he?" My boots dig against the wet, wet rooftop. Ready to run again. My knife hand tucks inside my tunic, bandage gripping the hilt. "Why is he giving you money?"

Dai just looks at me, his lips pressed flat. They're a strange shade of blue. He's been up here in the frigid rain way too long.

"Why can't you leave?" I try again. "If it's so dangerous for the Brotherhood to know who you are, then why do you stay here?"

He stands, faster than he should on such a steep ledge. Then he moves closer to me, mouth pulled tight.

For every step he takes, I take one back. "You're someone important, aren't you? Why else would you try to hide it from the Brotherhood? You act like a vagrant so they don't ask questions. Hide out in the open."

Dai shoves his fists into his pockets. Under the crescent shadow of his hood, I see that his lips aren't a razor line anymore. They're wrinkling and curving. Messing up his face. I wait for them to break apart. To tell me I'm wrong.

But he stays quiet and keeps walking. He steps around and away from me. His steps splash and slosh to the closest ladder.

I don't mean to, but I run after him. My hand slips from my knife. Reaches out. Snags the edge of his soaked sweatshirt. "I need to know, Dai—"

"No," he cuts in, "you don't."

He's both right and terribly, terribly wrong. I don't need

to know. But I do. I need a rock, an anchor. As much as I tell myself I don't, I need this trust.

Because I'm tired. Tired of running. Tired of always looking over my shoulder. Tired of fighting. Scraping by. Being alone. I'm tired of gangs and drug runs and empty searching. I want, so badly, to believe that Dai is good. That he deserves my trust. No matter what.

I want to feel safe.

Dai tries to keep walking, but I don't let go. My boots slide. Make a wake. He drags me a whole yard before he stops and looks over his shoulder.

"Let it go, Jin." He yanks his sweatshirt out of my fist. His arm flies back into a terra-cotta pot. It spins off its ledge, dashing the ground with dirt, shards, and withered leaves. "It's better for you if you don't know."

"How?" The air around me shivers. I realize I'm screaming. My shriek shreds through the curtain of drops—too tight, too high. "How is it better?

But if Dai notices how thin my scream is, how much I sound like a girl, he doesn't show it. He doesn't show anything. His expression is floating and still. A drowned thing.

"What you saw...it doesn't change anything about what we're doing at Longwai's. I trust you'll stay quiet about it."

*Trust.* The word feels sour on my tongue, like rotten meat. The boy in front of me says it so fast, so flippantly. As if it's something he perfected long ago.

My mind spins fast. Even if Dai refuses to let me in, I can still use what I saw.

"If I stay quiet and keep running, then I want more money."

"More money?"

"Yes. I need enough to let me buy time with one of Long-wai's girls." I look past him when I say this. My eyes focus on the ruined pot. Its spilled dirt looks a lot like blood. Swirling dark and spattered in the water.

His eyes narrow in a weird, frowning way. "You want time with his girls?"

"Yes." I try to make my voice sound extra throaty. Full of gravel.

"Why?"

"You have your business, I have mine. If you don't want me to tell Longwai, then you'll give me the cash."

"Fine. I'll give you half of my cut. But don't expect me to join." Disgust threads his words. I realize how awful my request sounds. Part of me wants to tell Dai what I'm looking for. Why I live in this awful, reeking maze. But secrets still wrap tight between us. Mine cling to me, his to him.

He moves for the ladder. I don't try to stop him.

And everything changes. The drops on my face become harder. Bite instead of sting. The rumble of the storm grows and swells. There's white. White all around.

Hail. It tears and claws. Rattles against the rooftop. The nightingales are shrieking now. The potted plants shred instead of wilt. Clothes drop from the lines like autumn leaves.

Dai's hunched form is fuzzy as he works his way onto the ladder. The air between us is blur and haze. Like a busted TV screen.

But I do see him pause, just before he disappears altogether.

He screams over the pound and pummel of ice, "There's a run in two days! I'll see you then!"

Then he's gone. I should leave, too. Before Kuen's lackey decides to come back with more knives.

The hail beats down with a new fierceness. White and cut and slice. It falls so thick I can't see the lights of City Beyond. I can't even see Dai's ladder. For the shortest moment I'm not in a city at all. I'm alone. Again and always. The air around me so cruel and free.

Dai. Feeling safe. That's not what matters. That's not why I came here. Not why I've survived.

I'll get through this storm. I'll find my sister.

# MEI YEE

The window-boy is tired. As soon as he appeared behind the bars and glass, I snuffed the lanterns so I could see his face more clearly. His cheeks and the snub of his nose burn with color, mixed bright by wet and cold. His dark eyes are shiny with water, the skin beneath them grayer than the rest of him.

But the sight of him still catches me—makes me prickle like cold skin meeting steam. Like panic, but stronger. It overwhelms everything: the ambassador's promise, the bruise on my hip, the Brotherhood's gold-toothed laughter. There's just the boy and his seashell. Me and my painted ceiling tiles. My brittle vase of flowers.

"I did it," I tell him, even though I wasn't planning on it. For hours I've been weighing the names. Their risk. It doesn't feel like such a small thing anymore.

The boy breathes out hard. His breath clouds everywhere,

reminds me of the mists that blanketed the rice fields in the most magical hour of dawn. For a moment it's so thick I can't even see him. It gathers on my window, rolls down like tears.

"I needed some good news this morning," he says through the ribbons of water and window fog. "I'm tired."

"Too many sunrises?"

"Not enough," he answers.

My hand rests over the window grating. There's a chill seeping through the glass, coiling around the bars. Winter creeping through the cracks like ants, slow and steady and gnawing.

The boy feels it, too. He's all shiver in his black zip-up hoodie. It's soaked through, like the many rags I used to clean out Jin Ling's cuts. It's little wonder his teeth are chattering.

I wish I could reach through the window. Not just to grab my seashell or feel the rain. I wish I could touch the boy, give him some of the warmth that's sweltering through my room, making me sweat.

Another impossible wish.

But even if I can't give him warmth, I can give him the names. Try again to bring a smile to his face. If he's handsome when he's frowning, I can't imagine what he looks like with a real, true smile.

"There were ten men there last night. And the mast— Longwai." Saying his name feels like the worst of sins, but I speak it and the boy doesn't flinch. "They didn't always use names. I only caught four of them."

The boy doesn't smile, but he doesn't frown, either. He's

looking at my fingers laced through the window's grate, as if he knows just how badly I want to reach through. "Which ones?"

"There's Fung. He's the one with the dragon on his face. He collects tributes for Longwai every month. And it's his job to...to deal with people who don't pay. They call him 'Red Pole.'"

The boy nods. "Go on."

"And Leung. He keeps track of a lot of the drug runs. There's a man with gold teeth named Nam. I don't know what he does. They called him the 'Incense Master.'" The unease planted in my stomach by the Brotherhood's sickly sweet opium fumes so many hours ago grows into a full-blown ache.

I don't have to do this. I can roll away. Pretend none of this ever happened. That I never really dreamed of seeing my sister again. Of visiting the sea. I can sit and wait and tell Ambassador Osamu *yes*.

These thoughts cause me to shift against the bed. My hip bone shoots pain. Remembers the harsh press of the ambassador's hand.

"Fung. Leung. Nam." The boy counts the names off. Three fingers poke out of his sleeve. "Who's the fourth?"

My breath feels stale in my body. I stare at his fingers, pronging through the cold air like antlers. They're smudged with dirt, knuckles raw and nails bit to the quick. I think of the way they held my seashell, so carefully, as if there were still life inside it, building chamber after chamber.

Those aren't fingers that bruise.

"Chun Kit," I say, breathless. "The last name is Chun Kit."

"Good," the boy says. "You're right."

"You...you knew?" A feeling swells up in my throat, like a balloon stretched to burst.

"Yes." The boy nods. Hair as dark as a raven's wing falls like feathers against his cheeks—softens the angles of his face. "I was testing you. To see if you really could get the information. You did well."

"So the other six names...you don't need them?"

"Well, yes. I do need them. In a sense." The boy bites his lip, something he must do often because the skin there is dry. "Tell me, was there a ledger?"

"Ledger?" The word rolls, fat and clumsy, off my tongue.

"It would probably look like a big notebook," the boy explains. "It's used to keep track of numbers and names. Official Brotherhood business."

I think back to the meeting, to the scarlet book that sat in the drug lord's lap. The one full of his black-ink scratchings. "The m—Longwai had a book. He was writing in it."

"Could you see anything he was writing down?"

"Yes," I pause, feeling the burn of shame stain my cheeks. "But I...I can't read."

"That's okay," the boy says, his voice soft. "The book... where did Longwai put it when the meeting was over?"

"I..." My voice fades out as I think back to the end of the meeting. The men didn't linger. Most of them left through the front hall. A few went to the girls' rooms. And Longwai...I strain my thoughts, trying to remember where the master had disappeared to after the dismissal. I'd been too busy trying to cement the four names into memory. "I don't remember. He probably took it to his office."

"His office?"

"It's on the second floor. I think. I've never been up there," I say.

"Do you think you can find out? For sure?"

Eavesdropping for names is one thing. But rummaging through the master's office...the game—the risk—has taken a plunge that makes my stomach lurch.

He must see this in my face, because he doesn't wait for me to answer. "Look, I know...I know what I'm asking is dangerous. I wouldn't ask you to do it if I had any other choice. But I need this. I need your help."

*Need.* His voice cracks at the word with a desperation that can't be faked.

"Why?"

"Because every morning I wake up and wish for a different life. And this is the only way I can have it. This is the only way I can go home." His voice is so raw, like his knuckles. It makes my hand press hard against the grate.

*Home.* That word flares in my chest, hot like a coal. I want to drink in the green of the rice paddies and distant mountain slopes. I want to find my sister and hold her in my arms. I want to be back watching for stars.

"We're...we're not supposed to think about home. It just hurts." The way the boy is looking at me as I say this, I know he understands. The same bittersweet golden agony barbs through his chest. "But I do it anyway."

"Where is your home?"

"I grew up in a place where there's lots of rice. And mountains. And herds of water deer that leap like fish through the morning mist." I pause, realize I've gone off track. "It doesn't matter. I can't go back. My father...he would just sell me again."

The boy's eyes go sharp. I can see his jaw working. Back and forth in an unheard grind of teeth. "Your father did this to you?"

"I wasn't much help on the farm. The rice crops were failing. We were starving." I hate that I'm making excuses for him. The man who left more scabs and bottle caps than he could count. We were starving, but he was thirsty. I know he drank away all the coins my flesh bought for him long ago.

"That's no reason—" The boy stops. I know he wants to say something more, something laced in fire and flame. But he holds it back. Lets it burn inside. "So where will you go? When you get out?"

I don't know the answer to his question. My stare settles back on the shell. I search the chambers of my heart for something, anything to tell him. But they all feel empty.

He follows my gaze down to the nautilus. Finds an answer for me. "I know you want to see the sea."

His hand comes up against the glass, mirrors mine. So close. Not even an inch apart. I shut my eyes for just a moment, pretend that the metal weave and cold between us don't exist.

"I want you to see it, too."

My eyelids open and he's still there. Eyes endless and brimming, night's void crammed full of stars. If I look just close enough, I can see myself in them. A tiny, trembling constellation. Just like the ones Jin Ling and I once traced.

"I'll try," I whisper. To find the ledger. To see the sea.

His smile stretches all the way to his eyes, where I am. The sight is radiant. That's the word Wen Kei always uses to describe the sun over the waters. I wonder if they're at all the same.

The boy's head jerks to the side, as if some distant voice just called his name. His name. I still don't know it. I don't know it and I feel closer to him than I do to the client who slides under my sheets every few nights.

"I have to go." The boy starts to move. "I'll be back in a few days."

"Wait." I press my cheeks into the bars, will him to stop. "I don't even know your name."

He pauses midstep, his foot hovering over the broken ribs of a rice-liquor bottle. "Next time. As long as you tell me yours."

And then he's gone. All that's left is the nautilus and window tears and my fingers against the lattice, still reaching.

# JIN LING

The hail doesn't reach the lower levels. Heat leaks through windows and pipes. Swallows the pellets before they land. By the time I reach the bottom of the ladder, I feel incredibly warm. A feeling that vanishes at the first sound of his voice.

"I was wondering when you were gonna come down."

My fingers freeze around the final rung. Stuck. Every muscle in my back clenches tight.

"No big kid and his gun to protect you now, you little shit. He's long gone." I hear the sneer in Kuen's voice. It drips from every word. "'S just you an' us."

Kuen's lackey must have run back. Told him where to find me.

I turn and jump at the same moment. Land in a crouch. Like a spider flung from its web.

He's right. It's just us on the street: me and Kuen. Blood

still crusts his face. Days old and dark. It looks like a dragon tattoo. Curling and twisting around his swelling purple nose. His mouth is the only thing that isn't puffy and bruised. It's still snarled. Teeth shiny and yellow.

But then I see what's in his arms and I forget all about his ugly face.

Chma is fighting—a mess of gray fur and squirm. Kuen's elbows crush tighter. My cat growls. The sound is low. All over. I hear it and my stomach drops like a stone.

"Let him go." As soon as I say these words, I wish I hadn't. They shiver through the street. Betray my weakness for everyone to hear.

Kuen spits a word that sounds like *vermin*. Seizes Chma by the scruff. My cat howls, claws, and writhes, but Kuen holds him far out. Like a sack of garbage. His free hand grabs the blade by his waist. A clear, silvery threat.

I start to move, but I'm too far away. I can't reach him in time.

Kuen's knife is fast. Flashing. Chma's angry growls turn into something too close to a human scream. It shreds the air, punches my chest.

I have no chance. I'm small and alone. There are probably dozens of his followers, more knives, hiding in the dark. But I don't stop.

Kuen must've expected me to slow or turn. He isn't ready when our bodies collide. My weight barrels him over. Drags us both to the hard ground. Even though I charged, I'm not really ready. I'm anger and impulse. Thrashing, hitting fists. But my knuckles are no match for Kuen's knife.

And, like most boys, he's stronger.

Kuen grunts and rolls to the side. I fall off his chest. My right shoulder slams hard into concrete. Somewhere in the chaos I hear Chma's screaming. He's still alive. Alive, but in agony.

Then Kuen is on top of me—muscle and violet-splotched flesh. From the corner of my eye I see the glint of his blade. Trimmed red with Chma's blood. It's falling, slicing through the air between us. Right down to my throat.

Years of being under my father's mad fists taught me how to dodge. Avoid the worst blows. I twist. The metal draws a thin line of fire down my neck. Pain bursts like boiling water across my skin. My left fist flies up. Catches the street boy's broken tender puff nose.

Kuen screeches, falls off me. I scramble away as far as I can. Stumble to the end of the street.

Other boys appear. I expect them to be jeering and angry, but the wrath I saw in Kuen isn't there. My eyes flick fast through them, searching for Bon. He's nowhere to be found. The rest look anxious, almost scared, as they watch their leader spring to his feet. He comes at me with a beastly roar.

The cut on my neck throbs. Clears my head of the anger haze. I leap to the side. Somewhere in the middle of jumps and pain-crafted curses, I find Chma. He's curled by a pile of trash. His beautiful, downy fur is soaked with red. I can't spot the wound, but then he moves and I see.

His long, sweeping tail is gone. Just a bloodied stump.

My first thought: *He'll live.* My first action: pulling out my knife.

There's no dodging Kuen the second time. He's reined in his wild rage, harnessed the pain into focus. His arms stretch wide. There's no side to step into, and I'm very aware of his followers at my back. All escapes are gone.

My calf muscles coil and spring. My body is a feather, light and spinning. Everything passes slowly. I see every detail of this filthy street. The chip on Kuen's second tooth. Limp, wet cigarette butts stewed with syringes and shattered bottles. Roaches skittering over mildewed walls. Chma, limp as a discarded scarf, eyes glowing yellow with pain.

Then all of it's gone. Blurred by my landing. Kuen's chest is bulky, hard as a board. I hit him. He shudders and steps back. His ankle catches on something, tugs him back to the ground.

There are sharp jabs of pain as we fall: glass, jolts, and fingernails. My knife is thrashing, trying to hit whatever it can. His blade is flashing, too. It whistles through the air. Sings of death.

There's an explosion of heat in my side, searing. Too much for silence. I open my mouth and scream, scream, scream.

*It's over.* For a moment that's all I can think. Kuen's knife is in me, sawing sinew and bone. Carving a path for my blood. The pain is awful. Everywhere. I wait for it to leave. I want my opponent to rip the metal out and stab again. End it.

But the new pain doesn't come. The old wound stays: a flower of flame and pain just under my arm. My vision flickers: blurry, sharp, blurry. If I could make my scream into words, I would beg. Why hasn't he pulled it out?

I look over. See the reason.

Kuen lies next to me. Mouth red-bright, eyes open. They're rigid, so still. My knife is deep in his chest. Only the hilt shows.

My sight mists over. Colors bleed into one another. Red, gray, black. They swirl. Spinning around and around. Until only shadows are left. The black becomes everything. And then it's all gone. Even the pain...

# DAI

I shove my hands into my pockets as I walk. Away from the window. Away from *her*. My teeth are still chattering from my sit on the rooftop. When I took in all that wet and cold and waited for the fall that never came.

My feet might be on solid ground now, but I still feel like I'm plunging. Or maybe it's more like I'm being pulled. The girl's eyes have latched onto me the way Jin's fist wrenched my hoodie. Both begging for truth.

I don't know how much longer I can keep lying to them. The truth is catching up to me. Especially when I'm outside the window—talking about home and needs and wants.

"Dai!"

So I wasn't imagining it. Someone *was* calling my name while I crouched at the window, searching for me with a single, crowing syllable.

"Dai! Dai!"

I find the voice in the form of a boy skulking by an empty handcart. It takes me a few seconds to recognize his drawn, bird-like face. He's one of the youngest vagrants, a part of Kuen's gang. Bon—the one Jin almost stabbed.

"Yeah?"

The kid looks scared. When I step forward, he slinks back, shoulders slumped. "Your friend, Jin. He's in trouble."

Suddenly I don't feel so cold. My skin flushes hot under my hoodie's soaked fleece. My hand slides back to the heavy, leaden form of my gun. "What?"

"Kuen—he'll kill me if he knew I told you," the boy sputters, flustered. His skeleton face is a strange mix of color. He struggles for his next words. "But I…I like Jin. I don't want him to die."

Something about the way the kid says this makes me realize how small he is. He belongs in grade school. Practicing his sum tables and stenciled characters. Kicking a football with his friends at lunch break.

I can tell, just by looking at him, that he's *too* young. Too nice. He hasn't mastered the rules of survival: keep your head down, let people die. No matter how much you like them.

And right now, I'm glad he hasn't.

"They were waiting for him to come down from the roof when I came to find you," Bon goes on. "And Kuen's mad. Real mad."

*Oh hell…*

"Where?" I don't need any more convincing. Not after seeing what that vagrant did to Lee. "Take me. Now."

191

Bon vanishes into a side passage nearly too narrow for my grown form to weasel through. Sweat mixes with the rain slick on my face as I leap after the boy. He darts and weaves faster than a rat through the streets, finally stopping at the edge of another dead-end alley. Bon's eyes are big onyx buttons as he points, wordless.

I step in, gun out and ready. I see the anxious cluster of heads, hear the confused voices of Kuen's gang gathered around, and I have the awful pit of a feeling that I'm too late.

"Move!" The word I scream is as effective as the bullet I fired last time. The kids scatter, a blurry movement of rags and half-drawn knives. Away, away—vanishing into shadows and the alley's mouth.

The ground at my feet is the worst color red. Puddles that were once sludge-brown swirl dark with it. Dozens of streams of blood twist over the concrete like feeder roots searching for good soil. Reaching for me like nightmares.

For a moment I forget how to breathe.

Jin looks smaller than I've ever seen him. He's curled up on his side, pale and done. His clothes are so soaked with scarlet that I can't tell where the blood is actually coming from. Or if he's even still breathing.

There's no question Kuen's dead. He's gaping like a fish on ice, hands still reaching for the knife in his chest.

Blood. Blood everywhere. My boots slosh through it. I almost drop my gun into the thick red sea at my feet as I kneel down, turn Jin over.

Things grow unsteady for a moment. Shadows flicker like

fire at the edge of my eyes. Memories of the night that changed everything flash back, mirror images of now. Too strong to swallow down. The blood. The cold tang of death in the air. My hand clutching a gun. Three broken bodies at my feet. Three murder charges to my name. Three reasons I can't leave Hak Nam.

But this is different. This is now. And this time, the boy is still alive.

My hands come up crimson and sticky. I look down at Jin. Too much blood. Too much. Just like my dreams. Even if it isn't all his. He might still be alive, but not for long. Not if I don't do something.

There are no doctors in Hak Nam for something this serious. An apothecary with dried fungus and powdered sharks' fins won't close up this knife wound. And my first aid pouch would just drown under all this blood. What Jin needs is past the Old South Gate. Beyond the rusting cannons. Into a land of law and justice. Where I can't go.

*Get rid of the boy. You don't need him anymore.*

Tsang's right. It's not like Jin will be running after this, not before ten days is up. He's useless to me now. I should just walk away, keep going. Leaving this broken, hurting kid behind. Out of sight, out of mind.

But they're never really out of mind, are they? My brother and Lee and the girl with the dragging hair…their faces haunt my dreams, their last words whisper and swirl. Like they were meant just for this exact moment.

My brother: *You're a good person.*

Lee: *Please! Don't leave me!*

And the girl whose escape went wrong: Only silence.

I look back down at Jin, notice just how white and sharp his face is. Like marble. Like the silent, dragged girl. Like death.

I can't save them all. But Jin...Jin is special. And I don't think I can handle another ghost.

My body doesn't feel like mine anymore as I slide my arms under Jin's back. The stick of blood burns my bare fingers. My insides twist with its scent of salt and iron.

My thoughts are spinning, trying hard to stay in the now as I lift the small boy to my chest, careful not to nudge the knife still lodged into his side. He's lighter than I thought. Almost nothing. No wonder he's so fast.

The Old South Gate is choked with people, running errands and making the most of their morning hours. They duck in and out of Hak Nam, hair slick with wet, shoulders flecked with hail. The storm has died down since I left the roof. Pellets—most no bigger than pastry sprinkles—line the street gutters and sidewalk gaps like cake icing. So thick they look like snowdrifts.

I keep to the edge of the street. Most who pass don't even give us a second glance. Those who do simply frown and walk on. Bloody vagrants—just another part of Hak Nam's status quo.

The cannons sit, taunting me with rust and invisible barriers. Visions of handcuffs and life sentences. *Can't stop. Don't stop.* I breathe air like courage and keep walking past the ancient arsenal, under the wooden gable, and into the strange, fresh layer of white.

I thought it would be different, the first time I stepped back into my hometown. I envisioned my return from exile as a loud, busy thing. Not a quiet, unnoticed slip into the streets.

Now that I'm actually out of Hak Nam, I don't know what to do. I stand here, getting *tap-tap-tapp*ed by the last of the hail, and realize that I expected someone to stop me. I never really planned to get this far.

I can't take Jin to a hospital. There will be too many questions, too much bureaucracy and paperwork. They'll let the boy bleed to death before he's processed. Plus, there's the possibility of cops. (Tempting fate is one thing, walking straight into its jaws is quite another.)

There's only one place I can go. One place where both of us will be safe. At least for a little bit.

The taxi driver I wave down is an old man with silver hair and wide, ugly glasses. He stares like an owl, black eyes tightening with fear when he realizes what I'm holding.

I manage to pull out a wad of cash. It's a lot. My month's stipend—meant for food and an apartment. Way more than he'd make in a week of taxi runs.

"No questions." I wave the notes at him. "Do you know where Tai Ping Hill is?"

It's a stupid question, because every citizen of Seng Ngoi knows where its richest neighborhood sits. But I find I'm usually more prone to stupid questions when I'm holding dying people.

For a moment the cabdriver looks like he's about to slam his foot onto the gas pedal and put as much distance between us as his engine can manage. But his eyes have latched onto the cash. The pack of bills I'm holding is thick enough to convince him otherwise.

"What address?" He waves me in, trying not to make a face at how much blood I'm smearing across his leather seats.

"Fifty-five." I toss the bills to the front and look down at Jin. His skin is as ghastly as the hail mounds outside. I can feel, just barely, his chest shuddering. Up. Down.

The cabdriver mutters to himself, words I can't completely hear over the chipper buzz of the radio. A woman's silky voice is sliding through the speakers, telling us this is the coldest, wettest winter Seng Ngoi has had in over a decade. I listen to her report and then some song by a popular, peppy girl band as the cab wheels its way to Tai Ping Hill.

Whenever I think about this place, I imagine it in the height of summer. When the hibiscuses burst into color—bright patches of red, yellow, and white lining the road up the hill. The roadside is so thick with evergreens and bamboo stalks you can pretend you're standing in a forest and not on a hill in the middle of a thriving metropolis. I think of the cicadas, how they clung to the red pine branches and chirped long into the night.

I'm so busy imagining how this place should be that when the cab stops, I'm startled. Through the fog-etched doodles on the window, I see it: the gate. It looks exactly the same, towering iron spikes set at the end of a long drive. Flanked by stone columns. Number fifty-five.

It feels like the hail that fell outside is tearing into my chest as I stare. This place looks unchanged. Untouched by my absence. But there's something different.... Like the bars are meant to keep me out.

"You getting out?" the cabdriver almost shouts, and I remember the urgency of everything. My hoodie is soaked through, heavy with blood that is and isn't Jin's.

My arms ache with the boy's weight as I climb out of the cab. Like he suddenly gained thirty pounds during the car ride. The taxi spins away, its tires spraying gravel and hail in their haste.

I trudge over to the keypad, hoping the entry code is still the same. My forefinger leaves smudges of blood against the sterling buttons. But I hear a beep and the churn of chains. The gate tugs apart. I move through before it's open all the way, leaving shallow pink steps in the hail drifts.

With so much still and white around it, the mansion looks like something from a movie set. It's too large and perfect with its ceramic roof tiles and high walls. I blink all the way to the wide, snaking veranda. Expecting it to disappear any minute.

I don't have to knock. The double doors swing wide. The man behind it looks distinguished, older. His hair is peppered with far more gray than it was the last time I saw him standing on this veranda.

"Dai Shing!" His stare centers on Jin, crumpled in the crook of my arms. His skin goes white as chalk, the way it did on the night that changed everything.

"Hello, Father."

# 9

The water is scalding, pouring over my hands and burning the crevices between my fingers. Jin's blood washes down the marble sink—first scarlet, then a lighter, rosewater pink. I watch it swirl away, leaving the basin as white as before. Like it was never there.

This washroom looks the same, with its neat wood floors and the rice-paper dividers lined with ancient calligraphy. Everything here looks the same: the foyer, the living room, the rock garden. Like my two years in Hak Nam were just some lucid nightmare.

I glance down and realize that my hands are still curled under the stinging water. When I pull them out, they're raw pink and shivering, like *momiji* leaves caught in an autumn gale.

I shrug out of my hoodie—still heavy with unseen red—and hold it gingerly. Everything here feels too clean. Or maybe I'm too filthy. My faint pink footprints on the wood floor suggest the latter.

In the end, I toss my sweatshirt into the sink, where the faucet is still spewing. Water bubbles up around it, the same color as the hard cinnamon candies my grandfather used to slip me when I was a boy.

"Dai Shing?"

I look over to the sliding door. Its copper lock gleams impossibly bright—the kind of luster you'd never find in Hak Nam.

"Is that you? Really?" The voice behind the door is my

mother's. She has the same accent as Osamu, but it's softer coming from her lips. If I close my eyes, I can imagine her face: eyebrows arched too perfectly, like a master calligrapher brushed them onto her skin; cheeks pale and powdered; lips painted the color of subtle, dark wine. She'll be biting them, the way she does when she gets nervous.

I reach for the latch, let the door slide open. There she stands, the mother I remember. She steps into the light of the washroom, and I see time's mark. More lines and creases by her eyes. The black of her hair is false, a darkness created by chemicals and dye. It's only when I study her that I feel like two years really have passed.

"Oh, Dai Shing. You're home." Her voice is tragic and light. Her arms stretch out, thinner than I remember—just skin, bone, and blue veins like streets.

I back away from her embrace. "Don't... don't touch me."

"But..."

"There's... there's blood." The explanation shakes out of my lips.

Her gaze travels down, like she's seeing the bloodstained mess of my T-shirt for the first time. And the scar. Still there, always there. Bulging and bright. A quiver passes over her face, rests on her lips. I know she's thinking of the same night. How the red on my shirt was tenfold. Some of it mine.

"It doesn't matter," she whispers. Her arms wrap around me: blood, stains, and all. "You're my son."

*The only one left...* I swallow back this thought, think instead about how I'm ruining her Gucci blouse. Sure enough, when she finally pulls back, there's a watery pink mark across the white silk.

She doesn't seem to notice. There are tears in her eyes as she stares at me. "Why did you come back?"

That's not the question she's really asking, because the answer is obvious. It's splattered on my shirt and stretched out in my parents' guest suite, trying not to bleed to death. What my mother can't understand, what she really wants to know, is why I would risk it.

I don't think I can tell her. Partly because I can't cram it into words, but mostly because I'm not so sure myself. The morning's adrenaline is gone—taking with it all the sharp clarity of emergency.

All I know is that I couldn't, wouldn't, let Jin die. I'm not the ruthless criminal Tsang thinks I am, the one I've pretended to be. I won't add another body to my count.

"Is the doctor here yet?" I have no idea how much time has passed in this steam-filled washroom.

"He's with the boy now."

"Good."

"I'll go get some clothes from your old room." My mother slides the door open wider. Steam slips out, reminding me that the world outside is clear. Cold. "And I'll ask Emiyo to bring you some tea."

She walks away before I can answer. Before I can remember and remind her that my old clothes won't fit anymore. Too much time and too many inches have stretched out since I last lived here.

This revelation echoes through me. Painting every corner of every room I walk through. I'm changed. I don't belong here anymore. This isn't my world.

All my time in Hak Nam—all those years standing on the edge of the rooftops, standing and staring—I'd been wishing, longing, striving for this place. Or so I thought.

Coming home isn't the answer. It doesn't bring me peace.

So what is my freedom? My escape? What will fix me?

The door to the guest suite is shut. Emiyo has already mopped up the blood. The floorboards are still slick with wet. I never knew what clean smelled like before Hak Nam, but now I can't ignore the sting of chemicals and lemons in my nose.

I stand in the last spots of wet and listen. For words, sounds...anything that might tell me if my friend is alive or dead. My ears are rewarded with a mess of footsteps and sharp orders. I can't make sense of them; they're jumbled, full of terms I don't understand. They never slow, the frenzy leaks under the door, mixes with the lemons. I can't stand still, so I pace, start walking circles around the sitting room. My fingers drum anxiously over the dark stains on my jeans.

My mother never comes with clean clothes, but Emiyo appears after a bit. A tray of green tea balances in her practiced hands.

"Master Dai?" She clears her throat and the teacups rattle. It's the set Mother brought from her home country. Fired in kilns, painted with visions of lily pads and lotus blossoms.

"Please, just Dai," I correct her. Even when I was younger,

the term *master* set me on edge. Now it just feels like an absurdity.

Emiyo simply smiles at me, like she knows better but won't dare to say it. "Your mother sent these down."

Tucked under her arm is a set of clothes. A white button-down dress shirt and slacks. Clearly my father's.

The maid places the tray down and holds the bundle of clothes out to me. Her eyes flick away and I follow them. In all my pacing, I streaked up the floor again.

"Thanks, Emiyo."

"It's good to have you home, sir." Our maid bows. "We missed you."

She's being so nice. They all are. With their hugs and smiles and fresh clothes. Acting like nothing ever happened. Forgotten and forgiven. I wish I could look at myself with the same rose-colored glasses.

Emiyo bustles out of the room before I can manage a reply. I finally allow myself to stand still, hands clutched tight around the expensive dress shirt. I'm just contemplating putting it on when the door to the suite slides open. The man striding out is immediately familiar: Dr. Kwan, our family physician. His sleeves are rolled all the way above his ashy elbows. The rest of the shirt is almost as stained as mine.

Dr. Kwan pauses in front of me, doing a double take before he asks, "Where is your father?"

"I don't know." I hadn't seen him since he rushed away to dial Dr. Kwan. But right now that's the least of my concerns. "How's Jin?"

He sighs, like he's inconvenienced by the question. "She's doing better. Lost a good deal of blood, but I got her stitched up. The knife missed all her major organs. It was a clean cut. I've already called the hospital for some blood bags. She'll need transfusions."

"Oh good. I—" The doctor's pronoun choices catch up with me. Barrel over, drill into my thick skull. "She?"

I realize my mouth is hanging open, but I don't care enough to shut it.

*She. Her.* It takes another minute for the words to sink in.

There's no way...

Maybe I say this out loud. Or maybe the doctor reads my face. "You didn't know? She went to pretty good lengths to hide it. But yes. She's definitely a female."

Jin's a girl.

And here I was thinking I was the one with all the secrets.

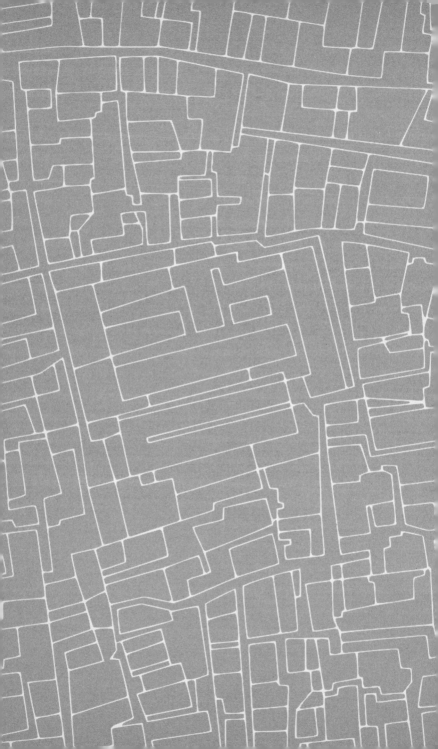

# 9 DAYS

# MEI YEE

I cannot sleep. Every fiber, every muscle of my body, is still full, floating high with window thoughts. When the boy left, my mind went with him, dashing through imaginary streets, all the way home.

I'm running down the dirt road, past fields and fields of grass as bright and green as a liquor bottle. Past the stray dogs that beg at farmers' steps for clumps of dried rice. Past the distant violet ridges of the mountains. I pass my father—back bent and splotched with sweat—knee-deep in the rice field's murky waters. I pass my mother—hanging laundry to dry under the breadth of her ginkgo tree, arms mottled dark with storm cloud bruises. I go all the way until I reach my sister, so we can be together again. Just as she wished.

Would I go home if I found a way to get past these bars? Or would I go see the sea? The expanding-chamber possibilities are terrifyingly endless, just like its waters. The thought of being out in the world—alone—is enough to make me stop breathing.

But would I be alone? There's the boy and what he said: *I want you to see it, too.* Something about his voice, his eyes, makes me think I'm not the only one whose insides are smoldering.

But I don't know. I don't know for sure. And the longer he's gone, the more these things start slipping, the way a dream fades with each waking hour of the morning.

My restless body is twisting, turning under every one of these thoughts when the humming starts. It's like the noise a spirit would make—soft and keening. It curls under my door, calls me to where she is.

The hallway is wrapped in dark, its lanterns hanging dim and smokeless. The sound—a thin, waiflike song—slips through the cracks of Sing's door, slides through Mama-san's lock. It brings bumps like small mountains over my flesh.

When I draw close, the wailing stops. There's scrambling, the sound of slippers on floorboards, and the heavy thud of palms against wood shaking the door.

"Please! Please, give me more." Sing's voice is loud. Too loud. "I'll be good! I promise!"

I'm frozen in the hall, looking at all the dead lanterns. They hang in rows, still and bulbous, like crimson moons that have been harvested and strung up to dry.

"Just one more! Please!" Sing screams. "I'll do anything! Anything you want!"

The door shudders again. The rage behind it grows as if

there isn't a girl there anymore, but a wildcat that's hissing, spitting, snarling to get to her cubs. But there are no cubs. There's only me, and somewhere in this maze of lanterns and dark there's a needle waiting to slide into Sing's veins and give her another few hours of relief.

"I need it!" Her growl falls apart into a sob. "Please!"

And in these words I hear all that Sing has lost. No matter how many times Mama-san brought a belt across her back, no matter how many men ducked in and out of her bedroom, Sing always managed to stay strong. Always dreamed.

*I need it.*

*I.*

*Need.*

*It.*

Her words echo and swell and flood, become the blood and marrow of this dark hall. So loud that I don't hear the footsteps that bring Fung to my side. He looms over me like a nightmare—a shadow stretched extra long. There's a syringe in his hand and a twist on his lips. His eyes are dark, dark, like the lumps of spent coals my mother used to dump behind our shack.

My body is all tremble, waiting for his shout or the quick slap of his hand, but Fung does neither. He stares a moment longer. The dark, dark eyes and the dragon above them betray nothing.

"You should go back to your room," he growls.

I obey. Walk back to my bedroom and its window full of bars.

There's no room for dreamers here. No room for risk.

And there's no room for me out there. Not really. As I told the boy: I can't go home, not even to see my sister. My father is waiting there, with a thirst and an itch and an empty wallet. He'd sell me again and my mother would watch again, her bruised eyes heavy with tears.

And I don't even know where the sea is. Or what I would do if I managed to reach it.

The ambassador does not make my heart sing, but I know every freckle on his body. I know his favorite dish is eel sautéed with mushrooms and bamboo shoots. I know he always hiccups three times in a row. I know he is the youngest child of two factory workers. I know that he'll still give me the apartment.

The boy won't even tell me his name.

I bury my head deep in my pillow, but I can still hear Sing. Her screams barrel through the door, punch into my eardrums like metal chopsticks. Haunt me with all the possibilities of needles and failure, what the unknown might actually cost.

Maybe I really am my mother's daughter.

# JIN LING

At first I think I've died. I open my eyes. Find my body swaddled in white cloth. Clean and crisp, like a burial shroud.

The room around me is nicer than anything I've ever seen. The floor and the ceiling are glossy, dark wood. Electric, rice-paper lanterns cast soft halos of light onto sparse, sleek furniture. Even the walls are pieces of art—painted with cranes and stunted fir trees.

It's not until I try to move that I realize I'm alive. The pain is still there. Hot and white. By my shoulder blade. There's a throb in my neck, too—reminders of all the places Kuen's knife went. Something tugs my hand and I realize there's a needle taped just under my skin. A clear tube snakes out of me, going all the way up to a full red bag. Blood.

I rest my head back on the pillow. Blink at the rafters. If one thing's certain, it's that I'm not in the Walled City. No place there is *this* nice. So how did I get out? How am I even alive?

"Oh good. You're awake." My thoughts are interrupted by a man's voice. A brassy one, like a temple gong.

I recognize him immediately. The way he stands in the doorway, shoulders set, is the exact same. There's no hood, but I know it's the man who met Dai at the edge of City Beyond. The one with the money.

"How are you feeling?" The man stays by the sliding door, hands tucked behind his back. I have to squint to see the finer details of his face. I'm not used to so much bright light.

"Confused." I keep scanning the older man's features. He's not pudgy or disfigured, like Longwai. He has wrinkles, but his face is sharp and sly. Like a fox studying a chicken coop.

Dai looks just like his father.

"I'll get the nurse." The man starts to turn.

"No—wait," I call out, and immediately regret it when the pain flares. "Is Dai here?"

The name does something to the man. Changes him. He no longer looks so sharp—the difference between the hunter and the hunted. He turns out the door, trying to hide it.

I wait in silence, wondering if the man will come back. I flex my hand, stare at the bag of blood. The thick red looks weird, hanging in a pouch, far from bodies and hurt. Almost like the sauce Mrs. Pak puts on her chicken dishes.

It takes me a moment to recognize Dai when he walks in. He's dressed like a rich man: white shirt, pressed pants, hair combed out of his face. He looks as if he belongs in one of those giant metal skyscrapers. All he needs is a briefcase.

212

But then he shoves his hands into his pockets and I remember who Dai is. The boy who sits on rooftops, his feet dangling, baiting fatal heights and concrete endings. The boy who spends hours under Longwai's knife, waiting for me to run back. The boy of scars and secrets.

Dai walks all the way to the edge of my bed. I know what he's going to say. I can tell by the way he's looking at me, eyes wary.

"You're a girl."

"And you're rich." My reply is thick, terse. I can't believe that, after all the things he's kept from me, he's actually angry.

Dai shrugs; his fists stay deep in his pockets. There's something tucked under his arm. Something long and flat and the same color as my boots. I can't get a good look at it, because he's turned away. He isn't looking at me or the mess of tubes around the bed. He stares at the fancy room. Stuff that belongs in a museum. "Didn't have much choice in the matter."

"Neither did I." I feel a scowl coming on. "Sorry to disappoint you."

"I…" He licks his lips, digs for the right word. "I'm impressed, actually. That's not an easy secret to keep."

I don't know what to say, so I close my eyes. My side is full of throb and pain.

"Why did you hide it?"

One eye opens, giving me a view of Dai's clean-cut face. His lips are almost a frown, which means his question is serious.

Talking hurts, but I do it anyway. "You've seen what happens to girls in that place."

"I mean . . . why did you hide it from me?"

"Same reason you hid all this, I guess. We all have our secrets. Had," I correct myself. "Besides, would it really have changed anything?"

His lips press together and he gives a small shrug. "So why do you want money to buy time with one of Longwai's girls? What do you really need the cash for?"

Dai's questions come fast. Rapid-fire bullets. They make me uneasy. I don't like being the one who gives up all the answers. I shouldn't be. Not when Dai's biggest deception is all around us.

"I'll tell you only if you give me some answers." Lightning pain forks into my side. I grit my teeth. Wait for it to pass. "Where are we? Who are you?"

I expect him to dodge my questions. Like every other time. Instead, Dai tugs a high-backed wooden chair over to my bed. He sets what he was carrying down on the floor. And just for a moment I glimpse it. A book.

"It's a long story." He perches himself on the lacquered wood. It doesn't look comfortable.

"That's good. Seeing as I'm stuck here." I lift up my needle-stuck hand, wave it at him. The scarlet tube coils with the motion. "You want answers, you got to give them."

Dai sighs. It's a heavy sound, full of years and silence. Something he's carried for a long, long time. Something he's ready to put down.

"I grew up here, in this house. . . . It was pretty much all I knew for thirteen years. Tutors. Mercedes. Private schools.

Trips abroad. Of course, I was a kid then, so I didn't really know how good I had it."

I can't even begin to picture the life he's describing—the world I'm staining just by lying here. What's even harder to imagine is how Dai lost it. Why doesn't he live here anymore? What happened to his tutors and expensive cars?

I ask him.

"I've told you before about my brother." Dai swallows. "The one you remind me of. His name was Hiro."

*Was.* This word feels like another strange drug pumped into my body. It makes me want to puke. I knew this story wasn't a happy one. I just didn't know it would be so close to mine.

"I lost him." Dai's head dips down between his knees. Hands muss up his hair. The way he isn't looking at me makes me think he's crying.

"We were two years apart. I was older, but Hiro had a better head on his shoulders. He was a good kid: straight As, star athlete, and all that. He could've been anything he wanted. I was trouble. Stealing cars for joyrides, cheating on tests, sneaking some of my father's liquor . . . if anything was against the rules, I probably did it. When we were little, Hiro would always follow me around and tell me not to do things. Like those little shoulder-angels in the cartoons. Sometimes I even listened to him."

He talks and I see Mei Yee. It's not the good times: the nights we huddled under the ginkgo tree and watched fog break over the mountains, or when our mother steeped used

215

tea leaves and served us weak amber water in chipped cups. No. What I see is the last time. The night the men came. The terror on her face. The ripping, shredding awfulness in my chest. The same awfulness I hear in Dai's voice.

"When I turned fourteen, Mother and Father sent me off to boarding school on the other side of Seng Ngoi. Mostly the kids there are rich and bored.... But there were a few in my year who were trouble. All the boys broke the rules. It was kind of what you did. We smuggled in cigarettes and liquor. Dirty magazines."

He pauses again. "I was young. Stupid. I started hanging around boys who were getting involved in things way over their heads. Blackmailing other students for money. Dealing drugs. It was fun. A rush. A sense of power. Other boys looked up to me. Wanted to work for me.

"It was good my first two years. No one got caught. We'd built our own little kingdom inside the school. Nothing could stop us. But then Hiro came to school. It didn't take him very long to figure out what I was doing. As soon as he found out, he tried to talk me out of it, like he always did. But I wouldn't listen.

"Anyway, we got into a big fight about it, just before one of my night runs to pick up the next month's supply of drugs. Hiro tried to stop me from going—he grabbed my hoodie and told me I was a good person. I tore away, left him at school, thought that was the last of it.

"We used Longwai as a supplier. His men would meet us out in Seng Ngoi and make the exchange. It was me and the mayor's son who had to go pick up that night. The kid—his name was Pat Ying—was really jumpy. He'd already taken a few hits before we snuck out. I liked to go on the runs clean. Have my head in order.

"Hiro followed us that night. I didn't know until…" Dai pauses. His eyes glitter with almost-tears. Behind them I see the tension of that long-lost night. How dark the streets were. The anger and fear fighting a cage match in his chest. How much he loved his brother. The heavy, heavy guilt that now bends his back. Breaks his voice.

"Things went…bad. There was a squabble over how much. Pat Ying got cocky and started arguing with Longwai's man. Pat Ying pulled out a knife, and I tried to stop him. He was too high to realize it was me, sliced my arm open." Dai winces at the memory, and I remember the scar that snakes up his arm.

"Longwai's man had a gun. The knife was enough to get him to pull it out and start shooting. Everything happened so fast. And my arm hurt. And suddenly Hiro was there, yelling. There was so much sound and then Hiro was on the ground. Pat Ying, too. And I couldn't see any blood. But there was the gun—right there, by my feet. Longwai's man dropped it somehow. I'd never shot a gun before, but something about seeing my brother on the ground not moving made me pick it up. Longwai's man jumped at me, and I didn't even think about it. I just pulled the trigger."

Dai closes his eyes. I can't tell if he's remembering or fighting. Maybe both.

"And when it was done, there was just me holding the gun. Everything was on the ground. The drugs. The cash. Hiro and Pat Ying. The man I killed.

"Hiro—" His brother's name hangs in the air for a moment, heavy with memory and sadness. "He was only fourteen. He could've been anything he wanted....He had his whole fucking life ahead of him! He believed in me, thought I would make the right choice. He died in my arms instead.

"I didn't know what to do. Pat Ying was dead, too. Both he and Hiro were shot with the gun I was holding. Longwai's man, too. I came back here, to the house. Told my father what had happened.

"I was sixteen. Old enough to be tried as an adult. Old enough to go to jail. My father knew all of this. Knew they would come for me. He didn't even think twice about taking me to Hak Nam. I'd never even seen him drive a car before.... But he shoved me in the back and took me to the Walled City. He told me to wait there until he could straighten things out, since the police couldn't arrest me there. I waited and waited. At first he came back every week to the Old South Gate with money and news. But the weeks dragged on and he couldn't clear my name. My prints were on the gun and three people were dead by its bullets.

"I've been a fugitive for two years now. If I step out of Hak Nam, the police can arrest me, take me to trial for murder and drug dealing. Even with my father's influence, I don't think it'll end well."

His story's a lot to take in. It makes my head spin. I'm

dizzy without even moving. "So...you killed one of Long-wai's men and now you're *working* for him? Aren't you afraid he's going to find out? And if your dad's giving you money, then why are you working at all? Why take the risk?"

"We never used names. I know Longwai could still trace it back to me, if he looked into it closely enough. I'm just hoping he won't." Dai swallows, Adam's apple bobbing. There's more to this story.

"Jin—" Dai catches himself. "Is that your real name?"

"Jin Ling."

"Do you know *why* Hak Nam is the way it is? Why it's exempt from the law?"

It's hard to shake my head in this immense fluff of pillow. I try my best.

"It used to be a fort. That's why there are cannons by the Old South Gate. About a hundred years ago foreigners came and bought up the city; but because Hak Nam was a fort, it wasn't a part of their contract. Governments got switched around and new laws were made, but Hak Nam was just for-gotten. None of the politicians or police paid attention to it, so it grew and grew into what it is now."

His talk about governments and politicians sounds like a foreign language. Hard to understand. I follow it as best as I can. Nod anyway.

"The foreigners' contract is scheduled to end at New Year's. A new city council has formed to guide the transition. They've decided to take over Hak Nam and demolish it. They just passed an ordinance that allows them to go into the Walled

City and clean it out. Raze it to the ground. As soon as the New Year arrives, they're sending in the Security Branch to take it back."

I try to grasp what he's saying. No more Walled City. No more Longwai. No more chances to find Mei Yee. "But... what about the Brotherhood? It's Longwai's city.... He's not going to just roll over without a fight."

"The ordinance has been kept very secret. Only a few officials know about it, so word doesn't get back to Longwai. They want to take him by surprise. But even if they arrest Longwai and the other Brotherhood members, the Security Branch has to have evidence to hold them. Right now they don't even know *who* to arrest. The Brotherhood keeps a pretty tight hold on its list of members."

"So how do you know about the ordinance?" I ask.

"It's no secret to the Security Branch that I'm camped out in Hak Nam. They know that the New Year's eviction is going to put me in a tight spot. And they know I have connections in the Walled City. They approached me a few weeks ago and offered me a deal: a complete pardon in exchange for a single piece of evidence."

"What's that?"

"Longwai keeps his records the old-fashioned way. Names. Bank account numbers. Deals. He writes all of it down in a book. His ledger. It will be the Branch's biggest piece of evidence against the Brotherhood. Something they can use to put the gang under for good. Longwai and his men have been arrested a few times, whenever they travel outside Hak Nam, but the Branch has never been able to hold them. Their eye-witnesses always bail; they're too scared to testify. Afraid of what Longwai will do to them and their families if the courts can't hold them."

*Afraid. They should be.* All I can think of is the drug lord's shiny hook scar, how the dragon on his sleeve shimmered when he laughed about a man being stabbed. "Why don't they just send a policeman to get the book?"

"They can't. Not yet. They have no legal jurisdiction in Hak Nam. If they sent an undercover cop to grab it, it would become illegally acquired evidence. Useless in court. And if they wait until they take the city back, they're afraid Longwai will see them coming and destroy it.

"I'm the loophole. If I get the ledger for the Security Branch, it stands as legitimate evidence. The Brotherhood has no chance of getting out on bail. I have to steal the ledger and hand it over to the Branch by New Year's."

Steal the drug lord's ledger? Just the suggestion shoots fear through my aching spine. No wonder they're offering Dai complete freedom. The job's impossible. "And if you don't?"

"Longwai and his thugs walk. And I end up in jail." He gnaws his lip. His foot bounces against the floor, the way it did in Longwai's brothel. "Or worse."

"So that's why you're sitting during my runs? You wanted a way into the brothel because that's where he keeps the book...." I trail off.

He nods. "I'm sorry I wasn't completely honest with you. I thought...I thought I could do it alone. They made me swear under oath not to tell anyone. If word gets out, if Longwai finds out about the raid, then it's pretty much over."

I should be angry. Furious. Dai put me in even worse danger than I realized. Failing a drug run is nothing compared with this. But the wrath, the fury I expect, doesn't come. I know, if I were Dai, I'd do the same thing. I guess, in a way, I have. I made him sit so I could try to find my sister.

"How long until New Year's?" It should be soon; the air's been cool long enough. This time every year City Beyond dresses in red and sets the sky on fire. Paper dragons dance through the streets. Lucky children—the not-vagrants—run around in new shoes, waving bright red envelopes of cash. Throw firecrackers on the ground to scare away the Nian: thief of children.

"Nine days." He spits the number out like a burning coal.

"Those were the lines in your apartment...." I realize. "But you—you're not in the Walled City now."

"No, I'm not."

Those three words tell me how much he's risked, bringing me here. His freedom. His life for mine. It's a strange, warm thought. My whole life I've always been the protector—the one rescuing people. I did it alone.

"I don't think the Branch will arrest me now," he explains, seeing the look on my face. "They want the ledger too badly."

"But it was still a risk."

Dai shrugs. The movement looks funny under his dress shirt. Stiff. Uncomfortable. "I-I couldn't let you die...."

"Yes, you could have." I glance back at the blood bag. It

222

seems emptier, the top frothing with beet-red bubbles. Life pouring back into me. "Most people would've walked by the alley. But you didn't. You saved me."

The look on his face. It's as if I just stabbed him or something.

"Thank you," I add.

He holds my words for a minute. Tasting them. The longer they sit the less wounded his face looks.

"You're welcome," he says finally, before changing the subject. "Your turn. I gave you my answers. How about yours?"

Suddenly I'm exhausted, heavy in the bed. As if Dai's whole story just landed on my chest. Pushing. Weighing.

"It's not such a long story, really," I begin. But then I start talking. I tell him everything. About the rice farm and how hard my father's fists hit. About my sister and that night with the Reapers. I relive every moment through my words: leaping onto the bike and following their van. Cutting my hair, becoming a boy. Looking, looking, always looking for my sister. Fighting tooth and nail. By myself.

My story's longer than I thought. Even Dai looks tired by the end.

"You think your sister's in Longwai's brothel?"

"I've looked everywhere else," I tell him. "What do you think will happen to the girls there? After the New Year?"

"Depends. If I get the ledger and the Branch arrests the Brotherhood, then they should go free."

"And if you don't?"

"The Branch might get a hold of Longwai for a time, but

he'll find a way to wriggle free, like he has in the past. And without the ledger's membership lists, the Branch won't be able to net the entire Brotherhood. There will be men left to... redistribute the Brotherhood's assets. Get the girls out and start the brothel somewhere else." Dai's face looks paler. As if the blood going into my veins is getting sucked from his own arm. "Your sister. What's her name?"

"Mei Yee." This is the first time in years I've said her name out loud. "Her name is Mei Yee."

Dai's hand moves over the bed, finds mine. Finger to finger. He's careful not to touch the tape or the tube or the needle. There's a strength to the way he cups my hand. His skin is startling and warm. Human.

"We don't have to do this alone, Jin Ling. I'll help you find your sister. If she's there, we'll get her out."

This is what it must feel like to have a brother. I think of all the times I used to wish for one. When my back ached over rows and rows of uncut rice. When my father's words all slurred into one and his knuckles split into me. When the Reapers came and there was no one strong enough to stop them.

I stopped wishing for that long ago. When the last of my mother's pregnancies ended in blood and I realized if she brought a boy into the world, I'd have to protect him, too.

But now Dai is holding my hand and I don't have to be the strong one. I don't have to be alone anymore. I squeeze his fingers in mine. The needle bulges in my veins, tugs against the tape. Stinging hurt.

"And I'll help you get the book," I promise. "Before the New Year."

Nine days fall over Dai's face. His hand flinches back. "You need to rest. Dr. Kwan says you need to stay in bed for at least two weeks. And nothing strenuous for about a month after that."

What he doesn't say out loud—what's written all across his expression—is that I'm going to be here for a while. I want to fight it, but right now even breathing hurts.

"I brought you something to pass the time." He bends down, picks up the book from the floor. A thin layer of dust coats its cover. He wipes this off. Hands the book to me. "Star maps."

It's weighty, this book. Heavy with so many things I don't know. So many things I want to learn. I set it on my chest, flip through pages that smell like gloss and years. The writing is in a language I don't recognize, cramped and squiggled. But there are pictures: velvet blue and white spiderweb lines. Connecting dozens of dots. If I squint close enough, I can recognize them.

"Cassiopeia's in there," Dai says. "If you get through that, there's plenty more like it upstairs. Oceanography, zoology, archaeology. A whole bunch of -y words. Hiro never could decide what he wanted to be...."

His sentence wilts. Sad. Like my father's fields after rainless days and weeks. I try to turn a chunk of pages, look for my rice scythe, but the burn under my shoulder flares. Makes my teeth grit.

Dai stands. His chair scrapes softly across the floor. "I'll have a nurse come in. Give you something for the pain."

I let the book of star maps slide to my good, fireless side. My eyes are shutting, surrendering to inevitable sleep. Never in my life have I been so, so tired. But there's one question I haven't asked. One answer I need to know. "Wait…did…did you see Chma? Is he okay?"

"Chma?" He pauses.

"Kuen cut off his tail." I see the knife. Chma's slick, wet stump. I'm angry all over again.

"You killed a boy for your cat?" It makes the fight seem too simple, too brutish when Dai says it like that: a boy for a cat. A heart for a tail.

*Not such a fair trade this time.*

Dai reaches the door, shakes his head. "I didn't see him."

He leaves. I stare straight at the pitch-black ceiling. All I see are Kuen's blank eyes, staring at nothing. Maybe he deserved it. Maybe my hand just slipped.

But he's still dead. Because of me.

Kuen is dead. And I'm alive.

So why does it feel as if I'm the one who lost?

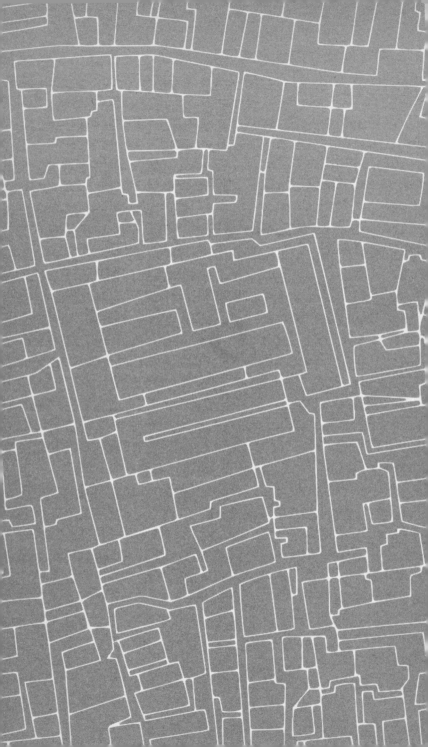

# 8 DAYS

# MEI YEE

I wait for the ambassador. Sing's cries are in my head, and the *yes* is on my tongue, filling my body with sparks and spit, like that firework our neighbors bought one New Year's. I'd never seen fire that color, a cherry red so bright it burned a hole into my vision. It was so beautiful, so not of my world, that I thought it was enough. But then the fuse ran out, shot up into the clear winter sky with a pluming white tail of smoke. The night's black filled with more colors than I could name: trails of sapphire, scarlet, and green.

The sight was so beautiful I cried.

And I feel as if I'm about to cry now when the door wheels open. There's so much inside—fear, loss, gain, unvoiced wishes, my *yes*—whirring and spitting and blazing like that firework. It's impossible to keep it all in.

But something about the way the ambassador enters the

room demands silence. He looks even bigger today, hulking in the fullness of his coat. The fabric is as black as a bear's fur. His arms are full of something I can't completely see. Whatever it is, it's not flowers.

There's no hello or formal nod. He walks over to the side table and grabs my vase by the rim.

"There were no suitable bouquets," he tells me over his shoulder. "And I wanted to bring you something special. To show you how sorry I am about what happened...."

*What happened.* I wish he would say it, tell me he's sorry for my bruises instead of bringing some other lavish gift. I wish he would keep to our routine, stick with flowers.

The ambassador steps away and I see he's replaced my browned carnations with a shallow pot. Out of its sandy gravel rises a tree. It's not a sapling, but a full-grown thing with limbs, bark, leaves, and roots. A tree that should be taller than me is no longer than my arm.

"W-what is it?" I stare, my *yes* momentarily forgotten, trying to imagine how a tree could be caged and shrunk. It seems like magic, impossible.

"A cypress tree." He leans over to inspect the leaves, brushing them with too-careful, manicured fingers.

"How—why is it so small?" I feel stupid, asking this. I've never seen a cypress before. Most of the trees in my province were long gone by the time I was born, cut down to make room for rice fields. Maybe all cypress trees are this size, and I just never knew.

"It's a technique called bonsai. Gardeners use it to keep the trees from getting too big and unmanageable. This way you can keep them inside. For your enjoyment."

I keep looking at the tiny tree. Trying to imagine what it would look like if it weren't confined to its pot. If men's fingers and shears weren't constantly picking at it, cutting it back.

"No more flowers?" I ask.

"They keep dying," the ambassador says as if I don't know. As if my room doesn't fill up with sweet rot stench every time the petals wither. "I thought you might appreciate something more permanent."

I'll have nothing to place in the window now. Nothing to warn the boy with.

This thought catches me—sharp and hard—like a sling-shot stone. It doesn't matter. It shouldn't. Soon there won't be a window. Or walls. Or plastic orchid blossoms and lop-sided stars.

As soon as I say *yes*.

The ambassador stops picking at the tree. His jacket comes off. Along with his coat. He moves over to my bed. The jostle of his body on the mattress shoots pain through my bruise.

"Have you thought any more about my offer?"

*Yes.* Just say it. Say it and all of this goes away.

My client sits beside me, but I'm still staring at the tree. Its tiny pot is ceramic, glazed blue. The same soft sheen the streetlamp makes on the boy's face. I find myself wondering if it's the same color as waves.

My lips part, but instead of my answer comes a question. The same one as before, "Would you take me to the sea?"

The ambassador frowns. He doesn't look handsome doing it, the way window-boy does. It only makes the wrinkles of his face deeper, more treacherous. "It wouldn't be good for people to see us together in public. But don't worry. You'll never have to leave the building. Besides, if it's the ocean you want, you can always see pieces of it from the rooftop. When you go to the garden."

"You...you can see it from the rooftops?" It steals my breath away, the thought that the sea was so close, this whole time, and I never knew.

"Yes. Seng Ngoi is a port city. We're right next to the water." His words come out quick and snapping. Like the noise that long-gone firework made. "Enough of this nonsense. What's your answer?"

The hairs on my skin bristle against the edge in his voice. I search for the *yes*—the one that was just on the crest of my tongue, waiting to be released—but it's deeper now. Unsure. Even the memories of Sing's shriek don't call it back. Instead of the pool and rooftop gardens and luxury food, all I can think about are the guards at the apartment door. How I'll never have to leave the building. There might be no bars there, but there's no boy, either. No one to promise a way out.

Can I trade one cage for another?

Are pieces of the sea enough?

"Mei Yee! Answer me." His voice is hot, too loud in my ear.

There's only one way home. For the boy. For me.

If I say *yes* now, I'll fail the boy, destroy his wish for home. I'll fail myself, destroy all of my hundreds of wishes.

There's only one way, and it isn't this.

234

"No." I expect my voice to be a willow branch: wispy, bending, and supple. The way my courage feels. Instead, I'm bamboo: made of splinters and stab.

The ambassador feels it. For the briefest moment he even looks as if he's been knifed. His jaw goes slack, his eyes glass.

"I want to stay here, with my friends...." The strength that was in my throat fades, wilts against the look that rises up behind my client's face. The storm cloud, the demon.

"You're cheating on me, aren't you? There's someone else! I know there is!" His shout is thunder and fire. It spews over the room, flecks into my face with the heat of his saliva.

"No!" I start to protest, but it doesn't matter.

Those arms, those fingers break their routine and pin me down, gripping with a power I never knew they had. The sharpness of my hairpins digs into my scalp as I'm shoved into the pillow.

So much sweat and skin. Everywhere. Wrapping tighter and tighter around me. And pain. I'm being pried, shredded, ripped. Opened and closed. Exposed and smothered.

*No. No. No.* Maybe I'm saying this out loud. Maybe not. I can't hear anything anymore. I can't see, either. My vision is covered in spots—like electric-blue lichen—the way it did when I stared out the window and waited for the boy.

It's only when the ambassador lets go and falls back that I realize he'd had a hand over my throat. The air that floods my lungs is thick with smoke. Breath by breath the world comes back. The dust-filmed plastic of the orchid petals. A dozen unseen bruises on my arm, my neck. The hot stick of scarlet trickling down my legs, staining the sheets.

He's out of the bed, piecing himself together with zippers and buttons. He doesn't look at me or the bonsai tree. The door opens and he's halfway out before he glances back over his shoulder.

I don't know how to read his face. His emotions might as well be inked characters—squiggles and dots. Whatever the feeling inside him is, it's intense. Like fear, anger, and love all thrown into a pot. Like the colors of my neighbors' firework.

"It doesn't really matter if you're here or there. You're mine. Remember that."

He shuts the door. The vase full of dead flowers leaves with him.

## 9

The ambassador meant to break me. This is what I decide when I hobble over to the mirror, see fingerprints smudged like ink around the base of my throat. I spend extra minutes with my makeup brush, piling layer after layer of powder against my collarbone. But no matter how much I put on, I can still see his marks. A shadow gone wrong.

He meant to break me. But I'm stronger than he knows. I'm stronger than *I* knew. The only thing the ambassador broke was himself—the image of him I built up over the months, the idea that he might be able to save me from this place.

There's only one way out. And it was never by his side.

The other girls notice the bruises, but they don't ask questions. It's a mercy, because I know I would never be able to answer. I could never tell them about the ambassador's offer—how I turned down heaven on a silver platter and he punished me for it.

Instead, they gather in my room and talk about the one girl who has a worse portion than we do.

"They're still making Sing take clients," Nuo tells us as she struggles to thread her needle. The cross-stitch is coming together—a carp with scales of fire and white, swimming against some sapphire current.

"The master wouldn't keep her here unless she was making him money." Yin Yu says this with her tongue concentrating on the edge of her lips. She's holding my hand in hers, wielding a wand of scarlet nail polish. She's made it to the final nail without a slip.

Nuo frowns. Her needle stabs hard into the cloth; she pulls the mandarin-tinged thread through.

"I think..." Yin Yu goes on. The brush slicks cool paint down to the edge of my pinkie nail. Drops off. "It's better than the alternative. She wouldn't last long on the streets. None of us would."

She finishes—both my nails and her words—and screws the polish shut.

"I should go," Yin Yu says suddenly. It's only when she's standing straight that I realize how thin she's become. "There's washing to be done in the west hall. Mama-san will be angry if I don't finish it soon."

I stand, too, trying to ignore the pain in my thighs. "You're cleaning too much. Let me take some of the rooms."

"You've helped enough. Besides, you shouldn't ruin your nails." Yin Yu waves me back down, vanishes through the dark of the door.

There are only the three of us now, sitting in silence. Wen Kei eyes the door as if it's the jaws of some sea beast, threatening to swallow her frail body. Nuo stabs the needle into the cloth. It slips, digs deep into her skin. A soft swear leaves her lips as she places the wounded finger between them.

"Yin Yu thrives off work," she says when she pulls her finger out, pinches it between the silk fabric of her dress. "It's the thing that keeps her going."

"I know." The other two girls are staring at me. Four eyes dark and full of question, bottomless wells. I can't hold their gazes for long, so I look at the crimson window covering. It matches the new shiny color of my nails.

I can still feel Nuo staring. "Why did you take over her duties? Do you want to be Mama-san?"

"That's what Yin Yu said," Wen Kei pipes in.

If there's any time I should tell them, it would be now. Memories—ghosts of the boy and his promises—file through my mind like a line of orange-robed monks. There's a fire in my heart, twisting, wanting to reach out and show them the light. The curtain's red looks brighter, more like blood than flames.

I want to pull it back, show them the shell. But every time I think of doing this, I hear Sing's desperate pleas, clawing and scrabbling inside my head. I know the others won't understand. The way I didn't understand.

238

They'll only try to stop me. The way I tried to stop Sing.

"The meeting is soon." I change the subject. "We should get ready."

Nuo lifts her finger to her face. The blood is still there, smoothed out like a second layer of red skin. Her needle must have gone deep. I think of all the many strings stretched tight across her zither, made of cruel steel. "Can you still play?"

She frowns, tucks the cross-stitch under her arm. "Do I have a choice?"

None of us speak, because we all know the answer.

## 9

This meeting my hands don't shake. The black lacquered serving tray is steady as I shuffle through the room, pouring wine and offering lights. So much smoke wisps up from the Brotherhood's pipes and cigarettes that soon enough I can't even see Nuo clearly. I only know she's there because of her music. Despite her bandaged finger, the notes stab through the air, steady and strong.

And despite the hurt in my legs, I walk straight, keep a smile pasted to my face.

We're stronger than they think.

Longwai holds the ledger close. It's small: the same size as those notebooks Sing used to sketch our faces in. As long as a brick and as thick as a thumb. The cover is a red as bright as Nuo's wounded finger, crowned with the crest of a shining gold dragon. Every few minutes he flicks through the pages, running over cryptic characters written weeks and months before. All through the meeting he fills it with notes; a few of the numbers I recognize—characters I learned when Sing tried to teach us how to read. Sometimes he's so focused on writing down inky lines and loops that the men have to repeat themselves to be heard.

When the meeting ends, I collect the empty glasses quickly, willing Longwai and the book to stay put until I can follow. The glasses clink together, their purple-red rims jostling for space on my tray. I try to move slowly, but in the cabinet's reflection I see Longwai heaving to his feet, the ledger wedged firmly in both hands. He starts walking to the far hall, in the direction of the stairs. I stash the glasses in the bottom of the cabinet, still coated with the stick of plum wine, and follow.

I've never been upstairs before. In fact, I've only seen the actual staircase twice. It lies at the end of the east hall, by the door to Mama-san's room. It spirals like my nautilus shell, up and up, into the dark.

I hang, uncertain, at the edge of the hall, waiting for the master to disappear to the second floor before I make my move. Every part of my body shakes as I push myself down the length of the hallway, farther into the dark.

I don't know if I can do this.

Deep inside there's a pull, a line of cowardice tugging, begging me to go back to my room. To sit on my bed and wait. To apologize to the ambassador and accept his offer. To apologize to Yin Yu. To tell the boy I can't do what he asks of me. To be my mother's daughter. To keep enduring.

But I remember the demon behind the ambassador's eyes, and I know things will never be the same between us. Even if he never bruises me again, every single touch will remind me of the night he made me bleed.

I silence every fear and keep walking, all the way down the shadow-drenched hall, all the way up the stairs. The door at the top is cracked open, streaming browned-gold light over the staircase. The air here smells different, heavy with mildew, leather, and ink. Scents both rich and spoiled. They catch in my throat as I rap my knuckles against the doorframe.

The door swings open. Longwai is behind it, his bulk filling up most of the doorway. Beads of sweat dot his brow, and his chest balloons with thick breaths. His eyes cloud and wrinkle at the sight of me. Girls never climb these stairs.

"What are you doing up here?" His words are tight and precise, as if they were cut out of him with a knife.

"I-I wanted to speak with you, sir." I bow a little as I say this, catch a glimpse of his room under the curve of his armpit. An entire wall of weapons—swords, pistols, rifles, knives. My eyes flick back and forth. No book.

My bow lasts longer than it should. I'm all too aware of this as I rise, feel Longwai's scathing study.

"I'm busy. Any problems you have should be brought to Mama-san." He waves a hand down the stairs. The movement creates another brief glimpse. I catch sight of a bed and a screen full of bright moving pictures. His television. Still no book.

"I—" My mind hurtles, searching for words and excuses that might keep me here. Give me enough time to spot that elusive ledger. "I can't go to Mama-san. I can't trust her with it."

Longwai frowns. "Is that so?"

My heart screams profanities in the form of beats. I'm not a spy, nor was I meant to be. The lies I have to feed the dragon, the ones I spent hours thinking of, feel slimy and rotten. Like something he'll spit back out.

I offer them up anyway.

"She likes to play favorites." I stand, ever so slightly on my tiptoes, trying to get another glimpse. There are no colors in the drug lord's bedchamber. Almost everything is black or some drab shade of brown. The furniture, the floor, the wall hangings. The only bright things are the television screen and a tankful of fish. These cast the entire room in a ghost light.

Finally, I catch it. The faintest glimpse of red. It's only a corner of something, poking out of a gaping desk drawer. That has to be it.

"Most people do." The master's booming voice snaps my eyes back to the floor.

"It's…it's Yin Yu." I stumble over my own terrifying words. My veins clog full of guilt, as if the very blood in them has stopped. "She—she's jealous that I've taken over her tasks. I'm afraid she's spreading rumors about me to Mama-san. And I'm afraid that you or the ambassador might hear something bad me. Something that isn't true."

"You think Osamu is paying for the quality of your character?" His mouth turns into a smile, then spoils into a sneer. "That I'm running some kind of etiquette school?"

242

I shake my head and push out more small, small words. "I don't want to end up like Sing."

"Then don't," Longwai says. "Is that all?"

"Y-yes." I take a step back, only to remember that the stairs are close. My heel hangs off the edge. At this point it might even be a mercy if I fell back. A few scrapes and bruises seem preferable to the way Longwai is staring at me now. Like a piece of meat.

"Don't bother me again," Longwai growls.

"Thank you, sir." I bow again, catch another look at the book. It's still there, wedged into the drawer.

Longwai grunts and closes the door. I navigate the stairs with coltish knees. They knock and shake with each step. Halfway down I pass Fung, who watches me with his dark, dark eyes. The stairs are tight and our shoulders brush. I have to shrink all the way against the wall to let him pass. We're so close he can't *not* see me shaking.

But the gangster doesn't say anything about it. His only word is a half-grunted "careful" before he keeps climbing, without looking back.

I did it. I spotted where Longwai keeps his ledger. I took the risk.

Jin Ling would be proud.

My heart is so swelling and full—with thoughts of my sister, the boy, the sea—that I forget about washing the dirty glasses in the lounge. I keep walking straight up the north hall. Past the tomblike silence of Sing's room. By Nuo's and Wen Kei's and Yin Yu's closed doors. All the way to the end.

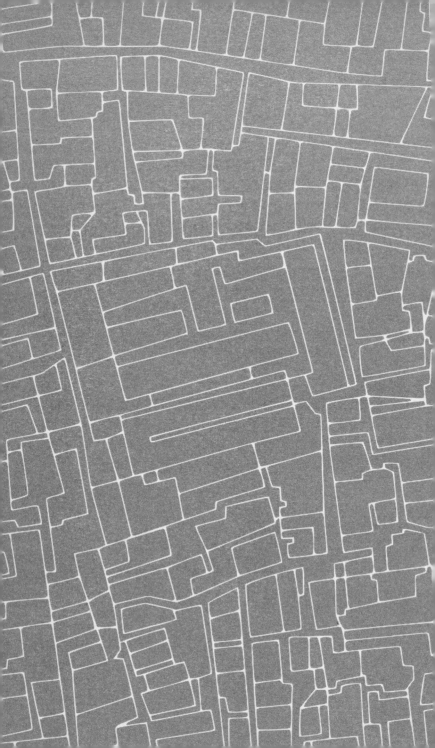

# 6 DAYS

# DAI

When I was younger and needed a place to think, I'd sit by the carp pond. It was one of my mother's indulgences—a reminder of her home country—installed at the rear of the house where an entire wall of glass looks out on the rock garden. Part of the pond stretches inside the house. The other half juts beneath the glass, into the yard of carefully raked gravel.

Koi swim to the edge of their small world and back again: fire white and liquid amber, scales shimmering. Their movement is smooth and streamlined, like some sort of jeweled hypnosis. It puts my mind at ease.

Whenever Hiro was tired of reading through his endless sets of encyclopedias, he used to come down here and toss coins into the water. They spun through the ripples—comets of silver, copper, and gold—down into the seaweed's tangled green. He never did hit a fish.

*Hiro.* I breathe in and dip my fingers into the pool. My confession to Jin—Jin Ling—was the first time in a long time I've said his name, or even thought it. I've spent so long trying to erase and forget. Cramming him into the world of night-mares. Trying to cut all ties with everything and everyone.

My brother's ghost is all over this house. Whispering *if onlys* in my ear. If only I'd listened to him. If only I'd been a better brother. If only . . .

I spent seven hundred and thirty-eight days in Hak Nam, doing anything I could to get out and find a way back home. But home isn't what I need. Talking to Jin—Jin Ling—telling her my sad story, only drove this truth deeper into my skull. A fancy mansion on Tai Ping Hill won't fix me. Trying to forget won't fix me, either. It will never earn my brother's forgiveness. Silence the ghosts . . .

I push my hand in deeper, the waterline up to my wrist. The koi scatter, scales streaking like torches in a night sky. I wonder if Hiro's coins are still at the bottom, hiding beneath years of algae and fish shit.

The pond is too cold, I decide. I pull my hand out and wipe it against my shirt. I would worry about stains, but I know Father won't wear this again.

After our conversation, Jin Ling slept, the drugs in her body forcing her through years of rest. Hiro's book of stars curled at her side, filling the catless space. I've never felt more awake. My mind whirls and spins with possibilities. Thoughts of Jin Ling and her sister. The girl and the ledger. The New Year and the six days between.

The girl...she's been on my mind a lot these days. How her eyes came to life when I gave her the shell. How her hand pressed up against the grate, mirrored mine. How, when I look through the window, I don't have to see my pieces; I see her, pulling them all together. How her words brought a smile to my face, tugged it out of nowhere like a rabbit from a magician's hat.

I haven't smiled like that in a long, long time.

I've never felt more awake.

The shuffling of feet causes me to look up, and I see Emiyo standing at the far end of the pond. Her knuckles are so white they look like exposed bone.

"Master Dai, you have a visitor." Emiyo's words are screws winched until they can no longer spin.

There's not much of a question of who's visiting me. I can smell the smoke from here. "Thanks, Emiyo."

My handler is in the foyer. He's pretending to be busy, examining a tapestry woven full of sparrows and cherry blossoms, when I walk in. The coal end of his cigarette glows dangerously close to the fabric.

"You shouldn't smoke in here," I say.

Tsang straightens, his stare flicking over to where I stand. He pulls the cigarette out of his mouth, lets it smolder between his fingers. "And you shouldn't leave Hak Nam. But here we are."

"How'd you know?" I let an eyebrow arch, try not to show the fear that's started to scurry under my belly.

"You missed our meeting. Plus the police processed a very

249

interesting call from a cabdriver a few days ago. Said he took two boys covered in blood to Tai Ping Hill. Didn't take long to connect the dots."

I missed the meeting.... Have I really been here that long? This house has a way of making time stand still. Days, months, years. Nothing changes but our faces. What else have I missed?

"I could have you arrested," my handler goes on, "if I was so inclined."

"I had to do something," I say. "My runner was dying."

"And you did something. Never mind that I told you to get rid of him," he growls. "Now you're just sitting on your ass. Wasting days. Watching the clock."

My jaw bulges. I can't look at his eyes, or the mole that juts out from the corner of his chin. Instead, I stare down at the cigarette and the ashes it's raining on the floor.

"I've been patient with you so far. But we're running out of time." My handler's wrist flicks, too jerky to be a mistake. White-hot ash explodes across the floorboards. From here it looks almost like snow. "I want you back in Hak Nam by tonight."

Because I'm feeling surly, I challenge him. "Or what?"

Tsang reaches into his jacket. At first I think he's going for another cigarette (he's running low), but he pulls out a fold of paper instead. He holds it up for me to see: my name, my crimes, my pardon. It's stamped and signed by one of the most powerful judges Seng Ngoi has to offer.

Fresh ink, flimsy paper freedom. So close I could reach out and snatch it.

"You get me the ledger—you get me Longwai's ass on a platter—you get this. If not…" Tsang pulls the document back, oh-so-close to the amber glare of his cigarette. The air around us singes and stinks. "All it takes is one phone call. One and you're done."

He thinks this will scare me, silence any further questions. It should. A lifetime of navy jumpsuits, cafeteria trays, always looking for shanks out of the corner of my eye is hardly something to scoff at. But all I can think about is the promise I made the girl. *I can get you out.* How I need it to be true.

"The girls in Longwai's brothel. What will happen to them?" I think of how easy it would be for them to slip through Hak Nam's thousands of cracks. Get sucked back into the rip current blackness of streets and men's lust.

"Don't worry about the whores. Worry about yourself." Tsang folds the paper back up (quite a feat with only one cigaretteless hand).

"What's going on here?" My father walks up to my side, but he doesn't look at me. All his concentration is poured into glowering at the Security Branch agent. His mouth is straight, but his eyes are sharp and snapping, like riled Dobermans. I'm sure it's the face he uses when he's trying to intimidate the party on the other side of the table at business negotiations for Sun Industries. It's the reason our family is wealthy enough to live on Tai Ping Hill.

"Just having a few words with your son here, Mr. Sun." My handler tucks his hands behind his back, blocking the cigarette from sight.

"It's getting late," my father says, even though it isn't. "Certainly you have work to get back to."

"I was just finishing up." My handler gives a smile that's too thin to be an actual smile. "I'll see myself out."

And he does. The door opens and closes, allowing in a howl of cold air that only sharpens the stink of smoke. The floor's ashes swirl and then die again.

"What are they making you do?" My father follows the ashes with his eyes. We stare at them together.

"Impossible things," I say, because it's shortest and easiest and true.

"There are other ways, Dai Shing."

"Are there?" I look up. He's standing close to me. Our shirts match, except mine is still damp with pond water. I notice, for the first time, that I'm taller than he is. "Even all your money can't buy my way out of drug dealing and three dead bodies."

Father shuts his eyes. His lids flutter, like he's in pain. "You can run. We have contacts overseas. Your English is good enough. I've already had documents drawn up."

Running. I wonder why he's only bringing this up now, down to the wire. He's asked me to wait so long, forced me to risk so many things to clear my name. Our name. The Sun family name.

The look on his face tells me all I need to know. If I flee the country, it will bring shame to our household. Any chance my father has at acquiring a pardon—of washing our social status clean (even if it is really just a technicality)—flies away with me on that plane. That's why it's his ultimatum. His last possible resort.

I could run. Start clean, away from Hak Nam and Seng Ngoi and my family. Away from the Security Branch and Longwai's ledger. Away from the girls.

*Don't worry about the whores. Worry about yourself.*

It's all I've done for a long, long time. Covering my own ass. Worrying, worrying, always worrying. Warning: Side effects of insomnia and selfish bastard may vary.

I think of how small Jin Ling's hand felt under mine. I think of the girl behind the window, with her midnight braid and faint glow of hope. I even think about that damn cat—tailless and alone in Hak Nam, probably still meowing like he owns the place.

These thoughts twist, twist, twist my heart. They wring out a single, undeniable truth: It's not just about me anymore.

Maybe it never was.

And suddenly I realize what I've been wanting all this time. The ache that coming home couldn't fix. Redemption. A chance to make things right. I can't resurrect my brother, but I can help the girls. Their escape is mine.

I can't trust the Security Branch to find Jin Ling's sister or free the girl behind the window. These are things I have to do myself.

I'm not walking away this time.

"I have to stay. I have to make it right." My father's eyes are still closed when I tell him this. "I'm going back to Hak Nam."

"There's nothing for you there," he says, voice tight.

Ten days ago he would've been right. But now...I don't close my eyes, but I still see the girl's face, feel the stir of her deep inside my chest—twisting the truth out—remember the smoothness of the shell under my fingertips.

My promises don't have to be empty. I might not be a good person, but I can become one. I can write in a new answer: the hero the window-girl sees.

I keep all this inside, because even if I say it out loud I'm not sure my father would hear. He was never the best at listening.

His eyes open, and instead of Dobermans, they remind me of ravens' beaks. Cunning. Sharp. They study me, prodding every detail like a needle's end. It's times like this I wonder why he doesn't hate me. Why he's kept me alive for all these years with wads of cash.

"I'll call the car around," he says.

# JIN LING

They give me drugs to take the pain away. Medicine that makes me feel as if I'm drowning inside my own head. Mostly it's darkness. Heavy, heavy black. I don't fight it. I don't really want to.

I know the days are different only when the nurse comes in with a new outfit. Hooks the tubes up to a full bag of medicine. Takes the empty one away.

...

...

...

Then Dai. Dai? He's standing by my bed. Talking. I try to listen, but sleep is crammed into my ears like cotton wads. I hear only a few words.

"Good-bye...going back...sister...need to rest...don't follow..."

Going back? Dai's going back? I want to sit up. Want to fight him. Make him take me. He can't leave me alone to sleep on some nice feathery pillows while he's getting Mei Yee.

I try to tell him this. Try to open my mouth, lift up my hand to grab him, but everything feels *so heavy*.

Instead of my grabbing him, he's grabbing me. Taking my hand. Squeezing it in his.

This time, I hear every word he says. "I'll find her. I'll get her back."

And for a moment, just before the black hits, I believe him.

# DAI

My apartment feels smaller. Like some giant leaned against the other side of the wall and crushed it in. This isn't the first time I've walked in and felt how empty it is. But it is the first time the emptiness bothers me.

I've got almost everything I need. Emiyo managed to scrub all the blood from my black hoodie and jeans. My gun is still tucked in my pants. There's only one reason for me to be here.

There are so many things waiting to be found: Jin Ling's sister, a ledger, a cat without a tail. I don't have time to stay. I've wasted so much already, and the girl behind the window is waiting for me. I don't even unlace my boots as I walk in. Three paces is all it takes to get to the wall. Four swipes is all it takes to erase the marks. My finger turns as black as my clothes. Never before have I wiped off so many at once.

Six.

It's time to end this.

# MEI YEE

The boy doesn't even have to knock. I feel him there, behind the glass, waiting.

I pull back the curtain, press my face against the grating. Something about the boy is different. I stare through the gaps in the metal, taking in the set of strong shoulders under his sweatshirt. That's the same. So is his hair, with its ends fringing by his cheekbones and jaw. He still looks chilly, with his hands shoved deep in his pockets.

It's nothing on the outside. He's the spitting image of his previous selves—like a painting rendered the exact same way three times. The difference is in his eyes and the way he steps close.

Like someone lost who's found his way again.

He's not the only one. I'm not the girl who sat behind this glass a week ago—breathless, afraid. I know all the things I want the most, the wishes I would make if Jin Ling were here. If the stars fell.

And I'll do whatever it takes to get them.

"Hello." His voice is changed, too. Each word is strong, confident. They echo through my heart like brass, shake me to the core.

"I found what you're looking for." It's hard not to be loud, but this news needs so much more than a whisper. "I was right. Longwai keeps it in his quarters. In the top drawer of his desk."

My words come out so fast I'm surprised the boy can even understand them. But he does. I know because I can see his eyes fill, brim over with the same light that's flooded my veins.

"His upstairs room?"

"Yes," I go on, spurred by the hope in his face. "The stairs are at the end of the east hall. By Mama-san's room."

The boy shuts his eyes, rests his head on the far cinder block wall. Still close enough that I can pick out each and every one of his sweeping eyelashes. His hands, I notice this time, are clean, dirtless. Though one of his fingertips is dusted black, almost as if it's covered in soot. I wonder what made such a mark.

I'm so engrossed in these little details, so lost in the features of my boy, that his voice, when he does speak, startles me.

"I don't know what to do," he says with his eyes still closed.

"You need the ledger, don't you?"

"Yes. It's...part of a deal I made with some important people. People who can get you and me out of here."

"How are you planning to get it?"

"I-I don't know," he says again, shoulders bowing. "I had a plan. But things fell through. My partner got stabbed."

*Pain. Disease. Death.* Longwai wasn't lying about the Walled City's streets. My breath dices into dozens of pieces. It takes me a moment to pull it back together, speak without a voice made of shake. "And if you don't get the book to these important people...what happens?"

"Nothing good."

Which means he'll stay out there and I'll be trapped in here. Choking on incense smoke and covering my bruises in powder, both chances at a different life ruined. I look over my shoulder at the door. At the cypress tree that will never grow.

I look back to the nautilus shell and the boy behind it. His eyes are still shut, his face turned skyward—as pale and flaring bright as a comet's tail. My fingers curl harder into the grate, longing for the other side, where he is.

Just one of my wishes.

Whatever it takes.

"I'll do it," I tell him. "I'll get the ledger."

The boy's eyes snap open, catch mine. The light behind them is gleaming, ferocious.

"If they catch you taking that book...if Longwai discovers what you're up to..." The boy's face looks grim, like a man who's just discovered he has only a week to live. "It's too risky. He'll end you. And I can't let that happen."

My skin shivers from the same want, the same *need*, that was in the ambassador's fingers. Trying their best to pummel, press, shape, and mold. Cramming me into his tiny, gravelly pot. Making me into something I'm not.

This is the only way.

And in my head I'm watching Sing twist, scream, and shout. I hear the slick of the needle under skin, see the dreamy look steal over her face. I feel the darkness of the hall pressing in, whispering the chorus: *I need it. I need it. I need it.*

Wishes cost so much more than dying stars.

"I know," I say, because I do. "But I can't live like this anymore. Sometimes an end seems so much better than my now. If there's any way out, any open door, I have to take it."

"Even if it seems impossible? Even if there are dragons behind it?"

*Even then.* I don't say it out loud, because the boy asked in a way that meant he already knew.

We're staring at each other. Eyes holding eyes. His gaze shatters glass, pierces metal. It hums through my body, charged and electric. Full of shine and hope and possibilities.

"I'm Dai," he says. "My name is Sun Dai Shing. What's yours?"

Dai. It's not the name I would have picked for him. It's too short, too blunt, too foreign. But I let it tumble around in my head for a moment. Let it settle into his hair, eyes, and skin. The more I think about it, the more I stare, the more it starts to fit.

The boy—Dai—shifts so the streaked sapphire light of

261

the far streets falls off his face. My eyes strain, struggling to pierce the new dark between us. I open my mouth, but no sound comes out, as if my throat is a drought-stricken well.

I am nameless.

Dai leans back into the light. Something about its eerie, electric blue comforts me. I start to breathe, pretending that the air around me isn't stuffed with incense and men's sweat. I think of the mountains instead. Of the ginkgo tree and how my mother called me by my name over and over.

It shouldn't be this hard to say my own name. But I think of the last few times I let my name slip to ears who did not deserve to hear it. To Longwai, who says it in a spider-creep way. To Osamu, who says it as if he knows me.

This boy standing across from me, with his folded hands and shadowed face, isn't Longwai. He isn't Osamu. He's Dai. And he trusted me with his name. So I must trust him with mine. With everything.

"My name..." I push past the hoarseness. My words become steadier, as clear as Dai's bottomless, electric eyes. "My name is Mei Yee."

# DAI

All breath leaves my lungs at the sound of her name. My back is against the wall, the water glaze is leaking through my shirts. Creep and chill. The winter is getting too much for just a hoodie. I should've thought to wear my jacket.

This is what I think about while I stare at the girl's face. Maybe because it's easier to wrap my mind around it. Warmth—a jacket—is something I can control. Something I can manage.

But this...her...she's more than warmth. She's fire, a soul, a name. *Mei Yee* reverbs through my head, my veins. Lodges like shrapnel in the far reaches of my chest. More powerful than a pound of C-4. Uncontrollable.

*Mei Yee.* Who grew up on a rice farm surrounded by mountains. Just like Jin Ling.

What are the odds?

I study her face again, searching for traces of sisterhood. It's not a perfect resemblance, but the harder I look, the more I see it. The way her lip quirks to the side when she's nervous. The thickness and slant of her lashes.

But it could be that I'm seeing things. Mei Yee isn't the rarest name, and a lot of times the brothel girls change theirs. I think of the placards on the doors. How the scarlet characters became almost invisible in the light.

There's no way I can know for sure unless I ask.

I push off the wall. "Do you have a sister?"

"I did," she says. "Before. Why do you want to know?"

That's enough. Enough for me to know. Her words are sad, but they don't carry the loss of death. They don't hold the same hollowness mine do when I talk about Hiro. Mei Yee's sister is still alive, somewhere. And I'll bet that somewhere is my father's mansion on Tai Ping Hill.

I can still feel Jin Ling's taped hand squeezing mine, straining at the sound of my oath. It seemed like such a solid, simple promise—up there on the hill, surrounded by gates and carp ponds. Here on the ground it's a different matter.

For a moment I consider telling her. But if Mei Yee isn't the sister—or worse, if she is and I can't get her out—I can't give her false hope. It's too cruel.

"Just a question." I try to say this as dismissively as possible. My heart is thrumming, struggling to work out this excitement. This fear.

My excuse to get into the brothel is now crippled, on

bed rest with Jin Ling, which means the book is out of my reach. And without the ledger, I can't guarantee Mei Yee her freedom. I can't get the book without Mei Yee. I can't get her out safely without risking her life. Without flinging her forward like a queen on a chessboard.

I think of the silent girl with dragging hair. The bloody, tattered escape gone wrong. My heart squeezes high in my throat.

I don't want to risk it. Risk her. But that's probably me just being a selfish bastard.

Funny how quickly things turn.

Mei Yee's fingers poke through the grating like tiny white seedlings. Tender, seeking out the sun. They push through so far I can see her nails, coated in slick red-hot paint. The color looks wrong on her. Too violent and bright.

"I'll get the book," she says, not quietly.

"We'll do it together," I tell her. "I don't want you snatching Longwai's ledger first chance you get. He'll miss it for sure. We'll need a way to get it out. Plus you'll need a distraction to get up there and back without being noticed."

My mind is like one of those mechanical windup clocks Hiro used to collect and take apart (in his *the way things work are cool and I want to be an engineer* phase). Only this one isn't scattered in pieces across his desk. It's working, whirring at its utmost speed. "How much time will you need? To get the keys and get upstairs?"

"Depends. Mama-san keeps the keys close almost all the time. Except…" Mei Yee pauses, twisting a hand along her lush starless-black braid. It wraps around her wrist like a rope. "Except when Yin Yu has them."

"Yin Yu?"

"One of the other girls. She cleans rooms for Mama-san, which means she has access to the keys."

"Do you trust her?"

Mei Yee's hand stops wrapping. I can't see her wrist anymore, swallowed in shiny, beautiful black. "Yes. If—if I can tell her why. Do you have money?"

Her question catches me off guard. "Some."

"The other girls can help, too. The ledger's pretty small. But it still won't fit through this grating." Mei Yee nods at the crisscross lattice. Not much besides a finger or two could slide through those gaps. "It'll have to go out the door. When I take it, you should buy time with a girl named Nuo. Wait in her room and I'll drop the book off there."

"These girls, Nuo and Yin Yu, how do you know they won't betray you?"

"A few weeks ago there was another girl, Sing. We knew she was going to run. Some of us even tried to stop her. But we never gave her away."

"Silence is different from actively stealing," I tell her. "But tell them if we get the book, I can get all of them out."

Mei Yee looks at me. The way she stares, without blinking, reminds me of kids at the zoo. I must be the animal, stuck on the other side of the bars, doing and saying things she can't completely understand.

"Is that true?" she asks finally.

I swallow, think of all of Tsang's ash and apathy. The police don't care about the girls, that's for sure. But once the book is out, once all the arrest warrants are in place, once I hand over Longwai's ass on a platter, there will be no one left to lock the girls' cage. No one left to keep them from running.

I nod. "I can't tell you more, because the secret is too big. But yes. Get the book and all of you will be free."

"The other girls will help," Mei Yee says, swift and certain.

"Just—be careful." My chest feels tight. Even trusting these two girls, these two sisters, is a stretch. Adding other, faceless girls into the mix seems too much. Too many variables, too many chances for something to go wrong. "Be discreet."

"When will we do this?"

Involving the girls changes a lot of things, but the biggest of these is the timetable. Before, when it was just my (and, I guess, Jin Ling's) neck on the chopping block, I wanted to find the ledger as soon as possible. But I could run, and the girls…they're mice snapped tight in a trap. If Longwai finds out who stole his book, he can—he will—crush every one of them.

And even if I acted alone—bought time with a girl or angled for an invitation—I wouldn't put it past Longwai to punish the girls anyway, take his rage out on those who would fight the least. There are too many things tying us together. For better or worse, we're all tangled now.

This is the only path we can take.

The turnaround has to be quick—so that Longwai won't

even realize his book is gone before the cops beat down his doors. Our swipe has to be at the last of the final minutes.

"New Year's Eve. Five days from now. I'll come to your window right before I swing back around to the lounge. I'll distract Longwai and your Mama-san long enough for you to get upstairs and out. Then I'll buy Nuo's time and wait in her room until you drop the book. I'll leave, and Longwai will be none the wiser. Then I'll come back for you."

Mei Yee swallows. "What about between then?"

"Keep him downstairs, smoking. Until midnight hits."

"How do I know you'll come back?" It's the question of a girl who's been left behind. Again and again and again.

The braid unravels from her wrist, and I see a mark there. A spoil of color in the midst of flawless white. Too odd to be a shadow, smudged like the ink fingerprint of a criminal. The signature of a certain middle-aged selfish bastard.

Goddamn Osamu.

I look at her face and it doesn't matter. It doesn't matter that her father sold her for pocket change. Or that she could be Jin Ling's sister. Or that my freedom, my life, now rests in her hands. Or that the seashell was made in a factory.

Even with her bruises, I've never seen anything as perfect and whole as her. As *Mei Yee*.

"I will come for you. No matter what it takes." These are the words of a goddamn hero pouring out of my mouth. The best of me—the part she woke—reaching to her through the glass.

I don't know if I've spoken truer words in my life.

268

# 9

I only had a few years with my grandfather, but there are some memories of him I can't shake. How he always froze at the sound of any airplane. How he always clutched a cane—the veins of his right hand bulging out like teal worms as he walked.

I was five when I finally became brave enough to ask him about his knee.

His chin trembled—cloud-white beard hair shuddered like the wind was combing it. "A long time ago, long before you or your mother were born, I was in a war. Did you know that?"

I shook my head.

"I was a pilot. Not the fighter kind, mostly dropped supplies to the men on the ground." He paused. Both hands gripped the cane, all his weight falling on that single piece of wood. "I was on a mission when my plane got shot down. I survived, but I was torn up pretty bad. Got a whole piece of metal stuck under my kneecap. I never could walk right after that."

It never made sense to my young mind, how a hurt from so long ago could keep a man from walking right. Stay with him the rest of his life.

But now that I'm older, now that I've fought my own wars and fired my own guns, I understand. There's a hurt in my heart as I walk away from Mei Yee's window, like the flare of an old war wound. An ache I can't really explain. An ache that won't let me forget.

I thought I spent these two years erasing. Getting rid of my pain, pushing it back to a place only nightmares could touch. But it was really just a deep freeze: hurt suspended in time.

I walk the old paths. Past factories and mills of exhausted humans working tireless machines. By the corner where a toothless old man huddles in a moth-gnawed blanket, hands cupped out like a bowl of flesh and knobby-boned joints. Past the prostitutes slouched in their doorways, shoulders bare to the winter. Children dash by, barefoot. I wonder who they're running to. Or what they're running from. If they're playing or fleeing.

I used to walk this track without feeling a thing. On and on and away. I looked at these faces—wrinkled, painted, deadpan, scared, hollow—and felt nothing. Not even a pin-prick. Now my heart feels ready to explode with hurt. Hurt for Jin Ling and Bon and Lee and Kuen and Chma and all the starving things on these streets.

But it's not just hurt that's waking. The ache goes even deeper, sears like lava in my bones. An anguish that makes me feel unbearably awake, alive. The agony of *her*, wedged inside my heart. Shrapnel that will never, ever leave.

I'm not very hungry, but when I pass Mr. Kung's glowing oven of *cha siu bao*, I buy a bagful. Their heat bakes through the paper, lighting up my fingers and palms. I think of Jin Ling. I should tell her—find a phone and call Emiyo.

Or maybe I shouldn't. She's supposed to be on bed rest—a rule she'd break in a heartbeat if she found out. And if my plan doesn't work, if we don't get the ledger ... it would be bet-ter for Jin Ling to never know in the first place.

A long, low howl erupts at my feet. Loud enough to make me stop and hope that I heard right. All through my walks, I've been scanning the streets. Looking, looking, looking for a feline sans tail.

I look down. At first all I see are puddles swallowing the electric lights of shops and spreading them like gold at my feet.

*Brrrrooow?*

I look to the side, by my right boot. Chma's yellow eyes glare back at mine. He slides over my leg, brushing my jeans with long, matted fur. The stuff of sneezes. It's speckled with dried clumps of blood. I see the stump Kuen's knife made. I've come across worse, but my stomach doesn't act like it.

"What are you on now? Your fifth life?" I ask, and kneel down in the middle of the street. Chma's dusky-pink nose pushes into the bag of stuffed buns. His whine grows longer, louder. I reach into the bag and pinch apart one of the buns. Chma swallows it all: dough, juice, and meat. It's gone in seconds. He noses the ground and then blinks at me.

*More.* It's not so much a question as a demand. Voiced with about as much authority as a tailless cat can muster.

"You pompous little—"

*Chma! Chma!* My term of affection is cut short by the animal's sneeze. He even manages to look dignified with a glaze of snot on his nose. *Chma!*

Seems Jin Ling was right. Cat sneezes do sound different.

I pull out more *cha siu bao* and wish again Jin Ling could be here. To see all that she's lost found again.

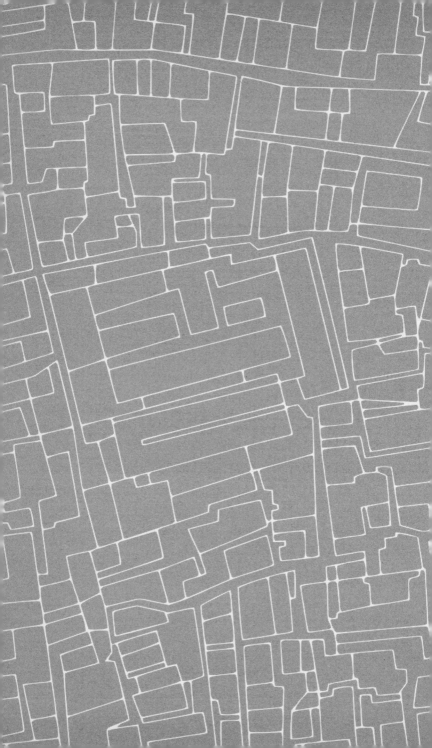

# 2 DAYS

# JIN LING

I've never slept this long. Nights in the Walled City are short. Dreamless. But here—swallowed in feathers, sheets, and tubes—I can't tell what's dream and what's reality. So many faces pass. Some visit and talk: Dai, my mother, Mei Yee. Others—the nurse and Dai's father—just stare and fill the room with their footsteps. Sometimes I feel Chma curled against me, warmth and purrs. Other times my father looms over the bed. When he disappears, I wake up soaked in sweat and shivering.

Then the waking truly hits. My eyes open and my head is clear. Fogless. I look up and see that the bags of medicine are finally gone. No more drugged sleep. I sit up, stretching my muscles slowly. There's still pain just under my shoulder. Hot and harsh, but bearable. My tendons and joints are stiff. Like rope left too long in the sun. Bones grind and pop all over my body.

How long have I been asleep?

"Hello?" My voice cracks. It must be days since I spoke aloud. Maybe longer.

My call echoes against the bare wood floors. It's weird to be in a place so quiet after years of city song. Even at the farm there was always wind blowing or the bubble of water boiling for tea.

This place is as silent as a grave.

"Hello!" I try again, this time louder.

A woman steps into the room. She's not old, but she isn't young, either. She looks the same age as my mother—just less worn. Untouched by sun and a drunken husband. I look for traces of Dai in her face. There aren't any.

She bows when she reaches my bed, and I decide she's the family maid. "What can I get for you?"

"Is...is Dai here?"

The maid frowns. "He left some time ago. I can get Mrs. Sun if you would like. She's here preparing for the New Year's party."

My stomach gives a sick, empty lurch. At first I'm not sure why. But then the memory leaks back. New Year's: the day everything will change. The day Dai has to get the ledger. The ledger I promised to help him steal.

Dai saying good-bye. Leaving without me.

"When...how long is it until New Year's?" I start clawing at the tape. My teeth grit as it tears back, tugging out hairs, jerking the needle under my skin.

"Two days." The maid's eyes widen.

I freeze. Half-peeled tape hangs from my hand. A brownish bruise peeks from under it. Two days until New Year's? That can't be right. I'm dreaming again. . . .

"You've been here for eight days," the maid says, eyeing the torn tape.

I stare at the old hurt on my hand. Try to understand what she's saying. Eight days. How did I lose an entire week?

"Are you feeling all right? Should I call in the nurse?"

My fingers tear the tape. This time it pulls all the way off. I tug the tube next. The needle slides out. I ignore the burn in my hand and the worse pain in my shoulder. Climb out of bed.

"What—what are you doing?" The maid puts her hands up. Tries to block me. Not that she needs to. My head spins, makes it hard to stay on my feet. I shut my eyes, wait for the spell to pass.

"I have to go back to the Walled City. Now."

The maid's face falls apart with panic. Her arms start flapping, like a bird dancing over a pile of gutted fish. "You can't go back. You're supposed to rest. The doctor wants you here another four weeks. He has to take out your stitches."

The world feels steadier when I open my eyes. I look down and realize I'm not wearing much—just a thin, cottony shift. *Rest.* I should rest. That's what Dai told me to do. My body still feels like chicken meat beaten tender with a mallet. But the window of time to find my sister is slipping . . . slipping away. And Dai might think he can steal the ledger alone, but I've been inside Longwai's den. I've seen how impossible it is.

"No!" I force out the word as loud as I can. I can't fail Dai now. My body might be hurt and aching, but I can't lose this last chance to find my sister. I'll rest when she's safe. "Where are my clothes?"

The maid frowns, moves between me and the door. "You're in no condition to be going back to that place."

My first instinct is to run. I consider dodging her. But the long, low burn in my side tells me not to. Plus I have no idea where we are. We could be miles, maybe even provinces, from the Walled City. Without my orange envelope and my boots, I'm as good as chained here.

The only weapon I have left is the truth. "I have to go help Dai. He has things to do before New Year's. Very important things." I swallow. My throat feels ground to its nerves. Raw from talking so fast. "If I'm not there to help him...it could end very badly for him."

The maid's weight shifts. Foot to foot. The floor groans under her. She's eyeing me like I'm a mangy dog. I wait for her to say no. To run for the nurse.

But she keeps shifting. It's as if the wood is talking to us in its own tortured language. Back and forth. Back and forth. Until finally, "I couldn't get all the blood out of your garments. I had to dispose of them."

I feel the thin shift under my fingers. I wouldn't survive ten minutes in this. "Is there anything else I can wear?"

"Hiro was about your size when he left for school. They're boys' clothes...."

"They'll do." I can't imagine going back to the Walled City in a dress. Not after all this. "What about my boots? The envelope and the knife?"

"There was no knife." Her look changes. Instead of a dirty mutt, I'm a wolf with bared yellow teeth. "The rest of your things are on that chair."

She's right. My boots sit on shiny wood—two beaten leather soldiers. The envelope is wedged between them. Still orange. Still fat. And behind that, the star book Dai gave me.

"I'll bring you some clothes. Then I'll see about getting you a car." The maid bows her way out the door.

I walk to the chair. My steps are slower than I'd like. Every breath reminds me of the fight. A flashback to the empty, gaping awfulness of Kuen's face. Of course my knife isn't here. It's back in some alley. Buried deep in his muscle and bone. Rotting away with everything else.

## 9

City blurs past the windows of the Suns' car. There's so much sky and sun. The only clouds above are the tiny scars left by airplanes, notching white numerals. Everything seems clean. Women walk around in pointy heels and nice dresses. Tiny white dogs pull on jeweled leashes. Men clutch their brief-cases, steering through sidewalks of food stands and electronics hawkers. Buses and taxis weave and merge across smooth asphalt. Lanes come together and part like zippers.

All around are signs of my lost time. Shops are covered with scarlet lanterns and elaborate paper cutouts of snakes. Vendors walk around with carts full of mandarin oranges and incense. In two days the streets will be bursting with red, cakes, and drumbeats. Fireworks will explode. Lions and dragons will dance over pavement—men in costumes warding off evil spirits.

The Walled City isn't hard to miss. Apartments stack high like shabby bricks. All of them are covered in bars. Cages on top of cages. After the Suns' mansion, the place looks uglier. I can't imagine how Dai felt, coming here after a lifetime on the hill.

The driver stays seated after he pulls up to the Old South Gate. I open the door, let myself out. Trash, mildew, and waste flood my nose all at once. They smell horrible. But they smell like home.

It takes a long time to reach the doorway to Dai's apartment. Every five steps or so I have to stop, catch my breath. The fire in my side grows. Burns my back and ribs. The air shimmers cool, but my face still shines with sweat.

The front gate is locked tight when I reach it. I slouch on the step, almost relieved. There's no way I could've made it up all those stairs. My head is swimming again. Blue and yellow bursts paint my vision.

There's a seafood restaurant next door. Full of sea salt, sliced fish, and smoking patrons. I watch the customers talk to one another over blue plastic tables. They pick at steamed snapper and garlic-covered eel with their chopsticks. Shove them thoughtlessly into their mouths. Like every other meal they've ever eaten.

Will this really be over in just two days? It's hard to believe. Sitting here, I wonder, if these people knew about the ordinance, what would they be doing instead? Would they search for new jobs and homes? Or would they carry on until change forced them elsewhere?

Both searching and carrying on seem too much for me—here on the step. I suck in the pain of my side and ignore the stars in my eyes. I can't run. I can't fight. I can't look for my sister.

All I can do is sit and wait.

# DAI

Two lines.

I stare at them, legs crossed, fingers twitching. They stare back, thin and black. Like a pair of burnt, limbless trees or the pupils of a cat.

I'm god-awful at waiting. Four days is a long time to second-guess a plan (or in my case third-, fourth-, fifth-, sixth-guess it). For four days I've sat, looping through our plan on repeat, playing out every possibility in my head. One hundred times I've ducked into the brothel, made away with the book. Taken Mei Yee's hand in mine and run. A hundred more times I've been caught, gutted on the end of Fung's knife while Longwai smiled on.

It could go either way, really. So much is on the wire. One wrong move and I'm done. We're done.

I make a noise at the marks. Chma lifts his head at the sound, ears pricked and paws edged straight in front of him.

He's been more than a little skittish these past few days. But I guess I'd be jumpy, too, if someone carved a chunk out of me with a blade.

I expected the cat to vanish into the next alleyway once he finished my bag of buns. But, like any self-respecting feline, he did the contrary—stuck close, claimed every inch of my apartment as his own. His fur wreaks hell on my allergies, but I don't have the heart to send him away. We'll all be out of here soon enough.

Chma stands, does an impossibly arched stretch that makes me want to move, too. A purr rattles the far reaches of his chest as he slinks over.

"Hungry?" My eyes stray over to the last meal we shared—a container of chicken drizzled in sticky, sweet sauce. One of Mrs. Pak's creations. It was finished off hours ago. "Guess it is about that time."

I haven't been hungry for days. There's so much worry in my stomach that there's no room for anything else. I buy food for Chma's sake, eat a little for the ritual.

"Downstairs then." Chma is already at the door. Eyes alert and expectant as I pull out my keys.

We trot the stairs together, twelve whole flights, before Chma breaks formation. I look down and he's gone, a silver flash. It's the first time he's left my side in days. My sinuses rejoice, but my eyebrows furrow. Something's off.

I can think of only one thing, one person who'd make him move like that. This thought makes me move faster down the final flight, so that I'm not really descending the steps but leaping them.

Chma's paws splay against the bottom door, claws making invisible needle marks in the water-worn wood. When I open it and unlock the gate, he pulls away, darts like a rat into the street.

No. Not into the street. Into Jin Ling's lap.

I don't recognize her at first. She's wearing Hiro's old clothes. They're a bit big on her—the jeans bulge out like parachutes and the jacket swallows her altogether. From the back—with all that baggy fabric and mussed hair—she looks just like him.

But then she turns. The illusion vanishes like that last question mark breath.

Not Hiro. Jin Ling. The one I saved.

Now that I know, I can't unsee her girlness. The turned curve of her nose, the slant of her cheeks. How her eyelashes curl up just so. It would be a mistake to think that any of these things mean she's fragile. The very fact that she's sitting here, eight days after being stabbed, is testament to that.

"Jin?"

Her fingers are running through Chma's sterling fur. She looks up at me. There's a smile on her face. "You found him."

"Yeah, I'm about one day away from becoming a crazy cat hermit. What are you doing here?" I look to her side—the one that was slashed like a victimized tire. There's no sign of hurt under the vinyl of Hiro's old winter jacket. But just because you can't see it doesn't mean it isn't there.

"I promised I'd help you get the..." Her eyes dart to the chewing mouths of the seafood diners and the noodle-makers covered in flour. "The thing you need to get."

"You should be resting," I tell her. Even sitting on this step she looks exhausted. An extra shade of white. "How'd you even get here?"

She ignores the question, squints up at me. "Is this because I'm a girl?"

"No. It's because you were stabbed with a knife. Only a week ago."

Her fingers are lost deep in Chma's fur. I can hear his purr from here. "I'm here. And I'm going to help you. I gave you my word."

"I never asked you to promise that. I'm handling it. You need to rest before your stitches tear open."

Hurt colors her face, stabbing me. Chma looks at me, too, with narrowed, too-bright eyes. They glare like spoiled sunshine, like I didn't just spend the past four days feeding him and trying to pour hydrogen peroxide on his tail stub while acquiring about twenty new scratches and two fresh bites.

Too stubborn to heal. Like cat, like girl.

"If you think I'm going to sit back and lose this one chance to find my sister . . ."

Jin Ling's last word pushes me to an edge. To tell or stay silent. I feel like a child standing on the center of a seesaw, trying impossibly to make it stay straight. I want to give her hope. But if it's false—if the Mei Yee behind the window isn't who I think she is, or worse, if she is and I can't free her—I don't know if I could take it.

"What?" Jin Ling straightens. She must see the tension playing through my face. I'm not as good at hiding this stuff as I used to be.

It's the secrets I can't take anymore.

285

"Your sister. Mei Yee?"

She looks at me like she's dangling over the rooftops, clutching only a rope and I'm holding the other end. My lungs freeze, like I'm being pushed deep into ice-cold river water. I'm barely able to get the words out.

"I think I found her."

# MEI YEE

I water the cypress tree every day. I've done this four times since Dai left. The tree is already dying; its green-laced leaves are spoiling. Dropping into the mud below. Maybe I'm watering it too much, but I don't think that's the problem. Trees weren't meant to be crammed into dark, smoky brothels.

A sigh leaves me as I place the watering cup back on the table. I don't know why I'm trying, really. The end is coming. Soon, whether we succeed or not, I'll never see this tree again.

The girls are behind me, sitting in their usual places. These last four days have passed with silence and waiting. They still don't know about Dai or the window or any of it. Four days is a long time to keep a secret in a place like this.

Nuo hears my sigh and the trouble behind it. "What's wrong, Mei Yee?"

I stroke the tree's tiny drying limbs. Leaves prick like

needles at my skin. "There's something I have to tell you. Something I have to trust you with."

All three of them are staring at me as I turn.

These four days have also seen me wondering, wavering on trust like stilts. These girls—these sisters—I know they've stared at the ceiling the same way I do. Wanting to be anywhere else. I've heard them talk about *home* and the sea and wall-less days with something like hope in their breaths.

But they also saw what happened to Sing. Stood beside me while she thrashed and screamed and drowned in pools of blood and heroin dreams. They felt the same fear I did, creeping through their veins like a drug of its own. A paralysis meant to last days, months, years. Meant to keep us here forever.

Telling them, trusting them with this plan, could go either way.

The one redeeming factor, the final weight in my decision, was their silence on Sing's behalf. How they said nothing when our friend ran. It feels like so many ages ago we were sitting in the same circle and it was Sing speaking. Her lips moved so fast I could catch only so many of her words. I was transfixed by how flushed her cheeks were, how bright her eyes shined.

They're quiet now, too. Waiting, waiting, waiting for what I have to say.

"I found a way out."

"What?" Wen Kei squeaks, so tiny by my feet.

The girls stare, blink in turn. Suddenly I feel too tall, so I move back to the edge of my bed.

"Well, really, a way out found me...." I say, mostly to fill the silence.

"What are you talking about?" Yin Yu's not sitting anymore, but halfway on her feet, like some cat ready to pounce.

My heart trembles, fills my head with a thousand warnings. The same ones that have whirled through my head, throbbed through my bruises these past two weeks.

*Too dangerous. Don't. There's still time to back out. Still time to say* yes.

So I do what I always do when the fears crowd in. My fingers dance across the crimson lengths of the curtain and pull.

The shell is still there. Outside looking in. Impossible to miss. My secrets through the glass, for the world to see.

"What—what is it?" Nuo leans into my mattress, trying to get a closer look through the grating. The way she's staring reminds me of how Jin Ling and I used to ogle the chewy, sticky slivers of rice candy in the province market.

Wen Kei answers for me; the word leaves her mouth more sacred than a prayer. "Nautilus."

Both of my friends stare at the window as if it's some kind of magic. But Yin Yu stays back. Her stare is different, not so much magical as wary. The way I used to stare at the stray dogs my sister always insisted on feeding. The ones that could turn and sink their teeth in at any moment.

"Where?" Wen Kei finally looks at me, the entirety of her small body turning in her excitement. "How?"

"A boy gave it to me," I tell them. "He's been coming to see me for a while now. We've been trading information."

"Information?" Wen Kei squeaks.

"About the Brotherhood." I make a point to look at Yin Yu as I say this. "I didn't take your duties because I want to be Mama-san. I did it because I had to spy. Get information."

"You've been"—Yin Yu stops, lowers her voice to even less than a hiss—"*spying*? On the *Brotherhood*?"

"What did he want to know?" Nuo asks.

"At first it was just names. Then he wanted to know where Longwai keeps his ledger." It's not until I see the three pairs of eyes grow wider at the sound of the master's name that I realize I've been using it.

"He says he's going to get us out. All of us." My words crash like stones into a still pond. They fill the room with trembling faces and ripples. Nuo and Wen Kei look at me as if I just unlocked the front door myself.

Yin Yu doesn't move. "What's his price?"

"We have to get Longwai's ledger."

Silence. More trembling.

"The red book? The one with the dragon on it?" Nuo's fingers dance over her thigh, playing some unheard song. "Why does the boy want that?"

I ignore the question I can't answer. It's easy for me to trust Dai—the electrifying burn of his eyes, the deep of his voice, and his *no matter what* through the glass. I know the girls won't take his mysteries as easily. "Longwai keeps the book upstairs, in the top drawer of his desk. We have to steal it tomorrow night. Well, I'm the one who's actually going to take it. But I need you girls to help.

"The boy is going to buy time with Nuo and wait in her room. I'll take Yin Yu's keys and sneak into the office while Wen Kei makes sure that Longwai and Mama-san are distracted. When I get the book, I'll drop it in Nuo's room and the boy will walk out with it."

Nuo and Wen Kei flinch at the sound of Longwai's name. Yin Yu is unaffected. Bangs fall, black and short, into her eyes. They mute some of her hard, hard stare. "And where's the part about us getting out? How do we know he's not just going to walk out and leave us? When the master finds out his ledger is gone…"

"The boy is coming back for us. He gave me his word." My voice fights against shake. I hope it's enough.

"And you're going to just trust some starving vagrant? He's using you, Mei Yee!"

"He's not!" I wish, now, that Dai had given me more words to work with. Something solid and concrete. I can't translate the feelings in my chest so easily. "There's something going on, Yin Yu. Something bigger than us."

Yin Yu rises, her serving dress gleaming red as hellfire. "Let the boy handle his own problems. We'll handle ours."

Her words are an absolute. A challenge meant for me to bow or quail. A few weeks ago I might have, but my spine is stiffer now. I stand as well.

"This is it, Yin Yu. This is our chance. There might never be another." I look at the other two girls huddled on my bed like chicks. "Even if you don't want to do this, you have to let them decide."

Nuo nods. "I'll help."

"Me too." Wen Kei's petite face pinches in a scowl. She's staring at Yin Yu. "I don't want to stay here."

"No." Yin Yu takes a step toward me, then pauses. "We're never going to leave! Don't you understand that! This is our life now. The only way out of here is on a beggar's mat or in a body bag. You saw what happened to Sing. Don't think the master won't do the same to every single one of us. We're all disposable!"

Eyes flash, blacker than night. Darker than a room without light. I look into them and realize she made up her mind a long time ago. When Sing screamed and thrashed and the needle burst poison into her veins.

I keep staring, trying not to get lost in the deep despair of her eyes. "We'll do it without you, then."

"No." She reaches out, grabs the door handle. "You won't."

The pit in my stomach suddenly grows, stretches as if it's outside me. I thought, at the worst, she would refuse. But now, seeing her long white fingers on the latch, pushing down, I know she's capable of much, much worse.

"Yin Yu. Don't."

I see all of it slipping away, sliding down with the handle. She keeps pushing.

"I can't let this happen again. I can't let you destroy us! Destroy them!" Yin Yu looks to Nuo and Wen Kei. "One day you two will understand. I'm doing this to protect us."

She looks back at me. "There is no escape, Mei Yee. The master will know. We can't fool him. He'll find out what happened, and then he'll inject each and every one of us. Maybe even kill us."

She keeps pushing the handle. Pushing, pushing, pushing. And a sick fills me, welling up like slimy black oil. It coats every fiber. Every vein.

I've never fought before. Not like Sing. Not like my baby sister. All fists, teeth, and dart. But something inside me snaps, propels me forward. Suddenly I'm at the door, shoulder slamming into its wood. My hip bone pins Yin Yu's wrist into the handle so hard that something cracks.

At first she's surprised. Then she shoves back. Her free hand flails, rakes at my face. I feel the sharp of her nails forging a path down my cheeks. I push out, use all my strength and more to slam her against the wall. Her tiny, wasted frame is no match for what woke up inside me.

"No." I hold her tight against the wall. "No, no, no, no."

It's all I can say. This one word. Even as I say it I see my chances, my life beyond this, my sister and her stars, Dai and his sea . . . I see all of it consumed. Swallowed by the dark of Yin Yu's eyes.

"What are you going to do? Kill me?" Her questions are calm and detached. The same way she floats through life here. "I'm *surviving*. That's all you can do here, Mei Yee! Keep your head down and follow the rules! Survive!"

I hold her there, every muscle straining. Every piece of me shaking. She's right. I can't stop her. Not without rousing Longwai and Mama-san's suspicions. Not without condemning Wen Kei and Nuo.

I can't hold Yin Yu here forever.

"We can get out," I manage. "We can go back home. See the sea."

The other girl looks at me as if I'm speaking some foreign language, telling her things she can never understand.

I look back at Nuo and Wen Kei. I let go.

Yin Yu steps aside. My door unlatches and swings loose. She slips into the hall, a flash of red swallowed into the dark.

"Mei Yee…"

My head doesn't feel like mine anymore. It swivels down toward the rug. Finds Nuo staring at me. Wen Kei is curled next to her, trembling.

"Go," I tell them. "Before they come back."

"It's not right. She can't do this." It's Wen Kei who's talking. I realize, from the way the words come out, that she's shaking because she's angry.

I kneel back onto the bed, knees bending in a half collapse. "Yin Yu is doing what she thinks is right. She's trying to protect you."

They look at me. Nuo's hands are fidgeting again. Wen Kei is breathing fast; her chest heaves in and out.

"Go," I say again. "Please."

"But what about the boy?" Wen Kei insists.

"It doesn't matter anymore. It's over."

Nuo is shaking her head. At first I think she means to disagree with me. Then I see the wet in her eyes. She leans in, wraps her arms around my shoulder. Her hair smells like cinnamon and cloves.

We don't say anything else. There's no time. I hug Wen Kei and then they're gone. Scattered like propeller seeds to the wind.

Dai's face appears in my memory—glowing and strong behind the window. I think of how he'll return and wait and never know. How I failed him.

The nautilus is still there, of course. Unchanged by this massive shift in my world. Behind bars and glass, still untouchable.

I look back over my shoulder at this room of useless, beautiful, dying things. Searching for something strong enough to break the glass. On the vanity is a jade hairpin, the ambassador's second gift to me. I bring it to the grating, its sharp end slides neatly into the gap.

I need to warn Dai. I need to touch it.

My hand jams against the pin, sends it through the window. For a short, stunning second the glass sings. Pieces fly and spin and scatter like jewels across the sill. A few of them even spit and shine across my bed.

Then comes the cold. It swarms through the hole, and I realize just how warm I've been. Winter slides under my skin, infecting me with feelings fresh and free.

My fingers slip through the grating, past the glass's angry edge. They reach all the way to the shell, keep pushing. And for a moment I'm touching the nautilus, feeling its smooth on my skin, hearing Dai's promises over and over:

*I can get you out.*

*I want you to see it, too.*

*I will come for you. No matter what it takes.*

Then the ledge ends and the shell falls, tumbling far from my sight. Lost and gone.

My finger catches the glass. I don't even feel the slice. But by the time I stuff one of my silk dresses into the hole, my finger is more blood than not. The curtain falls back for the last time.

I sit still on the edge of my bed, stanch the blood, and wait for them to come.

# JIN LING

There are moments you wait for. And then there are moments you *wait* for. Moments you spend every other moment preparing for. Points of your life that click and turn. Push you in a completely new direction.

Dai and I stand at the end of the alleyway. My breath is short and the never-ending burn keeps digging a hole in my side. I ignore these things. Look down the river of trash. Count how many steps it'll take to get to my sister.

My limbs shake with too much emotion. Dai leads the way and I follow, using one hand to steady myself on slimy stones. I'm glad Dai's ahead. I don't want him to see how hard it is for me to keep up.

A few feet in front of the window, Dai pauses. His body dead still. My foot lands on a loud, crunching soda bottle. His head whips back. Almond eyes narrow at me while he puts a finger to his lips.

My heart picks up: from trot to canter to gallop. Something's wrong.

We stand still. Listen into the shadows. I hear nothing. Dai takes a few more steps forward. Skips through the trash like a cat. The window's light colors him unreal scarlet. Dai looks at the shattered glass as if he's seeing a ghost. He crouches down, fingers diving through old wrappers and bottle caps, picking up something all curled and hard. A shell.

"What's that?" I hiss. "What's wrong?"

His jaw clenches. Another finger goes up to his lips and his eyes warn, *Be quiet!*

I'm angry, ready to hiss again, when a noise rises up from the other side of the jagged glass.

"Has she admitted to anything?" Longwai sounds oddly awake through the curtain. Smart, sharp, alert.

"Mei Yee? Of course not. She's just sitting there like a dullard." A woman is speaking, her voice thin and reedy. Horribly bitter. Hearing her say my sister's name makes me cringe. But it leaves no room for doubt. My sister used to be here. Behind this glass.

"And your search of the room?"

"There's a hole in the window. It was stuffed up with one of her dresses. No sign of the seashell, though."

Dai's fingers lock around my arm. He pushes himself flat against the wall, just under the window. I follow. My stitches slam into cinder block and I try not to cry out. I bite through my lip instead. Salt and iron swim across my tongue. The alley goes blurry with tears.

The light above us changes. Falling from red to a weak

yellow. Shadows spring on the opposite wall, shapes of Long-wai and the woman bending closer to the glass.

"Even if it broke by accident, why would she keep it a secret?" The woman's voice is clear. Close.

Dai's hand is still on my arm, squeezing tight. I don't dare move. Not even to look over at him. I hear Longwai's breathing. Heavy and thick. Unbearably close.

"Does she have a cut on her hand?"

"I—I didn't notice." The woman sounds startled. "Why?"

"Blood." Longwai says only one word. But it's enough.

"Do you think…"

"I'll send Fung outside to check the alley."

This time I do look over at Dai. He's staring at me, too. His face is a scarecrow's: lips stitched tight, patchworks of feeling all over. His eyes dart to the end of the alley. Keen and meaningful.

We have to get out of here.

"What should we do with Mei Yee?" the woman asks.

"Keep her where she is. I'll be in to see her in a minute."

"And if the ambassador shows up?"

"Tell him she's ill. Offer him another girl." He says this and I feel sick. I have to swallow it down. Keep that last little roll of rice and tuna the Suns' maid handed me inside my stomach. I always knew Mei Yee's hell was worse than mine. But listening to Longwai sell my sister like meat makes it very, very real.

My heart burns hotter than my stitches. I'm sick and murderous and ready to run.

The light sinks back into red. Voices trail off with footsteps, cut short by squealing hinges. Dai is on his feet, pulling me up. I feel like I'm moving in a dream: exhausting muscles and will, but not really going anywhere.

"Come on, Jin Ling." Dai tugs harder and I'm standing. "You have to go."

"We're just going to leave? But Mei Yee—"

He cuts me off. "You heard Longwai. Fung's coming."

I can't think straight. Not with the pain. Not with his tugging and pulling like this. "But Mei Yee. The book. We can't leave!"

"Jin Ling. Look at me."

It's the only thing I can do. Everything else is spinning like a child's toy top. I choose a point, the wrinkling gap of skin between his eyebrows. Focus on it.

"*We* are not leaving. You are." Dai digs deep into his jeans' pocket. Out comes a small wad of bills. "You get out of here and you take a cab back to Tai Ping Hill. Go to number sixty-two. Ask to see Ambassador Osamu."

The ambassador? The one who would show up for Mei Yee? Use her . . . My mouth goes dry at the thought. My shoulders start shaking.

Dai's hand grips tighter, steadies me. "Tell him Mei Yee is in trouble. He needs to come get her."

"That's all?"

"It's enough. It will get him to come." He crams the money into my jacket pocket. "It will give us the distraction we need to make things right."

I feel undone. My head is spinning the way it was that first

300

day in the Suns' guest suite. The world lurches even when I'm standing still. "And what are you going to do?"

Dai's walking again. His arm guides me like an ox pulling a plow. Trash churns under our boots while we make our way to the main street. When we reach the end, Dai lets go of my arm.

"The best place for me right now is inside that brothel."

I don't think I hear him right, but his hands return to mine. Metal—cold and hard—brushes my skin. Weight falls, sudden, into my fingers. I look down and realize what Dai has given me: his revolver.

"Keep this for me." He presses the gun into my palm. Heavy, heavy power in my grasp. "If Fung finds it on me, I'm done."

"No! I'm not leaving you here. I promised—"

Dai shoves the gun harder into my hand, cuts me off. "I know what you promised. And I know what I promised. But there are two of us, Jin Ling. That's two chances to get your sister out. If we go in there together, that's screwed; and I'll be damned if I'm going to let you go in first."

"But, Dai—" His name falls out of my throat. "Longwai. He'll kill you."

The older boy keeps talking. Doesn't miss a beat, "If he does...don't worry about the ledger. You get your sister out. Get as far away from this city as possible. Don't look back."

That was always the plan. But suddenly it feels like an impossible thing to do by myself. There are no words. I just look at the older boy. My throat is thick and my side hurts. My hands are heavy with his gun. His last protection given to me.

I'm shaking again. "I—I don't know how to use it."

"Pull the hammer, pull the trigger," he says sharply. "There are six shots, so save them until you can't anymore."

I don't want to leave him here. Alone. Without a weapon. I want to stay with him and fight. But my splitting side tells me that's no longer an option. I have to go. I have to let Dai do the things I can't.

"Get your ass back here fast. Osamu's, too." He swallows. Looks over my shoulder. Where the entrance to the brothel lies.

I don't know if I can do this. But I have to. My fingers close tight around the gun.

"Remember. Tai Ping Hill. Number sixty-two. Ambassador Osamu." Dai drills the information deeper into my skull. Not that he needs to. Every word is already there, blazed in challenge and fire. "And take these just in case."

He presses the keys to his apartment into my hand and lets go. Pushes me away. "See you soon."

I hope he's right.

I'm running, even though my side splits and I don't remember telling my feet to move. The gun is tucked deep in my jacket, slowing me with its impossible weight. Every step is awful. But my boots keep pounding. Through streets and shortcuts. All the way to the Old South Gate.

# MEI YEE

Half of me expected to be taken to the lounge, made an example of right there and then. I was ready for it—ready for the belt to choke up my arm. Ready for the syringe to slip into my vein and introduce me to an entirely different universe. I was ready for other things, too—the hard nose of a pistol against my head or the dead-thin edge of a knife across my throat. I was ready for it to end.

The only thing I wasn't prepared for was Sing's room.

Keys shake in Mama-san's bird-boned hand as she twists the lock, shoves the door open with her hip. Even with all the powder and paint, her face is clear; every horrible emotion she's ever felt is strung across it like prayer beads. I've never seen her like this, not even when Sing was bloodied and broken on the floor.

I think of that night. Of the snap and the scream when we

left her alone with Longwai. Of the bruises she tried so hard to bury with powder and sharp-tongued words. It doesn't matter that she's holding those keys. None of them lets her outside. She's just as trapped as any of us.

With the open door comes a smell not even incense can mask. Urine and waste and sick. The air is thick with it, clawing into my nose, down my throat. I smell all the days Sing has been here, rotting beneath a single flickering lightbulb.

The room is bare, stripped of all furniture and decor. The only thing that isn't walls or floor is a pile of filthy pillows in the corner. Sing's body—wasted from a fortnight of heroin and little food—melds almost invisible into the poor light and stained fabric. She's stretched across the floor with a stillness like death.

Mama-san seems not to notice, her nose long used to the stench. She looks at me and her face hardens. "You stupid girl!"

I expect questions. Or maybe a slap. But not this. Mama-san is glaring at me, lips pursed and coated with her fiercest shade of paint.

"You could have gotten out of here. If you'd played it right. You had the ambassador wrapped around your pinkie finger." She holds up her smallest nail. It's the same color red as her lips. "You had the chance and you wasted it. Threw it away like it was nothing!"

"I didn't do anything." I flip the switch inside me. The one I use when the ambassador crawls into my bed. The one that makes me feel dead inside and out. "Yin Yu is jealous of me. She's spreading rumors."

There's no guilt shifting through my veins when I say Yin Yu's name. Not this time.

"It doesn't matter. Don't you understand? Where there are rumors, there's hope. And when there's hope…" Her finely filed scarlet nail points to the heap on the floor. Where skin and bone and pillow stew in what's left of Sing. "It's not allowed in a place like this.

"Stupid," Mama-san mutters, and shakes her head. She doesn't even look at me again before she pulls the door shut.

There's even less light now. I feel as if I've been sealed up inside a tomb.

*Stupid.* Mama-san's word echoes in the new dark. Claws at me with its hints of truth. I never should have told the girls. Never should have expected them to have the same trust in a boy they'd never met…

A rattling breath rises from the corner, like a wind chime threaded with bones. Now that it's darker, the pile of pillows has transformed into a crowd of hulking spirits, calling me over. Wanting to devour me the way they've swallowed my friend.

The breathing grows louder, like hundreds of dried leaves tumbling and crunching against one another. One of the pillows lurches, falls on its side as something moves behind it. Then there's a loud, awful noise.

*Heeeeeeesh…*

"Sing?" I whisper on purpose, because I don't know if I really want her to hear me. I think of the last time I stood by this door, on the other side. How she threw herself at it like a wild creature.

305

But I don't think she'll be doing that now. The pillow-demons stay still. There's only the rasping struggle of Sing's lungs to let me know she's there at all. I take a few steps forward, wait for my eyes to adjust.

She's whiter than a set of bleached sheets. So much *lesser* and *faded* from the girl I knew: a husk. There's almost nothing left to her. I don't know if she could stand if she tried.

But she does move. Her arm reaches out and, even though the movement is slow, I jump back. It's a weak motion, taking everything she has to grasp out for my foot.

And the labored breaths turn into words. I have to strain to hear them. "M-m-more..."

"Sing." I crouch down, keep my distance. "It's me. Mei Yee."

Her eyes are open, but dull, as if they're not really seeing anything at all. She stares and stares. Her arm stays still, wrenched and twisted like a spare piece of string. She looks dead. Only her horrible, rattling breath tells me otherwise.

A shiver takes me, starting first in my neck and dripping down my back like rainwater. I go back to the door and sit, clutching my knees to my chest. My eyes shut. I wish my nose and ears could do the same.

The shell is gone. The boy is gone. And I'm like a star falling, falling, falling into darkness worse than death.

# DAI

It was a split-second decision, staying behind. One of those ideas you can barely process while your brain is stringing out cusswords a mile long. I'm standing in the lip of the alley, where the trash thins out into the trample of the wider street. There's no time for second thoughts, but they're there anyway, sticking me all over like hot acupuncture needles.

I have no idea what I'm going to do once I get through those doors. How I'm going to distract Longwai long enough for Osamu to get here. All I know is that Mei Yee's timetable has suddenly grown a hell of a lot shorter than mine. And I've got promises to keep.

My body feels so much lighter without my gun tucked into my jeans. Like a piece of me is missing. The nautilus shell is still jammed up a sleeve of my sweatshirt. More damning evidence. I kneel down and find an empty bag of dried seaweed bites. The kind Hiro and I used to toss at each other during study sessions. The logo—a cutesy cartoon cat licking its lip—is long faded. No one would bother to pick this up.

I slip the shell in—shove it to the far edge of the wall. The cellophane wrapper crushes hopelessly under my boot. Crunching against a wreath of shiny, jagged glass. The pieces are as sharp as a surgeon's scalpel. Perfect for peeling back skin, slicing veins.

My hand hovers over them, twitching as I weigh the risk.

I can go in there without a plan, but there's no way in hell I'm walking in without a weapon.

I grab the largest fragment of glass, shove it into my front pocket.

*Better not get caught in the alley.* My brain's adrenaline highlights this point. With double underlines and stars in the margins, the way Hiro used to mark up his biology textbooks. I take note (the way I never really did when I was actually studying), slip out into the wider streets, and start walking.

I'm not as far from the alley mouth as I'd like to be when Fung rounds the corner. For such a hulk of a man, he's fast. When he sees me, he shifts gears, lurches into double speed. I barely have a chance to flinch before he's next to me, seizing my hoodie like a dog's scruff.

"You," he grunts. "What are you doing back here?"

"I was on my way to see Longwai." I keep my voice level and long, like a ruler. Not the easiest feat when I can see Fung's gun not-so-subtly strapped against his hip.

"Yeah?" The gangster's eyebrow quirks, and the beast on his face moves like the New Year's dragon dances. The ones that will soon take place in Seng Ngoi's streets. "Funny thing. He wants to see you, too. You stood up his runs."

*Shit.* The runs. How could I forget? Not that there was much I could do in any case.

Fung doesn't let go of my sweatshirt. He tugs me back to the brothel's yawning door, pausing only to discard our shoes. I feel like a squirming rodent being dragged back to an eagle's aerie. Waiting to be torn apart by razor talons and beaks.

The lounge has a few smokers, but Longwai's couch is empty—just a stretch of threadbare fabric and sagging cushions. Fung pulls me through the smoke. We pass couches and the upturned corners of rugs and even serving girls. I look into their faces, hoping against hope that one of them will be Mei Yee. That the words we heard behind the window were a terrible, unreal illusion.

But she isn't there. Not holding a serving tray or behind the zither. She's not even lurking in the shadows.

My chest feels like someone's pumped it full of liquid lead. I see the same pain in the other girls' faces.

Fung keeps walking, dragging me through to the hall.

The east hall.

We stride past doors full of nameplates, to the end, where stairs curl up. At the bottom step, the gangster releases my sweatshirt, prods me forward with a growl.

"Up you go."

I conquer every step, trying not to think about whether Fung's got a gun pointed at my back. I think, instead, of how close I am to the book. How freedom has never felt farther away.

When we reach the top, my pulse is scattered and uneven. Just like Fung's thick-knuckled knock on the door.

Longwai isn't wearing his lounging jacket when he opens the door. He's dressed like Fung—only smarter. Buttoned-up shirt. A blazer. Slacks. All black. Like a Western businessman preparing to go to a funeral. Except Western businessmen usually don't wear gold chains around their necks or guns on their belts.

And I'm really, really hoping there won't be any funerals today....

The leader of the Brotherhood sees me. The knife scar on his face bulges along with his jaw, purple and shiny. This, with his smart dress, makes him look more like a predator than ever before.

"I thought I asked you to check the alley." He shoots a sharp look past my shoulder, at Fung.

"I did, sir," the guard says quickly. "Found this one skulking nearby."

"I didn't know Hak Nam's side streets were off-limits." I try my best to look bewildered.

"They are if I say so." There's no smoke weighing down Longwai's eyes. No subtle sloth to his movement. If he was a cobra before, now he's a mongoose. His gaze snakes back to Fung. "Keep searching. Leave the boy here for now. We're long overdue for a discussion."

310

My hands clench tight against my thighs as Fung walks away, moves back down the stairs. I feel the glass, sharp and pressing through denim.

Longwai walks away from the door, and the room comes into full view. The first thing I see are the guns and cruel-edged knives. A whole wall of metal and trigger, power and pain staring me in the face. The shard in my pocket is starting to feel like a bad joke.

I try not to stare at it too long. There are plenty of other things to look at. A large television screen crowned with rabbit ears and tinfoil. A tank full of aquamarine water and tropical fish that stretches across an entire wall. A hefty, lacquered writing desk. The top drawer with its delicate golden lock.

I'm so, *so* close. If Mei Yee is right.

*Mei Yee.* On my way up the stairs, I'd thought maybe she would be here. But the shadows of this room are empty things. She's somewhere downstairs, behind one of the many doors.

Longwai walks to the middle of the room, where a glass-topped table stretches out. Perfect lines of white powder streak across it: albino tiger stripes.

Every inch of me is alert—fighting fear and the very real sense that I'm prey. Prey in the deepest corners of the beast's lair. I put on the face I always wore when I was younger and my father decided to chastise me. Aloof, cocked brow. Like nothing in the world could stop me.

"Trouble?"

"Nothing that concerns you. Yet." Longwai stands over the table, and I realize that the glass is really a mirror, shining his

311

own towering height back at him. "I'm more curious about why you missed our last appointment. And the one before that."

"My runner got stabbed. I haven't been able to find a replacement. It's not easy to find vagrants willing to work with you."

"There's a reason for that." Longwai's hands rise up to his belt line, lifting the jacket up with it. His pistol gleams against the aquarium's tropical light. "You failed to honor our agreement. I'm not the forgiving type."

"So I've heard." I feel every ounce of blood in my head as my heart drills it through, beat by beat. But I keep my mask up. Stay cool. Don't look at the wall of sharp, sharp knives. "But you kill me, and it's a guarantee that no vagrant will ever run for you again. No matter how good the money is. Survival is the highest law."

"You're a dangerous boy. Clever." Longwai's hand pulls away from the weapon, goes up to cradle his hairless chin. "And here I was thinking you were the disposable one."

It's all I can do not to look over at the desk. So close. I'm so, so close. Just feet away from the book. All it would take was a distraction and a swift movement. Bullet or blade to the head.

But those guns on the wall probably aren't even loaded. Not like the gun in Longwai's holster. And even if I did get the book and get downstairs, I don't know where Mei Yee is. I wouldn't have time to look for her.

It's not the right moment. But what terrifies me is the very real possibility that the right moment will never come. That this is it.

"I like you, Dai," the drug lord says, "which is why you have all your appendages intact and a brain without a bullet lodged in it. You're smart. You work the system. Get things done. I need men like you."

Air grows stale in my lungs. I look down at the tabletop mirror. Where the lines of cocaine double, become more than they actually are.

"I need men like you," he repeats, "but I also need to know I can trust you. I need to know you have my best interests at heart."

"Is this an invitation?" I'm not faking the breathlessness in my voice. Out of all the things I was expecting when I was dragged through this door, an invitation to join the Brotherhood was not among them. Tsang would be peeing his pants right now.

"It depends on how you want to look at it. Try to see things from my perspective. Do you honestly think I can let you walk away from this operation? After how much you've seen? Anyone else would be in a body bag now. But you have guts and brains. I'd hate to let such assets go to waste."

"So...I join the Brotherhood or get carved up and shot?"

"Let's call it an opportunity."

"Well, I am an opportunist." I try to grin. I try not to think of Hiro and Pat Ying and Jin Ling and Mei Yee and all the other countless lives this man has destroyed. I try not to feel the endless pieces of shrapnel always shredding, always burning in my chest.

"Of course, there are the formalities before you become an

official member. Background checks and oaths and such. And there's the little matter of your loyalty. All my men must pass a certain *test*."

"Anything," I say.

"Anything?" His hand falls away from his chin, burrows into the pockets of his suit.

I nod and think of hundreds of things he could make me do. Hundreds of things I would hate.

"One of my girls has been giving me trouble."

*No. No. No. Anything. Anything but that.* I feel like a surgeon has sliced me in half, hollowed me out, my guts spilling over his blue gloves like stringy pumpkin seeds. My head spins and I try very, very hard to keep my smile on my face.

Longwai starts pacing circles around me. "I think she's been communicating with someone on the outside. We found a hole in her window just this morning, and one of the other girls claims she saw a seashell on the other side."

"What do you plan on doing with her?" I'm glad I gave most of my meals to Chma, because my stomach is churning like the waters at the stern of a ferry. A chaos of waves, cut to pieces by an engine's sharp blades.

"You don't keep a rotten apple in the bin. Though I'm beginning to think they're all rotten. It happens every few years. Some girl decides to run and all the others get riled up. I'll probably have to replace the whole lot." He shakes his head, like he's getting rid of the side thought. "But if she was talking to someone through that window...I need to know what she said. Who she was talking to."

"What do you need me to do?"

"You—" Longwai pauses and walks over to the corner where a miniature refrigerator hums away its benign existence. "You are going to help me get the truth."

The refrigerator door opens with the clink of bottles and a crack of too-bright light. Longwai grabs something I can't really see. It's small enough to fit in the palm of his hand, hidden as he nudges the door shut.

"I've already given her some time to preview her fate if she decides to keep quiet. You and I—we're going to go downstairs and ask her some questions."

"But what—what do I ask?"

"The questions are my job. If she doesn't answer, I want you to use this." His palm opens, like an oyster giving up its pearl. Only it's not a precious gem in Longwai's soft hand. It's a syringe, slim as a pencil, filled with liquid the color of beef broth. The drug lord is careful to keep the needle far from my skin as he hands it to me.

The syringe is cool poison on my palm. I try to keep my hand from shaking.

Heroin.

He wants me to inject her.

"Don't worry. It should be a simple-enough job." He's smiling as he says this. "After all, like you said, survival is the highest law."

# JIN LING

The cab I flag down isn't nearly as nice as the Suns' car. But I sit in its seat and feel as if I'm going in circles. Around and around. Backward, forward, back again. The city spins by, the same as before, except now it's night. When the cab starts climbing Tai Ping Hill, all of City Beyond is glowing. Neon fire blazing against black night. Dark sea. I try to look for Cassiopeia, but it's lost. Swallowed in electric fog.

The driver looks over his shoulder. "What was the number again?"

"Sixty-two," I answer, and try to pretend that my world isn't falling apart. That Mei Yee and Dai aren't trapped in Longwai's brothel. Surrounded by henchmen and guns. That I'm not there to fight for them.

*It's just like every other run*, I tell myself, even though I know it isn't. *Do it well and they'll be safe.*

But there's no quick exchange. No drugs for money and then done. I'm going to get a man who visits my sister. The man who pays money to Longwai so he can—no. I can't think about it. Not with a gun hanging heavy in my pocket.

I pick at a hangnail instead. Tearing and rooting at it with anxious teeth. When we pull up to number sixty-two, there's a chunk of skin missing from my thumb.

"Want me to wait?" asks the cabdriver.

I shake my head and hand him the cash. The driver leaves me on the side of the road. In the dark. Under stars and towering pines. By the open gate.

The house is up a hill, through a thick screen of trees. It's a building made more of glass than metal. Light shines through transparent walls, makes everything around it glow. Dozens of people mill inside, like tiny dolls. The women are draped in gowns. The men wear crisp black-and-white suits. A lot of them are foreigners—with light hair.

A party. The ambassador is throwing a party.

The people behind the glass move like fish, swimming round and round in a tank. This world—these people with their jewelry and drinks—is almost more terrifying than a line of Longwai's men. The men who are probably holding guns at Dai's and Mei Yee's heads.

I suck in a breath. Hold in the tears of fear and pain. I walk up to the door.

The doorman sees me. His smile turns into a frown.

"Please," I manage before he can say anything, "I need to talk to the ambassador."

"He's busy," the servant says. His voice is tart. Like his face.

"It—it's about Mei Yee."

"Young man, I don't know who you're talking about, but you have to leave." The door starts to close. "Before I call security."

I catch the door with my left, good side, and slip through. The doorman cries out. I give him a sharp kick in the shins and run.

I scramble into the middle of the party like a frantic piglet. A few of the Western women scream softly—words I don't understand.

"Osamu!" I yell, because I don't know what else to do.

The guests freeze. I feel more stares than I can count.

"What is the meaning of this?" One man surfaces from the rest. There's a quiet thunder to his words. Dim, controlled anger. "How did you get in here?"

He's older than I expected. His hair is silvering. There are more creases than smooth on his skin. More of an almost-corpse than husband or lover. Bile rises into my mouth. I swallow it back. Make room to speak.

"Ambassador Osamu, I need to talk to you." I bow, even though I feel more like pulling out Dai's gun and pointing it at this man's chest.

"This is hardly the time or place, boy." Those old, wrinkled lips pull tight. He's looking to the back of the room. To security that will drag me off at any moment.

I decide not to waste any more time. "It's important. It's about Mei Yee."

When I say her name, his eyes widen. His jaw grits. I'm not sure if it's fear behind his face or something else.

The ambassador grabs my bad arm, pulls me away. We pass the glaring doorman massaging his shins. We end up outside, in front of his house, by a trickling fountain. Our breaths cloud each other's faces.

"Where did you hear about her? How dare you come into *my house* and jeopardize *my honor* in front of *my peers* and *my wife*!" *My. My. My.* He spits the word over and over into my face. His saliva flecks my cheeks.

I look straight at this man. At the puff in his chest and cheeks. The hard pride in his eyes. I look at him and I hate him. The feeling spoils me, running through my arms. Curdling my chest and gut. It's as if every other hatred I've ever felt is pouring into me: Kuen, my father, Longwai. I can barely speak because of it.

"Mei Yee is in trouble. Longwai caught her doing something she shouldn't, and he's going to punish her. He doesn't want you to know." I treat every word like a world of its own. Try to balance it. Keep it even.

The ambassador's fingers clamp onto me, squeezing harder than a rattrap. There's power in his stare. He's trying to intimidate the truth out of me. "And how do you know this?"

"I—I run drugs for Longwai. One of the other girls in the brothel wanted me to tell you. She said it was urgent. A matter of life and death."

These final words seem to sway him. Osamu lets go of my arm and returns to the door. I look back to the window-walls, where a bunch of primped, pale faces gaze through the glass. Staring at me.

The ambassador exchanges words with the doorman and takes a thicker jacket to cover his party-wear. His fancy leather shoes cut past me with quick steps.

"Come," he calls at me over his shoulder. Like he's summoning a dog. I have no choice but to scramble after him.

He doesn't even look down when I reach his side. "I swear to the gods, boy, if you're wrong, I'll have you stashed away for a long time."

Threats mean nothing right now. My face is bathed in sweat. Side literally splitting. Hiro's old shirt is damp with my blood. I don't know if I can keep going.

I do manage to crawl into the ambassador's car, feel the lump of Dai's gun when I collapse against the leather seat. It digs into my side. Reminds me of the six bullets. Six chances at getting my way. Getting away.

# MEI YEE

For some time there's only dimness and the ragged tempo of Sing's breath. I begin to wonder if that's all there is. Just the in and out of her drug-riddled lungs, taunting me with her fate. The rhythm is almost hypnotic. After minutes and minutes of it, my eyes begin to close.

And then the door next to me opens—an explosion of wood and anger, jerking me awake. I struggle to my knees and then my feet, eyes full of the blurry series of legs filing in.

I stand and see their faces. The ones who've come to question and judge. Mama-san's makeup, Fung's tattoo, Nam's gold tooth, Longwai's violet scar. But there's a fifth face, one I have to focus on to recognize.

I see him and wonder if maybe I'm dreaming. But no, I rub my eyes and he's still there—in the flesh, without glass or metal between us. The golden skin. Hair peaked and jutting everywhere. Sharp face full of plans and cunning. Eyes that hum and shine like phoenix song.

Dai. What's he doing? Did they catch him, too?

Those eyes find mine. His chin quivers—side to side—in the smallest of shakes. I snap my stare down to the floor, away from him.

"Mei Yee." Longwai sounds disappointed, but thrills still manage to weave through my name. "Mei Yee. How could you do this to me? After everything I've done for you."

I keep my head down, study the crevices in the floorboards. There are years of dust and suffering wedged between them. Places even Yin Yu's broom couldn't reach. "I-I don't know what you're talking about, sir."

"No?" Longwai steps close. I feel his eyes all over me, as scathing and peeling as they were the very first night he inspected me. He reaches out, his fingers cool and clammy against my wrist. "Then how did you get this slice on your finger?"

He holds my hand up for the room to see. It takes everything I have not to flinch back from his touch.

"We know about the hole in the window. Who was behind it?"

*Down. Keep your eyes down. Don't look at Dai.* "No one, sir."

"You're lying," Longwai says, as if it's the most obvious fact in the world. "Yin Yu said you showed her a seashell. How did you get it?"

"Yin Yu is a liar. I've told you before. She's jealous."

"She's smart enough not to keep secrets." Longwai's

nostrils flare wide, like a horse that's run three *li* at full gallop. "I'm giving you a choice, Mei Yee. Tell me the truth and I'll let Ambassador Osamu take you away to Seng Ngoi. If you choose to keep lying…"

He gestures to where Dai stands, a bit apart from everyone else in the room. He's not looking at me, not meeting my eyes. I look into his hand and see why.

This syringe looks exactly the same as the one they stuck inside Sing's arm. Pumped full of liquid ruin and loss. The sight of it curled into Dai's fingers makes my heart clench.

Is it betrayal? Was he playing me this entire time? Plying me for information only to discard me in the end?

Every one of these questions feels like an arrow cracking through my breastbone. An entire quiver of sharpness splitting me open, right through the middle. I try, try, try to meet his eyes and find answers, but he doesn't look at me.

Longwai mistakes the wreckage on my face for fear. "I've allowed you some quality time with your old friend to make the gravity of your choice a bit more real for you. So, Mei Yee, it's the truth or that syringe. Which will it be?"

I could tell. All it would take is one finger, aimed straight as an arrow back at Dai's chest. One word, one point, and the needle's end would slide away. Guns turned on Dai.

Then what? If Longwai kept his word, I would be whisked away to City Beyond. Caged in the ambassador's penthouse for a lifetime of bruises and pieces of the sea. It's not freedom, but it's better than ending up as a living skeleton on Longwai's floor.

I look at the syringe, now almost completely visible under Dai's strained knuckles. The skin over his bones is a thin, sharp white.

It's a gamble. All of this. I have no idea, no guarantee that Longwai's promise will hold. And Dai...I focus on his fingers. How they shake.

It all boils down to a single question.

Do I trust him?

I look down the line. At Fung's offset jaw and hunched shoulders. At Nam's four peeling cheek scabs and gleaming eyeteeth. At Mama-san's body wrapped tightly in her slinky silk. At Sing's hair rippling over the floor like grease-drenched ribbons; her eyes are open, some shine returned as she looks at the syringe in Dai's hand. At Longwai's too-big belly stretched tight against the buttons of his shirt. Back at Dai.

He's looking at me this time. It's just a split second of our eyes locked together. And I know.

*No matter what it takes.*

"I'm telling you the truth." There's no shake in my words as I look back at Longwai. "There was no one behind the window. There was no shell. My window broke and I cut my finger stuffing the silk in it to keep the cold out. Yin Yu saw it and made up wild stories so she could profit."

This clearly isn't the response Longwai is expecting. His lips slide into an almost-frown. His eyes dart from Dai to me and then narrow. "And this is the truth?"

"Yes," I tell him.

The drug lord's head swivels back in Dai's direction. With

one hand, he grabs my arm again, the other he uses to wave my window-boy over.

Dai is so close I can feel the heat of him. So different from the clammy cool of Longwai's touch, or the slick sweat of the ambassador's chest. This heat is like a cooking fire on a winter night—the close, simmering comfort of home.

I close my eyes, bask in it as Longwai stretches my arm out straight. Somewhere I hear the snap of a band. Then I feel it, squeezing tight against my upper arm, choking all blood back down into my wrist, palm, and fingers.

My eyes open to see Fung tying a complicated knot into the band. Longwai is staring at me. Expecting me to beg: all quail and quiver at his feet. Instead I stare back, meeting the hollow hardness of his eyes.

"It doesn't have to be this way," he says.

"No." I feel every heartbeat slamming against the tightness of Fung's tourniquet. "It doesn't."

The spine in my voice makes him snarl, and I know it doesn't matter if he thinks I'm telling the truth or not. Mamasan's right. Courage and hope can't exist in a place like this. Longwai grinds them to powder under his heels.

It wasn't Yin Yu who did this to me, not really. It was this man.

He looks at Dai and points to the blue veins bulging beneath my skin.

"Do it."

# DAI

Back on my apartment wall there are two marks left, but it doesn't matter. I'm out of time. No days or hours remain. Not even minutes.

The numbers are different now. I add them up, doing quick calculations in my head as my fingers clutch the syringe.

Six people.

Three guns.

One syringe.

One shard of glass.

One book.

It's an uneven, impossible equation. No matter how many times I run through it, I can't come up with the perfect answer. The book and the girl don't go together. After the equal sign, it's only me or her. No us.

Longwai makes a living by lying through his teeth, but

he was right about one thing: I'm the disposable one. I'm the sacrifice, the queen in a brutal game of chess.

Turns out there's a law higher than survival. And I don't know what it is, but I feel it surging, throbbing, burning away the rest of my doubts and fears.

No book. No me. Just Mei Yee.

The syringe of heroin has lost the chill of the refrigerator. It shakes, filling with dozens of tiny bubbles in my hand. If anyone is looking at me, it should be all they see. Shakes and bubbles. But my left hand is sliding ever so carefully into my pocket, where the glass piece saws through denim. Its razor edge bites into my palm, ready.

There are so many veins in Mei Yee's arm—dredged to the surface by Fung's too-tight knots. She doesn't fight as the drug lord splays out her arm like an offering.

"Do it." Longwai points to the blue web under her paper-thin skin.

I take a breath, unclenching the syringe in my right hand while gripping tight to the glass in my left. If I time it just right, I can get the shard deep into Longwai's neck, grab his gun, and take care of Fung and Nam. A big *if*. And then there's the matter of every other Brotherhood member with a holster crawling through this place.

Getting out of here alive is a long shot, but it's the only shot I've got.

I pretend to watch the needle as I guide it close to Mei Yee's flawless skin. But really my eyes are searching for other veins, the thick cording ones gathered in Longwai's neck.

There's a cry and suddenly—a girl. A girl where I didn't even know a girl was. She rises from the corner, looking like a witch with her loosed black hair and gaunt face. Her eyes are both bulging and sunk in—fixed on one thing only. She lunges with a speed too fast and impossible for her bony limbs.

*"I need it!"*

The syringe is torn from my hand by this wild resurrection of a girl. I don't even have to pretend to stop her. Her fist clenches tight around the needle, jams it into her arm. But there's no vein to carry it through. Heroin and blood braid down her skin. The girl shakes, stares at it. She's trying to lick it up when Nam rips the hollowed plastic syringe from her palm.

I slip the glass back into my pocket.

"Get Sing out of here!" Longwai yells at Nam. I've never seen him like this, so angry his face is flushed full of autumn colors.

"But where—"

"I don't give a damn!" Longwai roars. "Put a bullet in her head for all I care! And fetch me another syringe while you're at it."

Nam grabs Sing by the hair and starts to drag. The girl's face shifts into a violent, ugly thing—as if she's possessed. From the way she moves, I could almost believe it: kicking, clawing, screaming, twisting. Nam's grip on her hair slides free and she's off. Out the door faster than a mouse.

*Now. The time is now.*

My hand wraps around the glass shard again, pulls up, and out to strike.

"What is all this?!"

A new roar causes my arm to freeze, midair. It isn't Longwai—the expression on his face is set and silent. He stares behind me, at the shadows crowding the doorway, blocking all ways to freedom.

For once I'm thankful this glass is so small. It hides perfectly beneath my knuckles, betraying nothing. I hold it tight and look around.

Osamu. My Plan B. Jin Ling did her job.

The ambassador is in familiar garb. I've seen him wearing the same style of tuxedo since I was too young to really know who he was. What always stood out to me were his gold cuff links, how they twinkled under the torchlight in our rock garden as he sipped cocktails and flirted with every woman there. Including my mother.

He doesn't recognize me—I doubt he even sees me at this point. Osamu's anger is bullish. So focused he didn't even remember to remove his shoes at the entranceway. His shiny leather oxfords stamp into the reeking room, shaking every floorboard.

"What's going on, Longwai?"

"Brothel business," the drug lord bristles, but the yell has left his voice. I notice his free hand is tucked to his side. The one his gun is hidden on. "None of it concerns you."

I'm so close to Mei Yee I can hear her breath changing. It gets faster in a way that the threat of Longwai or a heroin needle couldn't spur. It's the closeness of him—the way a rabbit's heart explodes under the stare of a hunter.

The ambassador's eyes travel up her arm, taking in Longwai's fingers still on her wrist, the bulging vein, and Fung's knots. "Mei Yee is my concern. I thought I made it very clear to you that she wasn't to be touched."

"I've respected your wishes for as long as it's been convenient. That time has long run out. Lest you forget, Osamu, I'm the one who owns this brothel and these girls. Mei Yee included."

The men stare at each other, like two silverback gorillas facing off on a single piece of territory. Ready to tear each other apart. A dramatic nature-show moment in the flesh.

Mei Yee shakes beside me. I wish hard, hard, hard that I had my gun.

Osamu reaches out, wraps his hand around Mei Yee's wrist. Their skin is so different—hers white as snow, his covered with age spots and wiry hairs.

"Name your price," he says, and I think of all the many bruises I saw on Mei Yee's skin that night at the window. How they match his touch exactly. I don't mean to, but my grip grows tighter, pushes so my skin is torn apart by the glass.

"It's not about the money anymore, Osamu." Longwai's voice is both hard and peeling, like callused skin. "She's up to something. Keeping secrets. I want to know what it is."

For a long moment all is stillness. There's the quick avalanche of Mei Yee's breaths. The old woman in her clingy silk, taking everything in like a spider on a web. And my hand tight on glass.

"Secrets?" Osamu is looking around, eyes wide and clearing, like a man who just woke up. Glimpse by glimpse he swallows the room: the filthy pile of rags, Longwai's gun, Mei Yee, me....

330

And then his eyes dart. Back and forth. Back and forth like one of those plastic table tennis balls, ricocheting between Mei Yee and me.

"I see how it is," he says softly.

I feel the heat of my own blood swimming across my palm.

"It's information you want?" Osamu's voice is a lake. Placid and calm on the surface, plunging to unknown depths. "You're not going to get it from Mei Yee."

His eyes set like stone on my face. "This is the one you want. Sun Dai Shing. What is the heir of Sun Industries doing flirting with the likes of the Brotherhood? I'm sure he has more than enough secrets to keep you entertained for the rest of your miserably short career."

Goddamn Osamu. Not a very good Plan B.

All the heat and threat that Longwai was pouring onto the ambassador shift, unload like dragon fire on my shoulders. The drug lord lets go of Mei Yee and draws his gun in a fluid, lethal, mongoose movement. The barrel stares at me—hard and unforgiving.

Game over.

He pulls the trigger.

# JIN LING

I can't keep up. The ambassador is gone. Vanishing into the Walled City before I can release my seat belt. Even that's hard. My right arm bursts with pain. Weakness. There's a dampness in Hiro's shirt; my side's bleeding again. Tears of pain fill my eyes. Make everything dazzle. The lights, the darkness, the flaring red lanterns of New Year's. Everything is shining. Mixing together.

I feel done. But my sister's face, her voice, is the clearest it's been in years. I see her smiling behind the steam-wisps of our weakened tea. I hear the lullabies she sang over me after Father's thrashings.

I think of Mei Yee and get out of the car. Leave the stink of rich cologne and leather. I'm walking, dragging through the Old South Gate. My walk feels like a twisted dream, into the heart of this unreal city. Through the last two years of my life:

The sewer grate where I made my very first camp. The shops I stole from, the stoops I haunted. The window I used to peer into every few mornings to watch cartoons. The alley where I rescued a gray kitten from his vagrant tormentors. The second alley, where I rescued him again. Mrs. Pak's restaurant and Mr. Lam's junk store. Mr. Wong's dentist chair. The hidden corners where I pitched my tarp. And on. And on.

Over soon. It will all be over soon.

The gun hangs heavy in my jacket pocket. All six bullets weigh my steps, make each foot forward seem more impossible than the next. I keep going. Because that's what I do. That's what I've always done.

Only this time—this crucial, final time—I don't think I have the strength.

My boots plow over puddles of ice. *Step, step, pain.* I stop. Lean against the apothecary's door. Try to focus on the dozens of jars with dried roots and bits of animals through the bars. My vision is double—smears of light and color and dark.

I'm almost there. One more turn and I'll be at the mouth of the dragon's den. It can't be more than twenty steps, but it might as well be a completely different country.

An empty can, riddled with rust holes, clatters down the street. Causes my neck to snap up, alert. I can't see much. Just the fog of my breath and the dark. Blurring together.

"There he is!" someone shouts, and I hear footsteps.

One by one, I see them. They come from all directions. A ring of boys and rags and knives. Their faces are pale and whittled. Carved by flickering lights. So sharp and bony that

I'm not even sure they're human. Maybe they're demons. Evil spirits come to swallow me down into the fires of the afterlife. To devour my soul for what I did to the jade dealer. To Kuen.

My hand fumbles, sliding from the doorframe down toward my pocket. Toward the revolver.

But there are more than six of them. Even counting through my double vision.

One of the boys comes into focus. He's squinting at me, lips screwed to the side. His blade is a sick shade of silver, slashing the night in front of him. "You sure it's him? Looks different to me."

"Got new clothes is all. Nice ones, too!" a voice calls from my left.

"Ho Wai's right," another boy says. "That's him. The one that gutted Kuen."

The boy directly in front of me steps closer. His knife moves with him; its edge hovers dangerously close to my throat. "Well, well, Jin." A grin splits across his sharp, starved face. "Fancy seeing you here."

# MEI YEE

Longwai's pistol points at Dai. I want to scream, but I can't find my voice. Or maybe I do scream and I just can't hear. The sound of the bullet leaving the gun pulses everywhere. Nothing—not the filthy gaps in the floorboards, not the makeup caked in the corners of Mama-san's eyes, not the aching, bursting vessels of my heart—escapes it.

So many things happen at once.

Dai is falling, falling, falling down. He's on the floor. Not moving. The floorboards under him seep out, stretch into a color like my curtain, like my nails. My ears hum and ring and scream, *This can't be right*. Longwai steps over the body, the pistol is pointing down now. This time it's aimed at Dai's head.

The ambassador's fingers are around my wrist. He's pressing the way he was before, breaking things unseen, calling up colors and hurt.

But he's not just pressing. He's pulling, too, tugging me away from Longwai's gun. Away from Dai. He yanks my wrist so hard my joint pops and sparkles pain. Sparks of light shiver like tadpoles across my eyes, follow me all the way out the door, down the hall, and into the lounge.

I could've touched him. We were that close.

"Hurry up." The ambassador drags me through this nightmare of smoke and couches. And I don't know how to fight him. Not when there was so much blood soaking the floor and I knew that Dai was there for me. *No matter what...*

Sing didn't make it far. She's on the floor of the lounge, her face pressed hard into the rug. Longwai's men are so busy with her that they don't even notice as the ambassador drags me through the room.

But someone in the lounge does notice. I stumble forward, watching Yin Yu watch me. The wrist I slammed into the door handle hangs limp at her side. Bangs fringe over her eyes, and I'm too far away to see the expression on her face. I can't tell if she's sorry or sad or completely vindicated. She doesn't move as the ambassador takes me away.

We're out of the lounge, down the south hall, heading toward the door. I've been dreaming of this moment for days, stepping out and away from this place. Only the fingers on my skin were gentler, as warm and endless and electric as his eyes.

We could've touched.

And then there's a noise that could end all other noises. Again it tears through everything: the winter air, the hallway's floorboards, my chest. It makes the ambassador jump even though we both knew it was coming.

The second gunshot rattles through my ears like cicada wings—over and over and over. Killing again and again and again. I squeeze my eyes shut, as if that could stop the noise. But all I see is Dai crumpled on the floor with Longwai's gun at his head. No chance of running.

"Let's go." The ambassador keeps tugging, as if I'm some stubborn donkey yanking against its halter. "Longwai might change his mind now that he's done with the boy."

*Done with the boy.* His words freeze my bones. As if the air whistling through the front door is actually cold enough to fuse my muscles together. I'm more ice than girl.

"What? Sad? Don't try to hide it. I saw the way you two were looking at each other!" The ambassador's hand crushes harder with every word, as if he can squeeze me back into submission.

"You killed him...." I don't mean to say it, but the thoughts slip out. Shock words as sheet white and shaking as I am.

"I just saved your life," the ambassador hisses. Pain shoots through my wrist like a thousand needles jammed at once. "Yours for his. You're mine. No one is going to stand in my way. Not Longwai, not Sun Dai Shing, not even you."

I wish he were wrong. That the tender blooms of courage and fight that have been poking out of the soil of my soul for the past few days hadn't just been torched at the sound of Dai's death. I wish I could stop him. Stop everything that's happened in the past few hours.

But some things just weren't meant to be. No matter how hard and how fierce you wish them.

# JIN LING

My whole hand is numb as it dives into the pocket of Hiro's old jacket. I must be touching the gun, but it's impossible to tell. My fingertips are clumsy and slurring. The way my father always was after bottle number three.

All the boys are closer now. As if they're the wheel and I'm the hub. Their knives could be spokes. Pointed against the jacket's vinyl.

"Where'd you get those clothes?" The vagrant they call Ho Wai edges in. Looks me over.

"Probably the same place he got the boots!" the center boy says. "Now shut up!"

"You shut up, Ka Ming!" Ho Wai barks back.

I can feel the gun now. The boys—Ho Wai and Ka Ming—aren't paying attention to me anymore. They're facing off. Like a pair of beta dogs. Putting on their best displays of snap and snarl for the group.

I take a breath of damp air. My sight is settling, coming together. There are eight of them—flanked around me like a half moon. Eight knives to six bullets and an unsteady hand.

Not good odds. Best just to answer them.

"I got these clothes from a house on Tai Ping Hill," I say.

Ka Ming and Ho Wai stop glaring at each other. All eight pairs of eyes are on me now.

"No way." Another boy to the left shakes his head. "He's lying!"

"How do you think I'm still alive?" I shrug. The vinyl of Hiro's old jacket sings friction. "Dai took me there. It's where he's from."

"Tai Ping Hill? The rich people's neighborhood?" Ho Wai frowns. His knife lowers just a hair. "Dai's from there?"

"Yeah…" I draw out my words. Let my mind work. If the boys were set on killing me, I'd be a corpse by now. Left to rot. But these boys…they don't have Kuen's claw and hate. They're just starving faces. Looking for a way out.

"Turns out he's a rich kid. Has a huge house and all that." I think of the cash Dai stuffed into my pockets. I wish I hadn't given it all to the cabbie. My own money in the orange envelope is sitting in the corner of Dai's apartment. Far from here. "And lots more clothes where these came from. You let me go and I can make sure you get some."

Wordless questions are thrown across the ring of vagrants. Glances bounce between knives and stone-cold faces. Most of them are aimed at Ho Wai and Ka Ming. It seems the spot Kuen left is too large to be filled by a single boy.

"How do we know you're telling the truth? That you

339

aren't just gonna run off?" Ka Ming's knife slashes the air to each of his syllables. Reinforcing every point.

I don't have the energy to come up with any more excuses. Any more lies. "You don't."

Ka Ming and Ho Wai look at each other. Stares sharper than razors. Thinking of all the reasons my life is worth keeping. Worth snuffing.

Another, smaller voice pipes up behind me. Bon, the kid I almost stabbed. "C'mon, Ho Wai. It's not like we actually liked Kuen anyway. I think Jin's telling the truth. Dai did take him out of the city.... I followed him that day. He's gotta have money."

Ka Ming's arms cross over his chest, his blade no longer flirting with my throat. "Clothes are nice. But not as nice as cash."

"I say we keep 'im hostage!" Ho Wai barks. "Find Dai and get 'im to give us some cash to keep his little friend alive. That way it's a guarantee, if Jin's telling the truth."

Dai—my throat grows thick as I think of him, somewhere in those glowing red halls, risking his life to save my sister. He needs his revolver. He needs me.

I don't have time for this.

My knuckles tighten hard around the gun.

# MEI YEE

Outside is a strange, new world where the air is threaded with an endless braid of smells: incense, seafood, decay muted by cool. Darkness is everywhere, pouring into the street corners and alleyways, crowding against the lines of electric shop signs. And the sounds...I'm sure there are more sounds, but all I can hear are both gunshots. Over and over again. They boom and crack with every heartbeat. Still ringing and singing the impossible in my ears.

Dead. Dai's dead.

*He can't be*, thrums my heart.

*But he is*, cries my mind. *He is.*

The thin silk of my dress means nothing to the winter air. Its chill curls into me the way a cat settles onto its master's chest. All the warmth Dai gave me is gone. As hard as I tried, I couldn't hold on to it.

But the ambassador is still holding on to me, pulling me

hard down the street. The numb of shock is wearing off. My wrist throbs and my silk slippers are useless against these paths of gravel and glass. My feet collect blood, cuts, and regrets with every step.

Osamu won. He got his wish while watching mine die, in a metallic flare of gunfire. And I could have stopped it. If I'd said *yes* all those days ago, Dai wouldn't have come for me no matter what. He wouldn't have stared down the barrel of Longwai's gun. He wouldn't be dead.

We turn a sharp corner, my wrist bending in agony. The ambassador stops, and I jostle hard into the stiff fabric of his suit, see the reason we've halted.

There's no room for us to keep going.

The path of cinder block walls, shop entrances, and hanging pipes is crammed full of street kids. The ones Longwai used to tell us about. They look nothing like Dai. They're stick and bone, pale as ghosts, and hung with rags.

Staring at us with nine pairs of hungry, dead-coal eyes.

"Out of my way!" the ambassador growls. His free hand waves as if he's swatting away a swarm of flies.

But the boys don't move. It doesn't take long for me to notice their knives, how they glint against the darkness.

"Move, you little bastards!" The ambassador's roar is barrel-chested. It rattles the pipes above our heads and shivers the glass around my feet, but it doesn't move the boys. The only thing that changes is their eyes. The hunger that was so leaden is now a gleaming thing. As bright as the golden cuff links on the ambassador's suit. As sharp as the daggers in their hands.

# JIN LING

Years of empty doors and hollow corners. Months of dark and black. Nights of shivering wet and dead rats roasting on a spit. Days of running and stabbing and running and snatching and running.

It was not for nothing. There's a moment where I can only stand and stare. Wonder how I ever doubted I would find her.

The first thing I see is her dress. As red as dragon scales under the streetlamps. Brighter than blood. Her hair is longer now. Braided to her waist. Her face is smoother, sadder. There's a heaviness in her eyes. A weight on her shoulders that wasn't there before.

But she's still my Mei Yee. Still my beautiful, beautiful sister.

My sister is a beauty, but the ambassador's a beast. Full of hot air and smoke. Puffed big and bad for show. For all his bellowing, Osamu reeks of fear. Vagrants know the scent well. The knives honed in on my throat now point at him. Eight strong.

"I'm a government official and my men are just behind me. If you don't move, I'll have them shoot you all on the spot," the ambassador snarls.

"He's lying." I speak clearly. Loudly. My hand is still tight on Dai's gun. "It's just him."

The ambassador notices me for the first time. His eyes pop almost out of their sockets. Like a rat skull crushed by a boot. "You! You set this up, didn't you, you little—"

My hand comes out of the jacket. It's not shaking or spinning like the rest of me. The revolver's barrel points straight at the ambassador's chest.

The gun does something eight knives can't. The ambassador falls silent. His face turns as pink as raw meat. Full of very real fear.

The revolver stays steady, but all my insides are shaking.

*Do it. Do it. Do it.*

But my finger won't move. Won't pull the trigger. I stare at the ambassador's meaty face, and all I can see is Kuen's leer. So horrible, blank, and red after what I did to him.

And just like that, my chance is gone. The ambassador clutches my sister. Hides behind her like the coward he is.

# MEI YEE

The ambassador is unraveling, like a ball of yarn no one can catch. All the perfectly selected masks he put on for me, for Longwai, have been shucked away like played cards. Now he's just standing in the cold—the age spots on his face are tinged purple, the way my bruises were—staring at the boy and his gun.

There's something brutal, something familiar about the boy with the gun. He's staring at the ambassador the way Jin Ling used to stare at my father: eyes full of poison, fists full of fight.

I think of my sister and find myself staring harder at the boy. *It can't be. . . . Not here . . .*

The ambassador tugs me tight to himself, crushing me into his girth so that it's my body blocking the bullet's path. As soon as this happens, the boy's features change, soften into the face I saw so many nights just by moonlight. When we shared the window together, hunting stars.

*It can't be. . . . But it is.*

The sight of my sister is the strength I need. She fills my insides with steel and bravery and the impossible. My freedom, my escape, is right in front of me. And I'm the only one who can seize it.

The ambassador's arm is locked around my throat. His hand is just by my shoulder, the tendons cording and taut. I sink my teeth deep, deep beneath his skin.

He howls and the taste of his blood fills my mouth: all salt and bitterness. His arm yanks away and I rush past the boys and their knives. They don't pay any attention to me. They close in around the cursing ambassador. I can see the ridged bones around their eye sockets. The knobs of their knuckles, too big around their knives. I think of the stray dogs in my old province. How hunger hollowed out their bones and created fierce, desperate creatures. Beasts that knew no fear.

My sister grabs me by the hand and starts pulling. We're running down the street, sliding into a dark alleyway, when the ambassador's screams start in earnest.

I'm not sorry.

Sometimes, when Father's rage became too unhinged and his hits were murderous instead of battering, we would hide. Jin Ling always led the way: out the door, past the ginkgo tree, into the vast maze of rice field rows. We would dip waist-deep into the water, slink like the snakes that actually lived in those long waves of green.

I feel like that now. But instead of rice fields, Jin Ling leads the way past walls of slime and over hills of trash. Through gaps I didn't even notice until she slipped into them, pulling me after her with urgent strength.

The ambassador's screams are long gone by the time we finally stop. Jin Ling is breathing hard, much harder than she should be, and sweat drips from the hacked ends of her hair despite the cold. She's still holding my hand, fingers wrapped tight around my thumb, the way she used to cling to me when she was first learning to walk.

We stop in a dark, empty corner and look at each other. Wordless. We stand, stuck in the moment. Staring and trying our best to believe.

"Mei Yee." She says my name and holds my hand so hard I don't think she'll ever let go. "It's me."

After all I've been through, all that's been done to me, I thought I had no more tears left. But the sight of my sister—the sound of her saying my name—is enough to break me. The water wells up, salty and free across my cheeks. "You came for me."

Jin Ling doesn't fit so well in my arms anymore. She's almost as tall as I am. Her face buries into my shoulder as it did when we were little, but she has to bend over to do it. And I feel her bones more easily, despite the jacket she's wearing.

When we finally pull apart and face each other, I study her. Not so many freckles anymore. And she's grown into her nose. And—

"Your hair," I gasp, and laugh through the rest of my tears.

"I cut it." She swallows and smiles, but her voice is shaky. "When I first came to find you."

"First?"

"I chased the Reapers' van when they took you," Jin Ling explains. "I cut my hair so I could pass as a boy. I've been looking for you ever since."

I don't have the words. I look at her—my fierce, fighting little sister—and tuck a strand of her hacked hair behind her ears. The thought of her cutting it all off and coming here to look for me is too much. Impossible, even though she's here now, saying it.

But I remember the way Jin Ling made her wishes. How she said *I wish we could be together forever* with the bite of a tigress. Nothing would be impossible enough to keep her wishes from being fulfilled. Not even the Walled City.

"How did you find me?" I say this and then stop. Know. I see the answer on my sister's face, feel it on the insides of my chest where I'm crumbling to pieces.

*My freedom cost so much more than a dying star.*

"Mei Yee…" Jin Ling is looking at me again. "The boy, the one who came up to your window…"

I shut my eyes. It's so, so cold, but I can't even shiver. People only shiver when they remember what it means to be warm.

"Dai." I say his name, but it doesn't help. It doesn't bring him back to me.

"Yes," my sister says. "What happened to him?"

"Dai." I say his name again, but the empty space is still there. Jagged-edged and howling, like the hole in my window, letting winter's chill slip in. I don't want to say what I'll say next, because if I do, what I saw will be real and true. But even words unsaid can't take back two bullets from Longwai's gun. "Dai's dead."

# JIN LING

My sister's words are like a knife to the gut. Hot and fast. Nothing but pain. It takes a minute for their truth to sink in. For the burn to start.

"The ambassador came and accused him of having secrets," Mei Yee says. Her eyes are closed. Lids fluttering and white like moth wings. "Longwai shot him."

Dead. Dai.

Those two words sound so alike, but I refuse to believe they go together. They don't fit. I was just with him. In the alley. He looked so strong. So sure. So red and alive under the light of the window.

But he knew it was coming. *You get your sister out. Get as far away from this city as possible. Don't look back.* He knew I'd have to do this without him.

Mei Yee breathes out beside me. Her breath sounds like

the shudder of dead leaves, the rip of paper. I hear it and remember that she's wearing nothing against the cold and her silk slippers are in bloody shreds. Dai might be dead, but my sister is alive. And I mean to keep her that way.

"Here." I shrug off the jacket. Hand it to her. It's drenched in my sweat, my blood, but the fabric still smells like lemon and green tea. Like Dai's house. "We have to go."

"Where?" Mei Yee whispers.

I don't want to go back to Dai's apartment. Face the vast, empty grunge of those tiles. The two black marks that will never be erased. But my orange envelope is there and Mei Yee needs good shoes. Proper clothes. And I have a feeling that Chma will be there, waiting. I can't lose him, too.

*But after that?*

I think of our father's house. Our mother's herb garden littered with bottle caps and liquor glass. Hollow windows and doors. I imagine Father leaned against the doorjamb. Waiting. Cheeks redder than the setting sun. Fists curled. And Mother behind him. Always behind him.

I'm not ready for that fight. Not with a burn in my shoulder. A gun in my hand.

I don't know where we'll go. Somewhere far, *far* away from here. Somewhere we'll never, ever have to look back.

"We'll figure it out," I tell her.

# MEI YEE

Jin Ling leads the way again and I follow, my mind numb. Trying not, not, *not* to think of Dai and those final, awful moments. What he gave up so I could be running and twisting through these streets behind my sister.

I'm so busy trying not to think of this when Jin Ling stops, motions for me to be quiet. We're in a sliver of space. It couldn't even really be called a proper alleyway with how tightly we're wedged in here. The cinder block scrapes against my back, my chest. If I breathe too hard, it will crush.

I want to get out because the stones feel as if they're suffocating me, but Jin Ling doesn't move. She stays wedged by the final opening and watches. The tower of free air in front of us is suddenly blocked, crammed full with a man's face. A dragon inked in savage scarlet.

Fung.

My heart stops, but Longwai's man doesn't. He passes our gap, dragging something behind him. There's the awful scrape, scrape of plastic and deadweight against the ground. My throat is lined with vomit, but I stand on my tiptoes, catch a final glimpse of the body bag as it's jerked past our hiding place.

I try to swallow back the sick, try to breathe, but the walls won't let me. Jin Ling slips her hand in mine, squeezes tight. As if she knows that her presence is the only thing holding me together.

The dragging sound stops too soon. Fung's grunt creeps into the alley as he lets the bag down, brushes his hands off.

"This is what comes of crossing the dragon," he growls at the body before his boots start their scuff back in the direction he came. "Better luck in the next life."

Jin Ling and I wait long minutes between the cinder blocks, listening and watching. Finally my sister edges out into the wider street nose-first, like a mouse emerging from its hole. Pulling me out only when she's sure it's safe.

The bag isn't even two arm's lengths away, a pile of sad black plastic. I don't want to look at it, the way it's shoved into a corner where a door stoop meets a wall. As if it actually contained garbage and not the boy who woke me up. Set me free.

My sister creeps up to the plastic and kneels down. Her fingers out and touching.

"Jin Ling—" I don't know what to say except that I can't be here. I'd rather remember Dai as the life outside the window. Not as the body in the trash bag, kicked to the curb. "Please."

Jin Ling frowns, her fingers digging deeper into the crumpled plastic. She starts tearing. The black splits apart easily under her nails. Like some sick cocoon: no wings, only death.

I catch a glimpse of skin—as white and hard as a china plate—and look away.

Jin Ling keeps tearing and the plastic keeps ripping. I keep looking at my bloody slippers, trying to ignore the sick emptiness of my stomach.

"Mei Yee…" There's a rustle and the pulling stops. "Look."

My eyes stay down, take stock of shredded silk and numb toes. I can't look up. *Don't make me look up.* This hurt—red skin and glass stab—is so much easier to take.

"I can't—I can't see Dai like this," I whisper.

My sister swallows. "It's not him."

# JIN LING

*Not Dai.* I stare at the bagged body. What the gangster just dragged through the streets—it's more skeleton than girl. Greasy hair. Wasted face. A single scarlet dot between her eyes.

"Sing," Mei Yee gasps beside me. "The second shot. It must have been Sing...."

I drop the plastic back over the dead girl's face. Look up at my sister. "What happened? The last time you saw Dai. Where was he?"

"We—we were in Sing's room. The ambassador accused Dai of keeping secrets, and Longwai shot him. He fell on the floor and there was blood everywhere. Longwai stepped over him and aimed the gun at his head. The ambassador dragged me away, and I heard another shot and I thought..." Mei Yee folds a hand over her mouth. Stares at the trash bag.

"The first shot. Where was Dai hit?"

"I-I don't know," she manages. "Somewhere near his chest. It all happened so fast...."

I stare at the crinkled black, too. But I'm not thinking about what's inside it. I'm thinking about my next move. Weeks ago I would've run—taken my sister out of the Walled City and never looked back. Part of me—the survivor who's kept me alive all these years—still wants that. Follow rule number one. *Run, run, run.* I've fought so hard, risked so much to get Mei Yee back. And now she's here. My work, the reason I came to this place, is finished.

But I remember the promise I made to Dai, even though he never asked me to make it. I promised to help him get his book. His freedom. As long as he's alive, that promise still stands.

Dai saved my life. My sister's. Now it's time for us to save him.

"Dai's probably still alive. He's got to be or else that gangster would've dragged two bags out." I look back at Mei Yee. She's standing still, swallowed whole in Hiro's jacket. Her cheeks are wet. "And if he is, we have to get him out."

I expect her to argue; instead she looks up from the bag to me. Her voice is so strong, so sure. There's a fire in her words—in *her*—that was never there before. "I know. How?"

*How.* That's the question. My mind is working. Spinning faster than a weaving loom. Taking all the individual threads and piecing them together. Braiding them into a terrible, delicate tapestry.

The ledger.

One more day until New Year's.

Mei Yee's scarlet dress.

Midnight.

Eight boys and their knives.

Dai's revolver.

So many pieces. Parts that could snag. Go wrong. The whole thing could unravel at any point. I try not to think of this.

Instead, I look straight at Mei Yee and tell her, "I have a plan."

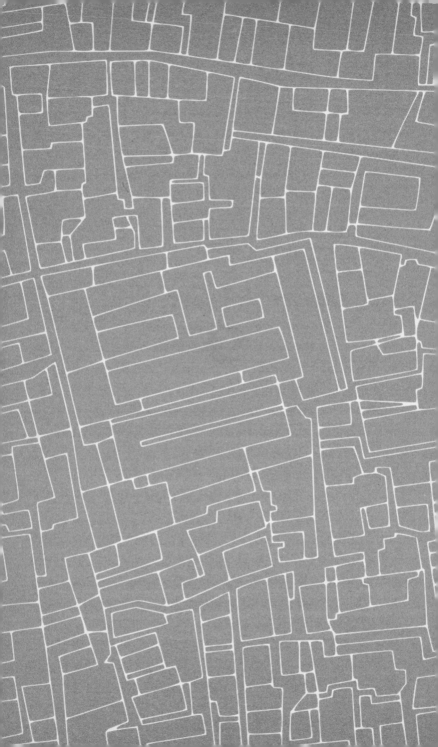

# 1 DAY

# DAI

The room is all dark. The kind of absolute black where you hold your hand to your face and still can't see jack shit. I've got no sense of time. If it's day or night. How many more hours of this I have to endure before Tsang's men come busting through to haul my ass off to jail.

The girls should be long gone by now. I wonder if Jin Ling used the gun I gave her. I really, really hope she shot Osamu—that son of a bitch.

It's thoughts like these that hold the pain at bay, keep my mind from snapping. I always used to wonder—in the long nights after the night that changed everything—what it felt like taking a bullet to the chest. I tried to imagine Hiro's pain: the hole inside him, letting nothing in, everything out. The fire and ice and numb all pressing down, calling out his final, splitting breath.

Soul and body cut apart. Forever.

I don't have to imagine it anymore. Turns out it's a hell of a lot worse than I thought. I didn't feel it at first. Just a heavy push into my right shoulder, my knees crumpling in shock. Then pins and needles and *sear*. So many pain synapses firing in my brain that I didn't really care that Longwai was looming over me. Waving death in my face.

But he didn't shoot. He didn't let me bleed out, either. (Who knew Fung was such a talented nurse? A gauze-wielding wonder.) Not so much a mercy as the fact that he wants answers before he stuffs me in a trash bag.

I'm lucky Longwai decided to start off light—just a few punches to the agonized mess that was my shoulder. He left me in here tied to a chair to "think about my options."

*Options*. With an *s*. Like I've got more than one.

As long as I stay silent, I stay alive. There's no way in hell I'm talking, not with just a day left. I want to see this bastard burn as much as Osamu. Hopefully, Tsang and his team will get here before Longwai gets more serious. Wants to carve out an eye or an ear with that infamous, eager knifework of his.

This thought makes me test my bonds again, but the ropes are still too tight, fat pythons coiled around my wrists.

But when you're flustered, like Longwai was, you miss things. Like the piece of glass tucked deep inside my palm. The one I clung to like life, through the gunshot. Through hit after hit after knuckle-ridged hit. I never let it show, kept my fists clenched even when Longwai landed the first punch, listened to me scream.

My hand unfurls slowly and the glass inches downward to my fingers. I work its edge back and forth, up and down. Longwai's been gone for a while, probably off to have a smoke or get some shut-eye. Every dark minute that goes by I expect to hear his footsteps again. I listen for them under the door as I saw at my bindings.

There's so much fire and pain in my shoulder that I don't even feel the ropes come off. My hands are just free, collapsing to my sides. I wilt to the floor, find the glass, place it back into my sweating palm.

When Longwai comes back, I've got to be ready.

I'm still on my knees when the footsteps start, padding closer and closer. I push up with my good arm, bolt to the wall by the door. My hand is tighter than ever on the bottle shard, ready for the lunge and stab.

The lock clicks and the door swings open.

# JIN LING

The stink of the sewer clouds my nostrils. Warm and jungle wet. I stand across from Ka Ming and Ho Wai. Keep a careful eye on their hands. Watch for knives. There's a faint glitter between Ho Wai's knuckles, but when I look closer, I realize it's only a golden cuff link.

"So do we have a deal?" I ask through the plume of sewer smoke.

"Sounds awful risky." Ka Ming shoots a glance at his partner.

*Risky.* Just one word to describe this cobbled semblance of a plan. I swallow back the tightness in my throat and tell them, "All good payoff has risk."

"Yeah, but risk and Brotherhood are two different things," Ho Wai points out. "How much did you say we'd get?"

"Ten thousand." I say the highest number that comes to

mind. Hope Dai's father is willing to pay it. "If everything works out."

The two boys stare at each other again. Talk with their eyes.

"Ten thousand," Ka Ming agrees. "No killing."

I glimpse Ho Wai's knife wedged into his belt. The edge is rimmed with pink; I look back to the cuff link in his hands. Raise my eyebrows.

"Not when Brotherhood's involved," Ka Ming goes on. "You understand."

I do understand. But I'm tangling with them anyway. With my crippled side and six bullets. With the speed of my sister's untested legs.

"It's a deal," I tell them.

# 9

I pass the noodle-maker's shop on my way back to Dai's apartment. Look at the clock on the back wall. A cartoon frog marks the minutes—his long tongue chasing a fly around the ring of numbers. Around and around and around. The old man beating the noodles into shape told me that when the tongue catches the fly at the very top, it'll be a new year. Our time will be up.

I try not to think about this as I push back through the door into Dai's apartment. Drag the plastic bag full of stuff from Mr. Lam's shop. Bought with everything I had left in the orange envelope. I took it easy on the stairs, but I still feel the steady weep of blood through Hiro's old shirt.

*Just a little longer. Just one more run.*

But my side feels as if it's been stuffed with pepper paste. Red and hot. I try to ignore it as I walk into the room. Toss the bag of goods onto the floor. Chma sniffs at the mess of plastic. Realizes it's not food and turns away.

Mei Yee comes over from her place by the window. "Did you get everything?"

"Yeah," I wince. Let myself down onto the floor. Never has hard, cold tile felt so good. "Talked to the vagrants, too."

"Will they help us?" My sister starts rifling through the plastic bag. Pulls out all the containers and brushes Mr. Lam stuffed into it.

"I caught them in a good mood...." I think of the cuff link. How it glowed like Chma's eyes through the gaps in Ho Wai's fingers. But this doesn't seem like something I should tell Mei Yee. Not yet. "And offered them a lot of money. So yeah. They're in."

The red dress is in the corner, folded neatly alongside Dai's other clothes. Even wearing boy's clothes—hair askew and eyes puffy—my sister looks pretty. I eye the growing pile of makeup by her knees. Start to doubt. I'll never be able to look like that. How can I think this plan even has a chance of working?

Mei Yee picks up a brush and opens the first jar. Peach dust fluffs into the air. Makes Chma sneeze: *Chma! Chma!*

I wish Dai were here to hear it. So I could tell him how right I was.

*Soon. Just one more run.*

366

"Shut your eyes," my sister commands. Stretches out the brush. "This will tickle a bit."

Powder sifts onto my face. I fight the urge to jerk away. Mei Yee takes minutes to make sure it's perfect, but she doesn't stop there. There are at least a dozen more jars. Colors for cheeks. Paint for lips, eyelids, and lashes. Long black clips of hair that isn't mine.

And then there's the silk dress. I slide it on fast, turned so my sister won't see the oozing wound under my shoulder. The one that's almost blinding me with its fire. Sooner or later it's going to catch up to me. I know this, but I still keep pushing. Hoping my body will stay together until all this is over.

I feel ridiculous. Cartoonish with this scarlet-shine dress and painted face. The fake bun pinned to my head clings like a terrified cat. It's not until I wrap my bindings around my bare thigh—slide the revolver into them—that I start to feel like myself again.

"You look beautiful," Mei Yee says when she sits back. Admires her work.

I look over to the window. The room's fluorescent light echoes back at us. Paints a perfect picture of the apartment. I don't see myself in it. Instead, there's a woman standing next to Mei Yee. A transformation of almost-curves and beauty.

I cock my head. The woman's head bends, too. My sister has done the impossible.

And now she must do it again.

The worst part of my plan—the part that makes my stomach turn and my knees weak—isn't the risk I'm taking. It's what I'm asking Mei Yee to do. I've thought through my plan again and again. A hundred times over. But there's no way this works without my sister.

I almost called the whole thing off, but she wouldn't let me. She's not the same girl who cowered in the corner of our father's shack. Who cried when a stray dog barked at her.

"It's almost time." I hand her my boots. "Are you ready?"

Mei Yee stares at the battered leather and laces. "Do you really think this is going to work?"

"I don't know." The lines are still on the wall. A perfect pair. I walk to the tiles and swipe one off. "You don't have to do this. I can figure out another way in."

"No." She shakes her head. "You can't."

I keep staring at the last line—forlorn against the off-white. It looks so odd by itself.

"And you're wrong. I do have to do this." Mei Yee sits down. Pulls the boots over her sliced feet. Her tongue edges out of her lips as she laces them up. "No matter what it takes."

Sounds like something Dai would say.

The final line looks so lonely. Because the numbers don't matter anymore, I reach out. Smudge the last charcoal strike away. As if it had never been there.

# MEI YEE

My feet are throbbing in Jin Ling's boots—singing blood and blisters against the raw leather. I try to focus on the pain in my toes, my heel. It's far better than the fear that's rising, sliding through every vein as I peer out of the shadows at the brothel's entrance. Where the dragon snakes around the door and a man with a gun stands guard.

"Are you ready?" my sister asks again in the tone that tells me she thinks I'm not. "Do you remember where to go?"

I know it's been only a few hours since I last saw Dai, but the moments between have felt like centuries. Every time I'm tempted to think of what's happened to him, what awful tortures Longwai has invented to get him to talk, I think of the route. The path Jin Ling showed me: right, straight, past the dumpling man, through a sliver in the buildings between the dog restaurant and the makeshift barber, right again, straight all the way to the cannons.

It's not a very long distance, but I'm not a runner.

I'm not, yet I must be. I will be. Because Sing is dead and Dai is still alive and this is the only way.

"Yes." My little sister is crouched in the shadows beside me, so I whisper. "I'm ready."

Jin Ling looks over at me. Even all the makeup I just brushed and dabbed on her face can't cover the strength there: smart, calculated, fierce. She reaches out, her hand gripping my shoulder. "I love you, Mei Yee."

I gather her in my arms, as I have so many times before. Only this time it's not blood but makeup I'm careful not to smudge. She's warm, too hot against my jacket even though all she's wearing is that useless serving dress.

I don't want to let her go. In the end, she's the one who does it—pulls away and looks me straight in the eyes. "We can do this. You can do this."

I nod and stand and try not to think of how my legs shake. I take one step and another, into the light of the street.

The guard doesn't notice me at first. He's distracted, kicking an empty noodle box back and forth. Battering its cardboard carcass into shreds with his boot. I swallow and keep walking. I'm close, almost too close, when he finally looks up. His eyes squint, then widen as he realizes who I am.

"Hey!" he shouts, but my aching toes already dig deep into the leather of the boots.

I start to run.

# DAI

The door opens and scarlet lantern light floods the room. The glass is deep in my good palm, ready for the softness of a wrist or throat. All those vital arteries I learned about in health class. I grip it tight and jump.

Our bodies collide and I realize too late that my visitor isn't Longwai at all. A serving tray spins to the ground, flinging a mess of cups and bandages and rice all over. And I'm tangled in red silk, my weight crushing the poor girl beneath.

"No! Please…" Her eyes are wide, and her shaking is about an 8.9 on the Richter scale. I look down and realize I'm still holding the emerald slice of glass against her throat. I pull it away.

"What are you doing here?" I look around at the ruins of her tray, answer my own question.

"You're Mei Yee's boy, aren't you?" The girl's eyes narrow. "The one who wanted the book."

Out of reflex, I look into the hall. Not that it really matters if anyone heard; this whole plan's gone to shit anyway.

"Something like that." I pull myself away, and the girl sits up, her bangs dropping like curtains over her face. She looks over at the chair, the frayed rope, and back to me, meat shoulder and all. I can see the waver in her eyes, the almost-yell swelling in her lungs, ready to warn the entire brothel about my escape.

She takes a breath. "You told Mei Yee you could get us out. Were you telling the truth?"

"Got her out, didn't I?" The adrenaline of the moment is wearing thin, letting the pain back in. And snarky-Dai with it.

The girl frowns. "And the book. You still need it?"

I slip the shard into my hoodie, keep my eyes fixed on the empty hall. It's only a matter of time before someone walks by. "Yeah."

She's studying me, like I'm some kind of viral strain on a microscope slide. Fascinating, dangerous if not handled properly. She reaches into the folds of her dress, pulls out a ring of brass skeleton keys. "Take these. The key to Longwai's office is the third one from the right."

The girl with the keys. Yin Yu. The one who ratted out Mei Yee. The one we never should've trusted.

I don't know if I should trust her now. She could be one of Longwai's puppets, baiting me to show my secrets instead of tell. I snatch the keys anyway. "Change of heart?"

"I never meant..." Her voice falters. She swallows and tries again, but there's still a rattle in her syllables. "They shot Sing right in front of me. Just like that. She was dead."

It's all she says, but I understand. I've seen dead bodies. I know how they change you, turn your guts inside out with their stillness and not-life.

This is what Sing's body did to Yin Yu. It undid her.

"I don't want to die here," Yin Yu says. "In one minute I'm going to scream and tell them you jumped me and stole the keys. Longwai's in the lounge facing the entry hall."

Of course he would be watching the way in. The way out. What are the odds that I'll get past him unseen?

"Go," Yin Yu says simply. "Your time is running out."

# JIN LING

Mei Yee's off faster than a hare. And the guard after her. I slip out of my hidden corner. Shuffle in battered slippers across the street. Through the dragon's door. My sister's advice loops through my head as I go: Take small steps. Fold your hands in front of you. Keep your head down.

I pass some of Longwai's men in the first hall. Walk by open doors where girls stare out. No one seems to notice the dirt under my fingernails. The coarseness of the horsehair on my scalp. The sad state of my silk footwear. The patch of blood blooming like a flower from my side. Subtle darkness on the fabric.

I want to move fast. Even though my side feels as if it's splitting apart. With every step, I fight the urge to run. It takes me longer than I'd like to reach the lounge. Longwai is on the couch, lips wrapped around the end of a long pipe. He doesn't notice me slink in from the entry hall. Mei Yee did her job well—my dress, hair, and makeup blend in. Seamless. I'm just another faceless serving girl.

*Book first, then Dai.* I trace out the plan in my head and skirt the edge of the lounge. Toward the hall on the right, where the ledger is. I'm almost there, just passing the girl playing her stringed instrument, when Longwai calls out. "You! Girl!"

I freeze. He's looking straight at me.

Before my hand can flash down to Dai's gun, Longwai lifts up his glass. "I need more wine."

Wine. He singled me out for wine. I scurry over to the serving cabinet. Try frantically to make sense of the mess of glasses and bottles there. I wish I'd been paying more attention to the way Yin Yu served it. The first time I was here.

"The bottle on the left," the girl at the instrument whispers. Her words are barely louder than the pluck of her strings. I glance over. Her eyes meet mine. She nods, fingers still moving, moving, moving.

It's so easy for her to tell I don't belong. What chance do I stand against Longwai?

I grab the wine bottle by its neck. Turn and get ready to pour. What I see stops me in my tracks.

It's Dai. Very alive and edging through the room's unlit corners. Hoodie up. Trying his best to get to the east hall.

"Is there a problem?" Longwai shifts on his couch.

"No!" My reply is sharper than I mean it to be. It steals the sleepiness out of the drug lord's eyes, makes him alert. He starts to stand.

One turn. One look behind his shoulder. That's all it would take for Dai to get caught.

I let go of the bottle. It plummets to the floor. Crimson wine bleeds across the rug, all the way to Longwai's slippers. He snarls. Stands up all the way.

"That rug is worth ten times what I paid for you!" Longwai seizes my arm. It takes everything I have not to pull away. Fight back. His fingers are freckled with spots of stale blood. I try not to think of where those stains came from.

"I'm sorry, sir." Saying these words feels like pulling out my own teeth with rusty pliers. I look down at my feet, where the wine bottle is still vomiting its contents. Push back the very strong urge to reach for Dai's gun.

"Sorry?" The drug lord leans down. Catches my eyes despite my best efforts to look away. "I don't remember asking Mama-san to assign serving duties to a new girl. In fact... I don't remember you at all."

My heart drops. There's a glint in his eyes. A tightness in his fingers. He's putting the pieces together—suspicions shaping up like potter's clay.

Maybe I'll get to use the revolver after all.

"Her name is Siu Feng." The girl has stopped playing her music so she can address the drug lord. "She was with the girls who came a few months ago. The group Wen Kei was with."

This throws Longwai off a bit. His brow furrows, second-guessing. Those fingers loosen. His back straightens. He points at the rug. "Fix this. And don't bother with the refill. I have business to get back to."

I look up, relieved to see that Dai is gone. The shadows are empty. Longwai doesn't head toward his office, as I fear he might. Instead, he disappears into the north hall.

The girl doesn't go back to her music. Instead, she comes over and picks up the wine bottle by my feet.

"Thanks," I tell her when she hands it to me.

She puts a finger to her lips. Motions to the lulling clients around us. Men so still I forgot they were there. "You're with the boy, aren't you?" she whispers.

I nod and glance back down the east hall. Wonder if I should follow Dai there. A wail of a scream rises from the north hall. A girl's voice babbles about attacks and keys, followed by Longwai's slurred roar, *Where is he?*

I'm about to race off. Warn Dai. But Longwai is already bulling through the lounge, face redder than the dragon on his door. His gun is out. Ready and trembling in his fingers. He disappears as fast as he came. Swallowed by the dim crimson glow of the east hall.

# MEI YEE

*Run. Run for Dai. For Dai. Run.*

It's been so long since I've moved like this. To tell the truth, I'm surprised I still can. Over heaps of trash, under ladders, around corners sharper than Nuo's embroidery needle. Shop lights blur past, puddles fly under my feet, and always, always I hear the guard breathing hard behind me, cursing with every other step.

I run, run, run until I can't feel my feet anymore. They're long past the pain of blisters and cuts. There's a new strength in my limbs—pure, hot energy. I feel that if I just stretched out my arms, I could fly. Out of these tunnels and up between the stars. This must have been how Sing felt before they caught her.

I think this, and suddenly my boot slips out from under me and the world goes flat. Pain jars my bones, becomes a part of me. The ground beneath my palms shudders with the weight of the guard's steps. There are no more wishes in my chest but hopes. I hope Jin Ling was right about those street kids. I hope I made it far enough.

A hand wraps around the heel of my boot, jerks me backward. My body slides easily through the puddle. I twist and see the guard almost on top of me. Before I really know what I'm doing, I take my free foot and slam it hard, hard, hard between his legs. He howls, releases me instantly. I scramble back just in time to see the shadows come.

The vagrants spring from every corner. Creatures of rags and knives and bone, swarming over the guard like maggots on meat. They're small, but with eight to one, Longwai's man doesn't stand a chance. They take his gun, kick it away.

"Better run, girly!" one of the bigger boys shouts back at me.

He's right. They're going to let him go soon—Jin Ling told me the vagrants could buy me only so much time. Even with their knives and numbers, they'll never harm a member of the Brotherhood. As soon as the guard realizes this, he'll be after me again.

I need to run so far and fast he'll lose me altogether.

I'm back on my feet and into the alley between the barber and the dog restaurant. Over bottles and bodies and so many other broken, unwanted things. Out and to the right. My lungs are fire and my legs feel like splintered chopsticks, but I keep going.

*For Dai. For Dai. For Dai.*

Straight as one of Nuo's zither strings, all the way to the rusted cannons. I reach them with nothing but gasps left in my lungs. I know I should follow Jin Ling's instructions—find a policeman, ask for help, stay with him—but all the energy that surged through me just moments before is gone. I lean hard against the rust, struggling for breath.

"Probably not the best night to be outside, kid. Get back inside while you can."

I look up. My eyes struggle to focus. At first all I see is the glow of a cigarette. Then the man in the trench coat behind it. Something about him feels wrong: the way he talks, the clothes he's wearing. He doesn't belong in the Walled City.

And then I see the row of vans lined up on the streets behind him.

*Reapers* is my first thought, followed by a sick lurch in my throat. But no, Reapers don't wear clothes like that. And they wouldn't be lingering so obviously in the streets of City Beyond.

The man pulls the cigarette from his mouth and checks the gold watch on his wrist.

"Is your kid coming or not?" A second man steps out from one of the vans. He's wearing a thick green vest, a navy hat with a silver badge pinned to the top. "We're ready to move in."

I look back at the caravan of black vans and suddenly I understand. These aren't Reapers. This is the police raid Jin Ling told me about. These are the people who were supposed to get us out. Dai and me. Together.

"Dai's in the brothel," I say.

The man in the trench coat looks up—startled. "And who the hell are you?"

"Mei Yee." My name brings no familiarity to his face, so I keep talking. "I was supposed to help Dai get the book for you."

The man's jaw edges out, his annoyance highlighted by the cigarette's brash light. "Supposed to?"

"Something went wrong and Longwai caught him! He's still in the brothel. You have to help him!"

His cigarette isn't even half finished, but the man tosses it to the ground and flashes another look at his watch. "At this point, sweetie, the only person who can help Sun Dai Shing is himself." He looks over at the man with the badge on his hat. "All right. The kid's not coming. Let's get moving!"

The van doors slide open and an army pours out. Men with body armor, searchlights, and guns longer than their arms. They jump out of their vehicles and start running. Past the old grandmother squatting on a blanket, hawking special bundles of New Year's incense. Past the snow-haired man and his basket of bean cakes. Past the young girl hauling a cart full of clean laundry across the rutted path. The whole world goes still, watching the men and their guns vanish one by one through the Old South Gate.

The man's words burn through me hotter than his cigarette: *The only person who can help Sun Dai Shing is himself.*

And because the man is wrong, I follow him back into the city of darkness.

# DAI

Pure luck got me through that lounge. I'm pretty sure I owe my life to the serving girl with slippery fingers, but I don't have any time to worry about that. The minute Yin Yu allotted me is vanishing fast.

I'm barely breathing as I reach the door at the top of the stairs. It's locked, just like Longwai left it. Yin Yu's keys shake in my good hand. There are so many of them, hanging from the brass ring like gilded skeletons. My nerve-strung fingers fumble, grip the third one from the right. I can almost hear the seconds counting down as I fit the key into the lock. Yin Yu should be screaming any moment now.

But the key is the right one, and the door swings open. The first thing I go for is a gun—one of the antiquated pistols on Longwai's display wall. It's light. Too light. A quick check proves my initial suspicions were right. He doesn't keep any of these weapons loaded.

I turn to the desk and then I see the clock.

Its numbers are digital, red pixels that scream like demons' eyes through the dim: 11:58 PM.

Almost midnight. Out of time.

*Tick, tock, tick, tock.* My hands twitch to the beat of vanishing seconds as I go to the desk, study the top drawer. There's a small lock—easy to break if you've got the right tools and strength. I grab the closest knife from Longwai's collection. Wedge and pry. The drawer pushes out, uneven and crooked from the force. Like a stray with a limp.

There are papers, pens, individual cigarettes, a tin of mints, and gold-colored paper clips. My hands tear and shuffle through all these things until I reach the bottom of the drawer. My fingers keep scrabbling, frantic, at nothing.

The ledger isn't here.

"There you are."

I turn to a familiar sight: Longwai stands in the doorway, his pistol out and aiming straight between my eyes. The knife sits on the desk. Inches from my fingers. Useless.

"I thought you'd be long gone...." The drug lord's voice trails off when he catches sight of the open drawer, the flurry of papers and pens and trivialities. The wide, book-shaped void in the middle of it all.

"Where is it?" he snarls, and pushes farther into the room. Those bloodshot eyes bulge wide as he seizes my hoodie by the drawstrings, yanks them tighter than a noose. "The ledger. What did you do with it?"

There's nothing left to hide, nothing left to risk, so I tell him the truth. "Nothing. It wasn't there when I opened the drawer."

"Impossible!" His pistol presses against my forehead, branding an O into my skin. "You have five seconds to tell me where it is."

So this is how it's going to end. A whimper and a bang all in one.

Better—I guess—than getting made into fish chum, piece by bloody piece. But only just.

*Five...*

For some reason, I thought I'd be seeing flashes right now. Scenes from my childhood maybe. Running around the Grand Aquarium with Hiro: my going gape-eyed at the electric eels; his reciting the scientific Latin names for every species he saw. Or making model airplanes with my grandfather.

*Four...*

There are flashes, but they aren't pieces of my past. Instead, I'm on a beach and my arm is wrapped around Mei Yee's shoulder, and we're staring far off across the waters. And Jin Ling is beside us, tossing shells into the waves. Not my past but my future. The one that's dying with every number that leaves Longwai's lips.

*Three...*

I might deserve to die for everything I've done. I even wished it in those black rooftop moments, when my legs dangled over the streets and my brother's final voice called me *good* and I knew I wasn't.

But now...now I'm not so sure Hiro was wrong. Now I want to live.

How's that for irony?

*Two...*

I shut my eyes.

*One...*

# THE NEW YEAR

# DAI

The shot sounds all wrong. It should be loud, clean. Like the one that went into my shoulder—cracking through the gun's chambers like a lone lightning bolt. Tearing time and matter apart in slow motion.

Instead, it's muted. Like a firecracker being crushed under someone's boot. An echo without fire or flare.

And there's no punch. No new pain taking root under my skin. Just my shoulder and its steady, reliable throb. The one that lets me know the blood in my veins is moving. Still inside me.

My eyes open. I'm still standing. My shoulder is still meat-mushed and throbbing. The cinches of my hoodie are still tight around my throat. Longwai is still standing in front of me, but his pistol has lost its resolve. The O is no longer marking my forehead. It's shifted, just like the drug lord's attention. He's looking over his shoulder, at the open yawn of the door. More shots pop through the dark, and screams tumble up the stairs.

The raid has started.

"What is this?" Longwai's question drifts through the open door, becomes lost in the growing tempest of noise.

The knife. I don't wait. I lunge with everything left in my body and grab the ornate, curved blade by its hilt. It's an old ceremonial piece, more for show than for actual cut and slice.

"What the hell is th—" Longwai is just turning back when I make contact. I throw myself into him, good side first, trying my hardest to bring him down. The drug lord is more solid than I expect, like his lounge slippers are actually cemented to the floor. He stays standing, but the gun hits the floor, spinning like a game-show wheel.

I land back on my feet, facing him. Trying to ignore how my right arm is noodle-limp at my side. How Longwai's gold-capped teeth are glint and snarl, ready to sink into my throat. How the blade in my left hand feels like nothing much.

Especially when I'm not left-handed.

Longwai is a fighter. He moves fast, throws a nasty version of an uppercut. Knuckles already covered in my blood come again for my face. But—this time—there are no ropes. I whip to the side, let him give the air a good thrashing. At the same time, I bring up the knife.

There's a *schick* and his black funeral shirt splits. A long cut runs down his right forearm—straight as a plumb line, neat as a surgeon's work. The red leaves him at the same time as his scream.

An arm for an arm. Now we're even.

But there are so many things this god of knives and needles has to pay for, so I keep fighting.

I throw myself at him again. He falls—cursing and howling and splintering in pain.

I land on top of him. My shoulder jars on impact; supernovas of pain light my vision. Star trails swim in my eyes, eating away Longwai's ugly face. I push through them, slide my blade up to the soft, soft skin at the well of his throat. It tangles with his gold-link chain, pulls a whimper out of him.

"It's over, Longwai." The growl that leaves my mouth sounds too animal to be mine, but I don't know who else would be saying these words. "You're over."

I'm over, too. They're here already, pounding up the stairs, filling Longwai's quarters with their floodlights and screams. They flood the room like locusts—scouring every corner with bright lights and rifles. Inspecting Longwai, the blood-edged knife at his throat, centering on me.

"Police! Drop the knife! Put your hands where we can see them!" someone says as the lights gather on top of me. Even the backs of my eyelids flare orange when I shut them.

I toss the knife to the floor, out of Longwai's reach. My good hand lifts high over my head. I brace myself. One of the cops grabs my arms and twists them behind me. The clicks and cranks of the handcuffs fill my ears. They close tight around my wrists—cold, metallic destiny.

# MEI YEE

The police are emerging from the brothel in ones and pairs. A mere trickle compared with the force that poured in minutes ago, like a broken dam of guns and searchlights. Almost all of them are leading people. Most, like Fung and the Brotherhood and the lounge clients, are in handcuffs. Others, like Yin Yu and Mama-san, are free. Some don't come out at all.

I don't see Dai or my sister anywhere. With every strange face that marches through the door, my heart drops another level, like air being slowly leaked out of a balloon.

*Please. Don't let them be dead*—I'm not even fully finished with this thought when Dai's face appears. He's being pushed out of the brothel, his arms twisted in knots behind his back. His face is twisted, too—pain, pain, pain. I see the cuffs and the policeman prodding him on; panic rises.

I run to the officer. "You're making a mistake!"

"Stand back," the policeman says with a stern face, and gives Dai an extra push forward. Hurt and wince flare on my window-boy's face, make me look closer at his shoulder. The sweatshirt there is tatters, torn and stiff with old blood. Underneath are bandages, white and rust. The same colors as my nautilus.

"No! You don't understand! He was in there helping. To rescue me." I move in front of them, blocking Dai's forced path with my body. "You can't arrest him."

The blank wall of the officer's face gives way to uncertainty. His eyes rove over Dai, and for just a second I believe I've convinced him.

"Ah. You found him." The man from the Old South Gate steps next to me. His hands are shoved far into the pockets of his trench coat. The half-finished cigarette between his lips makes his words mumbly. "I was beginning to think you were a no-show altogether."

"Sorry to disappoint." Dai looks from me to the smoking man. His words take on the same sharpness he used when we first met. "I was too busy being tied up and tortured."

The man sucks on his cigarette. It flares extra bright, like a lone dusk star. "It's not my fault you got yourself caught. Did you find it?"

Dai shakes his head.

The man with the cigarette stands still for a moment. He exhales: air made of ash and sigh and disappointment. When all the smoke has cleared, he nods at the officer. "If you see Chan, let him know the ledger is still missing. Tell him to keep an eye out for it. Take this kid out with the rest. There's a warrant for him."

"Wait! No!" I shout. "You can't do this."

Trench coat man pulls the smoking roll from his lips. The movement sends sparks swirling through the air. Some land, harmless but bright, on my arm. "He's a murderer, sweetie. We offered him his chance at redemption and he failed. Best say your good-byes."

"You want the ledger?" I look at the man—smoke fills his lips like a foggy morning, hazing the air between us. "It's in Longwai's office! In the top drawer of his desk."

Dai shakes his head. "It's not there, Mei Yee. The drawer was empty."

"But—but it can't be...." I keep talking so I won't have to feel the sinkhole growing in my stomach. "It was there. I saw it! I saw it!"

I'm staring at Dai now, pleading for him to believe me.

His eyes are even deeper than they were before. Somber and yawning and full. There's a smile on his face as he looks at me. "I'm glad you found her," he says, and nods somewhere past me. I look back to see Jin Ling behind me, limping and shuffling through the cold. The blood she tried so hard to hide is now an undeniable dark on her dress.

"Get him out of here!" the man next to me barks, and waves a hand into the endless night of these streets. They yawn on either side of us, like the great mountain caves in our province. The ones the spirits lived in, waiting for sacrifices that stopped coming years ago.

"No!" I reach out, try to grab him, but the officer shoves Dai forward, rougher this time, off into the crowd of people.

It's not the darkness of the street that devours him. It's the crowd of black suits and handcuffs that finally hides him from my eyes. Instead, I see Longwai—hands bound tight behind him, being dragged by police through the trash and dirt. His one arm is bent the way Sing's was so long ago, smearing blood and broken.

Part of me feels that I should be happy—seeing him like this. After everything he's done. To me. To Sing. To all the other shivering, sapped girls gathered under the lone sapphire streetlamp. But I can only look at such brokenness and feel it inside me, echoing long and far, deeper than the darkness between stars.

# DAI

The handcuffs are too tight. I can't feel my fingers anymore, but my shoulder is a different story. It's like the end of an unknotted rope: fibers twisting, pulling, fraying, coming apart. It doesn't really help that the cop behind me is shoving and jostling like a half-rate taxi ride. I know better than to complain, though. I had my chance. I had more than my chance.

I can only imagine what my father will say, if he ever comes to see me. I can just picture him, sitting with his flawless business suit and mostly gray hair. He'll stare through the inches of Plexiglas. All those years of masking his emotions at business meetings and cocktail parties won't be enough to hide the disappointment on his face. He'll lean close to his microphone and say, "You should have run."

I'm beginning to think that myself until I see Mei Yee. Her face is flushed, like she's been running. Even though she's dressed in my clothes, hair pulled back, everything about her seems brighter. More alive.

She doesn't even blink when Tsang calls me a *murderer*. She's still looking at me with her nautilus stare. Dusting the sand off my soul and seeing the best parts. The ones that Hiro saw. The ones he tried to tell me about.

And then I see Jin Ling behind her, hobbling desperately to be with her sister. Together again after so many years.

I see them, almost side by side (the way Hiro and I used to walk when we scoured the seashore), and there's no room for doubt.

*It was worth it.*

# JIN LING

I can't run and scream at the same time. There's too much hurt. Not enough air. I can barely even walk with the extra weight around my leg. The distance is short, but it takes me ages. When I finally reach Mei Yee and the smoking man, Dai is gone. Sucked into the tide of criminals and Security Branch.

"W-wait!" I'm wheezing, bent over. Trying to ignore my sunburst pain. The wound is catching up, draining me of my last, vital reserves. "Bring him b-back!"

"If you want to see him, you'll have to arrange a visitation at the correctional institution." A frown crosses the man's face. I think it's because he's almost done with his cigarette. "Can't tell you which one yet."

"I have what you want."

This seems to get his attention. He swivels around on

his heels. Looks at me. The extra skin of his neck bunches into his chin.

"And what might that be?"

I'm about to reach for it, but I take a longer look at the man's face. It's lit up. Orange and hellish. "Bring Dai back and I'll show you."

The man scowls and tosses his cigarette to the ground. He doesn't even bother stamping it out. He disappears into the crowd, calling after Dai and his officer.

I watch the cigarette die. Just one more piece of trash to step on.

Mei Yee stares at it, too. "Do you really have it?"

Before I can answer, the man is back. A bewildered officer and Dai follow him like toy train cars. All three of them stare. Waiting.

I reach down to the binding on my thigh, where Dai's revolver is wedged tight against the cloth. My hand grabs what it needs out of the thick, stretchy fabric. Pulls.

The man in the trench coat stares. His mouth is open, oddly empty without his cigarette. His hands stretch out. Reaching desperately for what I'm holding.

I reached for it the same way, when the music girl, Nuo, and a girl named Wen Kei showed me what they were hiding. After Longwai barreled through the lounge and blocked all ways to Dai, Nuo grabbed my wrist. Took me back to her room. Her chest was puffed up when she tugged the ledger from under her bed. The pride was in her words, too, when she explained how she snuck up Longwai's stairs while he was busy questioning Mei Yee. Used hairpins on the locks. A skill she inherited from a girl named Sing.

I pull the book back. Away from the man. The dragon's gold leafing shines almost green under the streetlights. I hug the soft red leather to my aching chest. It fits well there. "Let Dai go. Like you promised."

The man stares at the cornerstone book. There's something like relief in his eyes. In the part of his lips. He turns back to the officer holding Dai. "Uncuff him."

I wait until the cuffs are completely off. Dai's arms fall free. The right one heavy and awkward. Dai cradles it tenderly as I hand over Longwai's book of secrets. The cigaretteless man flips through the pages. His lips are together now. Pulled up into a smile.

"Longwai's ass on a platter," he says. Snaps the cover shut like a dragon's jaws.

"We good, Tsang?" Dai's syllables are dislocated, sweating with effort and pain. I can't listen to him without remembering my own hurt.

"It's after midnight. And technically you weren't the one to hand over the book. But…" The man—Tsang—reaches into his trench coat. Pulls out a white fold of paper. "I'm in a good mood. I'll give you this one, Sun Dai Shing."

Dai takes the paper with hungry fingers. Clenching so tight the edges rumple. He thrusts it deep, deep into the pocket of his hoodie.

Tsang tucks the ledger under his arm. Looks at each of us in turn. Eyes gleaming. "Take my advice, kids. Get out of Hak Nam. They'll be tearing it down. Turning it into a park."

"That's the plan," I tell him. I look back at my sister.

"Good luck with that." Tsang turns to go.

"Wait!" Mei Yee's cry stops him midstep. "What—what's going to happen? To Longwai? To all the girls?"

Tsang gives the book a fond pat, as if he's stroking a cat. "There's enough evidence here to put Longwai and his men in jail for a very long time. And the girls…" His eyes drift over to the streetlamp the girls are huddled under. A self-created, silk-clad herd. "They're free to go."

The girls churn and mill in their flimsy, colored dresses. They look so lost and trapped at the same time. Like the bright groups of fish crammed into restaurant tanks.

"Go where?" Mei Yee asks.

"Not my problem." Tsang shrugs and walks away. No one stops him.

I'm not moving anymore. But the pain is. I have to sit. It doesn't matter that the ground is covered with glass and spent cigarettes. I got what I came for. My family is whole and I'm done. Done running, fighting, and hiding. Done standing.

I end up on the ground. It's more of a fall than a sit.

"Jin!" Dai kneels down next to me.

"I'm"—I try to wave him off—"fine.…Do you have any money on you?"

"Money?" He frowns. "I gave you all the cash I had. What do you need it for?"

"The vagrants…Kuen's old gang…they helped get you out." I'm wheezing. "I promised to pay them."

"We'll get the money," he tells me. "Are you sure you're okay?"

I nod.

"You're bleeding," he says. Points at the dark, wet spot on my dress.

"So are you," I point to his shoulder. "I just need to rest. That's all."

He settles next to me. Lands straight on top of Tsang's discarded cigarette. "I think we all do."

# MEI YEE

They're all here: Nuo, Wen Kei, and Yin Yu. The girls from the other halls. Fewer than twenty in all, blinking and shivering and gaping in the blue, blue light. Even Mama-san hovers at the fringe of the group, where the reach of the streetlight fades—her face one part shadow, the other part shame. They don't recognize me at first, all bound up in a jacket and boots. When I step forward, they shy away, a single, shirking creature that's seen too many fists.

Wen Kei is the first to realize who I am. She pulls out from the pale, withdrawn faces, throws herself into me. "Mei Yee! You're okay!"

The other girls shift and start at the sound of my name. Nuo comes to my other side, buries her face into my shoulder. I hold them both tight, let myself breathe. All of us are shaking.

Even Yin Yu. She's trying to be unseen, slipping against the corner of my vision, but she doesn't go far enough. I can still see how her lips wrinkle against her face, trembling like the edges of my imperfect ceiling stars.

"You got us out," Wen Kei squeaks when she finally unburies her face.

*Out.* The other girls shift again. The word is not as holy to them; it doesn't settle well.

"It wasn't me." I look over my shoulder, over Nuo's stray wisps of angel hairs. My sister is still bent over on the ground, looking like a drop of blood in that serving dress. My window-boy is crouched next to her, and even from this distance—even through his pain—those eyes shine.

"What happens now?" Nuo asks.

I turn back and stare at the group. Nineteen faces. Nineteen beautiful, torn, *needing* faces.

*What happens now?* I spent so long thirsting, yearning, dreaming for this freedom. And now it's here and the streets are very dark and we're not the police's problem.

"I-I'm not sure."

"You're not sure?" The pierce of Yin Yu's voice is a needle of its own, filling me with fault and rattle. "Where are we going to sleep? What are we going to eat?"

Nuo and Wen Kei have pulled away, but they're still looking at me. They're all looking at me, waiting for answers I do not have.

And then, a presence. A heat next to me and a hand sliding into mine. Fingers meeting fingers. Warmth against warmth. The feel of Dai is so vastly different from anyone else I've ever touched. It makes my insides burst and soar, and I know, somehow, that things are going to be okay.

"Thank you for the keys," he says to Yin Yu. "And your silence."

She blinks at him, tilts her head so she's staring at him through her bangs. The way she does when she wants to watch without being seen.

Dai looks to me. His fingers are so gentle, threading through the empty spaces between mine, filling the gaps. "Are all the girls here?"

I look over their faces again. Only Sing is missing. The thought makes my heart ache and bloat. I nod anyway.

My window-boy clears his throat. His voice is so solid, so clear without the glass between us. "I know none of you really know me—besides Mei Yee and Yin Yu. But I wanted to let you know that if you want somewhere to stay tonight, somewhere safe, you can come with me. There will be food. And tea. And mats for sleeping. If you want."

The girls all stare at him as if he's a wild thing. I wonder if this is how my face looked that first night he tapped on my window and I saw another life stretching out, calling me into a different chamber.

I think of the tiny room with the tiles colored like a smoker's teeth. How just Jin Ling and the cat and I felt like a crowd. "But your apartment isn't big enough for all of us."

"We're not going to my apartment," Dai says. "We're leaving Hak Nam. We're going home."

405

*Home.* He says the word like a song. Something different from wilting rice fields and knuckle-laced nights. Something worth singing about.

"You trust him, Mei Yee?" a girl from the south hall asks.

I stare back at this boy whose hand I'm holding. Whose hair is mussed and whose eyes are lined with tired gray. Who's smiling in a way I've never seen before. It looks the way his *home* sounded: safe and whole and full of warmth.

This answer comes easy: "With my life."

Dai's fingers tighten in mine. His smile grows and he looks back at the other girls. "If any of you want to come, then follow me."

Wen Kei steps out first. Then Nuo. The rest of the girls wash after them—a wave of color and timid steps. In the end, there's only one left. She stands alone in the island of lamplight.

"Mama-san." My fingers slide from Dai's and I walk back to her. "You can come, too."

"There's no room." The old woman sounds different out here in the open air. The dragoness has vanished from her voice. It's so soft, almost lost.

"You heard Dai. We can all go," I tell her.

Mama-san shakes her head. Her tight, tight bun is coming undone, wisps of hair falling free into her face. She pulls them back with fingers like rakes.

"There's no room out there," she says again. "It's not our world. People like us belong in the shadows. I'm staying in Hak Nam."

I know the look—the way her shoulders are hunched, the

way the whites of her eyes go wide. She's been caged too long. It's the open, unknown door she fears. Just like my mother.

I reach out my hand, will her to take it. "Mama-san—"

"Go." She cuts me off, edges farther from the streetlamp. "You'll find out soon enough."

Dai and the girls are waiting for me, and Mama-san keeps shrinking. Away from my outstretched hand, away from the light and into the shadows she thinks are her own. And the dark keeps coming, envelops her until she's gone.

Now I'm the one who's alone. Adrift under the lamp, in the blue pool of light.

Dai's next to me again. "Are you okay, Mei Yee?"

"I can't—" I swallow back the sick helplessness in my gut, keep staring into the darkness. "I don't want to just leave her here."

"This is her choice," he says softly, "and thanks to you, she's free to make it."

My window-boy is right. No matter how much I want to grab Mama-san by the wrist and take her to a safe place, I can't. The choice is hers alone.

"Are you ready to go?" he asks.

Our hands come back together, tight. I can't tell if I'm the one clinging to him or if he's the one holding me. I think— maybe—it's both. I look over to the girls and my sister. To the road that's folding open—ready to take us *out* and *away*.

I choose not to stay in the dark.

"Let's go home," I say.

# DAI

I support Jin Ling's weak steps with my good arm, taking her all the way to the Old South Gate. Just like before. Only this time her blood isn't on my shirt, and I don't have to run. I've got all the time in the world.

Mei Yee walks on my other side, by my wounded shoulder. It throbs whenever she presses too close, but I ignore it. Some things are worth the hurt.

The rest of the girls trail behind her—an exodus of wide eyes and shiny dresses. I can only imagine the look on my father's face when I knock on the door of 55 Tai Ping Hill this time. I'm guessing he'll have something to say and I'll have something to say back. We'll seesaw the way we always do, and in the end, the girls will stay. All twenty of them.

Of course, it's not a permanent solution. But right now I'm not thinking much further than the next twenty-four hours: a visit between Dr. Kwan and my shoulder, a good dose of pain meds, a hot meal, and a firm mattress.

And after that…

I don't know, but I have a feeling it's all going to work itself out.

An extra silhouette has joined us, bobbing tailless over rubbish heaps and door stoops. When the shadows run out, he trots close to my ankles, yowling louder than any cat should.

"Don't worry." I look down at Chma when our strange procession reaches the rusted cannons. He leaps up on top of one of the ancient artifacts, piercing me with his yellow head-light eyes. "We won't leave you behind."

The streets of Seng Ngoi are alive, pouring over with parades and happy drunks. Everything is bright gold and vibrant poppy-petal red. There are lanterns and sweet cakes and children dancing with new shoes, delighted to be up past their bedtime. One old man walks past, offers me a swig from his bottle of rice liquor. I shake my head, but he smiles anyway, showing his absence of teeth.

"Happy Year of the Snake!" He takes a swig of his own and teeters off into the festivities.

It's too much for Mei Yee. I can tell by the stun on her face. She's staring at the flare and color of the street, fingers half covering her eyes to shield them from the brightness. The sky is no longer black, but streaked with every color. Fireworks thunder and sparkle above us, showering the streets of Seng Ngoi like magical rain. We stand and watch them, even Chma.

"They're beautiful," I hear Mei Yee whisper, even though each boom of color makes her jump like a nervous rabbit. "This whole place is so beautiful. A city of lights."

"In a few days I'll take you to see the sea," I promise.

The colors of the evening's celebration flash over her face. She smiles and looks over at me. *Sees* me. My heart is full and burning—brighter than this night. "I'd like that."

I look down and realize that despite all the noise and chaos around us, Jin Ling has fallen asleep. She's leaning into me—every ounce of her featherweight—her face smudged and shameless against my hoodie. Reminds me of how tired I am. How tired all of us are.

I look at Chma and my two girls. I take in the fires of the sky. Fresh colors to mark a new year. A new day—day one of the rest of my life.

Our lives.

Let's get started.

# EPILOGUE
## 180 DAYS LATER

# MEI YEE

The first time Dai took me to see the sea, I couldn't speak. The sun was shining off the waters like the fireworks that had laced the sky so many nights before. It glittered and gleamed all the way to the horizon. So much water spreading out in all directions.

The waves were small that morning, lulling and calm. The water stretched under the sky like a mirror, reflecting the infinite. I felt that same wide vastness inside my chest, washing in and out of me. Wind—stiff with winter and salt—licked against the leather jacket Dai's mother gave me, but I didn't shiver. I stood on the edge of the world and wanted more.

So I come back—again and again—and the sea always calls the way it did that first time. Singing with the gentle hush and lap of waves. Whispering possibilities with every tide.

Our world changed fast after the New Year. It took Dai's

gift of persuasion and a small army of taxis to get all of us up to Tai Ping Hill. He walked up to the mansion with his good shoulder set, as if he was ready for a fight. The people who opened the door—Mr. and Mrs. Sun—ran out and hugged him instead.

What followed was a chaos of days and doctor visits and phone calls and Mrs. Sun and Emiyo bursting through the front door with more shopping bags than their own weight combined. Clothes in all sizes, for all the girls.

But Dai's mother didn't stop there. She sat with us in the rock garden, listened to our stories. When we told her—when she asked about our homes, our parents—that we could not go back, she understood. And then she went to work.

And so a new charity project was born, funded by Sun Industries's generous donations, managed by Mrs. Sun herself. A boarding school was founded for all the children the Walled City spat back out—Longwai's girls and ladder-ribbed vagrants—complete with classes and counselors and doors that lock only from the inside.

Even all this didn't stop some of the girls from leaving. I thought that final night in Hak Nam—when I stood under the streetlamp and watched Mama-san vanish—that all our choices had been made.

But it's not just one choice made in one moment. It's every time I wake up in my dormitory room sweating from nightmares of needles and Sing's screams and Jin Ling has to grab my arm and tell me I'm safe. It's every time I feel the fear washing up, creeping into me for no reason at all, even though

416

the sky is blue and Dai is laughing at one of Jin Ling's jokes. It's every time I see a man with silvering hair and think that maybe Ambassador Osamu hasn't really gone missing as all the news sources say he has, that maybe he's just biding his time, waiting for the perfect moment to come for me.

The counselors Mrs. Sun hired to talk with us, they tell me these things are normal. Symptoms of something called PTSD. And most of the time I believe them. But sometimes, sometimes, I hear Mama-san whispering: *It's not our world. People like us belong in the shadows.*

And sometimes, sometimes, I wonder if maybe she's right. If I do not deserve the wide of the sea or the electric hum in Dai's eyes, which crackle and spark in my heart, or everything Mrs. Sun is giving me.

The other girls feel this, too—this war of choices. Yin Yu was the first to slip away. Our fourth morning at the Suns' house, we woke up and her mat was empty. All the clothes Mrs. Sun had given her were left in neat folds. More empty mats followed, and—later—a few dormitory beds: girls from the other halls. Always, always they end up back in Hak Nam, surfacing in scarlet-lamped doorways, back to the old ways. Back to the shadows.

The counselors tell us this is normal, too. Every two weeks they go with Mrs. Sun back into the Walled City—issue their invitation with cups of icy, sweet *yuen yeung* and smiles. They have not come back with any of the missing girls, but they do come back with news: more Security Branch raids, a wave of evictions. Slowly, steadily, the government is draining the city, preparing its body for dissection. I haven't been back to Hak Nam, but every once in a while, its picture will appear on the folds of Mr. Sun's newspaper. It looks the same as ever: bricks on bricks and bars on bars. Openings gaping like sockets in a skull.

It's hard to imagine how a place like that could ever be a park—all green and sunshine and growth. Where things like bright red hibiscus and magenta bougainvillea bloom.

But it will be. One day.

And Dai. He's stayed in his father's house, studying with tutors to make up for those lost years. There's an entire unknown world at his fingertips—universities and traveling. He likes to talk about it a lot. He also likes to use the word *us*.

Our world changed, but one thing stays the same. As constant as the tide.

Every Sunday at noon we take a car to the south of Seng Ngoi—away from the city's smokestacks and crowded shoreline—where the beaches are hidden things, with rocks and unbroken shells. Jin Ling curls up on a blanket with her ever-present pile of books, flipping through pages and sounding the characters aloud—transforming the slashes of ink into words. It makes me jealous how quickly she's learning. We're in the same classes—along with Nuo and Wen Kei and a lot of the vagrant boys. But it won't be that way for long. Jin Ling's already finished the first three books our teacher gave her, and she's always hungry for more. I think it's because she's at the top of our class that our instructors let her keep Chma at school. The cat is almost a part of her wardrobe. She even brings him here, to the beach, where he sits patiently on the edge of the blanket, stalking the tiny crabs that sometimes inch out of their holes.

He's watching one now, the ends of his fur all bristled and gray. If he still had his tail, it would be twitching.

"Hey, Mei Yee!" Jin Ling's face is wide as she looks up from her book. It's one from the stacks in Hiro's old room. The pile Dai gave her. "Did you know that there are whole mountains under the ocean?"

I shield my face and look back out at the water. Try to imagine the tower of mountains beneath it. I remember how we all laughed when Sing told us the very same thing. How it seemed so impossible that such a height could be swallowed by such a depth.

I look back at my sister and am struck by how much she looks like my old friend—crouched on this blanket with a book, the light of words in her eyes. She even tries to wear her hair in Sing's old braid. She asks me to braid it for her every morning, so I do. It's still far too short, and the end result is nothing more than a stub. But I take the three strands of Jin Ling's hair anyway and twine them into something whole. Something as strong as she is.

Some scars stay with you. Like the medallion of shiny skin that punctuates Dai's shoulder. Or the furious violet welt curled into my little sister's side. If you looked at me now, you'd see nothing—no bruises or cuts or lumps made by old hurts. All the blisters and bloody toes I got running from Longwai's guard are long gone. You can't see my scars, but they're there all the same. Sing—her death—is just the tip of it. The more I talk with the counselors, the more I find. Wounds that float up faster than they seem to heal.

But they are healing. Step by step. Day by day. Choice by choice. I'm tearing down the bars and bricks.

I'm becoming new.

"It says so right here!" Jin Ling jabs a finger at the shiny page. At the exact same moment, Chma jumps, plows nose-first into the sand. From the looks of it, he didn't catch anything. He's only grown fat and lazy now that he doesn't have to hunt rats the size of himself. "See?"

"Maybe instead of reading about the ocean, you should go experience it." I'm only teasing her, but my little sister leaps up anyway, starts sprinting across the sand all the way down to the waterline.

"Where's Jin going?"

I look back over my shoulder to see Dai walking up, barefoot in the sand. His jeans are rolled up to his knees, and his white V-neck glares against the afternoon sun. So bright I have to shield my eyes.

"Off."

"I got us some lunch." He kicks the sand off his toes, settles onto the blanket beside me. The brown bag crinkles against his lap, and I catch the familiar, delicious smell of stuffed buns.

Chma isn't the only one who's been getting plump.

"Should I call her back?" I glance back in the direction my sister ran. The tide is low today, shirking back to show an entire carpet of seashells. Jin Ling tiptoes through them like

420

a ballerina, bending down and picking some up. When she finally reaches the water, she starts tossing them back, watching them land like gulls in the rough blue. I've never seen my sister act so much like a kid. Even when she was one.

"No. Let her be. She's having fun." Dai shakes his head and grins at me. "I'm not hungry yet, anyway."

That smile is just like the sea. I'm not sure if I'll ever grow tired of it. I shut my eyes and feel the warmth of the summer sun on my skin, my face. The rawness of remembering Sing starts to fade, along with all the other things. Mountains covered by the depths of something greater, more vast than I could ever begin to fully know.

Dai's arm slides around my shoulder and I lean into him. Open my eyes and stare ahead. Where my sister stands in that carpet of shells, chucking them one by one into the sea.

"That's funny," Dai murmurs next to me.

"What?"

"Nothing.... It's just that I've seen this before." A not-quite frown appears on the edge of his lips, stays there. "Déjà vu."

The word sounds foreign, but not like the English I'm studying. "Is that bad?"

"No," he says, and looks over at me. "Not bad. Perfect. It's absolutely perfect."

Our lips are so close, just a breath or sigh away.

My window-boy—he's always so careful, so gentle. He always waits for me to choose, to reach out, to let him in. I lean closer, and the softness of his lips grazes mine. Fire-flare bursts in my chest, full of life, life, life. Dai pulls in. His fingers are feather-light on my cheeks, brushing and swirling and teasing like a phoenix in flight. We linger together—in this space without grating or glass. In this place I want to be.

And even when it ends, it doesn't. I see so much reflected in the brown of his eyes: my sister and the sea. Heights and depths. Horizons and possibilities. Flights on fire. I see these things and I feel the vastness calling, deep inside my chest.

It's times like these I know—in my deepest core, in the marrow of all that is me—that Mama-san is wrong.

This is my world. Wide and open and waiting.

# JIN LING

I am running. This time there are no boots. No sliming puddles or cigarette butts. Just sand like velvet between my toes. Spray and salt and sea.

It feels so different—running without a reason. Without knifepoints or purple-veined shopkeepers at my back. I turn around and all I see are Dai and my sister on the blanket. So close to each other they look like a single person under the sun. Chma is still rooting through the crab burrows, his tailless rump raised high. Hunting for the fun of it.

There are no shards of broken glass under my feet. Just things the sea washed up: kelp, crab claws, and shells. A lot of them I recognize from Hiro's book. Mussels, sea snails, Arabian cowrie. I bend down. Pick them up. Check to see if there's still life inside. Hiro's book said that sometimes the shells wash up and dry out. Before the next tide can save them. Every time I see a snail's sealed up yellow end, I throw it back. *Plop!* White foam and sink.

*Plop! Plop! Plop!*

It's a small thing. A toss for a life.

My life has been full of these small things. Clothes without holes. Boots that fit. My first real mattress. Chma lounging in sun slants and dust motes. New, not-molding books. Bowls of rice porridge every morning. Classes with chalkboards. Dai rumpling my hair every time he sees me and talking about how long it's getting. My sister smiling again.

The small things add up.

One day I'll find a way to pay it all back. I'm learning all I can—books and books of words. Mrs. Sun says I'm "exceptionally gifted." I can be whatever I want. A doctor or a diplomat or a lawyer. I don't know for sure what I want to be yet, but I know I want to help. I want to find a way to go back for my mother. To face my father without a gun in my hand or a bruise on my face. To show her she doesn't need him.

For now, I'll keep throwing.

"Jin!" I look back over my shoulder. See Dai waving a brown paper bag over his head. Like I'm a taxi he's trying to flag down. Chma is on his lap, begging. "I got stuffed buns!"

My stomach squeals the way Chma used to whenever I accidentally stepped on his tail. It's never hungry the way it was before—all gnaw and teeth. But the stuffed buns always taste just as good as they did that morning on the roof.

"Coming!" My voice gusts back over the sand.

There's one last shell by my toes. All curled and coiled the way Nuo wears her hair. So big my palm almost can't hold it. I pick it up anyway. Toss it far, far, far into the sea.

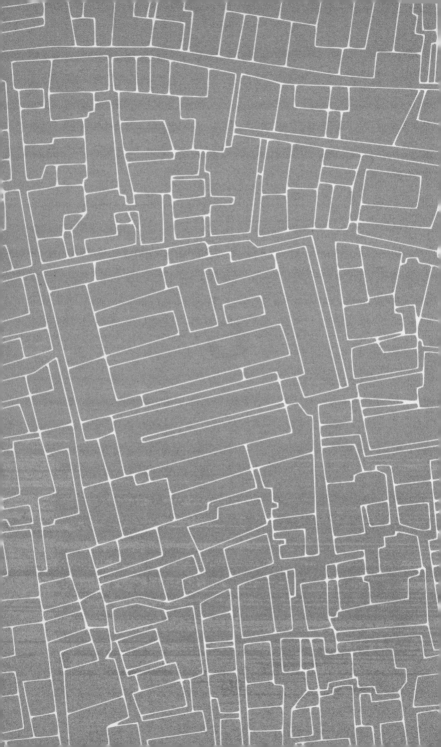

# AUTHOR'S NOTE

The Walled City was real.

A very real, unreal city.

I first learned about its existence when I went to hear a woman named Jackie Pullinger speak. She spent nearly twenty years living and working in Hong Kong's Kowloon Walled City. The place she described—a sunless, lawless shanty-town overrun by gangs— sounded like a setting straight out of a dystopian fantasy. My imagination began racing (as it tends to do). I started thinking about all the different types of people who lived in the Kowloon Walled City: the street kids, the prostitutes, the fugitives, the ruthless gangsters. Storylines rose out of nowhere. Wove together into a story I couldn't put down.

This book does not fit into the category of historical fiction, and was never intended to. While I did extensive research on the actual Kowloon Walled City, and tried to portray it as closely as possible, I also employed artistic license to convey the story I wanted to tell. This can be seen in the name changes (Hong Kong became Seng Ngoi, for example), the timeline of the Walled City's eviction and demolition, Seng Ngoi's judicial system, and the specific operations of the Brotherhood of the Red Dragon.

Another thing savvy readers might notice is how I handled characters' names. Names in the Kowloon Walled City were generally in Cantonese, with a single-syllable surname (such as *Sun*) and a double-syllable given name (such as *Jin Ling* or *Mei Yee*). In Hong Kong today, it's not unheard of to shorten the given name to a single-syllable nickname (as Jin does, to maintain her disguise), though back when the Kowloon Walled City existed, this practice was not common. But for the purposes of the story I wanted to tell, I chose to shorten some names throughout. Some of the names also had Japanese or Mandarin origins, depending on where the characters are from. I also feel it's worth mentioning that although the term *Mama-san* has negative connotations in the US today, it was the traditional title used for women who managed brothels in the Kowloon Walled City, where there was some Japanese influence because of Japan's occupation of Hong Kong during World War II.

Apart from the things mentioned above, I do believe the reality and the fiction are not all that different. Both Hak Nam and Kowloon started their lives as military forts. Both grew so thick and fast that the sunlight could no longer reach the streets. Both housed powerful gangs and over 33,000 people in their cramped borders (it was 6.5 acres, only 0.0102 square miles). Both were eventually torn down by the government and turned into a park. In fact, the decision to demolish the real Kowloon Walled City was announced on January 14, 1987. The exact day and year I was born.

Although I was never able to see the real Walled City, I was fortunate enough to visit the park built in its place. The space is small and manicured, filled with remnants of the neighborhood: cannons, the crumbling ruins of the South Gate, a metal replica of the old city, a bonsai tree garden, and even (on my visit) a tailless cat. Should you ever find yourself in Hong Kong, it's well worth taking the time to visit this site.

The Walled City might be gone, but human trafficking is not. According to a 2006 UNICEF report, nearly two million children have been trafficked into the sex trade. Some, like Mei Yee, are even sold by members of their own family. To learn more about this issue and how you might be able to help, I suggest visiting the website of the International Justice Mission, a human rights agency dedicated to rescuing victims of trafficking and providing them with legal protection. You can find it at ijm.org.

# ACKNOWLEDGMENTS

Writing this book was a raw, intricate process. I felt as if I were plucking out pieces of my soul, spinning them into delicate strings, knotting them into a tapestry of words. But writing this book was not a lonely process. So many people supported this project and ultimately became a part of it. Strands of their own.

There are those who knew it as Cutthroat Novel—Lydia Kang, Amanda Sun, Kate Armstrong, and Emma Maree Urquhart. Those who read it as WALLS—Kelsey Sutton, Justina Ireland, Christina Farley, and Caroline Carlson. Those who encouraged me to keep working even when it seemed foolish—The Lucky 13s and Aimee Kaufman.

There is my brilliant agent, Tracey Adams, who loved the strength of sisters and mountains beneath the sea. There is my phenomenal editorial team—Alvina Ling, Amber Caravéo, Bethany Strout, Nikki Garcia—and all the publishing teams, who worked tirelessly to bring this book to the world. There are the readers—Mio Debman and Amy Chaw. Mio especially provided invaluable cultural insight and helped me paint a more vivid picture of Hak Nam.

There are my friends and family, whose love and encouragement constantly remind me that *the braid is always stronger than the strand*. There is David, who sits on rooftops and seashores with me. Who talks about stars and home, and stretches my heart full.

And through it all there is God, who weaves all things together: my stories and my life. Soli Deo Gloria.

The author posing with a model of the Kowloon Walled City.

The Kowloon Walled City in the early evening, glowing from the
illuminated homes and shops of some of its 33,000-plus residents.

An aerial view revealing the unmistakable density and shape of
the Kowloon Walled City.